39 Plus One

A novel by Ragh Bir

Grosvenor House
Publishing Limited

This book is published by
Grosvenor House Publishing Ltd
Link House
140 The Broadway, Tolworth, Surrey, KT6 7HT.
www.grosvenorhousepublishing.co.uk

This fictional novel is based on real-life people and events. Names, characters
and businesses have been changed to protect the privacy of the individuals.

A CIP record for this book
is available from the British Library

ISBN 978-1-80381-198-7

The adventures of a thirty-nine-year-old singleton who lives in Royal Windsor. She appears to have everything apart from a significant other. How many frogs will she have to kiss to find her true prince...

Contents

Dedicated to
K.D.B.
My one true love
See you in the morning...

FACT – The Quest is real

This novel is based on the true-life experiences of the author, although some events, situations and characters have been created and imagined, allowing the story to unfold. It has been condensed to fit the year that the main character, Rachel, has dedicated to find her significant other. Whereas, in real life, this was undertaken over a number of years. Names, characters and businesses have been changed in order to protect the privacy of the individuals.

Chapter One

The Quest

Next year I enter the fourth decade of my life. It's a dirty word for me, known as the 'F' word amongst my close friends; whenever they try to talk to me about what I'm planning for my fortieth, I silence them and say, "Don't mention the F word." They just laugh at me. By the way, most of them have already been there and find it amusing that I'm taking it so seriously; they are all married with 2.4 and living the imperfect dream, apart from Vince and Harry who think a good bonk solves all life's miseries. Getting back to the 'F' word; yes, I'm in complete denial, I know, but how I remember those days dancing to Wham's 'Young Guns' for the end of year school concert in the summer of '83 thinking how, someday, I would be married to my Andrew Ridgley lookalike, only to discover my Andrew Ridgley lookalike used to like whamming his fists into me and I decided it was time to say goodbye to my Wham days.

So, here I am, just turned 39, single, and for the past 7 years, I haven't really had a serious boyfriend. I admit

I have not explored all avenues. The thought of speed dating or even communal dinner dates horrifies me; the queuing up, the name badge, the viewing and then the bids are cast. The image that comes to mind is that of cattle lining up to be auctioned; *ooh yes, the rump looks good on that one*, or *noooo too old to bear children.* Okay, I'm being cynical, but just the thought of standing around with a group of humanimals all waiting to be sized up and examined, all suffering with the same affliction is not my kind of fun. It's the desperate yearning look, the wait to see if someone has put a bid on you, the anticipation that this time the farmer has noticed your prize-winning qualities. No! It's another walk back to the fields. So, yes, I know that I'm being very unfair; how can I possibly give an opinion on something I refuse to try.

Then, there's the internet. Well, remember as a child when your birthday was approaching, you'd get the Argos catalogue out and look through the pages and list all the things that you'd like, and then place the list where everyone can see it, normally stuck to the fridge door? Then, when eventually your birthday comes around, you open your presents, imagining which one from the list it is, only to be disappointed with yet another set of pyjamas which 'you'll grow into', a pair of socks, and a box set of bath foam and soap on a rope. I have, on a couple of occasions, registered on dating sites but what a lengthy process! Boredom sets in by the time I get to the type of qualities I'd like in my ideal partner and before I know it, I start comparing the virtues of internet dating with the traditional method and suffice to say, my Argos days are over.

It's not that I can't get a boyfriend, I'm just not that good at keeping them. I've been told that I'm too fussy, too pretty, too nice, too independent, and, once, even that my standards are too high. I mean, *really*!

So, I've decided to go on a quest for the next 12 months to find my perfect, imperfect soulmate. To explore all avenues. To accept all invitations, even if they're not to my liking, i.e., too short, too fat, smelly, players and haters, etc. You get my drift? I say perfect, imperfect soulmate because, let's face it, nobody's perfect and although it's all very cosy and lovey the first few years of a relationship, after a while, all the things you tolerate for the love of the man, becomes the things you absolutely hate in him. Like the face shavings left in the sink, the smelly, wet clothes strewn everywhere, and I know you won't believe me, but once, on entering the bathroom, I found poo halfway down the outside of the toilet bowl and I'm not talking a little spot. I'm talking a great lump, the size of a golf ball, just clinging on to the side for dear life. The explanation I got was that it had fallen off the loo roll during the wiping process and landed on the outside of the toilet. Well! I can't really talk about that anymore, but my point is that if you really love someone, and find that perfect, imperfect soulmate, then what you do is laugh about it and put up with all his poo.

So, my quest to find my perfect, imperfect soulmate begins...

Three Days Earlier

It all began with my journey back from work. I decided to stop at this new store that had recently opened; it was one of those organic deli-style shops. Anyway, there I am trying the little titbits on offer at the antipasti counter; I was rather peckish after work and, as I'm popping the third feta stuffed olive in my mouth, I feel eyes on me, so I turn and catch a glimpse of him. He's pushing his little trolley around the corner of the aisle, but I know it's his eyes watching me stuff my face. Or am I just being paranoid? "Would you like to try the jalapeno stuffed—" I hear a voice from over the counter ask.

"No thanks, I'll just take a small tub of the feta olives please, seeing as I've eaten most of the ones on the tray," I say, chuckling to the young lad who's serving me, but it goes over his head.

I study his face to calculate how old he could be; he looks up and catches my eye as he passes the tub over the counter.

At 39, I don't think I look too bad; a couple of grey hairs or so hidden under my brunette locks, no wrinkles yet, unless I smile too hard, and apart from a slight muffin top when I wear low-rise jeans, everything's in the right place. "Anything else, madam?" he asks, as I pop the tub in the basket.

No! Not now you've called me 'madam'. "No thank you," I reply, as I walk away and turn into the aisle where, a few feet away, I'm faced with the one whose eyes were on me when I was olive-eating.

He looks up and smiles and I pretend not to notice him as I walk past and then I hear a French accent. "'Ello."

I turn to look at him and he's cute-ish; the accent is much cuter. "Hi," I say, half-smiling and walking on. Oh God! I hope I don't have any of those olives stuck in my teeth. I make it to the cheese counter and check my teeth with my tongue and then notice the tray of cocktail sticks with cubes of cheese attached and grab one, wolf it down, then use the stick to clear olive debris from my teeth.

Then I hear a familiar voice. "Can I help you with anything, madam?" It's the deli counter boy; he must have rollerbladed over.

"No thanks," I mumble, trying not to look like I'm eating my way round the store. All I need now is a drink, and as I turn into the next aisle, there's an organic wine tasting table. I smile and think, *you don't need to go out to a fancy bar with your girlfriends, just turn up at the organic deli store and you can have a quick catch up over nibbles and a glass of wine while you browse. No purchase necessary.* I smile to myself and head on over to sample what's on offer; there's an elderly couple there chatting to the wine promoter lady, so maybe I could do a drink and dash without being noticed. I help myself to the weeny glass of red, knock it back and nod my head pretending that I'm listening to her narrative on the virtues of drinking organic wine and then help myself to another when she turns, looks at me and asks my thoughts. "Oh! Well, it's jolly nice," I say, as I pop the empty vessel down and scoop up another thimbleful of happiness and then I turn to the elderly couple and ask them what they think as I edge my way back to let them take centre stage.

I can see Mr French Accent at the end of the aisle looking at something on the shelf, so I fake a hello and raise my hand as if to wave to him as I calmly walk away. I'm not going to shy away; the vino has helped to ease my demeanour. Besides, I haven't had a date in ages and as we pass, he stops and introduces himself as Francois. "Hi, I'm Rachel." I feel a bit awkward when I notice a lady close by glance over, raising her eyebrows and smiling as she snoops in on our conversation. I catch Francois taking a nose of my feta-stuffed olives in my basket; he looks up and smiles at me. He's not very tall but has a nice smile and accent and after a little small talk about the new store, he asks me if I'd like to go out sometime. I give him my number, say goodbye and, as I walk away slowly, I can hear him say that he'll call. I pay for my olives and, whilst walking to my car, I think of how we ever managed before mobile phones were invented. I mean, how great not having to go in search of pen and paper or try to commit to memory names and numbers that could be your destiny. It starts to rain and is chilly out but there's a spring in my step.

Later that evening I receive a message from Francois saying that he wants to meet on Saturday at 6pm at a café that's close to where he lives and then go into town for dinner. FUUUUUCCKK! That's only two days away. What shall I wear? Where are we going? Casual or dressy? This calls for an emergency Friday night with the girls to discuss.

Harriet and Naomi meet me at our usual Friday night hangout called 'The Drinking Ole'; it's a little Spanish bar in Windsor that serves great tapas. I order a bottle of wine and three glasses and wait for them to arrive. Harriet is the all-important party girl who can handle her drink until she passes out, of course. She has a well-paid job that can afford her to buy whatever designer piece she likes and would not concern herself with how much she has spent. Once she showed me a simple hair clip and told me that she had paid £15 for it; to me it just looked like a plastic hair grip, but what do I know. Naomi is the quiet, doesn't-drink-too-much, practical earth mother type who hasn't been shopping for herself in years and would rather go without than be a fashion-conscious victim. I have known them both since school; they both married young to their childhood sweethearts, and I suspect they think the grass is greener. Sometimes it is and sometimes it isn't. "French? I don't much like the French!" exclaims Naomi. "Too arrogant; they think they're the bee's knees, and what's the thing with the snails?"

"Well, I think they're romantic, charming and that accent is so sexy," Harriet purrs. One for and one against. Great! "Look, you haven't had a boyfriend in ages; he could be the one," continues Harriet.

"Well, as long as you don't serve us snails at your wedding, I'm fine with it," Naomi chips in, rolling her eyes.

"Oh, for God's sake! It's only a date," I add, laughing.

As I suspected, I'm none the wiser after meeting up with them, but I should remember that they haven't dated in years, and I guess wouldn't have a clue anyway. And me? I feel like I've been dating for a lifetime, and I still don't have a clue. I do have rules for dating – nothing major – but, firstly, if a man has asked me out to dinner, then I expect him to pay, if there's a second date, then I will offer, unless he absolutely objects to me contributing. If I like him, and want to see him again, I will let him pay, if I know I won't be seeing him again, then I will insist on paying half and then I won't feel so bad when I say that I'm not interested in seeing him again. Secondly, I never kiss on a first date, not for any reason but I just think it's always good to wait, unless they're totally irresistible and we just click. Then, that kiss has got to be the sweetest kiss ever, no tongue-swashing saliva faced kiss which has been unleashed way too soon, as I have experienced on past encounters.

Chapter Two

Pepé Le Pew

It's Saturday, late afternoon, and I have half an hour before meeting Francois. The tornado that hit my bedroom earlier has finally settled as I pick out my first-choice outfit from under the pile of clothes on my bed. My light blue jeans with a white halterneck top accompanied by some strappy, pale pink heels and a dark blue woolly coatigan.

I meet Francois at a restaurant; he's standing outside as I drive into the car park, and I notice that he's in exactly the same clothes that he was wearing in the supermarket a couple of days earlier. I park the car, unbuckle my seatbelt, and Francois has jumped into the passenger seat and is lunging toward me. I lean back a little as he says 'ello in that soothing French accent and kisses me on both cheeks.

"So, have you just finished work?" I enquire.

"Non, I had the day off today," he replies.

I can't believe it! He's been off all day and turns up for a date wearing tired old jeans, and a bobbly black jumper that's reserved for rainy day walks; I'm not impressed! Still, I've got to think that things can only get better. I open the car door and start making my way out. "Shall we make a move then?" I say, looking back at him still seated in the passenger seat.

He nods, and I realise that he's expecting me to drive. He must have seen my jaw drop as I stepped back into the driver's seat. "Or, if you prefer, I can drive; my house is two minutes away," he offers.

I nod my head in approval. "Yeah, sure, okay," I respond, *and a change of clothes wouldn't go amiss either,* I say in my head as he jumps out of the car and disappears. *Was that mean of me?* I ponder. He did ask me out, so therefore he should be picking me up, and it was his idea to go into town; we could've just gone to a local restaurant. Oh why, oh why am I overanalysing? That's it! Just enjoy the evening.

After giving myself a talking to and reapplying my lip-gloss, I feel excited to see that Francois has returned in a jeep. I pick up my coat, and bag, lock the car, and with a smile, climb into the passenger seat of his car when an overpowering smell of wet dog invades my nostrils, and not to mention the doghair everywhere. Oh no! What have I done? "Hi," is all I can muster as Francois takes my hand and starts kissing the top of it whilst mumbling something in French. Damn! I wish I'd taken my French lessons at school seriously now.

Our journey into town is relatively painless and I've become nose-blind to the wet dog smell. Francois, as well as driving, is doing most of the talking. He's a masseuse in his spare time, his full-time job is at a cinema in Fulham, and he says he also reads palms. He drives down a side street and parks up. "This is where I work," he says, as he points to a cinema that we've just passed on the main road, he gets out his phone and makes a call. "I'm calling my friend, Nadia, she lives close by, maybe she can join us," he says, as if it's quite normal to invite another lady on a date.

What! I want to shout out, but all that comes out is, "Sure, why not?" I can't believe that I'm on a date and the guy is calling for reinforcements before we've even begun. Right! I'm pissed off now. There's no answer from Nadia so Francois curses in French as he jumps out of the car and asks me what movie I'd like to watch. Well, I had no idea that we were going to watch a movie; not a good option in my book for a first date really, but never mind, 'what do I know'.

But before I could answer, he says, "Wait in the car and I will pick up the movie list." Then he disappears.

As I sit in his smelly car feeling itchy and scratchy, I make a call. That sexy French accent is wearing thin, that's for sure. The answer machine clicks in; 'Hi, Vince 'n' Harry are busy bonking so leave the usual and...' This is so typical of Vince and Harry; they never answer because they want everyone who calls to listen to their message. "You fuckers! Pick up, it's me, Rache, I'm on a date with this guy who's—"

A second later, Vince answers. “Rache! What’s happening? What the fuck’s going on?”

“I’m on a date with this guy who’s left me in his smelly car; he works at the cinema and— ”

“What’s going on? Where is she?” I can hear Harry shout out in the background.

“She’s in a smelly car, she’s on a date,” Vince shouts back to Harry. “Look, Rache, get your arse out of the car, get into a cab and get round here.”

“Oh shit! He’s back, got to go, call you later, love you.”

As I ring off, I can hear Vince shout out, “You better call, or I’ll be— ”

Francois opens the driver’s door and with a smile he hands me the movie listing. Whilst looking at it, he produces two tickets for the 8 o’clock showing of Munich. I look at him in astonishment. *Why bother asking me what I’d like to watch if you’ve already bought tickets*, I think to myself. He asks me if it’s okay and, to be honest, I really don’t care; I want the date to be over already. “Sure, it’s fine,” I reply as I get out of the car.

We walk up the road and stop at a noodle bar that’s opposite the cinema. Great! *Time for a large glass of wine to soothe my senses* is what’s running through my mind, and as I scan the menu, I can hear Francois order two green teas. I can't believe it; did he just order for me? He's speaking in French to the waitress. I continue looking at the menu – pretending to, anyway – as I'm listening to their conversation, peeking over the top of it. Oh yeah, they're definitely flirting with each other. I have no idea what they're talking about, but I hope those green teas are both for him. I decide to order the king prawns in garlic and chillies with noodles, and as I pop my menu down, the French-speaking waitress smiles at Francois, picks up the menus and walks off. I look at Francois and say, "I was thinking of having the king prawns in garlic—"

He then butts in, saying, "So I have ordered something quick because we only have 45 minutes before the film..."

"But the film doesn't start 'til 8 and then there'll be 15 minutes for trailers and..." I try to say, but it falls on deaf ears.

"We should get there early, Rachel," he interjects. He then reaches across the table, takes my hand and starts kissing, starting from the top of my hand all the way up to my elbow. I pull my arm in and away from him and he mumbles something in French. All that my mind conjures up is that French skunk in the Looney Tunes cartoon, Pepé Le Pew, swooning the reluctant feline oblivious to her disgust for him.

I drift off in my thoughts momentarily when I hear Francois call out, "Rachel!" I look up and the waitress places down two steaming mugs of something

I suspect is non-alcoholic, "I love green tea, it's very good for you, non?"

"Well, I love wine," I butt in before he can finish what he's saying. "They say drinking a glass of red wine a day is actually good for you," I conclude.

"I do not drink," he says, cupping the mug of green tea in his hands.

I'm pissed off, I don't want to be here, and this must be the first French person I've met that doesn't drink wine. "Oh, really, why's that?" But before he can answer, the waitress is upon us with what looks like two bowls of noodles. Francois and the waitress exchange small talk and smiles as I look down into the bowl. "Hi, I'd like a glass of red wine please," I murmur, looking up at her but she hurriedly leaves.

"Bon appétit," Francois says as he takes the chopsticks in his right hand, and with his left hand reaches over to take my hand. Oh no, not Pepé Le Pew again. He starts kissing my hand and with each kiss, his lips aim higher and higher up my arm. I must have a look of horror on my face as I notice the couple from the next table side glancing at us and smiling. I pull away, half-smiling, and I'm trying to be polite but can't help but feel embarrassed to find myself in this situation.

"So, what is this?" I ask, looking down at the noodles. "As I'm pretty sure it's not the garlic king prawns that I was eyeing up on the menu," I say, with slight sarcasm.

He seems too preoccupied with his food to notice that I've even spoken, so I make a start on the noodles with the least amount of conversation exchanged. My mind has been overtaken with thoughts of alcohol and although I quit smoking years ago, I find myself in need of one right now. I finish the noodles, the green tea, and start scouring the restaurant for wine-drinking single men who may need company. The small restaurant is busy and noisy, and I start thinking back to Vince telling me to get my arse in a cab and get round to theirs; how I wish I had the courage to leave then.

I come out of my stupor to find Francois talking to the waitress again. She has brought the bill over and Francois proudly announces that it's only £15, as if he's managed to secure a huge discount. I exaggerate my look of surprise, reach for my purse and start rooting around, waiting for him to say 'no, it's okay, it's on me', but instead I hear, "It comes to £7.50 each."

I don't bother looking up as I draw out a tenner, leave it on the table, get up and walk out into the crisp air that's filled with the sweet smell of freedom, and, mmm, the passing aroma of marijuana. I inhale as much as I can as I watch Francois hand the cash over to the waitress and bid her a French farewell. He leaves the noodle bar beaming from ear to ear – maybe he's just secured a date with her too – and then he takes my hand and dashes across the road as if on a mission as he enters his place of work.

We head up the red-carpeted stairs, and he produces the tickets to the attendant, and they chit-chat for a minute before we make our way into the main screen. We settle into our seats and thankfully the cinema is not busy, and no one is seated close by to us. I feel relieved that it will soon be dark, and I'll not have to exchange small talk with Francois. I know that I won't be seeing him again and I don't want to know anything more about him. The lights go down and once the film starts, I'm engrossed and find myself drooling over the leading man, Eric Bana. I can feel Francois try his best to inch closer to me but each time he does, I shift further away from him and when the film ends, the lights come on and Francois reaches out to take my hand, I immediately stand up and start shuffling out of the row. "It was good, non?" he remarks as I sidle out into the aisle.

"Yes it was," I reply.

We head out and the car journey back is long and arduous, his driving is much slower and, although he's occupied with singing along in French to one of his CDs, I'm feeling weary from the evening's events and recall back to the excitement I felt earlier on in the day and how differently it has panned out. We eventually arrive back to where my car is parked and as I unbuckle my seatbelt and open the car door to step out, he grabs my hand, his lips making a move toward the top of my hand. I instinctively shout out, "No, Pepé!"

The astonished look on his face amuses me as I realise what I've just said, and as I recoil out of his car, I mumble goodbye and make a hasty retreat to my car, stopping at the petrol station on the way home to pick up a bottle of red wine and a pack of cigs.

When I arrive home, I give Vince a call and relay the story of my date with Francois; I'm on speakerphone so Harry can hear too. Harry is the calm to Vince's storm. Vince screams with laughter when I tell him of the Pepé Le Pew kissing, and Harry simply says, "Rache, you're too nice, you should've just stood up and walked out as soon as he didn't let you order a glass of wine and your meal of choice."

I laugh with them 'til my stomach hurts and say, "Another one bites the dust," before bidding them goodnight.

'Another one bites the dust' is something I always say to my friends when they ask, 'how'd the date go?' to signify that there won't be another one. Sometimes, I am even known to sing it, hum it or, like tonight, play it whilst drinking a large glass of Malbec.

Chapter Three

Mamma Mia!

A few days later, after my first date of the Quest with Francois, I decided to recharge my batteries by going for a swim at the local leisure centre. Here I met Ryan, his tanned, toned physique made me look twice as I was treading water in the deep end of the pool, and as he approached, I swam off. I really didn't look my best wearing swim goggles, and after a couple more lengths, I stopped to catch my breath. *If only I hadn't smoked those cigarettes the other night*, I scolded myself. Then I heard the sweetest Irish accent say hello and as I turned around, I saw the brightest blue eyes staring back at me. Okay, so he looks a bit older than I'm used to, with his perfect white teeth and full head of silver hair, but we strike up a conversation and after discovering that he's a police officer and has just come back from a month-long holiday – hence the gorgeous tan – he asks me out and we make a plan to meet back at the leisure centre car park later that day.

Seeing as it's not cold out, I decide to wear a dress with heels and take along a jacket. Ryan arrives looking smart in jeans, shirt, and a huge smile, I can't help but stare at his beautiful white teeth against his tanned skin, and while we stroll into town, he tells me of his recent trip away to Vietnam when I enquire how he managed to get such a lovely colour. I start feeling positive about this date despite the obvious age gap. Ryan is cultured, experienced and is in great shape, and we have a shared interest in swimming. We arrive at an Italian restaurant that I've not been to before, it's newly opened, and everything looks fresh and sparkly. The waiter greets us as we walk in and shows us to a table, and I notice we're the first to arrive. "Ah, this is nice," Ryan says, smiling at me.

"Yes it is," I reply, as I take my seat.

He orders a bottle of wine, and we share our stories. He tells me about his job in the police force, where he's devoted almost 30 years' service and is close to retirement, his wonderful holidays alone since he's been divorced for the best part of five years, and his two teenage boys who live with him. The wine is helping with the flow of conversation, and I feel a buzz between us, then he reaches out his hand across the table and I have a flashback to Pepé Le Pew but thankfully he just takes hold of my hands and asks me to close my eyes.

"What?" I snap, surprised by his request.

"Just close them for a moment, Rachel," he whispers in that seductive Irish accent.

"Okay," I say, surrendering to his request, my imagination running wild.

I close my eyes for a nanosecond before hearing his voice say, "Okay, open."

I open my eyes and watch Ryan's thumb and index finger reach into his mouth as he proceeds to remove the top half of his teeth. The look on my face at seeing such an act must've been a picture because Ryan starts laughing uncontrollably and starts repeatedly slapping the back of one of his hands into the palm of the other hand whilst still holding onto his teeth.

"Oh my God!" I gasp, as if my entire world has just crumbled. I'm rendered speechless and try to partake in the joviality of the situation but cannot. I reach for my glass of wine just as the waiter arrives with our food and Ryan promptly pops his teeth back into their home. The waiter offers black pepper, parmesan, and wine, to which I can only nod my acceptance, and as we prepare to eat he tells me that as a younger man he was tackled whilst playing rugby. I nod and smile sympathetically and make the necessary reassuring noises that I'm not the least bit disturbed by what he just did, in public, on a date! On a first date! I quickly glance around to see if anyone else was witness to the incident but luckily the other diners are not close enough to have noticed. The only person who may have witnessed it is the waiter, who's smiling at me.

I look away feeling a little embarrassed and tuck into the penne arrabiata and my mind wanders back to earlier when we met and how I noticed how wonderfully white and straight his teeth were. The buzz from the wine and our earlier energy has worn off for me, but Ryan is still guns blazing and I listen to him talk about the musical *Mamma Mia!*

We finish our pasta, and the waiter returns to take our dishes. He offers dessert and coffee to which I refuse, and I make my excuses that I have an early start. We walk back to our cars and that awkwardness hangs over me where I know that I'm not really into him but feign interest so as not to hurt his feelings. I mean, he's a nice guy but after the denture thing I'm no longer... My thoughts are distracted with Ryan's voice. "So would you like to see *Mamma Mia!* sometime?"

His smile from the moment of us meeting has not diminished one bit. "Maybe? I'll let you know," I reply, hardly able to breathe. I feel like I'm back in the swimming pool, gasping for breath after having swam a length. I'm relieved that he didn't attempt to kiss me, and I drive home safe in the knowledge that at least I can let him down gently at a later date.

Exhaustion from the day's activities and a midweek date leads me straight to bed; a good night's sleep is in need. However, I wake up after having the worst night's sleep with dreams of giant white teeth chasing me down a dark alley.

As I rush out of the door for work, I hear the phone ring. I almost leave it but head back in and I answer, "Hello."

"Well, top of the morning to yer," the voice on the line responds. I panic. It's him. I can't escape and say wrong number or pretend to be a housemate and say that Rachel is not at home, never will be, has emigrated or visiting a sick relative in the Outer Hebrides. He has recognised my voice from one hello.

"Rachel? It's Ryan."

"Hi," I say, pausing, not sure what to say next, "I thought I gave you my mobile number, Ryan?" I stall, trying to think back to yesterday evening when he asked me for my number. "Anyway, I'm running late for work," I blurt out, annoyed at having to speak with him so soon after our date. I thought it would've been at least a week before he decided to make contact.

"Okay, I'll make it quick then, I've booked us tickets for *Mamma Mia!*," he says.

"What?" I interrupt his flow. "I said that I would let you know, Ryan."

"Well, you see, I got a last-minute deal and thought I'd surprise you. Have a think about it and I'll call later, okay, bye." Sensing my annoyance, he ends the conversation by putting the phone down. I croaked out an inaudible bye and put the receiver down with a slam in shock at what just happened, and I'm quite sure that I didn't give him my landline number.

My mind is in a whir as I leave for work and my entire day is consumed with feeling ambushed and annoyed at myself for not having said 'NO'. I should've walked out at dinner when he pulled his dentures out, I should've said no to seeing him again on our walk back to the car after dinner, and I'm going to say no when he calls later.

I call in to see Vince and Harry on the way home from work partly because I need some light relief. Also, the thought of going home and anticipating the call from Ryan is making me feel queasy. Vince and Harry are both rolling around on the sofa laughing. "I don't think there's anything wrong with him having dentures, Rache," Vince exclaims, "besides, there's a lot he can do well once those pearly whites are in a glass sitting on the bedside table at night." He winks at Harry. "Just putting a positive spin on it," he concludes with a snort of laughter.

I leave Vince and Harry's still undecided as to what to do but feeling a little lighter about the situation, and I start thinking if I'm being unfair to Ryan. I mean, we did get along and he has a great body and we do have common interests before he extinguished them all by displaying his toothless grin. My walk home is filled with thoughts of us kissing and the possibility of his dentures coming loose and ending up in my mouth. Urgh!

I reach home and my mobile phone starts ringing. I scramble around my handbag trying to find it, but it rings off before I get to it. As soon as I enter the flat, the landline starts to ring, and an uneasy feeling rises in the pit of my stomach, I imagine it's Ryan, so I pick up and say, "Hello."

"Hiii, it's Ryan here."

"Oh, hello, Ryan, how are you?"

"So, I was thinking that we can meet at Waterloo station at around five, have a bite to eat before the show and a drink or two, how does that sound?" he says.

"Ryan, I did say that I would let you know whether I could make it and actually—" But I'm interrupted.

"Yes, yes, I know, but the tickets are such a good deal and I thought I'd surprise you and—"

"Yes, but—" I mumble.

He speaks over me with his Irish charm. "So, which train do you think you'll be catching?" he adds.

"I'm not really sure, I haven't had a chance to—"

I'm interrupted again. "Well, there's one at 4:25 that will get you into Waterloo at 5:15," he says.

"Oh, right," I reply, completely flabbergasted that he has even planned my train journey. I can't believe that I'm being bully bashed into a second date. I feel deflated and defeated at this point and I fall silent for a moment, trying to think of how to say no.

"Okay, see you tomorrow at Waterloo, bye," Ryan says, promptly ending the call.

"Tomorrow?" I scream down to a dead phone tone. I'm not one bit excited about seeing him or *Mamma Mia!* tomorrow and after a glass of red, some toast and a couple of cigarettes, I head to bed hoping that I'll wake up and find it was all just a bad dream.

I wake with a knot in my stomach and spend the morning at work thinking of ways where it would seem quite understandable to cancel, like a family member has been rushed into hospital or my single best friend has chopped off her finger whilst de-stoning an avocado and I have to take her to hospital, or the neighbour's cat has been run over. I know it's useless, even my brain is going into overdrive and shuts down. I sit at my desk with my hands over my face, peeking out through the space between my fingers and let out a sigh.

"Are you okay, Rache?" I hear a voice ask from across the desk and as I look to my right, one of the sales guys is sat there on the phone looking at me with a concerned expression.

"No, yes, not sure," I reply.

"You don't look so great; have an early dart and I'll cover for you," he says, winking at me. I don't need to be told twice as I grab my handbag, blow him a kiss and head for the door.

When I reach home, I sit down on the balcony of my flat which, overlooks Peascod Street in Windsor and light a cigarette and enjoy my coffee when my mobile rings; it's Harriet. "Hello, Hattie," I answer.

"Hello, love, just wanted to see if you were free this evening for a drink?" she asks.

"Would love to but I've been bamboozled into a second date with the dentures!" I exclaim.

"What?" Harriet screams out in laughter. I briefly recall my first date with Ryan and in amongst her laughter and disbelief are comments like, 'you should've said no' and 'you're such a softy, Rache', and lastly 'you should've just put the phone down on him, Rache'. "Oh well, look at it this way; you get to see the musical that you've been wanting to see for ages, you get dinner and drinks thrown in and, you never know, he might surprise you and you may even enjoy the night," she says, trying to lift my spirits.

"I think I've had enough surprises from him, Hattie."

"Look, it'll be over before you know it and you'll be home in your bed tonight, knowing that you'll never have to see him again," she concludes succinctly. Trust Harriet to put her spin on it, although, I must admit, I do feel a lot better after our chat and decide to make the most of it and start planning my day to catch that 4:25 train to Waterloo.

I arrive at the train station with 10 minutes to spare and strike up a conversation with the girl standing next to me. She's a pretty redhead and I noticed her checking me out as I walked down the steps to the platform; not like a man checks you out but the way another female checks you out – discreetly checking out your clothes, hair, heels, make-up, etc. So, I smile at her and when she smiles back I start talking to her, telling her that I'm going on a date with Ryan who I met a few days earlier. I tell her about the first date and the dentures and how he has bamboozled me into a second date to see *Mamma Mia!*. She was laughing so much as I was telling the story that by the time the train pulled in to the station, I had made a train buddy.

We sat down beside the window opposite each other, and she said, "So when we get to Waterloo, he'll be waiting for you?"

"Yes, I expect so," I say, rolling my eyes.

"Oh good, I'll be able to see what he looks like then," she says.

"Yes, you will but—" As I'm speaking, I can feel someone staring at me, and as the train starts slowly moving, I turn to my left and I jump with fright. OH MY GOD! Ryan is standing there, looking at me, he starts laughing, smacking the back of his hand into the palm of the other. The look of shock and horror on my face is clear to my flame-haired friend as she realises this is the man I'm meant to be meeting at Waterloo. Ryan sits down beside me and once he's stopped laughing and backslapping his hand. He explains that he wanted to surprise me so he caught the train at the previous station which would have meant he had to change trains and platforms twice, rather than take the train direct to Waterloo from where he lives. WHY! WHY! WHY! I'm totally caught off guard and am gobsmacked. I can feel my ginger friend's eyes piercing into me and I'm trying hard not to catch her gaze as I know once I do we will both start giggling so I feign a look of happy disbelief and resign myself to the fact that I no longer like surprises.

As me and Ryan make small talk, I turn to look out of the window and catch the eyes of my train buddy who looks like she's about to burst out laughing, I smile at her and keep my head toward the pane of glass that separates me from freedom, trying desperately not to laugh, although cringing inside. The journey to Waterloo felt painstakingly slow, the train stopping at every station. My mind wandered back to that conversation with Harriet when she said, 'it'll be over before you know it' and 'you'll be back in your bed tonight, knowing you'll never have to see him again'. I take comfort from her last sentiment as we arrive at Waterloo and as we disembark, my ginger friend mouths 'good luck' to me with a wry smile. I smile back with a look of hopelessness, and we go our separate ways.

Ryan and I exit the station and on our walk to the theatre, we stop at a pub for an early dinner. He tells me again of his imminent retirement from the police force, of his divorce and his two children that live with him, both in their late teens so can look after themselves, he adds. He talks of the improvements he's made to his house and of the hot tub that he's had installed. Thankfully, on the next table to us are another couple who we discover are also going to see *Mamma Mia!* so most of our time is taken up engaging with them and before long, it's time to go. Me and Ryan split the bill, and we all leave together. After a short stroll, we arrive at the theatre, say goodbye to our fleeting friends and make our way to our seats, which are located in the upper circle next to the aisle with no one sitting directly in front or behind us. It's perfect. Ryan takes the aisle seat and I slip in beside him.

The show begins and I sit back in my seat and enjoy watching the story unfold and not before too long, the interval has arrived. We make our way to the bar and as we walk in, I notice a table with two drinks and Ryan's name beside it. I'm pleasantly surprised at his thoughtful act of organising interval drinks so that we wouldn't have to queue at the bar. "How sweet of you, Ryan, thank you," I say, expressing a look of gratitude. We chat about how good the show is and when Ryan pops to the loo, I start thinking that maybe he isn't that bad; he's kind and considerate, he's just a bit full-on like an excitable puppy and just needs a bit of getting used to.

"Rachel." I hear Ryan's voice and snap back to reality. "The show's about to start." We make our way back to our seats and settle in.

The last 15 minutes of the show, ending with the musical ensemble, is amazing, I could see people jump up out of their seats to dance and when the group of ladies a few seats away from us shot up, I did too, half expecting Ryan to join me. I turned to look at him, only to find him with his head flung back, mouth wide open and snoring away. It was at that point I realised there was no way that I could be with him. How could he be sleeping through the music and all the singing going on? So, I decided that I would make a getaway and tried carefully sliding sideways past him, but his legs were so close to the seat in front. I managed to get one leg over the first hurdle whilst still trying to maintain a rhythmic movement to the music. My thinking was to leave him snoring, run and catch the train home and say that I tried waking him but just couldn't. I got both my legs over his first leg so that I was standing in between his man-spread with my back to him, I tried to dance over the other leg, but he awoke to find my gyrating buttocks in his face. It was all so embarrassing as I tried to explain, over the music, that I was desperate for the loo.

I made my way out to the toilet, reapplied my lipstick and giggled to myself at the absurdity of it all. I dreaded leaving the toilets and having to face him but there was no other escape route, so, with a huge smile on my face, I walked out and found him standing outside waiting for me. "Hi, did I miss much?" I said, trying to sound and act casual.

"No, it was over anyway, you should've woken me."

The group of ladies that were sat close by to us walked past singing and laughing as they made their way out of the theatre. We followed them out and made our way back to the station. I was filled with dread at the thought of him wanting to kiss or asking to see me again. As soon as we arrived at the station, I could see my train sat there at the platform with people rushing to board. Ryan looked at the board and his train was due to depart 10 minutes after mine. I started to make my way to the platform and as I turned to say goodbye, I gave Ryan a kiss on the cheek and said, "Thank you for a lovely evening."

"But it's not over, Rachel!"

"Whatever do you mean?" I spat out.

"Well, I thought I'd accompany you home on the train—"

But before he could finish his sentence, I walked through the barrier and shouted back, "It's fine, you don't have to, goodnight." I didn't wait for a response as I stepped on board and walked down the carriage hoping to find an empty seat in a corner so I could hide. I found a seat beside the window opposite an elderly couple who were dressed so smartly I'm sure they must've been to the theatre too, whether they saw *Mamma Mia!* is a mystery.

The next few minutes, as the train stood motionless, waiting to depart, were excruciating. The image of Ryan walking down the carriage toward me, laughing and slapping the back of his hand into the palm of the other terrorised me. The train pulled away and I breathed a sigh of relief. It was over. I smiled when I finally made it to my bed and drifted off.

The following morning, I'm awoken by the sound of the phone ringing and as I pick up, I presume it must be Harriet calling to catch up. "Morning, Hattie, a bit early for you to be calling."

"Well, top of the morning to yer," Ryan chuckles.

No! No! No! This isn't happening. I'm still sleeping, this must be a bad dream, I want to pull the duvet up over my head and assume the foetal position. "Good morning, Ryan, sorry I thought you were someone else," I reply, but Ryan is not listening to a word I've said and rambles on about how he's planning a BBQ at the weekend and that I must come and meet his children.

"It's only going to be a couple of people, a few of the neighbours, my kids, their girlfriends, and bring an overnight bag for a sleepover and a bikini too so we can test out the hot tub," he says excitedly.

My future life with Ryan flashes before my eyes and a feeling of suffocation overcomes me and before I know it I've blurted out, "No! I'm sorry, I won't be seeing you again, Ryan, thank you, goodbye," I place the phone down and pull the duvet over my head.

Chapter Four

A Farter For Starters

"Another one bites the dust," I say, when I meet up with Harriet and Naomi a few days later at The Drinking Ole. We share a bottle of Rioja, well, me and Hattie do seeing as Naomi isn't much of a drinker and always tends to go for a white wine spritzer. They've both gone from laughter to gasps, wide-mouthed, jaw-on-the-ground expressions, back to laughter from me recalling my first two dates of the quest with Francois and Ryan. "Whose idea was all this dating malarkey anyways?" I say, smiling.

"Yours!" they both answer simultaneously.

"It's only been a few weeks, Rache, it's just a blip," Naomi offers.

"Yes, you know what they say, third one's a charm," Hattie remarks, winking at me.

The barman appears at our table with a bottle of wine in hand and says, "It's compliments of the gentleman." He motions with his head to a table where three men are seated, looking over at us. Hattie sticks her ring finger up to show the wedding band adorning her hand at which point Naomi and I start giggling. Two of the men are in suits and the third looks a bit rough around the edges, with cropped red hair. Hattie sends the bottle back, smiles and nods at the men as we all get up to leave.

One of the suits comes over to us and offers his apologies. "Sorry, ladies, didn't mean to offend, I'm Jeremy."

"No offence taken," Hattie responds, "but I have to get home to my husband."

The ginger one appears and offers his hand out towards me. "I'm Ricky."

I don't really like shaking hands with complete strangers, so I smile and say, "I'm Rachel, and we were just leaving but thank you for the—"

But before I could finish, Naomi interjects, nervously whispering, "I really have to get home and get started on dinner, Rache."

The tall dark suit named Jeremy is chatting with Hattie and as me and Naomi make a move to leave, Ricky says, "You don't fancy going out for a bite to eat, do you, Rachel?"

I'm momentarily stunned into silence, then turn to Naomi with an expression of 'help me' but Naomi mutters, "The quest."

I turn to look at Ricky. "What? What quest?" he says.

"Oh, no, nothing, I'll explain later," I reply.

"I'll take that as a yes for dinner, then?" he says, beaming like a Cheshire cat.

"Sure, why not," I answer, trying not to sound too indifferent. I wave and mouth 'bye' to Hattie who's still chatting to Jeremy. She blows me a kiss and I give Naomi a stern look as the three of us leave. I can't be mad at Naomi, I did say at the start of 'the quest' that I wouldn't reject anyone who asks me out regardless of how I feel, what I think of them or how they look.

Me and Ricky walk out onto Peascod Street, and he mentions that he's not really familiar with the area and asks where I'd like to go for dinner. I suggest the Indian restaurant next door, The Raja, which he's happy with. The restaurant is dimly lit and in need of updating, but it's popular with the after-work crowd on their office outings. I notice a couple of smaller tables either side of the entrance, which the waiter directs us to and offers us a menu once we've taken our seats. The decor is basic and consists of a wooden bar area, and dark wooden tables and chairs. The chairs are clothed in dark red velvet and the carpet is also a shade of red with a yellow design but is worn and badly frayed. The food, however, is delicious and even though there's a raucous table of office workers at the far end of the restaurant, they're not in any way close enough to disturb us. Our waiter returns promptly and takes our drinks order.

"I'll have a beer," Ricky pipes up and then realises that he hasn't thought to ask me first and looks over to me apologetically. I smile and shake my head to signify that it doesn't matter and look up to the waiter and order the same. I'm feeling a little awkward as Ricky is not my type at all; I've never gone for the close shave, bad boy look before, however, he seems pleasant enough and he does have a cheeky cockney way about him. "So, what do you do?" he asks.

"I work as a PA for an office supplies company; not remarkably interesting but I enjoy it and it pays the bills," I reply. "And you?" I enquire.

"I'm in-between jobs at the minute; that's what that meeting next door was all about. Hopefully I'll be doing some work in this area for a bit. I used to be in the army but got discharged so any job, cash in hand, I can get is a bonus."

"Oh really?" I say, intrigued, wanting to know his story but the waiter appears with our drinks and asks if we're ready to order. "No sorry, haven't had a chance to look at the menu yet," I reply.

"No problem, madam," he says in a thick Indian accent and leaves.

We both scan the menu and agree on the sharing platter for starters and as soon as we put our menus back down on the table, the waiter returns with a small wicker basket of poppadoms. We place our order and enjoy the cold beer. I'm feeling a little tipsy, so I make a start on the poppadoms and chutney, as does Ricky. I don't really want to ask about Ricky's discharge from the army but can't help myself.

"Okay, but first you have to tell me what the quest is." he says.

"Well, basically if someone asks me out, I've made it a rule to accept all invitations, no matter what, in pursuit of finding my perfect imperfect soulmate."

"So, I wouldn't have got a look-in, then?" he says.

I burst out laughing. "No, I'm not saying that; I'm saying that I'm willing to explore all avenues that I probably would not have walked down before," I say, smiling at him.

He chuckles softly, his cheeky smile melts me, and I wander off in my thoughts that maybe he's not all that bad; I mean, isn't this what the quest is all about? His packaging is not to my preference but maybe his character, personality and, most importantly, the chemistry might be. I'm bought back to the moment with the waiter placing our starter platter onto the table. "So, what's the story with the army then?" I say, whilst helping myself to an onion bhaji.

He takes a big glug of his beer, plates the starter and in-between mouthfuls, shares his story. "Okay, so I was on leave for a week and thought I'd surprise my girlfriend and basically I walked in on her with another man in our bedroom at it like rabbits," he says casually.

"Oh no!" I gasp.

"The worst part was that I knew the guy; he was from the same neighbourhood as me in Hackney where I grew up and there'd been bad blood between us. The thing is that they just carried on when they saw me standing at the bedroom door."

"What?" I shrieked.

Ricky went on with his story. "So, I grabbed him and kicked the shit out of him and booted him down the stairs. He was naked and tried to fight back but I dragged him out of the house and—"

"Stop! Please, stop!" I couldn't bear to listen to any more; one minute I was feeling sorry for him and the next sickened, hearing of his abhorrent behaviour, especially as he had a smug look on his face whilst recalling the events as if his actions were justifiable. I couldn't eat another bite and just sipped my beer as Ricky, seeing that I was clearly shocked, tried to explain his actions.

"I got nicked, did time, got discharged from the army. You see, my girlfriend locked the front door once we were outside and called the filth so by the time they arrived, he was in pretty bad shape."

I fell silent and watched as Ricky continued eating. "Wow! That's a story," I remarked, trying to lighten the mood as I wasn't sure what else to say, but from my demeanour he could tell that I wasn't impressed.

"Haven't you done something that you completely regret and wish you could go back and change, Rachel?" he says, as he devours the remaining meat on the platter.

Yes, agreeing to have dinner with you is what I regret comes to mind. "Yes, of course," I nod, feigning a smile.

The waiter arrives just in time to distract me from the awkwardness I find myself feeling. He clears our starter dishes and asks if we'd like to order our main course. "Yeah, yeah," Ricky says, "and another beer."

When the waiter leaves, Ricky half stands up as if he's about to do a squat. He pushes his chair back with the back of his legs, sticks his bottom out and lets out an enormous, long fart. He bursts out laughing, turns and walks away, saying, "I've been wanting to do that all evening."

As soon as he's out of view, I grab my handbag, stand up and walk calmly toward the door. I catch the waiter's eye as he walks to our table, beer and menus in hand, but my focus is on escape and as I get closer to my exit, I take a final look around, satisfied that I haven't been seen and I open the door and run.

My heart pounding, I run out onto Peascod Street and duck into the alleyway running down the side of the restaurant trying not to lose my balance on the cobbles, and I breathe a sigh of relief. I can feel my heart pounding out of my chest so fast, but I feel lucky to have had the opportunity to get away from him until I hear someone shout out my name.

"Rachel!"

Oh my God, it's him! I hurriedly walk a few steps and seconds later, I hear him calling out again, it sounds closer this time, as though he's seen me in the alleyway. Sheer panic envelops me, and I can hardly see where I'm running when I collide full on into the arms of a stranger.

I feel safe, warm in his arms and I can smell his aftershave mingled with the aroma of garlic and herbs, then suddenly I hear footsteps approaching and the stranger see's the panic in my eyes and senses the tension in my body. He pulls me in close and I instinctively kiss him on the lips. The footsteps pass us by, but I remain lip-locked until the footsteps have faded away. I feel uplifted and as I gently open my eyes and pull back slightly, I become aware of the familiar taste and smell of a cigarette. "Are you okay?" he asks.

I whisper, "Yes." I gently nod as if I'm transfixed in this bubble with him. His eyes are a deep brown, he feels familiar to me and as I step back to look at him, I hear footsteps approaching; panic overcomes me and as I release my hold on him, I whisper, "I'm sorry," and run. I can hear the stranger shout out to me "senorita" but as much as I want to run back to his embrace, I also don't want to run into Ricky and my objective now is to make my way back to the safety of my flat.

I'm ten feet away from the front door and I have already prepared the keys in my hand to make my entrance as swift as possible. I slide the key in and push open the door as if my life depended on it; I'm home, I'm safe and feel elated and relieved at the same time as I climb the stairs to the flat. My mind is racing, and my heart is doing backflips as I think back to the brief moment spent in the arms of the stranger, the sound of someone pressing the buzzer to my flat startles me and I return back to panic mode. Is it Ricky? Did he see me and follow me home? My mobile phone pings a message and I notice that one's from Naomi asking how dinner is going and the other is from Harriet, who's downstairs. I buzz her up and open the door to the flat and watch her as she climbs up.

"Well, what the hell happened to you? That bloke you went off with came charging back into The Drinking Ole about 10 minutes ago asking if we'd seen you."

"What were you still doing there?" I asked, as I filled the kettle.

"Well, that gorgeous Jeremy and his friend kept me entertained. We had some Tapas, another glass of wine and discovered that we had mutual friends from his previous life in advertising. Then just as I stood up to leave, that guy you left with came in looking panicked. Said that he'd popped to the loo and came back to find you gone; he thought you'd gone to the ladies and asked the waiter who told him that you'd left."

"Yes! I ran out, Hattie." She burst out laughing as did I.

I made some coffee, poured us a brandy and took it outside on the balcony. "I told him that you obviously weren't interested in him, said my goodbyes and walked here." She looked at me with amused puzzlement.

"He was so gross, Hattie, he told me that he got discharged from the army because, whilst on a week's leave, he went home and found his girlfriend shagging another man in their house; he beat him to a pulp and did time. If that wasn't bad enough, he pushed his chair out and did a humungous fart just as we'd finished our starters, mumbled that he'd been waiting to do that all evening, laughed and went off to the loo. At which point I—"

"Where were you?" Hattie cut in with a look of disgust followed by a face full of laughter.

"Next door at The Raja." I paused for a moment as I took a sip of brandy and smiled at her when a feeling of excitement came over me thinking of my encounter with the stranger. "So, I ran out down the alleyway, the one that's next to the restaurant, and collided into this man and I had the most romantic kiss with this total stranger." I finished telling Hattie the rest of the story and we swooned over the mystery man.

I called Naomi once Harriet had left and recalled the evening's events. "He did look a bit rough though, Rache, didn't he?" she said.

"Yes! He did, Nomes, and thanks for mentioning the quest and pushing me to have dinner with him. I was going to say that I had other plans before you—"

But before I could finish she jumped in. "Your quest, Rache, and, besides, he had asked you out and you did say no matter what, whether big, fat, bald, smelly, etc., etc."

"Yes, okay," I sighed in defeat.

"Look, come over to mine on Monday after work for dinner and you can tell me more about the mysterious kiss with the stranger."

"Okay, night, Nomes."

"Another one bites the dust, Rache." She rung off and, with that, I went to bed. A kiss with the stranger on my mind as well as on my lips.

Chapter Five

King George's Arms

I awoke from my slumber feeling warm and fuzzy; running into this stranger last night has left me dizzy with excitement, he may be the one to put an end to my quest and my pursuit to find my perfect imperfect soulmate. I need to find him, I need to go back to that alleyway, maybe he lives or works close by, I might run into him again... But, No! I can't! Suppose I bump into Ricky. What would he be doing there? He might be working close by and see me. No! I can't go back; I just have to hope that I'm lucky enough to run into the stranger and his lips again. My internal dialogue has gone into overdrive and determined the outcome of my dilemma.

The weekend passes by uneventfully and although it's quiet, my thoughts of my encounter with the stranger has me in a dreamlike state so that, come Monday morning, I still have a smile on my face and a feeling of giddiness remembering the kiss whilst on my way to work. Since I've arrived a little earlier than usual, I pop the kettle on and make coffee for the small team of sales guys I look after. There are four of them in total; two are married and the other two are in relationships. They're nice guys and inevitably I always hear the stories of what they get up to on their work trips away and sometimes see the odd photo of a naked body part that's been taken at the end of the night when one of them has passed out from the excesses of alcohol.

My day rolls on in a dreamy haze and before I know it, it's 5:30 and I remember my dinner plans at Naomi's. I arrive just as Naomi's husband, Neil, is leaving with their two girls. "Hello, Rache, how the devil are you?" he shouts out as he's strapping the girls in the back of the car.

"Yes, really good, Neil, and you?" I shout back as Naomi opens the front door.

"Yes all's well, okay, you two have a good night," he says as he climbs into the driver's seat.

"Hello, you," Naomi says, as she ushers me into the living room.

"Are you still working?" I say, noticing her laptop still up and running on the coffee table.

"No, but I will be showing you something on it later," she replies, looking at me coyly.

"Ooh, sounds intriguing," I say.

So, after dinner, she says, "I want to show you something, Rache. Please don't get mad, I know you're hanging on and waiting to see if you'll bump into the mystery man from Friday night, but you need to keep doing the quest and—"

"Okay, okay, what is it?" I interrupt as we get up from the dining table, wine glass in hand, and I follow her into the lounge where we sit down on the couch. She picks up her laptop and a page pops open; 'My Gorgeous Friend'. I scan the page and read out the text, "*My gorgeous friend, Rachel, is 39 years old and before she reaches 40, must find the love of her life...* Are you crazy!" I cry out. "Naomi, you cannot be serious!"

"Look," she says, "you're on a quest and you have to try this too. It's just another way of meeting guys, that's all, and I know you won't make the time to sign up to it and fill out all the stuff they want you to, so I did it for you and this one's free for the first two months. What have you got to lose? Besides, there's this cute guy on there that I think you'll like."

I can't argue with her as she's right, so I succumb to her wishes. "You'd better pour me another glass of wine," I demand, which she does happily and as I take a sip, she shows me the profile of one of my matches.

"Look, this one's handsome. He has his own business, his name is George, he lives about 15 miles away and he owns a pub called the King George's Arms," she says.

"That's original," I remark, rolling my eyes.

"Look at his photo, Rache, he has a full head of hair, it says that he's 5-foot-10 – that's not too bad – and just think of all the free booze and parties we can have at the pub!" she says, excitedly.

"Okay, Nomes, so what do I do?" I say, as I scroll down to read a little more about George. His face looks a little plump and round, but he does have lovely blonde hair and a beautiful smile. It says that he plays badminton, pool, and loves dancing. Okay, so far so good.

"Well, I've already done it, Rache!" exclaims Naomi.

"What have you done, Nomes?" I almost yell out at her.

"You're meeting him at his pub at eight on Wednesday," she says.

"What!" I scream. "That's only a day away."

"Yes, I know, the thing is that you don't want to meet him on a Thursday, Friday, or at the weekend because he might be busy working, so I chose Wednesday which is midweek and hopefully it'll be quiet," she remarks.

"Well, I would've thought that he'd have staff to serve if it got busy, Nomes."

"Rache, just think of the excitement of it all, you could be the future King George's Arms landlady," she says, looking wistful.

"I think I've had enough excitement to last a lifetime if the last few weeks are anything to go by. Okay, what's the address of the pub?"

"Yay!" she screams out.

As I'm leaving, she hands me a note with George's address and the login details to the website. "I've saved a couple of other profiles that you matched with just in case this one doesn't work out," she shouts out as I'm walking down the drive. I put my hand up to wave goodbye and make my way to the bus stop.

Before long, I'm home in my bedroom, scanning my wardrobe for an outfit for the pub. It's late October and although it's dry out, it can get a little chilly later in the evening, so I opt for my trusted jeans, t-shirt, and leather jacket, with heels. I'll be driving so won't have more than one drink as I don't know the area or the pub and, with it being somewhere in the sticks, those country roads can be a bugger to drive down in the dark.

A day later, when I get back from work, I make myself a quick dinner of beans on toast, grate some cheese on top, splash on a couple of dashes of Worcester sauce, and start getting ready.

I set the satnav to the address of the pub and get going; it's 7:30 so I should get there in plenty of time.

I drive out of Windsor and 20 minutes later, find myself going deeper into dark winding country roads and I start imagining a cosy pub with a roaring fire, good wine and ales, home cooked food with a pine wood aroma clinging to the air.

I arrive at the destination, it's a quiet road, dark and dimly lit, but there's no pub in sight. I reapply my lipstick and check the address that Naomi gave me with what I've typed in the satnav; it's all correct so I venture out of the car and see a little sign with an arrow that reads 'King George's Arms'. "Oh, thank God!" I say aloud as I walk to where the arrow is pointing and find myself walking towards a bungalow, the sound of shingle underfoot making a loud crunching noise that as I walk I find the heels of my sandals sinking down into the stones. I make it to the front door in one piece and tap on the knocker. The hallway light flicks on and through the top half of the frosted glass door, I can see a figure walking up. As the figure gets closer, it appears to get bigger and then the door slowly opens. "Oh, hello, sorry to bother you, I'm looking for a pub called—"

But before I could finish, she interjects, with a chuckle, "King George's Arms!"

"Yes," I say, as we both smile at one another. She's wearing a white nightie with pink slippers; at least it looks like a nightie but could be a dress. It's tight fitting around her rotund body and she has a full head of golden tight curls that come to her shoulders.

I can see someone peering from around a door at the end of the hallway behind her. "Yes, love, you want to take the side access path that's next to the drive and you'll see it," she says, with a sparkle in her eyes.

"Thank you very much, it's so dark I must've missed the sign for it, sorry to have troubled you," I say, as I turn and walk away out of the drive.

"Everyone does," I hear her say as I crunch my way out of the driveway and turn into the path.

I walk about 10 metres before I see a sign that reads 'King George's Arms' above a building that looks like a barn. The hairs on the back of my neck stand as I get closer and I realise that what I was imagining on my drive here is nothing like what I'm standing in front of and, as I take stock of the situation and am about to turn around to leave, the wooden door flings open and a man who looks exactly like the woman who answered the door to the bungalow appears wearing the same smile with a head full of golden hair and the waistline to match. "Rachel, hello, and welcome to my pub!" the voice bellows out at me.

I feel like a rabbit caught in headlights that's about to get run over. Motionless, I can only manage to squeak out, "George?"

"Yes," he says, as he ushers me in with open arms to what I can only describe as a make-believe pub, a man cave, a big double garage that has everything a boy would enjoy. I scan the room, unable to move away from the entrance and into his lair. To my left on the wall is a dartboard which is next to a pinball machine then there's a jukebox. In the top left corner is a bar area with four high bar stools placed around a wooden counter, and then my eyes move to the next objects. There are two gold thrones where a king would sit with his queen. I can feel my mouth opening in disbelief as my eyes continue in a clockwise motion, scanning the room. Next to the thrones in the top right corner is a pool table and at the 3 o'clock position is a two-seater sofa. Then, as I look to my right, I see a square wooden table and chairs with board games. George is standing right in the middle of the room on a black and white chequered floor area which I'm assuming is the dancefloor. "So! What do you think of my pub, Rachel?" George asks, opening his arms as prideful owner.

I realise I'm still gaping and quickly change my expression of shock to that of amazement and say, "Wow! I've never seen anything like it before in my life, it's—"

"Everybody loves it," he interrupts excitedly. "That is, my friends and family, of course," he continues, as I nod slowly thinking back to a couple of nights earlier at Naomi's where this nightmare all began.

I can feel myself tense up, I need to leave, I could just turn back around and say 'sorry, I've made a mistake' and walk out calmly, or run... *Remember, it's dark and the gravel, yes, just calmly walk out...* But as I turn my head slowly to discreetly check out my escape route, something moving catches my eye and I turn back to George, who says, "Talking of family, here is Mum and my twin sis, Georgette."

I slowly turn to my left and there's the lady who opened the door to the bungalow and beside her stands the person who was peering round the door at me. They're both wearing the same outfit stretched over their round body's and are laughing loudly. I feel like I'm in an episode of the *Twilight Zone* and join in the laughter, masking my true emotions, my mind screaming, *RUNNNNN!* But my body unable to carry out the action.

"She looks just like in her picture George, doesn't she?" his sister, Georgette, remarks, as if I'm invisible and George and his mum both smile and nod.

"So, have you offered her a drink then, George? his mum enquires.

"I was just about to when you two turned up; I told you not to come until later," George replies, looking sternly at his mum. I watch them talking and there's no mistaking that they share the same genes; as well as looking alike they have the same laugh and mannerisms. They all turn and look at me as if they've just read my thoughts and George asks if I'd like to sit on the throne, he then turns toward his mother and sister and cocks his head to the side, motioning for them to leave.

"See you later, Rachel," they both say in unison, giggling as they waddle off, much to George's delight.

"SOOO, what would you like to drink, milady?" he says, as he strolls to position himself behind the bar. I follow him tentatively and sit down on a stool. His hand reaches down behind the counter, and he retrieves a gold plastic crown and places it on his head. I can't control myself and inadvertently burst out laughing which releases my nervous energy and somewhat relaxes the farcical predicament I find myself in. Luckily, King George doesn't take offence. "Treason!" he screams. "Off with her head!" he says, laughing. He has a pretty face and a good sense of humour although could do with shifting about 10 stones – all of them could. I start to wonder about how I'm ever to get out of here, when George asks, again, still in character, "What would my fair maiden like to drink?"

"Oh, Sire, I'm afraid I do not drink," I reply. I think it's best that I don't drink; I need a clear head. I'm not sure what my fate will be if I get trapped in this lunatic asylum and I'm conscious that Georgette and the mum might make another appearance and then I'll be outnumbered, and my escape will be hindered.

"Oh!" he replies, sounding a little miffed.

"Yes, I have allergies," I blurt out. What am I saying? Think! Think! His face looks unconvinced and so I continue, "Yes, I tend to come out in a rash and so I take these allergy tablets and..." I pretend to start scratching my neck and arm as if I'm having an allergic reaction. "So, I only partake on special occasions like weddings, birthdays, or parties and then it's only ever half a glass," I pause, "of champagne." I need to stop talking, the king's face is looking at me disbelievingly. "I'll have a lemonade with ice and a slice," I finish saying.

"Okay, I think I can rustle that up for you," he says, as he retrieves two glasses from behind the bar. He places ice in both, followed by a slice of lemon and then turns, picks up a bottle of Beefeater gin from the shelf behind him and pours a generous measure of gin in one of the glasses. "Why don't you pop some music on, Rachel? The jukebox has a good selection," he murmurs, gin bottle still in hand.

"Okay," I reply as I step down from the stool and walk over to the jukebox. I feel certain this is a ruse to get me away from the bar whilst he finishes preparing the drinks. I can feel his eyes poring over my body then I hear the fizzing sound of a bottle being opened and I turn toward the bar and watch him pour.

He looks up and smiles. "Found anything you like?"

"Oh yes," I say, tapping any old digits on the jukebox, and as I walk back to my stool, 'Tainted Love' starts playing.

"Tuuuuune!" he bellows out, gyrating to the music.

He hands me the drink and we clink glasses and say 'cheers' and I take a sip. I can taste the gin. I knew it! I am totally pissed off now. I mean, suppose I really did suffer with serious allergies; I could be having a reaction right now! This could, however, work to my advantage, I start thinking. I could start scratching and say that I'm feeling unwell. A plan is coming together, I think to myself. I take another sip of the drink and watch George move from around the bar, drink in hand, singing, "Tainted love, ohhh, tainted love." He begins to swing his arms around rhythmically. I must admit, I do love this song but not here, not now and not with him.

I watch him dancing in the middle of the chequered dancefloor, drink in hand, his tight-fitting white t-shirt clinging to his body, wet patches forming under his armpits, and his moobs bouncing from side to side. He catches me staring at him and beckons me over to join him and I shake my head to say no but then realise I must show some interest in order for my plan to work, so I down the lemonade on purpose, and reluctantly join him on the dancefloor. I start to dance, feeling embarrassed as I imagine what Harriet, Naomi, not to mention Vince and Harry would say if they could see me now, but desperate times call for desperate measures. "This tainted love you've given. I give you all a boy could give you. Take my tears and..." George belts out the song, looking and gyrating in my direction. I feel scared for a moment then join him in singing whilst hatching my escape and just as the song comes to an end, I start scratching my neck and bend over, gasping for breath, clutching my throat. "Rachel! Are you okay?" he shouts out.

"I just felt a bit out of breath for a moment and my neck is feeling hot and itchy," I reply, laying it on thick and breathing erratically.

"Oh, dear God! I hope everything's okay," he says, walking back to behind the bar, his voice now sounding panicked.

"Maybe I could use the bathroom, please?" I say, slowly walking back to the bar, retrieving my handbag. I can see fear in his eyes and realise this is it.

"Yes, yes, of course, I'll show you..." he says.

"No, it's okay, I already feel embarrassed, just point me in the right direction and pour me a glass of water please," I say, casually trying not to alert him to suspect me in any way.

"Okay, just take a right out of the pub and go in through the back door of the bungalow and the loo is the first door on the left," he says, his face stricken with alarm.

"Thanks," I mumble as I hold myself together and walk out closing the wooden door to King George's Arms as I leave. I hurriedly tiptoe up the path, trying not to make a sound and then start to imagine that Georgette and his mum might be watching me and jump out from behind the fence at any second. As I get closer to my freedom, I turn back. It's so dark I can't see a thing. I breathe a sigh of relief and cross the gravel driveway, trying desperately not to make too much noise. I can see my car and start walking faster towards it when a light from inside the bungalow comes on. I run for my life, hand fumbling for the car keys in my jacket pocket.

I jump into the car and start the ignition, feeling terrified that at any moment, the three of them will be running out and surround my car. The engine kicks in and I release the handbrake and drive off slowly. I turn to the left and look at the bungalow as I drive past, and I can see two figures standing on the doorstep, their body's blocking any light from escaping the house. I put my foot down and drive away, feeling a sense of calm come over me the closer I get to Windsor.

Chapter Six

The Spirit's Behind You

The sweat is sliding down my back as I'm running. I'm running so fast that my breath can't keep up with my legs, I feel a panic like I have a fever that I can't sweat out. My fear is palpable, and for whoever is chasing me, it's advantageous, their hands grasping at my clothing. I can hear music, I run faster towards it hoping that someone will save me. "Don't touch me please, I cannot stand the way you tease." The music gets clearer, and I gasp for breath. My eyes pop open as I shoot upright in bed with the alarm beeping. I lean across, switch it off and lay back down. I take deep breaths to calm myself and fall back to sleep when I'm awoken with my mobile ringing. I let it ring off and then the landline starts to ring, so I bumble out of bed and pick up.

"Oh! Thank God! You're alive. I've been trying to get hold of you, I called twice last night, no answer and again just now on your mobile. Where have you been? Or did you get lucky?" Naomi blurts out.

"Nomes, I'm alive, I was asleep and, no, not lucky, in fact, I'd say that was the worst hour of my dating life so far," I say calmly.

"I called you last night, I sent you a message, and I even called your work, I was about to call the police when—"

"What! Why? What time is it?" I scream down the phone.

"Rache, it's 9:30."

"FUCK! I'll call you later, Nomes."

I hang up, jump in the shower and make my way to work. As it happens, when I sneak in at 10:45, no one even looks up, so I creep over to my desk and sit down and busy myself. Two of the sales guys are away on business and the other two are on calls.

It's a small, family-run company that employs about 20 people and I have endured five years, although I have also enjoyed it. It's a bit dysfunctional at times, as the owner is hardly ever in, and his two daughters practically manage the day-to-day business. One of the daughters, Sharon, is married to Geoff, who's the sales manager. He's a sleaze and he looks like a shorter version of Barry Manilow. I always tease him by singing 'Copacabana' whenever I'm feeling mischievous, much to the amusement of the sales guys. They tell me of the antics they get up to on their business trips away and Roger, whose desk is a few feet away from mine, always wheels his chair over to me and tells me everything, warts and all.

He told me that, once, on this business trip away with Geoff, they were staying at this ropey old hotel in Leeds. After a few drinks in the hotel bar, Geoff invites two ladies to join them at their table. A few more drinks later and one of the ladies, who Roger described as looking like a transvestite, says to Geoff, "I know who you remind me of, you look just like Barry Manilow." She then proceeds to snort with laughter, pushes her seat back and barfs on the floor in front of them all. At this point Roger decides to call it a night, but in the morning, gets to hear what happened after he left. So, neither lady would leave the other alone with Geoff, so both ended up in his hotel room and he ended up shagging them both.

"Ewwww!" I cried out as Roger was recalling the night. "What? Even though she had barfed, he still shagged her?" I said disgustedly. Roger bursts out laughing. "I feel sorry for Sharon; just imagine if she knew," I added.

"She must know what he gets up to, Rache. From what he says, I don't think that she lets him near her anymore in that way," he replies.

After Roger relayed this gem to me, I couldn't help but tease Geoff by singing 'Copacabana', although he must suspect that I've heard the story but doesn't let on and just smiles and goes along with it.

After work, I decide to go for a run, but before leaving, I give Naomi a call and revisit my encounter with King George as briefly as I could and thank her for her choice in men. The sarcasm in my voice is evident and as she apologises and, just before hanging up we both say, "Another one bites the dust!"

My run through Windsor Great Park is exactly what I needed. I feel exhilarated and as I come to slow my pace, I start thinking back to the morning and the dream I had of being chased. It seems that, lately, all I've been doing is running; running away from people and situations I find myself in. I start chuckling to myself when I think back to last night with George, the dancing, his sweaty moobs, his deceitful prank in lacing my drink and my eventual getaway. This quest is turning out to be quite an adventure. What is the universe trying to tell me? I guess getting older is making me reflect on my life more; maybe I do need to move out of my comfort zone and stop being so picky, put myself out there for this quest to succeed. Yes, but isn't that what I'm doing? I need to be more positive then, and, in doing so, I'm sure to attract the same positive soul. Yes! After giving myself a little pep talk I snap back to reality and lose my footing when a dog strays across my path.

"Monty, over here, boy!" I hear the owner shout. "Sorry," they continue, as I fall forward and stumble but fortunately catch myself and manage not to splatter myself on the ground in front of the gates to the castle. I glance around to see if anyone had witnessed it and find a smiling face looking in my direction. I half smile back, mortified, and continue walking. "Hi." I hear a voice close behind me and as I turn I see the smiling man approach me. "Are you okay?" he asks.

"Yes, thanks," I chuckle. "Those bloody little dogs, always trying to trip you up," I say as we continue to walk and talk, and just pass the time for a few moments until we have to part ways. After we say goodbye, I continue on my walk home.

A few seconds later, I feel a hand on my shoulder and as I turn, I find the smiling man. "Hi again, I just thought, if you're free sometime, would you like to go out for a drink?" he says, blushing. "I mean, it's okay if you don't want to, you can say no, or you might be in a relationship."

He talked so fast without taking a breath that I started to laugh. "Okay, sure," I reply, and we exchanged numbers.

"I'm Graham, by the way."

"Rachel," I reply as we say goodbye and part ways a second time.

I think of the stranger that I ran into as I take that alleyway where it all took place; although it's early evening, it's noticeably quiet apart from a few people returning home from work. I walk onto Peascod Street and pass The Raja and The Drinking Ole and then remember Ricky, so I start a steady jog back home.

The stranger is still on my mind, and I find myself scanning every man I pass on my way home. His olive skin, warm brown eyes, and dark hair. I find myself back in that moment and can smell his aftershave and the taste of his mouth. I arrive home and feel good after my run and after taking a shower, I decide to relax and pour myself a glass of red, pop George Michael on and prepare dinner.

The phone rings and I let it go to the answer machine. I turn down the music and hear, "Sometimes I feel I've got to run away; I've got to get away," followed by laughter. I recognise Vince and Harry's voices singing Tainted Love and pick up the phone and start laughing along with them.

"Is that a true story, Rache?" Vince asks.

"You poor thing," I can hear Harry say in the background.

"Yes, all true," I reply. "Nomes has obviously been in touch then?" I continue.

"Yes, she feels really bad about the whole thing and is never going to set you up again," Vince says. "Anyway, she's coming over on Saturday for dinner, Harriet can't make it as she's had a better offer so come round at six, darling, no excuses, see you." He hangs up quickly so I can't decline and say I've other plans.

Just as I hang up, my mobile pings with a message from Graham. *'Hi, it's Graham, it was lovely to run into you earlier and I thought I'd get in touch sooner rather than later and see when you're free to meet up'.* I turn George back up and carry on with dinner. I'm not in the mood for meeting up too soon so I text back and arrange to meet the following week at a pub that's a halfway point for the both of us.

Dinner at Vince and Harry's is always fun. They live in an old Victorian house in Windsor that's styled and decorated as you'd see in a magazine; it all looks awfully expensive, but exudes a homely and cosy feel. They're great at hosting, and the evening is always full of copious amounts of alcohol, food and laughter. I am, of course, the chief storyteller of the night as they all want to hear, in detail, of all the dates I've had since the quest began, which dominates the entire evening. The evening ends with Vince putting on Soft Cell's 'Tainted Love' when I visit the bathroom. I walk back to the living room to find the three of them singing and dancing along; they look up as I enter the room and double up laughing. I join in, of course. I fail to mention my upcoming date with Graham intentionally when I'm leaving as I'm really hoping that, this time, this one will be normal.

I arrange my date with Graham the following week on a Thursday and when it comes around, I'm not in the usual crazy, bouncing around the room, pulling out different outfits mood. I simply put on my jeans, boots, a jumper, grab my faithful black leather jacket, and walk to the pub. It's only a mile away and the walk will do me good, also I can relax and have a couple of drinks too. I'm feeling good about meeting up with

Graham; we've met in the old-fashioned way, and he was brave to come after me to ask me out, which shows courage and I like that in a man. I arrive on time to find Graham already seated at the bar on a stool with a bottle of beer.

"Hello," I say as I walk over to him.

He steps down from the stool and gives me a kiss on the cheek and says, "How lovely to see you, Rachel." I say thank you and take a seat on the adjoining stool. "Are you okay with sitting at the bar?" he says, as I settle into my seat.

"Yes, this is fine," I reply. The barman arrives and asks me what I'd like to drink. I point to what Graham is drinking and say, "I'll have one of those, please."

Graham is just a little taller than me with blue eyes and short fair hair, he's clean shaven and he has a good wholesome feel about him. We're sitting close enough to each other for our legs to occasionally touch when we move, but with enough distance that it doesn't feel overfamiliar. The conversation and laughter is flowing so well between us, and he tells me that he's stopping over with a friend who lives in Eton as he's just got back from spending six months in India. He seems very worldly, loves travelling and learning about different cultures and is very much in touch with his emotions and spirituality.

I tell him that my life sounds depressingly boring compared to his adventures and so I take my leave and pop to the loo. We've had a couple of bottles of beer already and as I walk back I don't feel at all tipsy, maybe I'm high on the excitement of how my date is going. When I return to my seat, Graham is ordering another round and I insist on paying since he's got the last two rounds in. The barman returns with my change, and I whisper to Graham that I think he's undercharged me. "No, that's right, Rachel, the non-alcoholic beer is cheaper," he whispers, to which I nearly spray him with the contents of beer from my mouth.

"Oh! I wondered why I wasn't getting a buzz," I say, feeling foolish.

"Are you okay with that? Or shall I order a real one for you?" he says.

"No, it's fine," I reply, trying not to sound too disappointed. "It's not that bad actually," I continue, lying through my beer.

As Graham continues to talk, I take a sneaky look at the bottle and there it is; 0% alcohol. My fault, I think to myself, I should've just ordered wine. What was I thinking trying to act so cool, saying 'I'll have what he's drinking'. Surely, he should have made me aware that it wasn't a real beer. Thankfully, he's still talking and didn't notice that I had wandered off into my own thoughts. I tune in to what he's saying. "So, it's been about three years now since I stopped drinking, it was shortly after my mum passed away."

"Oh, I'm sorry," I say.

"That's okay, she was unwell for a while, and it was her time. She was a medium, so I grew up with people in and out of our house at all hours visiting her, wanting to make contact with loved ones that had passed over and who needed answers or some comfort. My dad, on the other hand, had had enough of it and thought it was a load of mumbo jumbo, so, one day after school, I came home to be told that he'd packed his bags and had gone."

"Oh no," I squeezed in, feeling sad listening to his story.

"It's okay, we had enough money from what Mum took from the readings. She used to say that I had 'it' and that I should go into clairvoyance, but I never really wanted to and, besides, what really hurt at the time was that my dad never said goodbye, didn't even leave me a note; I never saw him again." Graham stopped talking and smiled at me, but he has a sadness in his eyes. I feel sorry for him about his dad just leaving like that. I smile back and think of how open and in touch he is with his feelings, especially for him to share this with me on a first date. I get to thinking that I'd definitely like to see him again.

"Graham, that's such a sad story—"

As I was talking, Graham's eyes light up and he says, "There's someone behind you." I turn my head around and don't see anyone apart from a few tables that are occupied. I turn back to Graham looking at him puzzled. "There, there she is," he says, and I quickly turn around again. There's no one there and as I turn back to face him, bewildered, he says, "I can see an old lady behind you, she keeps coming and going, she's standing right there now behind your right shoulder, she could be your spirit guide." I gaze over my shoulder again as I'm starting to feel a little creeped out. Graham carries on talking but I'm distracted and so slyly peek at the time on my phone; it's just gone 7:30, so if I leave now, I can pick up a takeaway from the Thai house on the way home and put a movie on – preferably not a horror, I think, and I smile to myself.

I dip in and out of listening to Graham talk about his next trip to Peru as my thoughts are fixed on ordering a pad Thai and some spring rolls or— I'm interrupted mid-thought by Graham saying, "There she is again!"

I instantly turn around and feel stupid. When I turn back, I pick up my handbag, stand up and say, "Peru sounds interesting."

Graham follows suit and as we make our way to the door, he says, "So, I'm away for two weeks visiting friends in Bath and then I'll come back to Eton and would love to see you again, Rachel."

"Yeah, sure," I say, smiling at him as if the last half hour hasn't been creepy at all, but knowing full well that I will not be meeting up with him again.

He kisses me on the cheek and as I give him an awkward half-hug, we say goodbye, and I make my way over to the Thai house. I place my order and don't have to wait too long before I'm on my sober walk back home, picturing a glass of red waiting for me. Then I get spooked walking in the dark when the old lady standing behind me comes to mind and unnerves me for the rest of the journey. I make it home in one piece, not for the lack of constantly looking behind me.

Another One Bites the Dust.

Chapter Seven

When Things Get Dark, You Need To Put Your Shades On

I never did hear back from Graham, which is good as I wouldn't have had the heart to say that I wasn't interested in seeing him again. Naomi urged me to get back to the online dating site that she'd set me up on as I had a free month left, so I checked out the matches that she'd saved and one evening after work, I went through them. One of the matches was Robert, who had sent me a message a week earlier saying hi. His profile said that he's six-foot tall with dark hair and in his pictures he's wearing sunglasses and a denim jacket. There's a couple of pictures where he's not wearing sunglasses but he's standing too far back to get a good look. His body is medium build and in the one picture which is a close up, you can only see one side of his face, but he looks very handsome and manly. I make contact and after a few messages, we make plans to meet up the following week. He says that he works most nights, so I agree to meet at his local, although this is not my preferred choice as he's on home ground. Since he's working that night, I decide I'll drive and meet him for a drink straight after I finish work; we can always meet up again if things work out but, most importantly, my car will be outside if, judging from previous dates, I need a quick getaway.

As I'm packing up to leave a little early from work, one of the sales guys walks into the office. Kevin's desk is next to mine and as he takes a seat, he says, "Hey, Rache, how you doing?"

"Yeah, I'm good, thanks, Kev, leaving a bit early today unless you've got something you need me to do?" I reply, as I take out my leftover lunch of two Ryvita with cheese and pickle and try to eat it without completely messing up my clothes whilst still trying to look professional.

"No, you crack on, Rache, got anything interesting planned?" he asks.

I finish my mouthful of food and, with my index finger, touch the corners of my mouth to make sure I'm crumb free. "Well, actually, I'm going on a date," I reply, making it sound like my single life is so wonderful.

"Ooh, who's the lucky git?" he says, glancing up from his computer.

"Oh, this guy I saw online, his name is Robert and we're meeting at a place called the Baylis Clubhouse; have you heard of it?"

"Thought you didn't do all that online dating stuff," he says. "Let's just say that I'm exploring all options now that I'm getting on. So, do you know it?"

He looks up at me as I continue eating with an expression of deep thought and says, "Isn't it the place in the trading estate? It sounds like the working men's club in Slough Trading Estate."

"What! A working men's club? What's that?" I screech. Thankfully, there's no one on our side of the open plan office to hear.

Kevin tries to stifle his laughter as I look at him with a grim expression. "Look, I could be wrong, Rache. Anyway, why are you meeting there?"

"He said he's working a night shift and that's his local and I just agreed to it. Oh, what have I done?" I sigh.

"It's probably not the place I'm thinking of, I'm sure. Besides he should be picking you up and taking you out, a classy chick like you," he says, trying to cheer me up, but the look of despair on my face has Kevin in fits of laughter. I decide to leave and freshen up my make-up in the loos. "I want details tomorrow, Rache!" Kevin shouts out, I raise my hand to say goodbye.

After a quick freshen up, I set the satnav to Baylis Clubhouse and Kevin's right, it's in the trading estate in Slough, which is a huge industrial estate full of factories, businesses, shops and apparently a clubhouse. *It can't be that bad, can it?* I start thinking on my drive over but as I get closer and find myself in this industrial town, I'm feeling maybe I might be a bit overdressed; my black suede knee-high boots and frilly pale pink shirt, teamed with a black skirt, might look somewhat out of place, but I'm pleased I have my black wool coat to hide under.

I pull up into the car park of a two-storey building and notice some men in suits with sports bags walking in. Okay, so it's a clubhouse with a gym, a spa, maybe, with a bar and restaurant. I don't feel too out of place now. There are also a few ladies dressed as if they're going to a nightclub at the far end of the car park; they could be on a girl's night out or a hen do. I feel as though a weight has been lifted off me and I breeze into the clubhouse and realise I have no idea where I'm meeting Robert, so I hang around the entrance just in case he hasn't arrived. I check my phone for messages and reread his message which just says *'5:30 @ Baylis Clubhouse. Robert x.'* It's now 5:40 and more men are arriving and heading straight up the stairs to the bar.

I decide to be brave and when three more men walk in looking like they've just finished work for the day, I follow them up the stairs. If I don't see Robert then I'll know that I made the effort and I'll get the hell out of dodge. I reach the top of the stairs and one of the men holds the door open for me and as I walk through, I smile and say thank you. The room is buzzing with testosterone. Straight ahead is the bar and to the right of it I can see two doors, one has a sign for the toilets, and on the far right-hand side of the room is a stage spanning the width of the room. I walk tentatively past the tables, feeling eyes on me as I manoeuvre around them to reach the bar; the edge of the room has cushioned seating booths and then I notice a man standing at the end of the bar wearing a denim jacket and sunglasses smiling at me. I walk over to him and say, "Robert?"

"Hi, I'm so sorry, I wasn't sure where to meet you," he says.

"Yes, I was waiting downstairs," I reply.

"Oh, I feel terrible," he chips in.

"Look, it's okay, I made it here, nice to meet you," I say, feeling rather uneasy as if we're being watched. I take a look around the room; there's a mix of clientele, some men are in suits, and some are dressed as if they've just come off a building site.

"What would you like to drink, Rachel?" Robert asks as the bartender looks over to me.

"A glass of red wine, please," I reply.

"You look lovely," Robert says, and I wonder if he can actually see anything with the sunglasses on.

"Thanks, I've just come straight from work, didn't have time to go home and change."

I notice Robert is wearing exactly the same clothes as in his profile picture, double denim with a white t-shirt and sunglasses. Our drinks arrive and I follow him to the closest table, which is three feet away.

"I'm on the juice seeing as I'm working later," he says.

"Yes, I remember you saying, so where do you work?" I enquire.

"Here," he says.

"Oh!" I say, sounding mildly surprised. I haven't addressed the elephant in the room yet and feel a little uncomfortable bringing it up, so I take a sip of my wine and as I'm about to ask about the sunglasses, he looks to the side and takes them off. I can only see the left side of his face and he has lovely green eyes, and as he turns to face me, I flinch. "I'm sorry," I say, "I didn't mean to do that, I..." I didn't know what to say. His left eye was artificial and badly scarred.

He pops his glasses back on and says, "That's why I wear them."

"I see," I say, without thinking. "I mean, I understand." I try not to seem shocked but I'm sure he can tell that I am.

"I've always worked in clubs and pubs as a bouncer and many years ago I was in the middle of breaking up a fight and all I remember is the back end of a cue stick..."

I put my hands over my face in horror at hearing his fate. He stopped talking and my heart sank. "That's terrible, I'm so sorry," I say, offering some sort of futile comfort.

"It's fine, it happened a long time ago now, you just learn to adjust, and I've gotten so used to wearing the glasses now that I don't even know they're on," he says.

"So, what do you do now?" I ask.

"I work here in security, looking after the girls."

"The girls?" I say, looking at him puzzled.

"Yes, this is a lap dancing club and I look after the girls, make sure no one bothers them, you know," he says.

Well, actually I don't know and all I can manage to say in response is, "Oh right," as I'm not sure how to respond. It's not really the type of career I would expect my life partner to have and from the resigned look on my face, Robert realises it too.

We chit-chat for a bit longer until he says that he'll be starting work soon and so I finish my wine and stand up to leave. He stands up and offers to walk me out, but I tell him I'll be fine. "I hope you have a good night, Robert; it was lovely meeting you," I say, holding out my hand to him.

He takes it and pulls me in close and whispers in my ear, "Thanks for not laughing, Rachel, you're beautiful and you're way out of my league." I smile sweetly at him, give him a kiss on the cheek and leave.

By the time I've reached home, showered and put my jim-jams on, I feel a lot better. However, that part of me that's a sucker for a sob story is gnawing through my heart and although I feel as if I didn't give Robert a chance, I also know that I'm changing and have to reinvent myself. The old Rachel would've gone out with Robert for a few weeks, maybe a couple of months, because she felt sorry for him, not wanting to hurt him, hoping that it might work out but knowing in the back of her mind that one day she would have to break it off because he wouldn't be enough. I'm constantly learning about myself and in one way, feel relieved that I have respected myself and Robert, in knowing that this was not what I want and having the courage to walk away. As I mosey around the flat, I feel a sense of calm and serenity overcome me and, for the first time in a long time, feel happy to be alone with nothing special to do.

Chapter Eight

Excess Baggage

My feeling of calmness extends well into the weekend, where I find myself doing as little as possible, simply enjoying the alone time and focusing on me, with running in the morning, cooking and having early nights, making calls to reassure those who had left messages that all was well. On Sunday evening, I put my laptop on and logged onto the dating site as there were a couple of weeks remaining and, after an earbashing from Naomi on the phone earlier about how much time she'd spent on completing my profile and uploading photos etc., I thought it best not to deny her the glory of me actually finding someone suitable on her website of choice. So, as I trawled through the matches, I came across a lovely sight; tall, fair haired, divorced 45-year-old Dimitri, has a daughter aged 14, has his own business and, apart from living 30 miles away, looks very nice. We spend the next half an hour chatting online and I start getting a good feeling about Dimitri, so we make a date to meet up for a drink the following Wednesday.

He lives in St Albans, which I've heard is a bit posh, so he must be doing okay for himself.

At work the following morning, is the first time seeing Kevin since my date with Robert last week and he's intrigued to find out how it all went. When the business of Monday morning winds down, Kevin whispers, "Rache, how'd the date go at Baylis Clubhouse?"

I give him the 'look', you know, the raised eyebrow, stern look and he smiles, even more intrigued to find out. "Well, Kevin, I turn up in this industrial estate where, in the middle of all these factories, stands a lap dancing club cleverly disguised as a leisure centre." At this point, Kevin's smile has extended from ear to ear and so I continue. "Then I walk in, hang around the entrance for 10 minutes waiting for my date to arrive before making my way upstairs, only to find my date, Robert, standing at the end of the bar with shades on."

"What!?" Kevin spits out.

"After getting a drink, we sit down and he tells me the reason he's wearing sunglasses by showing me his glass eye and, not only that, but he also works at the clubhouse as security for the lap dancers."

I stop there, as Kevin is now shaking from laughing so much that he's crying. Eventually, after composing himself, he asks, "So, will you be seeing him again?" He bursts out with laughter, at which point my middle finger involuntary shoots up at him.

"He was a really nice guy, Kev, he just had some bad luck and lost an eye but, no, he's not for me," I reply.

"Rache, you're in different leagues, you need someone in a good job, solvent, who's gonna look after you," he says.

"Yes, I'm working on it, Kev."

Kevin's a lovely married man, in his late fifties and his wife, Nina, always makes him a packed lunch for work. He told me once that he walks around the house in the nude sometimes. "As long as you don't frighten the neighbours," I said to him when he decided to divulge this information to me.

The next couple of days at work fly by and when Wednesday arrives, I'm actually feeling a little nervous and have butterflies. I haven't told anyone about the date with Dimitri as I don't want to jinx it and we're only meeting for a drink. He seems more on my wavelength from the messages we've been exchanging. I opt for blue skinny jeans, strappy black heels and a black top with my faithful leather jacket, arriving in good time at the bar that Dimitri has chosen. As I make my way out of the car, my phone pings through a message from Dimitri to say that he's just arrived. I reply, *'yes me too'* and with the sound of a car door closing I look around and see this tall, slim figure about 15 feet away. It's a little dark out but the streetlights give off enough light for us to recognise each another and as we start strolling toward one another, a fuzzy feeling comes over me.

"Hi," we both say simultaneously and then Dimitri moves forward and kisses me on the cheek. He is even more handsome in the flesh.

"So, you found it okay, Rachel?"

"Yes," is all I can muster. I feel like my lips are glued together and I've lost my voice, my mind is racing along with my heart.

We walk through this lovely courtyard, which has seating with outdoor heating, Dimitri holds open the door for me to walk through first and he follows closely behind as we make our way to the bar. "You look lovely, Rachel," he says. "I always get a bit worried as sometimes you meet people and they look nothing like their profile pictures, but you actually look..." I'm smiling so much as he's talking to me that we both find it hard to stifle our laughter.

"Thank you, I feel exactly the same," I say, "and I've had a few shockers lately." I feel like we're already a couple; the easiness in our demeanour with each other and the closeness of our body's makes me feel like I want to hold his hand already. We order our drinks and settle in a cosy little table by the fire, and I cannot believe how happy and excited I feel being sat here with him after the last couple of months of disasters.

The next hour passes so quickly, with endless chatter and laughter and a little flirting, that I don't want it to come to an end. Dimitri walks me to my car and asks,

"When are you free for dinner, Rachel?" As I look up at him I wish I could fast-forward to a place in the future where we're already a couple and kiss him as if he's mine. "Rachel?" he says.

"Yes please," I say, snapping out of my dreamlike state at which point he starts chuckling which sets me off. "Oh, I'm sorry, Friday is good with me," I reply.

"Friday is perfect," he says. As I open the car door and turn toward him to say goodbye, he leans in and this time he kisses me on the lips, our lips softly touching for a second. I want more, he does too, but we both pull gently away, smile and say goodbye.

My drive home is so quick that I don't even recall certain parts of the journey as I'm consumed with joy at meeting this lovely man. I realise that Friday is only a day away but I'm basking in this euphoric feeling that I decide to panic tomorrow. When I reach home I get ready for bed and the phone pings; I can see that it's a message from Dimitri. *'Rachel, it was lovely meeting you and I'm looking forward to getting to know more about you on Friday. Dimitri x.'* I climb into bed and feel warm and snuggly. I reply to Dimitri's text but find it difficult to get the right words; I don't want to sound desperate but then I don't want it to seem that I'm not interested. My reply to him reads, *'It's been such a long time since I had so much fun on a date that I'm looking forward to Friday too. Night x.'* I send the message then read it back and wish I'd spent more time on it. I close my eyes as soon as my head hits the pillow and realise that, for the first time in a long while, I didn't run away, try to escape or have to be rescued. This calls for a catch up with my besties but not until after my dinner date on Friday with Dimitri. I want my Thursday evening to remain free for me to de-fuzz, pluck, exfoliate, cleanse, polish and condition my entire being in preparation for the second date.

Dimitri gets in touch the next day and asks for my address saying that he'll be picking me up at seven and for me to make a reservation at a restaurant of my choice. I book a Moroccan restaurant that's just around the corner from me, text Dimitri my address and then spend the rest of the day at work deciding on what to wear and whether we will still like one another. I'm not sure I actually got any work done apart from answering the phone.

That evening, with a face mask on, conditioner in hair, exfoliating and plucking all complete, I relax on the sofa when the phone rings. It's Vince. I'm trying not to speak too much as we exchange pleasantries and then let slip about my Friday night dinner plans. Oh, what have I done? The problem with married couples is that they want to know all about their single friends' dates inside and out, details and dramas, so they can feel smug and happy that they no longer have to endure the dating merry-go-round. However, Vince and Harry aren't like that at all; they'd love to see me settled, happy, married and have already designated themselves as the wedding planners. I manage to get off the phone and assure them that they'll be the first to know of any developments in that area. I continue my beauty regime and go through my closet and pick out a couple of dresses, my black faux-fur jacket, and some heels, and lay them out in preparation for tomorrow.

The entry phone to the flat buzzes at exactly 7pm the next evening as Dimitri arrives on time; I pick up and say hello. "Hello, Rachel, I'm just outside," he says, sounding a little nervous.

"On my way down, Dimitri," I reply. I pick up my black suede clutch and keys, and pop my jacket on, have a final check in the mirror and leave the flat. I walk down the stairs, open the door and Dimitri is standing with his back to the door and as he turns around, he smiles and takes my hand as I step down onto the pavement.

"Wow, you look amazing," he says, taking my breath away.

"Thank you, so do you," I say as he softly kisses me on the cheek.

We walk down Peascod Street and I notice how good he looks and how good he smells; he's wearing dark blue jeans with black shoes, a black blazer and black t-shirt that oozes a sexiness and complements my dress of choice, which is a black halter neck that falls just to my knees. "So, where are we off to?" he says, taking my hand gently and I point to the Moroccan restaurant a few yards away.

"Is that okay with you?" I ask.

He smiles and says, "Yes, that's great."

Mo's Moroccan Kitchen is a small, intimate place that has live music on a Friday night. I say that with a pinch of salt as the two musicians are great but later on in the evening, they leave the mic open for anyone to come up and sing. In most cases, the musicians have no idea of what they're being requested to play but the singing is mostly so bad that it doesn't really matter.

We enter the restaurant and Mo is at the door ready to greet us. "Good evening, please come in," he says, with a twinkle in his eye.

"Good evening, I have a reservation for 7, under the name Rachel."

"Yes, please come this way."

We follow him to a table at the front of the restaurant in the corner by the window, which is a little private. I know Mo very well but have told him that I'll be on a date and not to go fussing around us. Mo pulls out the chair for me and before I sit down I take off my jacket and pop it on the back of my seat. "Wow, you really do look sensational, Rachel," Dimitri says.

I smile at him and say, "You look rather handsome yourself." The sexual attraction between us is evident and I start to blush, so I take the menu and start fanning myself as Dimitri picks his up and starts looking through it.

Mo arrives back at the table with a small plate of olives and sets them down and says, "Rachel, are you okay? Would you like me to put the AC on?"

"No, I'm fine, Mo, just a bit flushed, I'll be okay, thanks," I reply.

Dimitri orders a bottle of wine and then asks if I'm okay too. I assure him that all's well and when he comments on how friendly the staff are, I come clean and tell him that I know Mo very well and had asked him not to fuss over us. Dimitri laughs and says, "I want you to be comfortable, Rachel, I don't mind at all that we're at your favourite restaurant and they can be as attentive and fuss as much as they want, it all adds to the charm of the place." I look wistfully at him and think to myself how lovely he is, and when Mo returns with our bottle of wine I introduce him to Dimitri.

The evening was the most wonderful second date I could ever have imagined, from the food, the wine, the laughter and getting to know more about Dimitri; even the dreadful singing from some of the diners made it even more memorable. Dimitri was the perfect gentleman; when the bill arrived he took care of it. I did offer but he just smiled and said no with a look of surprise that I should have even offered.

On our walk back to the flat, my head is whirring with questions. *Should I invite him up?* and *does he expect me to put out just because he's paid for dinner?* He takes my hand and walks me to the front door and as we face each other, he leans in and kisses me. I respond, longing for more but knowing that I need to take things slow, so I quieten my thoughts and enjoy the kiss, my arms inside his jacket wrapped around his body and his hands gently draped around my neck. I'm not sure if it's because Christmas is a few weeks away, but everything feels magical and just perfect. We both pull back and look into each other's eyes and smile and just as I'm about to ask if he'd like to come up, he says, "I have to go, I'm working tomorrow but would love to meet up next week."

"Yes, I'd love that," I reply, and we both commence kissing for a moment longer.

I watch him walk away and before he turns the corner, he looks back and holds his hand up to say goodbye; I wave back and excitedly run up the stairs to the flat. My heart is racing; I savour the kiss that remains on my lips. I want to call someone and tell them that I've found him, we've found each other, he does exist, the quest is over, but instead I make a coffee and change into my PJs and sit on the balcony watching the Friday night revellers make their way to the nightclub.

I awake the next morning feeling like my life has more purpose than the day before. I notice a text message from Dimitri which reads, *'What a great evening I had with you, Rachel, and I'm looking forward to seeing you soon, let me know which day next week suits you. Demi x'*. He's signed off with his nickname, Demi. OMG! I love him even more. I want to text back and say that I'd like to see you today, tomorrow and forever but settle for, *'Hi, Demi, it was a lot of fun, and I don't think I've laughed so much on a date before. I can do Tuesday if that works for you. Rache x'*.

Demi gets back to me later that Saturday when I'm cleaning up the flat. His message reads, *'Tuesday won't work for me, but Wednesday is good, so I'll come to you for 6 if that's okay x'*. I reply that it's good with me and then go into overdrive with cleaning the flat with the thought that I'll definitely be wanting him to come up this time. I put the radio on to distract me as my thoughts about Demi absorb everything I do.

Later on in the afternoon, I call Vince and Harry and tell all, much to their delight. "When can we meet him, Rache?" Harry asks.

Vince shouts out in the background, "Let her meet his Trojan horse first!"

"Vince!" I shout back, in response to his smutty remark but laugh all the same.

Harry chides Vince and says, "She's never going to let us meet him if you carry on like that, Vince."

"He's right, though, I would like to get to know him a little more before I dare unleash any of you lot on him," I say.

"Good luck for Wednesday, darling, we want all the deets," Harry says.

"Bye." I ring off and go to the bedroom and start packing an overnight bag ready to make my way over to Ascot to stay with Mum and Dad; it's their wedding anniversary and they're having a little party at the house. They have a party every year and invite a handful of people. They say that special days should be celebrated every year with special people, so I always invite Harriet and Naomi as Mum and Dad absolutely adore them and think that they're such a good influence on me with being married and settled.

"I just don't understand how a beautiful girl like you, Rachel, can't find a decent man," I can hear Mum say.

"Mum, there are no decent men left in the world; they're already married and if they're not, they probably don't want to be, seeing as they can have a different wife each night of the week. There's a shortage of men in the world," is normally my response.

When I arrive, I find them in the living room, holding one another, slow dancing and staring into each other's eyes as if it's the last time that they'll see each other. I watch tenderly until Dad catches me standing by the door and opens his arms and says, "Hello, love, come in." I throw my arms around them both, wish them a happy anniversary and think of Demi; if only I'd met him a few weeks earlier he could've been my plus-one. Mum shakes me out of my thoughts and whisks me away to the kitchen to try the salmon mousse that she's made – that she makes every year – which is just as delicious as the year before. The doorbell rings and the first of the guests arrive. I rush upstairs and pop my bag in my bedroom, quickly freshen up and make my way downstairs.

The open plan kitchen-diner is professionally laid out with a buffet and drinks; Mum outdoes herself every year. It's very relaxed and everyone invited knows just to help themselves although I always help out to begin with by offering drinks when the guests arrive, which gives me just enough time to exchange pleasantries before Harriet and Naomi arrive. They arrive together and I leave them to greet Mum and Dad whilst I grab a bottle of champagne, three flutes and head over to the sofa. I open the bottle and decide to top up the champagne drinkers as my last chore of the night before settling on the sofa and waiting for them.

Naomi saunters over with Harriet a few steps behind, who's shimmying to Baccara's 'Yes Sir, I Can Boogie', laughing as she plonks herself down. "SOOO!" Naomi says as we clink glasses.

"SOOO!" I respond looking at her quizzically.

"A little birdie told me something of interest earlier today, Rache," she says, cocking her head to one side.

"Okay, okay, I was going to tell you, but I didn't want to jinx it," I respond.

"Do tell," Harriet purrs, curious to know what Naomi is referring to.

I spend the next 20 minutes talking about Dimitri and our wonderful date, with Naomi and Harriet acting like we're teenagers again, giggling with giddiness as I recall the dates, the kiss and our upcoming third date.

"I'm the maid of honour!" exclaims Naomi.

"What!" Harriet says. "Now hang on a minute," she continues in jest.

"That's why I didn't want to tell you so soon, you're worse than Vince and Harry," I say, rolling my eyes.

"Well, I'm the one who put you on 'My Gorgeous Girlfriend.com'," Naomi says, pouting, "and so I should have first dibs," she concludes. Harriet and I burst out laughing and start singing 'Tainted Love' to remind her of her previous choice for me from the dating site.

Our evening continues with much joviality until we're the only ones left drinking and dancing. I call a cab, bundle them into the back and leave them arguing with each other as to who's going to be dropped off first.

My Sunday is spent helping Mum and Dad clean up from the party, catching up over lunch, then leaving them to enjoy the rest of the day as I eventually make it back home by late afternoon.

The next two days at work are busy, which is good as I can't get Demi out of my head and our upcoming date on Wednesday. I keep myself alcohol-free so that I look and feel my best and on Tuesday evening decide to go to a hot yoga class to detox and to dispel the nervous energy spiralling through my body. I completely forgot how excruciating a 90-minute hot yoga class can be when you're not 100% focused. I feel as though I want to run from the room but once it's over and I'm in the shower, I feel it was all worth the pain and as I'm walking home from the studio, a feeling of satisfaction comes over me from the sheer endurance of surviving the class. I arrive home and as I open the door to the flat, I hear my phone ping a message through. It's from Demi so I pop my bags down and get comfy on the couch and read his message.

'Hi Alison, please talk to me. I really love and miss you and promise that I'll never go on anymore dating sites again. We're having a baby, please don't shut me out. Love Demi x'

I have to read the message again as my whole body has gone limp and I suddenly feel lightheaded. I realise that Demi has accidently sent me the message meant for Alison who I'm assuming is his ex and is having his baby. I can't breathe. I feel a lump in my throat and as I try to stand up from the couch feel wobbly and fall back down. The phone rings, it's Demi, I don't answer and then a few minutes later he rings again. I leave it on the coffee table as I go to pour myself a glass of wine and pop to the bedroom for my emergency jumper; the big oversized fluffy jumper that makes you feel safe and warm as if an angel is giving you a hug. I take my wine, phone and emergency cigarettes and open the door to the balcony, sit down and for a moment just remain still. My peace is interrupted when my phone pings through a voice message, I take my time, finish the cigarette and enjoy the red wine which, on an empty stomach and after a hot yoga class, has gone straight to my head. In my heart I know it's all over with Demi before it's even begun so there's no need for me to rush to listen to his message; I know I can't be with someone who's still in love with their ex who's also expecting.

I finish the glass of red and listen to his message. 'Rachel, someone has taken my phone and I think they may have sent you a message, please call me.' His voice is shaky, and the message sounds insincere. I take my glass and head inside and start preparing dinner, eating my salmon salad in the silence of my flat. After cleaning up, the phone rings again, I refuse to pick up although I want to speak with him, but I'm upset and I don't know him well enough to unleash any kind of negative emotion, and I have to think about what I'm to say to him.

When I'm getting ready for bed, he calls again; it's 10:25 and this time I decide to answer. "Hello, Demi."

"Hi, Rachel, I've been trying to contact you, someone picked up my phone and I think they may have sent you a message." He sounds nervous but is talking much slower now than the frantic voice message he left earlier.

"Yes, I think you may need to give Alison a call," I reply.

"Look, Alison is my ex and she's gone a bit crazy, she took my phone and—"

"So, when is she expecting?" I quickly butt in.

"In two weeks," he says.

"Wow!" I say, sounding incredulous. "Like I said, Demi, you need to speak with Alison."

"No! I don't want to be with her." I can hear the despair in his voice. "Rachel, please," he pleads.

"Demi, you're expecting a baby in two weeks with Alison, who apparently you love and miss, who you've made a promise to that you wouldn't go on anymore dating sites again. This is the text message I received, whether it was sent by mistake to me by you or whether Alison did take your phone and send me that message, I'll never know."

"Rachel, please listen to me, she's a psycho, she wanted to have a baby, I didn't, she wanted to trap me and now here I am."

I felt sorry listening to him. For me, all the shine and glow from meeting him has now been tarnished with this text message. I would've preferred if he'd just told me on Friday the situation he was in. "Demi, I'm not sure what to think at the moment and I have to go so just give me some time." He agrees to this emphatically. I ring off and go to bed.

My Wednesday at work feels like a 'blah' day; I can't wait for it to be over so I can meet with the girls. Naomi sent me a text earlier in the day to wish me luck for my date with Dimitri and I told her it wasn't happening; that's when she decided to summon the troops to assemble at mine for 6 o'clock.

When they arrive, laden with the essentials – wine, pizza, and chocolates – I'm blown away. "Listen, it was only a third date, guys," I say, whilst fetching wine glasses.

"Yes, Rache, but you really liked him and tonight would've been the night when you would've let him have a taste of your cherry pie," Vince says, snorting with laughter.

I nod in agreement, tilting my head to one side and half smiling. "Look, any excuse for a drink and a catch-up, Rache," Harry pipes up.

We all get comfy and after I play back Demi's voice message and update them on our conversation from last night, we all conclude that there's no way I should give him the time of day. That is, apart from Naomi, who quietly says, "Well maybe he does really like you and his ex is a psycho who got pregnant, and they could've met up and he might've told her about you and when he wasn't looking she took his phone and sent you that message to stir things up."

"Well, whatever the story is, Rache, do you really want to be with him knowing that Alison, in two weeks, will be popping out a baby Demi?" offers Harriet.

"No, I don't think I do," I say, sounding a little unsure.

"At the end of the day, Rache, you have to decide whether he could be the *one* and then if he could be, and you start a relationship with him, can you handle all the baggage that he'll come with? And would you be able to trust him, more importantly," Harry says, presenting his thoughts.

"It's not like I'm in a relationship with this guy anyways so I'm just going to give—" The phone rings just as I'm mid-sentence. We all look down at it sat on the coffee table. "It's Demi," I say, and then everyone looks up at me.

"Answer it, Rache," says Vince.

"No, I can't, I don't know what to say."

Harry picks up the phone and hands it to me. "Yes you do, Rache," he says. I answer the phone. "Hello."

"Hi, Rachel, it's Demi."

"Hi, Demi," I say, standing up and walking out onto the balcony.

"How are you?" he asks.

"Yes, I'm okay, and you?"

"I've had better days. We would be on our date right now and I don't want to push you, but I would like to see you," he says.

"What, now?" I say.

"Yes, you see, things haven't changed for me, I would still like to see where this could go. Don't you?" he asks.

I'm silent for a moment. "Um, well no, not now, I don't. You're a lovely guy but... It's too much baggage for me," I reply.

"Everyone has baggage, Rachel, we all do. You can't go through life not accumulating any baggage."

"Yes, Demi, you're right, but you have excess baggage."

"Excess baggage!" he says, indignantly.

"Well, yes, with a baby due in two weeks, Demi." There's silence on the phone and I turn around and Vince, Harry, Naomi, and Harriet are all quiet, trying to catch the gist of the conversation.

"Okay, Rachel, I'm not sure what to do or say to—"

"Nothing," I interject, as I don't want to talk about it anymore. "Look, it was lovely meeting you and good luck, Demi, bye."

"Rachel—"

I hang up, turn and walk back into the living room. I feel sad but also relieved as I remember a line from that text message that said *'I promise not to go on anymore dating sites'* and it makes me think that he could be one of those guys that goes on dating sites whilst in a relationship to see if there's anyone better. Or maybe Alison did get his phone and she did send the message to me intentionally warning me that he was already in a relationship and that she was expecting his baby. Oh, I don't know, I'll never know the truth, I'm just glad I'm out of his drama.

"Sooo?" Vince says, snapping me out of my thoughts. I relay the conversation to them and after another drink, lots of hugs and 'there's more fish in the sea' type of cliché remarks, they all make their way to the door to leave. Naomi turns back as she's walking out and we both mouth, *another one bites the dust.* I half smile and nod.

Chapter Nine

A Crying Shame

A few days later at Naomi's, I saw Gregory. He was there doing some work; he's one of those handymen who you could say is a jack of all trades and a master of none. I'd seen him a few times before at hers but paid him no mind, but today, as we sat in the kitchen chatting, making plans for Christmas, I noticed him. He's not very tall – we'd be the same height if I was in heels – looks physically fit and he has a gentle, softly-spoken way about him that always intrigued me. I looked at Naomi once he'd left the kitchen to say, "What's his story?"

She whispered, "Not sure, doesn't talk an awful lot, which makes him seem a bit mysterious."

I stayed longer than I wanted and missed the bus, so decided to walk the two miles home even though it was cold out; after the two cups of mulled wine and mince pies, I was feeling toasty and definitely in need of the exercise and fresh air. Naomi, without fail, every year starts Christmas in mid-November; the tree and decorations are up, there'll always be a pan of mulled wine ready to be put on and she will have bought enough mince pies, strudel, eggnog, and any other Christmas delights that she and the kids took a fancy to at the supermarket. She wants the kids to enjoy Christmas for more than a couple of weeks and so every year she starts as early as possible. Poor Neil doesn't even bother objecting anymore as he's outnumbered and just thinks that, as long as Naomi is happy, who is he to argue.

I eventually reach the bottom of Peascod Street and can't help but look up to the top; Christmas decorations add to the enchanting backdrop of the statue of Queen Victoria and the castle. It's late Saturday afternoon and Windsor is busy with shoppers, people buzzing around the stalls, and then I notice a man in the crowd who looks familiar. Is it the stranger? I can't be sure. My heart thumps through my chest and I have to focus and breathe as shoppers bustle past me. I scan the area for him, but he's gone. I wildly walk toward the sighting, surging past shoppers, when my toe hits the cobbles and my whole upper body flies forward into the oncoming path of an elderly couple. "Oh gosh! I'm so sorry, my foot hit the cobble and..."

"It's okay, dear, no harm done," the gentleman says, as they smile and walk on.

I look around and search for the stranger but there are too many people and so I retreat and make my way back home feeling foolish but hopeful that I may still one day run into him again. I reach the flat and settle into my Saturday evening with a glass of red, sitting out on the balcony looking down on Peascod Street, hoping that being higher up might give me the advantage of spotting the stranger in the throng of shoppers, but it's a hopeless exercise. A message pings through on my phone from Naomi. It reads, *'Rache, passed your number on to Gregory when you left, he's not seeing anyone and thinks you're very pretty. Let me know when he gets in touch. Love N x'.*

Oh wow, I completely forgotten about Gregory.

The next day I began ironing my clothes for work, which, incidentally, is my least favourite chore. I could go so far as to say I *hate* ironing. I think it may have something to do with the fact that when I was a young girl, one of my cousins placed a hot iron on to my bottom when I was lying face down on the bed and, needless to say, the bright yellow polyester trousers I was wearing stuck to said bottom. Anyway, during my least favourite chore, a message pings through on my phone which reads, *'Hi, Rachel, Naomi gave me your number and suggested we should get together for a drink, get back to me if you'd like to. Gregory'*. I text back, *'Hello, Gregory, yes that sounds like a plan, how does next week work for you?'* We arrange to meet the following Thursday; I give Naomi a quick call to let her know that Gregory has made contact and that we've made plans for Thursday. I finish the ironing and momentarily think of Demi.

The next three days at work pass by and when Thursday arrives, Gregory picks me up at 8. We walk up Peascod Street to the top where, just to the right of the castle, there are a few smaller pubs tucked away in the cobbled side streets. It's much quieter there as the Christmas office parties are in full swing and we settle down with our drinks at a small table; I take my red wine in hand and look around at the Christmas decorations and then set my gaze on the open fire. "So, you've done quite a bit of work at Naomi's now?" I say to break the silence and the slight awkwardness between us. I don't really fancy him but he's not unpleasant to look at, with dark brown hair and brown eyes and a weathered builder's look about him.

He says, "Yes, I'm sure I've seen you there a few times now when I've been round hers working."

"Promise I'm not stalking you," I say, laughing. He laughs back, and we relax a little.

I feel like I'm chatting to a hairdresser as we discuss holidays we've been on and places that we'd like to visit. I discover that he's never been married, has no children and that he's 47, has two brothers who are both married, and his mum and dad are divorced and that his mum lives in one of those care assisted complexes not far from him. He seems like a nice man and on our walk back home, he gently takes my arm so I don't trip on the cobbles, which endears me to him. It must be the joviality of Christmas, along with the decorations and lights, which has enhanced the attractiveness of everyone and everything that we pass. Or it could be the two large glasses of red that I've just had, or even the remnants from the Demi situation that has made me feel a little sentimental, so much so that, by the time we reach my flat and I look in Gregory's eyes, I just want him to sweep me up in his arms and kiss me. "So, thanks for walking me home and for a lovely evening," I say, lying about the lovely evening. I don't feel any chemistry between us but maybe that's okay since things with Demi didn't go to plan and we had plenty of it.

"Yes, thank you, too, it was nice to eventually meet you properly," he replies, looking a little downhearted. I lean in towards him and give him a kiss on the cheek and as I pull away, he says, "Would you like to do this again sometime, Rachel?"

"What, the kiss or drinks?" I reply, with a cheeky grin.

"Both, if you'd like," he says, chuckling.

"Yes, why not," I reply.

We say goodbye and I walk up to the flat and I know that Naomi will be itching to find out how it went so I give her a call to say that all was okay, no big fireworks but we will meet up again. She's satisfied that I'm at least going on another date; I'm satisfied that he didn't do anything foul to put me off.

My second date with Gregory is a few days later on a Sunday, it's a lunch date, so when he picks me up at midday, we go for a walk in Windsor Great Park. I discover that we don't really have much in common, but we do share the same sense of humour, which is a start, and over lunch he tells me more about his life, which leaves me feeling a little sad for him. He doesn't have many friends and his two brothers only contact him when they need work doing to their houses and then usually renege when it comes to paying; as does his closest friends who are a married couple who treat him pretty much the same. "They do cook me dinner and let me stay over whilst I'm doing the work, seeing as they live an hour away," he says.

"Oh, that's okay then!" I say sarcastically.

After lunch, we walk back to my flat and I invite Gregory in for a coffee, he accepts although I hope he doesn't think that I'm inviting him in for more than just coffee. It's been a while since I've been with anyone and when it happens, I really want us both to want it and enjoy it, and now, with him, doesn't feel like the right time, plus I hardly know him. "You've got a really nice little flat, Rachel," he remarks when I give him the grand tour.

"Little being the operative word," I say, laughing.

Gregory doesn't stay too long after our coffee. He seems very shy, which I do like about him and before he leaves, he invites me to dinner around his place, which I accept. I'm feeling a little more positive now. Maybe it doesn't need to be all hearts and butterflies to begin with, maybe this one will be a slow burner and with Christmas looming, it will be nice to have someone to share the holidays with. I call Naomi and give her a progress report, which excites her more than me.

The following day at work, I receive a text message from Gregory asking whether Thursday evening is good for me and checking if there's anything that I don't eat. I like that he cares to ask; it's been a long time since anyone has cooked for me on a date and since it's at his house, I'm thinking that he might want to get intimate. Thursday feels like ages away seeing as it's only Monday but being busy before the Christmas break keeps me occupied and the week flies by.

I leave work on Thursday and rush home. The weather is drizzly but not cold so I decide to dress in my favourite casual outfit of jeans, t shirt, leather jacket, with heels. After redoing my hair and make-up, I give Naomi a quick call to let her know about the dinner date at Gregory's, she wishes me luck – or did she say she hopes I get lucky, I'm not sure – as I order an Uber.

The car comes to a stop outside a cottage which looks quaint and rustic from the outside but when Gregory opens the door, I can see that it is deceptively spacious and nicely decorated. "Well, hello, Rachel," he says smiling. He looks nervous and steps to the side to let me in.

"Hi, how are you?" I say as I step right into the living room.

"Yes, good thanks," he replies.

The gas fire is on, and the room is warm and cosy. Gregory willingly gives me the grand tour of his three-bedroom cottage, which he's proud to show off. We enter the kitchen and I involuntarily start opening the kitchen cupboards to see what's inside whilst he's busy opening a bottle of fizz. I realise what I'm doing and spin around to find him looking at me. "I'm so sorry, what am I doing going through your cupboards?" I say, embarrassingly laughing.

"It's fine, carry on," he laughs back and pops the cork. We clink glasses and he seems a lot more relaxed, which makes me feel at ease.

He turns and pops the bottle back into the fridge which leaves me checking him out and as he turns back, I quickly look away but I think he may have clocked me and so I ask, "So, what's on the menu, chef?"

"I was thinking of ordering a Chinese," he says.

"Ew no! I'm not a fan of Chinese cuisine," I say, making a face of disapproval which makes Gregory laugh out.

"No, I'm only kidding," he remarks.

"Oh, thank goodness," I reply, giving him a soft poke to the side of his body.

He pops his flute down on the worktop and opens up the fridge and says, "Okay, so I was planning to pan-fry some fish in a garlic and herb butter. I have cod and salmon – you choose, or both if you're feeling very hungry – accompanied with green beans, baby sweetcorn and some potato dauphinoise."

"Wow! I'm impressed!" I reply.

"What, at the menu?" he says.

"No, that you can pronounce dauphinoise," I say, laughing.

He laughs back and takes the bottle of Prosecco out of the fridge and tops me up. "So, what will it be?" he asks.

"Salmon," I reply.

Gregory takes the food out of the fridge and as he starts to prepare the fish, I start prepping the vegetables. He pops the oven on for the dauphinoise and puts on some music. I'm feeling easy and comfortable in his company now that the nervous energy between us is dissipating, probably helped by the alcohol, music and preparing the meal together. His face looks less stressed when he's smiling. Normally, when I've seen him in the past at Naomi's, he has always looked worried and unhappy which makes his forehead very furrowed as if he's frowning all the time but tonight there's not a frown in sight. "So, where did you learn to cook?" I ask.

"Um, I'm not sure that you would class this as cooking, I'm only pan-frying some fish, you're prepping the veg and Mum told me how to make the potato dauphinoise," he says.

"Oh, really?" I say, looking up at him with a slightly amused grin.

"Yes, before today I had never made them, and she talked me through what to do and obviously how to pronounce 'dauphinoise'. Are you impressed?" he says, laughing.

I laugh back and say, "I'll let you know when I am." I pop the veg into the steamer and then lean back against the counter and pick up my glass of Prosecco and watch Gregory pan-fry the salmon. He turns around and smiles at me which makes me go a little weak at the knees.

I take my leave and pop to the cloakroom to freshen up before dinner and when I return I find Gregory setting the table. He pulls out the chair for me and as I take my seat, he returns with a bottle of wine. I was rather tipsy, so dinner was welcomed. Gregory takes a seat, and the evening, so far, has been lovely. I'm enjoying the meal too and as I look up to tell Gregory that I'm impressed, I can't help but notice his eating habits. His head is hovering over his food with his arm semi-circling the plate and he has not looked up once, all the while shovelling the food into his mouth with his fork. He reminds me of someone in jail, a prisoner at chow time protecting his plate of food from being stolen by the other inmates. I stop for a moment, put my cutlery down, pick up my glass of wine and take a drink whilst watching him and then say, "I'm impressed."

He looks up and says, "Thanks." He takes a drink from his glass of wine before resuming the attack on his dinner. I was not even halfway through my meal by the time Gregory had finished his; he offers me more of the potato dauphinoise, but I'm quite satisfied with my portion and decline. I continued in my own time eating whilst Gregory hoovered up the remaining food. Speaking fondly of his mother; he tells me that he speaks with her every day on the phone, sometimes more than once and visits her once a week at her apartment in the complex where she lives. Once I've finished eating, he takes my plate and we both head back into the kitchen where he tops up our wine and we make ourselves comfortable in the living room on the sofa.

The lights are dim and without thinking, I blurt out, "Were you ever in prison?"

"What?" he spits out, and from the shocked expression on his face I realise what I have just asked him.

I quietly say, "It's just that I went on a date with this guy who was in prison for assault, and I just need to know before—"

"No, I have not," he interjects, sounding rather bemused. Okay, so he's not been inside, then why does he eat like a jailbird? My mind starts pondering on this point when he asks, "Rachel, would you like dessert?"

"No, not just yet, thanks, I'm so full after dinner, which was really lovely if I didn't say so before," I reply.

He looks chuffed and we make small talk about his work and then he comes out and tells me that he'd always fancied me and every time he would go to Naomi's to do work he would hope that I would be there too. I said that I had no idea and asked him why he didn't say anything before. "I just thought you were way out of my league, Rachel, you always looked so smart and fit and, to be honest, I thought you were probably taken so I was surprised when Naomi gave me your number." I smile at him; I'm flattered by his honesty and blush a little at being complimented.

I excuse myself and pop to the loo and, on my return, see that Gregory is in the kitchen retrieving the bottle of wine from the fridge, so I pop in and say, "Are you trying to get me drunk?"

"Yes, is it working?" he replies.

I want him to grab me and take me in his arms and kiss me, but we just look at one another as if our eyes are doing the kissing. Then suddenly my body reacts to my thoughts, and I step forward and start kissing him gently on the lips. He responds instantly and then stops for a moment, steps in closer so his body is pressed up against mine and we continue to kiss gently at first, then wildly as our bodies react to the rush of energy and pleasure, yearning for more. It's been so long since I've been close and intimate with anyone and now I know how much I've missed it, so I take Gregory's hand and we head back into the lounge.

I slip off my heels, lay back on the sofa and watch him kick off his shoes as he climbs on top of me and slides his body up in between my legs. We continue to kiss, our bodies pressing hard against each other's. I'm feeling so elated that I'm here in this position and start slowly lifting up Gregory's t-shirt. He lifts it up over his head as I unbuckle his belt and pop the buttons on his jeans open, and he pulls them down and off. He lifts up my t-shirt and pulls it up over my head whilst I unzip my jeans, which he helps me slip out of as we continue our intimate dance. I feel so excited at the prospect of having sex that I'm enjoying every kiss and touch, my body aching to be entered as we dry hump. Then, I feel something slide down my cheek. I open my eyes to witness the most horrid look on Gregory's face, his eyes squinting as if he's in pain and then tears fall from his eyes onto my face. With that, he jumps up and runs out of the lounge, clutching his crotch over his boxer shorts, leaving me on the sofa in bra and knickers, stunned, bewildered and horny, wondering what on earth I did to cause such a reaction.

I lay there for a few moments and then I hear the shower running upstairs, so I pop my jeans and t-shirt back on feeling completely unsatisfied. I wonder if I should just put my heels back on, grab my bag and leave. Why, oh why, was he crying? What did I do? I rack my brain as to whether I did or said anything and with that thought, the shower stops and a couple of minutes later, Gregory walks back into the lounge with nothing, but a huge bath sheet wrapped around his waist. He's dripping wet, and he takes a seat on the armchair a few feet away. I look at him and say, "Are you okay? Did I do something to upset you?"

"No, no, it's not you," he replies, and after a short pause he continues, in a childlike manner, "It's Daphne!" And with that, he bursts out crying like a baby blubbing. I'm in complete shock and ponder whether I should go over and console him but am unable to as I find his behaviour a turn-off and I leave him to his tears.

"Who's Daphne?" I ask.

After a moment, he composes himself and says, "She's my ex; we broke up a few months ago and—"

I am furious so I cut in, "And you chose to think about her whilst we were—" I stop there as I'm afraid of what I may say next. I stoop down and start popping my heels back on.

"I'm sorry, I've messed this all up. You see, Daphne used to only allow me to have sex with her if I did some work at her house, like decorate or put a fence up in the back garden and if I didn't do it as she wanted then she wouldn't have sex with me; it was like a reward and punishment kind of thing," he says. I'm astounded at his explanation and can feel my jaw slowly drop in disbelief as he continues talking. "She used to call me a gimp and said I walked ten to two."

The look on my face of puzzlement at this statement has him stand up and demonstrate, he positions his feet out like a penguin at ten minutes to two.

"Oh!" I remark.

He continues, "She once locked me out of the house and called me a cunt."

I had to cut in as I found his language vulgar. "How long were you together, Gregory?"

"Six months," he replies.

"Six months!" I blurt out incredulously. "And when did you break up with her?"

"She broke up with me once I finished all the work on her house; about three months ago now."

The look on my face must have given Gregory the indication that I was not impressed with his sorry story and for his tantrum at such a moment. He tried to suggest we try again but, for me, the moment was now lost and after hearing all that, I was turned right off him. "I'm afraid I can't see you anymore, Gregory, I really think you need more time to get over your ex and—"

"But before I could finish, he butts in. "Please, Rachel, I'm sorry."

"I can't start a relationship with someone who's this messed up and still carrying baggage from their last relationship; that's not fair on me. The only thing I can do for you is offer you friendship," but as soon as I said it, I realised that it was a mistake. I can't be friends with Gregory, but I couldn't backtrack now; he was already nodding his head in agreement to my proposal.

I left as soon as the Uber arrived, feeling frustrated and annoyed at myself for suggesting we could be friends. By the time I had reached home, I had already received three text messages from Gregory. The first one read, *'Rachel, I'm so sorry, please forgive me'*. The second one read, *'You're right, I need to work through some things'*. The third one read, *'I hope you got home safe and sound, I'll call tomorrow'*. I didn't respond. I made a hot chocolate and sat on the balcony wondering what the hell just happened. I text Naomi and Harriet for an emergency Friday night meeting at The Drinking Ole.

The following day at work was never-ending and by 4:30 a lot of the staff had left, so I made a dash for it too and went home to refresh before meeting the girls. Naomi was the first to arrive and was eager to hear how dinner at Gregory's had gone, so when I relayed last night's events to them, she was completely horrified. Harriet burst out laughing and when I got to the part where Gregory jumped up and darted out of the room holding his crotch, Harriet's reaction gave me a fit of giggles, much to Naomi's annoyance, and then my phone started to ring. I retrieved it from my handbag and saw that it was Gregory. "Answer it!" Harriet demanded, smiling cunningly.

"No! What would I say?" I reply.

"I'll answer it, I want to give him a piece of my mind," Naomi jumps in angrily.

"Hello," I answer, whilst watching Harriet stifle her giggles.

"Hello, Rachel, it's Gregory."

"Hi, Gregory."

"I just called to see how you are and to apologise again for yesterday," he continues.

"Listen, Gregory, I'm out at the moment so this is not a good time for me to talk."

"Oh, okay I'll try later, then," he says. I hang up.

"What happened? What did he say?" Naomi asks.

"You know, just the usual; 'how you doing? I'm sorry again about what happened last night'," I say.

"You didn't say goodbye, though, you just hung up on him!" Naomi says questioningly. Harriet scoffs at Naomi's remark.

"Look, he's on top of me, we're kissing and just about to get down to it when he starts crying, jumps off me, runs out of the room holding his meat and two veg, has a shower, comes down with a bath sheet wrapped around himself and cries some more and then tells me that he was thinking of his ex, Daphne. So, forgive me for not saying goodbye to him, Nomes."

"Here, here!" pipes Harriet in my defence. "You know what I think," Harriet continues, "I'm quite sure that you got him so excited, Rache, that he came in his pants and didn't know what to do and so started to cry." She laughs uncontrollably.

Naomi is flabbergasted as I burst out laughing, too, joining Harriet. "No! Stop it, both of you," Naomi says. We're laughing so much that the tears are running down our faces.

"That could well be the reason for the shower, yes! He prematurely ejaculated. I remember now, when I looked up and felt the tears drop on my face, he had the come face." I mimic the face he made. Harriet starts crying with laughter again which sets Naomi off too. "The worst part is that I said I couldn't go out with him because he needs to work through his shit but then offered him friendship. Why did I do that? It just came out of my mouth and before I could take it back, he was agreeing to it like a nodding dog."

"It'll be fine, Rache; he'll probably be too busy or embarrassed to keep in touch anyway," Naomi says reassuringly.

"I'm not so sure, Nomes, given the fact that he's just called. What does he want now?" I say, exasperated.

"Well, just tell him to do one," Harriet says, still chuckling.

"Nooo, I still need him as my handyman," Naomi says desperately.

"Oh crap! I forgot about that, Nomes. Look I'll chat with him and in a few days, weeks... It'll fizzle out, I'm sure," I conclude.

We all leave the bar and Harriet walks me home, still laughing about Gregory's mishap and as we turn the corner, I notice a box on the step outside the flat. It's addressed to me and so I stoop down and open it to find a rose plant in a pot. Harriet grabs the note inside the box and opens it up and reads it out loud. "Rachel, please accept this gift as my way of apologising for ruining a perfect evening. Gregory x."

"Oh my God! He must've just dropped it off," I say, looking around.

"Maybe he's watching us right now," whispers Harriet. We both look at one another and proceed inside to the flat without looking back.

Once inside safely, Harriet walks out onto the balcony to see if anyone is standing around. "I'm glad you're here, Hattie, I'm not sure what I would've done if he was standing there too and I was by myself," I remark.

"He may have just dropped it off and left, Rache."

"Yes, I suppose, maybe that's why he was calling earlier to see if I was at home," I reply.

"Well, he's either creepy or he's genuinely sorry and wants you to give him another chance, darling, but the ball's in your court," Harriet says, as she scans the street below.

Once Harriet has left, I give Naomi a quick call and run it by her. She's ecstatic that he's made such an effort to make up for the previous night and she really wants me to give him a second chance. After speaking with Naomi, I send Gregory a text message saying thank you for the rose plant, however, as soon as I've sent the message, he rings. "Hello," I answer.

"Hi, Rachel, it's Gregory, I'm glad you like the plant and I'm pleased you got it okay; I wasn't sure about leaving it on the doorstep."

"Yes, it's here in the kitchen, safe and sound, thank you," I reply.

"Oh good," he responds and then after a pause he continues, "um, so, okay, I'll guess I'll catch up with you soon."

"Okay, bye, Gregory."

"Night, Rachel."

As I hang up, I feel tense, and I find myself cringing from the awkward conversation. *I hope that's it and he doesn't call again*, I think, as I head to bed.

With Christmas two weeks away, work gets busy; my downtime is spent socialising and shopping and dating takes a back seat. Our office Christmas party is literally a lunchtime event at a local restaurant and then those who want to stay on drinking can and anyone who wants the rest of the afternoon for last minute Christmas shopping can slope off. I decide to slip away and on my way home, I check my phone and have a missed call from Gregory. I'm in too much of a good mood and am feeling a little tipsy from the office party to call him back straight away, but as I reach the flat, I hear footsteps behind me and a voice shout out, "Rachel!"

I turn and see Gregory half-running towards me. "Hi," I say, as he stops in front of me, out of breath and looking flushed. "I just saw your missed call," I continue, "what's up?" I ask.

"No, nothing, all is good, I was Christmas shopping and thought I'd let you know, see if you were free for a drink," he says, having regained his breath.

"Oh, right, well, I've just finished work early, it was our office Christmas lunch and I wasn't planning on... Look let me just pop my things inside and I'll be down in a minute," I reply, and I leave him on the doorstep and go inside the flat. I'm a bit annoyed that he's ambushed me into going out for a drink with him, but I'm also in the Christmas spirit so easily persuaded.

We walk up Peascod Street and pick up a couple of cups of mulled wine from one of the stalls and just walk; it's busy with shopper's so it's difficult to hold a conversation, so we head out to Alexandra Park where there's an ice rink and sit on a bench and watch the skaters. Gregory doesn't mention what happened that night at his place again and neither do I. Our conversation is based around Christmas and family and although a little awkward, the mulled wine is making it bearable.

After a long silence, Gregory suggests ice skating to which I flatly refuse as I've had too much to drink and will probably fall flat on my face or break my neck. However, I don't need much persuasion in the pursuit of fun and find myself, 10 minutes later, putting skating boots on. I do love to try to ice-skate and to start with, I stay close to the side until I'm confident to venture out alone, but Gregory is hopeless, and I end up propping him up initially. We mostly end up on our behinds but it's enjoyable and once we've got to grips with balancing without grabbing one another, our time is up. As we head to the exit, I decide to skate a little faster; as I turn to face Gregory, he's coming straight at me and collides into me. He has me pinned, my back against the barrier and his body pressed against mine. I feel a rush of sexual excitement run through me and as he looks up, apologising, I start to laugh and hold onto him as we make our way out.

Our walk back to the flat is mostly quiet on my part as my mind is racing with thoughts of wanting sex. "Rachel," Gregory says, awakening me from my lustful thoughts.

"Sorry, I was miles away," I respond.

"I was just wondering; would you like to go for another drink?" he says.

"Oh, I'm not sure that I should have any more," I reply.

"How about a bite to eat then?" he presses.

We reach the flat and I turn to him and say, "I really need a tinkle."

We both head inside and I leave him in the lounge as I pop to the bathroom to freshen up. I reapply my lip gloss and fix my hair. A rush of sexual feelings comes over me again and as I leave the bathroom, I find Gregory standing, waiting for me, like a puppy waiting for its owner to return, all happy and doe-eyed. I walk over to him and place myself in front of him, not too close but close enough for him to grasp the intention. "So," he says, as he looks into my eyes.

"So," I reply, trying to sound all provocative.

"Well, would you like to go for a bite to eat then?" he asks again. He hasn't picked up on my carnal desires.

"No, I think I'm going to give it a miss."

"Okay, Rachel," he replies.

As he walks toward the door to leave, he turns around and we hug. I hold on and press my body against his, he reacts by gently pressing his body back, unsure of the signal I'm emitting. Then I softly brush my lips past his cheek to his lips, which triggers him to start kissing me. I just need my desires to be satiated without a repeat of his last performance. We continue kissing whilst walking to the sofa, where we slowly take off our clothes, he slips in between me, and we just fuck. For the brief moment of pleasure, I'm satisfied, but it was over all too quickly, and my body is eager for more. Gregory moves his body weight off me and starts kissing me on the lips again, caressing my breasts. As I turn slightly toward him, I groan in pleasure; I wasn't expecting a second go. I can feel him getting hard again and it excites me so that I completely let go and enjoy being touched by him. I want him inside me again. All of a sudden, my mind comes to realise the consequence of this act and inside, my head is screaming, *no! What have you done?* It's too late and I'm selfishly enjoying it.

When the deed is done again, I nip to the bathroom and scold myself for crossing the line with Gregory all because I was tipsy and feeling the need to be touched. I freshen up and walk back into the lounge to find Gregory still on the sofa; he holds out his hand to me as if to pull me back into his arms, but I pretend not to notice and go in search of my underwear and start getting dressed. "Well, I wasn't expecting that," he says, looking pleased as punch.

"I'm so sorry, that wasn't meant to happen, Gregory. I had a few too many drinks and— "

I try to continue but Gregory interrupts. "It's okay, Rachel, I understand," he says.

"You do?" I question.

"Well, after what happened last time, you said that you couldn't go out with me and that I need to work through some things and I'm sorting myself out now; so, we can be friends in the meantime," he replies. I'm not sure how to respond so I don't say a thing and I continue putting my clothes back on; thankfully, Gregory does the same. "So, thanks for a wonderful afternoon," he says, smiling like a Cheshire cat as he walks to the door to leave.

I follow him down the stairs to the front door and as he steps down on to the pavement, he turns and gives me a hug and leaves. I run back up the stairs and think about calling Naomi to confess my naughty deed but decide against it as she'll only admonish me for using Gregory for my selfish pleasure. Nonetheless, feeling satisfied with the outcome. Although, I have a feeling that I may have created a situation which I fear may lead to more tears for Gregory.

The weekend spins by with last-minute Christmas shopping, catching up with the folks and putting up the Christmas decorations. With the Christmas break just over a week away, the excitement is building and my Sunday evening of listening to Christmas songs and decorating the tree is disturbed when the phone rings. It's Gregory. "Hello," I answer.

"Hello, Rachel, it's me," he replies.

"Oh, hello, me," I say back.

"How are you?" he asks.

"I'm very well, and you?" I reciprocate.

"Yes, really good..." he replies.

When I eventually hang up the phone to Gregory, I scream out, "That's 30 minutes of my life I will never get back!" He droned on about his problems in his last relationship, spending Christmas with his family and also relayed the conversation he had earlier in the day with his mother. Maybe this is karma for my Friday afternoon of pleasure; it must be. I used him for physical attention, and now he's using me as an emotional sounding board. I shake him out of my head and settle down for the night.

It's my last week at work before Christmas and all is very quiet; most of the family who work there have already left for the festive break, so that leaves a handful of us in the office, which is pleasant, especially since we always tend to leave a little early every day. By the time we get to Christmas Eve, no one bothers coming back after lunch, which is a bonus of working for a family-run business; they value time spent with loved ones.

Christmas Eve is always reserved for drinks and carol-singing, visiting the local haunts around the castle. I meet up with Harriet and Naomi at the Castle Arms and after telling them the latest on the Gregory saga, Naomi responds with, "Oh dear!"

Harriet smiles and with a raised eyebrow, says, "Well, when a girl needs a jump start..." I burst out laughing and when we both turn to look at Naomi, who is not impressed, we laugh even harder.

"So, how is it left with Gregory now? Are you seeing him?" Naomi asks.

"God! No," I blurt out, "he's a nice guy but I really don't want to take on a project. I was in need of a service, and he was there, and I'd had a few to drink and I couldn't help myself. Besides, he's been calling me nonstop, I feel like Dear Deidre listening to his problems."

"Poor you!" Harriet pipes in.

Naomi is not so forgiving. "I don't want to lose him as my handyman, Rache." This makes Harriet laugh even more.

"Look, Nomes, I'm sure that won't happen, he understands the score and, besides, he's not ready for a relationship if he's still hung up on his ex. I didn't force him to do anything, I'm just glad he didn't cry and run away this time."

A couple of pubs later and I eventually arrive home and start on dinner when the door phone buzzes. I pick up and say, "Hello."

"Hi, it's me."

What is he doing here? I think to myself, a little annoyed that he's here uninvited. "Hello, Gregory, what are you doing here?"

"I just thought I'd pop by and drop off a Christmas present for you," he says.

"What? I wasn't expecting you to..." My cheery mood is slowly disappearing after being bamboozled by him again. I buzz him up, open the door and watch him climb the stairs with a huge grin on his face and a big bag in his hand.

"Hi," he says, as he reaches the top.

"Hi, what's all this then?" I enquire, as he reaches out his arm and hands me the bag.

"You'll have to wait and see," he says.

"Gregory, you really shouldn't have. I mean, I wasn't expecting you to buy me anything, we're not seeing one another and— "

I'm cut short when he says, "Yes, I know we're just friends, but I saw this, and I wanted to buy it for you and it's nothing to do with what happened the other day between us. It's Christmas, it's just a gift from one friend to another." I am speechless for a moment as the gravity of my amorous actions last Friday afternoon just slap me in the face with the realisation that Gregory will stop at nothing in pursuing a friendship with me.

I thank him, accepting his gift, and offer him a drink, which he accepts. He sits down on the stool in the kitchen with his arms resting on the counter, watching me pour the wine and he notices the vegetables I was in the middle of prepping for dinner, and says, "Oh, sorry, did I disturb your dinner plans?"

I pass him a glass of red and reply, "I was only making a veggie lasagne, but it can wait." I take a sip of wine and start to feel guilt-tripped into having to invite him, so I ask him if he'd like to stop for dinner and before I have even finished the sentence, he has already accepted my invitation from his continual nodding.

I continued preparing the lasagne as he sat talking about Christmas Day at his place with his mother, two brothers and their wives. He spoke continuously for the entire time it took me to prepare the lasagne, pop it in the oven and prepare the salad. I drifted off in my own thoughts until I heard him call my name, at which point I looked up and he said, "So what do you think?"

"Sorry, think about what?" I said, a little embarrassed that I had switched off.

"Coming over to mine on Boxing Day. My mum will be there and my—"

"I'm afraid I won't be able to as I'll be in Devon visiting family," I cut in quickly.

"Oh, it was just a thought," he said and then carried on talking. I topped up his wine and carried on with dinner, my thoughts firmly now on how fast he had moved on from a few days earlier when we had slept together, to inviting me over to his place on Boxing Day and meeting his family. I try not to read too much into it as I set the table, pop some music on and serve dinner.

As we settle down to eat, Gregory looks at me and says, "Thank you for a lovely evening, Rachel, I'm feeling really positive about life and I'm looking forward to next year and what it may hold."

I raise my glass and say, "Cheers." However, my thoughts are hoping he's not including me in his plans for his future happiness.

I watch Gregory eat like he's guarding his food, one arm encircling the plate, the other hand holding the fork, and as he comes near to finishing, I offer him a second helping which he accepts. He refuses a third glass of wine as he's driving and once I have finished eating, I get up to clear away the plates. Gregory is occupied on his phone which, leaves me free to clean up after dinner, after which I place a bottle of Champagne into a bottle bag to give to him when he leaves, which I feel obliged to after accepting his gift. He realises he's outstayed his welcome when I emerge from the bedroom in my comfy clothes. He stands up, apologises and starts making his way to the door. "No need to apologise, Gregory, big day tomorrow and..."

"Yes, of course, I still have a lot to do, with wrapping presents and..." He pauses for a moment and looks at me intently and says, "It's been really lovely, Rachel, thank you again for dinner."

"You're welcome, thank you for the present," I reply, as we both stand at the door. Then I remember what happened a few days earlier when we were in this position, and I was drunk and horny.

I retrieve the bottle of Champagne and hand it to Gregory and wish him a Merry Christmas. "What's this? You shouldn't have," he says, peering inside.

"Nor should you have," I respond smiling.

We hug goodbye and that feeling rises up in me as Gregory holds me, pressing his body against mine. I look up at him and am just about to say that we can't do this again, when I feel his hardness and, before I've realised it, his tongue is massaging the inside of my mouth. My back is against the door and my legs have been gently parted by his and he's softly grinding his body against mine. I'm enjoying it and can't stop, even if I wanted to. He stops for a moment and places the bottle of Champagne down on the floor and resumes his act. I am wet, and as he undresses me, he places his fingers inside the front of my lace knickers and touches me, his other hand reaches under my sweatshirt and softly pinches my nipples. I can't contain myself and groan with pleasure as I unbuckle his belt and reach in and take hold of him, but he then kneels down, slips my knickers off and places his head in between my legs and licks me 'til I orgasm. I plead with him to fuck me and as he enters me, my body completely surrenders under his control. A minute later, his body jerks and slumps on top of mine and as we lie on the floor, I can hear my inner voice screaming *what the fuck have you done!*

"I can't believe we've just done that," I whisper.

"I know, it's great," he whispers back as he slides off me and turns on his side to face me.

His hand wanders to my breasts and he starts caressing them and I can't stop him, as I'm in lust; not with him, but with sex. I turn my head towards his and we start kissing again. The palm of his hand slides against my nipples and the sight of him getting hard again drives me to climb on top of him and sit astride as he enters me again. He cups my breasts and sweetly sucks my nipples, his teeth biting softly as I move slowly back and forth. He's deep inside me and I'm delirious with pleasure as his fingers rub my clitoris until we both climax. I stay on top of him until the pulsing inside me stops and then slip out and make my way to the bathroom.

When I return with my dressing gown on, I find Gregory already dressed which pleases me as I didn't want a sleepover. "So," he says.

"So," I say back, "let's chat about this another time, Gregory, it's late."

"Sure," he replies, with a huge grin on his face. "You're a very sexy lady, Rachel," he whispers in my ear as we say goodbye for the second time that evening.

"Have a lovely Christmas, Gregory."

He walks out of the door and down the stairs. I refuse to entertain any thoughts of regret just yet, as my body is still in that beautiful state of bliss, buzzing with electricity at the thought of what it had just enjoyed, twice. I go to bed and fall into a sweet slumber.

I wake up on Christmas morning and put some coffee on as I take the present that Gregory bought me and open it to discover a beautiful Mulberry purse. *He must've paid quite a bit for that;* I think as I investigate to see if it's genuine. It looks like the real deal and then I find the gift receipt inside which confirms to me that it's genuine. I'm shocked and in disbelief that he has spent so much money on a present for me. I resign myself to forget about it for now and get ready to head to Mum and Dad's for Christmas, which is the same every year for the three of us, unless I bring a boyfriend, but that hasn't happened in years.

I arrive around 11:30, give them both a big hug, pop the presents under the tree, and take my luggage upstairs. Dad prepares the drinks, then I put the television on in the kitchen whilst helping Mum with dinner. She has already prepared canapes. Dad is in charge of the turkey and we all just enjoy the day in our own joyful way. At 3pm we watch the Queen's speech with a glass of Champagne – my third or fourth by then – and eat 'til we're fit to burst. Dad will slump in front of the television watching any old film that's been on a hundred times and after a nanny nap, will find us in the kitchen getting the cheese and crackers, Christmas pudding and chocolates ready. After this, we will usually get round to opening presents and playing a game of scrabble.

The next day we all head down to Paignton in Devon where Dad's brother lives with his family. It's a family tradition that we always visit them on Boxing Day, stay for a few days and come Easter, they all head to Ascot for the Easter break. It's the only family on my dad's side, so spending quality time with them all is important. It's more like a drunken haze with my two younger cousins and being so close to the beach is the bonus.

During the journey down to Devon, a text message pings through on my phone whilst I'm driving. Mum offers to read it out to me to which I swiftly reply, "I'll get it later, Mum."

"Okay, dear," she responds.

The thought of her reading a message that Gregory may have sent which might mention the other night is not something I wish to be aired. When we stop at the services, I get a chance to read it. It is from Gregory and reads, *'Hello, Rachel, I hope you had a lovely Christmas, thank you for the Champagne, I'll be saving it for New Year's x'*.

My response reads, *'Hi, Gregory, you're welcome. Christmas was lovely and quiet with the folks. Thank you for the beautiful present but I can't accept it. It's way too much, I'll catch up with you when I return in the New Year'*. I didn't think it right to leave a kiss at the end of the message as I don't want him reading too much into it, especially since I've already blurred the lines between us.

He responds with, *'Okay, have fun and see you soon x'*. I don't respond as I really don't want to encourage him to continue to text me during my break in Devon.

Time spent with the family in Devon is always busy, filled with daily walks on the beach, picnics in inclement weather, playing boardgames by the open fire, eating delicious home-cooked food, and, for me and my cousins, visits to as many pubs as we can fit in before it's time to go home. It all ends far too quickly and before too long, we're heading back to Ascot, laden with presents, sandwiches and a flask of tea for the drive home.

On our journey back, I receive a text message from Vince who wants to make sure that I'll be back for the New Year's Eve party that he and Harry host every year. Their New Year's Eve parties are always Champagne-fuelled fun. We always used to pile into their local pub but when they started charging an entrance fee for the privilege of drinking there on the last night of the year, that's when they both decided to welcome in the New Year at theirs. This is a lot more civilised, with the bonus of not having to dodge the blokes in the pub who are just after trying to cop a kiss and a feel, holding a bedraggled bit of mistletoe over your head hoping you're drunk enough not to care.

Three and a half hours later we arrive home and after packing my car with my Christmas gifts and luggage, I make my way home, desperate to relax in the bath and have an early night. As I lay in the bath, I close my eyes and think back to three months earlier when my quest began and all the dates I have been on; how quickly the time has passed by and then I wonder what the New Year will hold. I think of Gregory and how I know in my heart that he's not for me but how much I enjoy the physical part with him, but is that because I just miss that intimacy with someone? I hope he understands where I stand, although maybe I should reinforce my position next time we speak as the last thing I want to do is mess him about, especially as his ex has already done that. I feel excited about the new year and continuing my quest, so I finish off my soak and head to bed.

The next morning, I decide to go for a run in Windsor Great Park, my last run of the year. It's drizzly but not cold and seeing as the last two weeks have seen me indulging in good food and copious amounts of alcohol, it's only fair to partake in a healthy pursuit of exercise to ensure I'll slip easily into my black dress tonight.

I arrive at Vince and Harry's at 6 o'clock on the dot with my Laurent Perrier Rosé in hand – their favourite drink any time of the day – and a bottle of red. The house is warm and smells like a bakery. The aroma of herbs, garlic and bread baking engulfs my nostrils, and as I hug them both, I can hear Harriet's familiar laugh. I walk through the hall towards the kitchen, which is laden with trays of canapes on one side, champagne flutes and wine glasses on the other side next to the fridge; the oven is whirring away with the delightful smell invading the house. "Hello, gorgeous." Harriet welcomes me, sweeping me up in her arms and we hug tightly.

"Hattie, how are you? Hello, John," Harriet's husband is waiting keenly to be the next in line for a hug. "She let you out for the night?" I say, motioning toward Hattie as we hug.

"Yes, for my annual catch-up with you all," he quips.

A hand appears with a glass of Champagne and as I take it, I look across to see Vince smiling and giving me a wink. We clink glasses and I'm introduced to a couple of new faces and say hello to some familiar ones too. Naomi arrives with Neil not long after me and us girls leave Neil and John in the kitchen talking about golf and head to the lounge for a catch-up. "So, what's happening with you and Gregory, Rache?" Naomi asks excitedly.

"No, nothing much, although I did end up shagging him again – by mistake, of course. He came over after our get-together on Christmas Eve with a present and after a couple of more drinks..." I raise my eyes to the ceiling. "Anyway, I'll be returning the present."

"Why?" Hattie asks.

"He spent a lot of money and—"

Before I could finish Naomi butts in. "Well, what did he get you?"

"A Mulberry purse," I reply.

"Ooh, lovely," Hattie purrs.

"Yes, but I hardly know him and we're not going out, we're just..." I pause for a moment. "Shagging, as far as I'm concerned."

Naomi looks disheartened and says, "Well, maybe something might develop?"

"No, I don't think so, Nomes, he's seems like a lovely guy but I'm just not into him like that and, besides, he knows the score, so we're just FBs for the moment," I reply.

"FBs?" Naomi says looking lost, until Hattie whispers in her ear and she nods. "Well, I better let you know that—"

Naomi is interrupted by a voice shouting out her name and we all turn around. I am confronted with Gregory standing in the hallway outside the lounge with Vince. Naomi walks towards them and then turns and mouths 'sorry' to me. I look at Hattie who is smiling at me, trying hard not to laugh, as she says, "Surprise!"

"What's he doing here?" I ask, but Naomi arrives with Gregory.

"Hi," Gregory says, as Naomi introduces him to Harriet and then he turns to me and says, "Hello, stranger, how was your break in Devon?"

"Hello, Gregory, Devon was wonderful," I reply, trying to sound casual but seething inside at Naomi. "I got home late last night. So, how are you doing?"

"Yes, very well," he replies.

The awkwardness between us is palpable, so Naomi quickly butts in. "Gregory had to pop by today to finish up on some work at ours and didn't have any plans for tonight, so I thought I'd..."

I feel someone poke me from behind; I let out a shriek and turn to find Vince hovering around with a grin on his face. "Sorry, Nomes, you were saying?" I say apologetically.

Before Naomi can continue, Vince takes me by the elbow and announces, "I need your advice on the soufflé, Rache." I am relieved, to say the least, to be rescued and eagerly oblige, whispering 'excuse me' as Vince whisks me away, sniggering like a schoolgirl. "Oh my God! What was she thinking? It had nothing to do with me, hun, she got the impression that you two were an item and before you know it, Bob's your uncle, Fanny's your aunt, and she's asking us if it's okay for him to come along, and to be honest, darling, we weren't sure what to say, so we told Naomi the decision was yours," Vince said without taking a breath, so that, by the time we reached the kitchen, he nearly passed out.

"I am pretty pissed off with her, she didn't ask me and, furthermore, we're only shagging, I don't want a relationship with him. Besides, he's got too many issues," I say as Vince tops up my flute.

"He's not for you, Rache, he's bit of a drip," remarks Harry from across the kitchen, as he takes the bread out from the oven.

"I'm not going to let this spoil my night," I say, as Hattie walks into the kitchen.

"Where are these soufflés, then?" she says, howling with laughter.

I bum a cigarette off Vince and stand outside in the back courtyard; it's lit up with so many fairy lights and looks positively inviting. "I didn't know you smoked," I hear someone say, and turn to see Gregory standing by the back door halfway in, halfway out, not committing to either.

"Only on special occasions," I say, with a wry smile. He steps out and I put the cigarette out.

"Look, I'm sorry if I've cramped your style, it's just that Naomi was asking how things were going between us and I said they were going great and the next thing she's asking me what I was up to tonight, and when I told her that I didn't have any plans, she invited me along," Gregory says sheepishly, looking at the ground.

"It's okay, Gregory, it was just a bit of a shock when I saw you. As I said, I only got back last night from Devon and hadn't caught up with Naomi 'til tonight and she hadn't gotten round to telling me that she had invited you."

"Right, I see, of course," he replies. We both head back indoors to the warmth of the kitchen and top up our drinks.

The evening swiftly passes by without too many mishaps apart from when Gregory tripped up on his way back into the lounge, launching face first into Artisan Sheldon's humongous breasts, much to everyone's amusement and laughter. She was not impressed and slapped him hard on his arm and then felt guilty and pursued him for the rest of the night, much to mine and Hattie's enjoyment.

Artisan Sheldon, Sandy, for short, was an old schoolfriend of Hattie's. She was the nerdy ugly duckling at school until she got a boob job in her early twenties, which saw the start of her transformation. The more attention she got, the bigger the boobs and bum got, but it also came with its drawbacks as she became a raging alcoholic and would always insult you one minute and with the next breath, want to be your best friend and shower you with compliments.

After much drinking, eating, and dancing, the television was turned on for the countdown and the firework display in London. Gregory managed to escape Artisan's clutches for a moment and came over to wish me a Happy New Year with a kiss before his pursuer noticed and stood behind him, waiting her turn. "Happy New Year, Gregory," I said, before Artisan pounced on him. "I'll be leaving soon, so I'll say goodbye to you now," I managed to say, whether he heard or not is a mystery as I left shortly after, catching a ride with Hattie and John who dropped me off home. It was lovely getting home and climbing into bed, I could hear fireworks going off, music playing, and I felt content. I switched the phone off and drifted sweetly into a new year.

I wake up to a beautiful, bright morning on New Year's Day in 2007. The year I turn 40, there, I said it without feeling afraid. "Forty! Forty! Forty!" I turned the television on and headed to the bathroom. On my return, I switched my phone on and as expected, am bombarded with ping after ping of 'Happy New Year' messages. One from Mum says, *'I hope you've not drunk too much, Rachel, and see you for lunch'*.

There are also a few texts and missed calls from Gregory. *'Hi, where are you? The guys said you left, shall I come over?'* His voice message, from what I could make out with all the noise, music and what sounded like Artisan in the background calling for him, said just the same, asking where I'd got to and wanting to come over.

I sent him a text message saying, *'Happy New Year. Had to leave early as I have a lunch date with the folks today. Turned my phone off last night so only just picked up your messages. Hope all is well'*.

I make a coffee and catch up with the morning news, watching the replay of the celebrations and firework displays from all the major cities around the world; it makes me feel hopeful for this New Year and I start to ponder on all the things that I'd like to embark upon. The phone pings and I'm bought back to reality with a message from Naomi asking if I'm up and free for a chat, so I give her a call. "Happy New Year, Nomes."

"Happy New Year, Rache," she says, sounding a little sheepish. "Where did you get to last night? I went in search of you and then thought you might be with Gregory until I saw him with Artisan and then Vince said that you'd already left."

"Yes, lunch plans with Mum and Dad today and I didn't want to feel totally wrecked, so I left early with Hattie and John shortly after midnight."

"Gregory was asking me where you were too, although Artisan wouldn't leave him alone; she was her usual pissed self, all boobs and fur coat. Not letting him out of her sight, poor bloke." I laughed out loud, picturing it in my head. "It's not funny, Rache, I think he was quite traumatised by it all," she said, chuckling herself.

Naomi went on to apologise to me for inviting him without asking whether I was okay with it. I made peace with her, and she promised never to interfere again and then she went on to say that she had overheard Gregory tell Artisan that he was in a relationship with me. He was probably trying to spurn her advances, I told her.

We hung up and I resolved to get ready early and head over to Mum and Dad's, much to their surprise, as me arriving late is usually the case on New Year's Day. Lunch was followed by a long walk around Virginia Waters; it was a lovely quiet afternoon and feeling thoroughly exhausted after the walk, I made my way home.

I slipped into my jogging pants and t-shirt and snuggled on the couch with a throw and popped the TV on. Heaven! I sighed as the fleece throw felt soft and warm around my feet, warming me up as I lay there, my upper body propped up with the cushions. *Ben Hur* had just started and although I must've watched it more times than I care to mention, who hasn't? It became my film of choice for the next three or so hours of my life; it's one of my favourites and the good thing is that I can have as many loo and snack breaks, and still feel as though I haven't missed anything.

I'm startled by the sound of my mobile ringing, and I instinctively pick up and answer, sounding a bit groggy. "Hello."

"Hello, Rachel, did I wake you?" Gregory says.

"Gosh! What time is it?" I say, as I look across to the clock in the kitchen.

"It's just gone 6," he replies.

"I must've crashed out whilst watching TV. Happy New Year, Gregory."

"Happy New Year. What happened to you last night?" he says, sounding a little annoyed.

"I thought I'd mentioned that I'd be leaving early as I had lunch plans and didn't want to get too wrecked, I did say bye to you when we wished each other a Happy New Year last night," I replied.

"Oh! I must've missed that; I had that crazy girl follow me around all night," he says.

I burst out laughing. "Artisan?" I said, knowing full well it was her.

"Yes, she wouldn't leave me alone, I even told her that I was in a relationship with you, but she wouldn't buy it," he went on.

"No, she's a clever cookie, is Artisan. Oh, I'm so sorry, poor you, but you did launch yourself on her boobs and that's a come-on to our Sandy," I said. We both laugh.

"That was an accident, I tripped up," he said.

"Yes, tripped up as you were walking into the lounge looking at those huge mammas. It's okay, it's not the first time it's happened to Artisan, but I think that was the first time that someone actually went head first into them," I say, laughing uncontrollably.

"Rachel, stop teasing me," Gregory says, laughing too. "I really need to know what's happening," he adds, desperation in his voice.

"Happening?" I say, sounding puzzled.

"Yes, between me and you," he replies. I pause for a moment. "Look, can I come over and see you?" he asks.

"What, now?" I reply.

"Well, yes, I'm in Windsor and—"

Before he could finish talking, I interrupt him and say, "Gregory, I thought we agreed that we'd just be friends and have a bit of fun and see how things go without putting any demands on anyone, especially since you're working through your issues," I say, exasperated. This was not the way I wanted my new year to start and now I was wishing I hadn't answered the phone.

"Yes, yes, I know we're just friends but..." There's a long pause and I start feeling a little sorry for him, so I ask him where he is. "Just around the corner," he replies.

"Okay, pop over, then, but I'm warning you that I'm in my comfy clothes and you have just woken me."

I don't get a chance to finish what I'm saying as Gregory butts in, saying, "Okay, see you in a bit."

I jump up and go to freshen up in the bathroom when the entry phone buzzes. I let him up and continue to the bathroom, opening the door to the flat on my way. Whilst freshening up, I can hear Gregory enter the flat. I call out that I'm in the bathroom.

"Okay," he says, as I take a swig of mouthwash, swish, spit, put some lip gloss on and leave the bathroom to find him standing by the balcony with a huge bouquet of flowers in his hand. "Hi," he says, looking a little worse for wear.

"What d'you do that for?" I say, looking at the flowers.

"I wanted to," he says, blushing.

"Well, they're lovely, thank you," I say, retrieving a vase from the kitchen cupboard as Gregory follows me, bouquet in hand. Then he leans in and kisses me full on the lips. I pop the flowers in the vase with some water and start feeling a little aroused from his kiss. *Maybe he does understand that I just want a physical relationship and nothing more*, I think as I offer him a drink.

"No, I don't really fancy a drink," he says, looking at me intently.

So, I resume my position on the couch under the throw. He takes his shoes off and sits at the other end stroking my legs and then, after a few moments, slides up behind me, our bodies spooning. *Ben Hur* is still on, and I continue watching, as I'm in no mood for conversation. Then I feel his hand reach around under my t-shirt and cup my naked breast, his thumb and finger gently rubbing my nipple. I can feel that familiar surge of excitement build up in me as he continues, his hand stroking my breasts whilst he kisses my neck. I feel him getting hard and I reach my hand behind to touch him; he groans with pleasure and whispers in my ear, but I can't make out what he has said so I turn towards him. He positions himself on top of me, I unbutton his jeans and we undress, eager to enter the blissful state of union. I momentarily think that I will have to end things with Gregory soon as he's getting too needy for my liking, but, for now, I dismiss these thoughts and enjoy the sexual encounter.

Once we are both satisfied, we resume our position on the couch and continue to watch the movie. Gregory starts talking about his mother and how her 70th birthday is a few weeks away, whilst he strokes my hair. Then his phone rings, which startles us, but also gives me the opportunity to jump up and start putting my clothes back on. I turn to him and the expression on his face is that of a rabbit caught in headlights. "Are you going to answer it, then?" I say, hunting around for my t-shirt.

He jumps up and says, "Yes, yes of course." He walks over to the kitchen worktop and retrieves his phone. I feel relieved, the expression 'saved by the bell' comes to mind, as I really don't want the postcoital sentiment.

I pop my clothes back on whilst he chats on the phone and then make my way to the bathroom; I can hear him talking but I'm really not interested in eavesdropping until I hear him say, "No, Mum, not yet." This intrigues me. I flush the loo and press my ear to the bathroom door, trying to listen to what he's saying but his voice has gone from talking normally to whispering, so I quietly open the bathroom door and walk out, which startles him. He's still naked and I can sense his feeling of embarrassment as he sits down on the couch and searches for his boxer shorts. He cuts the conversation short, saying, "Okay, mum, I have to go, I'll call you later, bye."

I make myself busy in the kitchen as Gregory hurriedly dresses. "Would you like a drink, Gregory?" I ask, as I pop the kettle on.

"Um, no, I'm okay, thanks," he replies.

He seems preoccupied in his thoughts, so once the kettle has boiled, I make myself a mug of tea. "So that was your mum, then?" I ask, not really bothered about who he was talking to but the fact that he was whispering has got me thinking that it's something that he didn't want me to hear.

"Yes, indeed it was," he says, as he slips his shoes on and stands up. "We're, um, planning her 70th birthday, nothing too big, and I was going to ask if you'd like to come as my plus-one. It'll just be family, a few friends, er, a small affair," he concludes, glancing over at me as I squeeze my teabag and put it in the bin.

"Oh, well, I don't really do the family thing, Gregory, unless I'm in a serious relationship with someone, but thanks for asking."

Gregory looked stunned at my abrupt answer and slowly makes his way to the door to leave. I follow him, and I can sense his disappointment as he turns to say goodbye. "Well, if you change your mind, Rachel, let me know."

"I will, thank you for the flowers and..." He rushes down the stairs and as he opens the door onto the pavement, shouts out bye. Wow! he is definitely pissed off with me, but I have purposefully emotionally detached myself from Gregory, as I don't have strong enough feelings for him to pursue a relationship. He doesn't make me go weak at the knees, the butterflies are not fluttering away in my tummy and, if I'm being brutally honest, witnessing him crying like a baby when we were first getting it on still makes me cringe.

It's New Year's Day and I'm determined not to waste time and the need to resume my quest takes precedence. I take my mug of tea and take the throw and wrap it around my body and head onto the balcony, sit down and light up my last cigarette, another thing that must come to an end. I ponder on what the next nine months may hold in store for me 'til my big birthday and the end of the quest. I say goodbye to what has been and gone, to all the men whom I've encountered so far and smile to myself, with a feeling of content, that all is well.

A few days passed and I hadn't heard from Gregory. I hoped I hadn't wounded him by my response to his invitation to his mum's 70th birthday, so I thought I'd give him a call on my way to work. There's no answer, so I left a voice message. "Hi there, Greg." *Greg! Greg! When have I ever called him Greg?* I think to myself. "Just on my way to work and thought I'd say hi, hope all's okay with you, chat soon, bye." Ouch! That was awkward.

My first day back in the office and apart from catching up with emails and booking visits for the sales guys, all was pretty much easy-going and drama-free until my phone sprang into action with a call from Gregory. "Hi," I answer, light-heartedly.

"Hello, Rachel, sorry about before, I was busy with a client."

"That's okay, just thought I'd say hello and hope that I hadn't upset you the other day when you were over."

"No, no, but I did want to ask you if you've had any more thoughts about accompanying me to Mum's 70th?" he says.

"Oh!" was all I could manage to fit in before he went on.

"You see, we need to know numbers and she was asking me about our relationship, where it was going, and I didn't know what to say to her, so..." There's a long pause. My mind went blank as my brain was trying to fathom what Gregory had just said. "Rachel, are you there?"

"Um, yes, sorry, so your mum needs to know where this relationship is going?" I repeat back to Gregory, unaware that I'm speaking a little louder than usual and when I look up, I realise everyone in earshot is looking at me. I get up and creep out of the office and as I look back, I can see Kevin smiling, almost laughing, with a look to say he wants the whole story when I return. "I'm in the office, Gregory, so I can't talk about this now," I say, as I walk into the staff kitchen.

Gregory starts bumbling away, saying how sorry he was and how his mum wanted to know the status of our relationship. I feel like I've been transported back in time to when I was at school and the roles have been reversed and I'm the boy in this situation being asked by the girl that I've been snogging where the relationship is going. Fast forward 25 years and the man is asking, on behalf of his mum, where the relationship is going. What have I done? I stayed too long, I kept saying that I needed to end it with Gregory, sooner rather than later. No wonder his ex was so brutal with him.

"Gregory, let's talk later, I can't talk about this at work, bye." I hang up before he could respond and sneak back into the office; thankfully mostly everyone is busy on the phone apart from Kevin, whose eyes light up as he watches me take my seat. “I’m not talking about it now,” I snap, “maybe I’ll fill you in later, and that’s a maybe with a small ‘m’,” I continue, and look over at him making puppy dog eyes at me, eager to laugh at my current dating disaster.

On my way home from work, I get a call from Naomi who insists I join her at our usual hang-out, which I accept, and less than 20 minutes later, I walk in to find Naomi and Artisan sitting at a corner table on the couch. “Hi,” I say, sounding surprised at the sight of them both; Naomi didn’t mention that she would be there.

“Hi, Rache, I bumped into Sandy on my way over here and she—”

“Invited herself,“ Artisan interjects, laughing coyly.

“Yes, something like that,” Naomi says, sheepishly.

“Ah, okay, well how nice to see you so soon. How’s tricks?” I say, looking at her with mild curiosity as I take a seat.

“I am super, darling,” she says, her breasts heaving with exasperation as she sighs.

“Oh, well I must say, you’re looking a lot better than when I saw you last week at Vince and Harry’s,” I remark.

"Yes, yes, darling, how's your boyfriend?" she asks, shuffling her position on the couch nervously.

"My boyfriend?" I reply quizzically, knowing full well who she's referring to.

"Gregory," Naomi responds, "she's talking about Gregory."

"I wouldn't quite call him that, we're just friends," I say, as I stand up to go to the loo. "Be back in a mo." I walk away, looking back at Naomi with a look of irritation.

On my return, I find Naomi alone on the sofa and so I order some drinks and sit down. "What was all that about, Nomes?" I blurt out.

"No idea, she called me this afternoon asking after you and Gregory, wanting to know if you two were an item. I think she may have a thing for him after they snogged on New Year's Eve, then she wanted to— "

"They what!" I spat out, nearly spraying red wine over Naomi. "They snogged?" I said, shocked. "Well, Gregory failed to mention that when he called in to see me on New Year's Day."

"She wanted to meet up and ask you directly," Naomi continued.

"Oh well, she's welcome to him. Where is she, by the way?" I said, looking around to make sure she wasn't lurking behind me, ready to bash me with her bosoms.

"As soon as you went to the loo, she rushed out of here saying she had a meeting to go to," Naomi says, rolling her eyes.

I told Naomi of the conversation I had earlier with Gregory, about his mother's request about the status of our relationship and about the invitation to her 70th birthday party. "Isn't that supposed to be the other way round? The girl asking the man where the relationship is going?" Naomi says.

"Right!" I reply, emphatically.

"Well, I'm not surprised that you're not interested in him, Rache."

"I'm going to pop over to his and speak with him before his mother starts calling me," I say, and we finish our drinks and head out onto Peascod Street.

Naomi drops me off outside Gregory's house and as we sit in the car, I apologise to her for things not working out with him, just in case she finds that she loses him as her handyman. She laughs and tells me not to worry about it. We kiss goodbye and as I walk up to his front door, I notice the lights on upstairs and I hear music playing and a women's voice in the background.

Oh, I do hope it's not his mother, I think as I knock on the door, there's no response and so I knock again, a little harder.

The music stops, the hallway light comes on and Gregory opens the door. He looks stunned, eyes wide, and stands still for a moment with his mouth half-open before spluttering out, "Rachel, what, er..." Another pause. "What are you doing here?" he eventually manages to croak out.

"Well, hello to you too, Gregory," I reply, and then I notice the top of someone's head peeking from around the kitchen door. I cock my head to the side to look around him to see who it is, and he shuffles nervously glancing around. It occurs to me how stupid he looks standing there and I think of the number of times that he's called on me unannounced. "Not going to invite me in, darling?" I say, loud enough for the other person to hear, but before he can even answer the huge breasts appear from around the kitchen door. Artisan tries to look nonchalant as she reveals herself, but I could tell that she was afraid due to her reluctance to come any closer. Gregory looked as though he wanted to be swallowed whole by a sink hole, his face turned red and was all screwed up with that look of when he came in his pants and cried. He was motionless, speechless, and looked pathetic. "Really, Gregory!" I said, with a hint of distaste and then I raised my hand to swish my hair back which made him flinch and he stepped back as though I was about to strike him. "I see you have a date for your mum's 70th birthday now." I turned around with a smile on my face and sashayed up the path and out of the garden, not looking back.

My walk home seemed a lot quicker than I imagined and half an hour later, I stopped off at the local chippy, the need for comfort food, my fluffy slippers and a glass of fizz was imperative for my soul. As I reached home and entered the warmth of the flat, I kicked off my shoes and changed into my PJs. My mobile started ringing but I was too eager to eat so I ignored it and thought how differently my encounter with Gregory had panned out; it was such a stroke of luck that I went over when I did and caught him with Artisan. I enjoyed my dinner all the more and once finished, I checked my phone to see that it was Naomi. She'd left a voice message saying that Artisan had called and told her of the evening's events. I gave Naomi a call and recalled the incident to her.

"I can't believe that two-timing snake and as for Artisan, no wonder she was eager to see you earlier. I think this must be the lowest she's ever sunk to," Naomi says vehemently. "He won't be coming here to do any more work for me, that's for sure," she continued.

"Nomes, don't say that; I was going round to let him go but, as it happened, things worked out brilliantly for me, so I feel relieved and not one bit guilty. He was too needy for me, and I think they'll make a better match. I'd love to be a fly on the wall at his mum's 70th birthday, just to see her face when she meets Artisan and her boobs," I say, with a chuckle. We hang up and I take my glass of fizz and say, with relief, "Another one bites the dust."

Chapter Ten

Randolph the Red-Nosed Stockbroker

Most of my morning at work the next day was spent filling Kevin in on the events that had unfolded the day before, from when I had received the call from Gregory. Kevin needed to know every detail, not an abbreviated, short bullet-pointed presentation, but a full-blown, warts and all account from the first meeting to the ending, with Artisan rearing her boobs from around the kitchen door. Retelling my brief affair with Gregory, made me aware of how funny it actually all was, neither of us got much work done through his incessant probing and laughter after which he said, "Rachel, I was chatting to Nina about you..."

"Really!" I blurt out. "What about?"

"Well, if you let me finish," he says, rolling his eyes to the ceiling. "She has an old friend from uni days that she's recently got back in touch with, and he's divorced, works in the City as a stockbroker, has a fair bit of money, I would say, seeing as he lives there too, and she was thinking about getting you both together."

"Divorced!" I say, grimacing. "They always have so much baggage."

"Well, yes, Rachel, people do get divorced if they don't get along anymore or fall out of love or for many other reasons. Besides, your last one had more baggage than most and he hadn't even been married," he says, smirking.

"Okay, okay, fair point," I say, conceding. "What does he look like? Have you met him? And why does Nina think that I'll be suited to him?" I fire off, eager to know the answers.

"No, not met him. Don't know what he looks like, but Nina always used to say that, at uni, he was a Kevin Costner lookalike, but I'll forward a picture once I speak with her, and not sure why she thinks you'd be a match," he says, looking dumbfounded. "But, if I were to hazard a guess, I'd say because he's solvent, cultured and wants to settle down with someone and enjoy companionship again. I think he's in his mid-50s."

"Woah! That's a lot older than what I'm looking for, Kev."

"Yes, but from what I gather, he's young at heart and still out there keeping up with his younger counterparts," he says, tilting his head to one side and shrugging his shoulders with an expression of 'give it a go, what have you got to lose'.

"I'd have to see what he looks like, Kev."

"Okay, I'll sort that out," he says excitedly. I get back to work and make arrangements to have a catch-up with the girls a couple of days later on Friday, after work.

Later that evening, I receive a message from Kevin with a photo of a man named Randolph. He's wearing a blue suit, white shirt, a pink tie, and he's holding a glass of Champagne. He's not exactly my cup of tea in the looks department and I'm not sure which part is supposed to look like Kevin Costner, apart from the fair hair. He has a slim build, but I can't tell how tall he is from the picture; I guess he must be all right if Nina has endorsed him. I get back to cooking dinner and start thinking that maybe I do need to venture out of the Windsor area and meet different people with different lives, be flexible and spontaneous. Randolph must have an exciting lifestyle, being a stockbroker, work hard, play hard; and taking a trip into London wouldn't be a bad idea. So, I take another look at the picture and text Kevin back, saying, *'Okay, I'll go on a date with Randolph, although I'm still looking for the Kevin Costner resemblance'*.

Kevin texts back straight away, saying, *'Brilliant, I'll get Nina to forward your number on'*.

I look across to the beautiful vase of flowers on the kitchen counter and momentarily smile as I think of

Gregory and Artisan together and then banish any further thoughts of him and enjoy the peaceful evening to myself.

The next day at work I receive a text message from Randolph saying that Nina had passed on my number, how lovely I was and asking if I'd like to meet up. I reply, saying yes, and we arrange to meet the following week at Waterloo Station. I'd be getting the train in, so settle on the Wednesday after work, saying I'd let him know what time the train would be arriving once I'd had a look. It all sounded a bit romantic, me stepping off the train at Waterloo and walking down the platform to find him standing there, wearing a pink carnation in his suit lapel. "Ha!" I laugh out loud, picturing it.

Kevin is not in the office for the rest of the week, thankfully, as I'm sure he'd be doing cartwheels. The next couple of days pass by uneventfully and, come Friday afternoon, I'm gagging to leave the office to meet up with Naomi and Harriet. Friday night drinks after work always tends to be fun, everyone you pass has that feel-good 'weekend's here' face, where they're glad the working week is over and now it's time to relax and hang out. I'm the first to arrive at The Drinking Ole, so I order a bottle of red, a white wine spritzer for Naomi, some nibbles and I secure a table for us. Hattie arrives next so I pour the wine and we make a start. I fill her in on the final episode with Gregory and Artisan; mid story Naomi arrives, and she contributes her summation. We all agree, after much hilarity, that they were destined to be, from the moment Gregory's face landed on Artisan's boobs that fateful New Year's Eve a week ago.

I took my phone out of my handbag and pulled up the picture of Randolph; both of them stared at it displaying a look of indifference. "Don't all speak at once," I remark, with a giggle.

"Well, who is he?" Hattie says, smiling curiously.

"His name is Randolph, he's a stockbroker who lives in the City and I've got a date with him next week."

"Looks a bit older than—"

"Yes, I know, he's been around the block, you'd say, divorced, no kids, around 50," I cut in, before Naomi has a chance to finish. Why am I defending him? I don't even know him.

Harriet's face says it all; she looks like she's chewed a wasp. "He looks a little washed-out, Rache," she says.

"He does, doesn't he? Apparently, he used to look like Kevin Costner. One of the sales guys at work, his wife used to go to uni with him, says he's a good one, so I'm trying to rise above the old haggard look that he's got going on. After Gregory, maybe someone a bit more mature might be what I need," I say, trying to convince myself more than anyone else that it's worth a try. I take a look at the picture again and start laughing, which sets them off too. "I'm just trying to see the Kevin Costner in him."

"Well, look, Rache, at least you'll have a night out in town and, who knows, he might book a Michelin star restaurant, or he might take you to a rooftop bar for cocktails," Harriet concludes.

We enjoy the rest of the evening and call it a night once we've finished the wine. I walk back to the flat and enjoy the start of the first weekend of the year in a quiet sense of calm, catching up on reading. I'm in the middle of *The Power of Now*, which I'm enjoying immensely, although I've been reading it for two months now and have to read the same page twice; first time to read it, then a second time to reinforce what I read the first time. So, it's taking me a long time, but I don't care, it's my go-to book at the moment.

My weekend of not doing much passes by easily and the start of my working week has me mentally organising an outfit for my date with my Kevin Costner lookalike. I leave extra early on Wednesday afternoon from work with toothache, to get home and get ready for my trip into town. I decide to dress up and forgo my usual date night jeans, just in case Randolph has booked a swanky restaurant or rooftop bar, and I opt to wear a dress with knee-high boots and my faux fur jacket.

The train journey to Waterloo takes about 50 minutes and I arrive with 10 minutes to spare so I take my time disembarking and retrieve my mirror from my handbag and check my hair, reapply my lipstick, then make my way off and saunter up the platform towards the terminal. The station is busy with peak-time commuters and as I pass through the ticket barrier, hoping to see Randolph waiting for me, there's no sign of anyone who looks remotely like the man in the picture. I slowly wander through the throng on the lookout but no one who matches his photo catches my eye. So, I make my way to the exit and then I notice a man standing with his back against a pillar, looking down at his phone. He's wearing the exact same outfit as in the picture that Kevin sent me, and as I hesitantly approach him, I stop. I'm about 10 feet away from him and don't want to move forward. He hasn't noticed me; maybe I can turn or walk straight past him, I think, but just then he looks up and sees me. He catches my gaze and I feel like a gazelle caught mid-motion by a lion and I'm snared. He slowly starts walking in my direction and my fake smile must be a giveaway for the discontent that I'm feeling. "Rachel?"

"Yes, hi, Randolph, is it?" I say, hoping that a mistake has been made and he'll say no.

"Yes, call me Randy," he says as we shake hands.

He's not much taller than 4-foot, 5 inches, maybe 4-8, he has a huge, bulbous red nose, the old and haggard look was enough to compete with, but this is too much. What was Nina thinking? Wait 'til I get to the office; Kevin will get a piece of my mind.

We both walk out of the station and head towards the South Bank. "So have you just finished work, Randy?" I say, trying hard not to sound too upset as I look down at him. With my boots on, I must be over a foot taller than him.

"Yes, I have," he bumbles, walking fast, ahead of me. We ascend the steps and walk on a little further and he stops just before Festival Pier on the River Thames, points at the restaurant, and says, "Will this do?"

"Um, yes, sure," I reply, without even looking, my mind still focused on how I should have just instantly spun around or walked straight past him at the station. It's a Brazilian restaurant, it's busy, lively and loud, which suits me fine. Luckily they have a table, and we take our seats; there's no small talk with Randy, he takes his menu and starts looking through it. I take a look around the restaurant, then look at him and wonder how I ended up here. The waitress arrives to take our drinks order.

"I'm ready to order," he says, looking up at her.

"Oh, I haven't had a chance to look at the menu yet," I say, as I quickly scan the options whilst Randy places his order with her. "May I have a caipirinha and the prawn and coconut stew please," I say, smiling at the waitress.

"So, Rachel, what do you do, then?"

"I work as a PA for the sales team with Nina's husband, Kevin."

"Oh, right, of course," he says.

The waitress arrives with a bottle of red wine and the caipirinha. She opens the bottle and pours a little into the glass for Randolph to try, which he refuses with a shake of his head and says, "It's fine." He motions with his hand for her to pour. The expression on her face as she walks away at his dismissive behaviour makes me cringe.

"I hear that you're a stockbroker," I say, taking a sip of my drink. Randy takes a huge gulp of his wine and starts to talk about his job, how he's been doing it for over 30 years and would've retired by now, but got divorced five years ago, how he had the best times making so much money and enjoying the high life. As he's talking, I can't keep my eyes off his nose; it's big, red, has huge porous bumps and then there's the thread veins around his cheeks. I take my drink in hand to avert my attention from his facial features but it's futile, my eyes are transfixed.

Then he asks, "Would you like some wine with dinner?"

"Yes please," I reply, as I look down and realise that I've polished off my caipirinha, but it has taken the edge off of sitting across from Randy, listening to his life of luxury as a stockbroker. Randy pours me a glass of the red and decants whatever's left in the bottle into his glass and continues talking about his lavish lifestyle that his job has afforded over the years. I get the feeling that maybe he's trying to impress me, but I'm actually irritated by his boastful and wasteful use of money.

Our dinner arrives and Randy orders another bottle of wine. I look at him and realise that his stockbroker lifestyle is embedded in him. Dinner, for me, is spent enjoying my prawn stew and enduring Randy talking, in between mouthfuls of steak and wine, about his ex-wife, and how she cleaned him out when they got divorced. "Did I mention I've been divorced for five years now?" he says again. I made the mistake of asking why they got divorced and how I wish I hadn't, as that can of worms cannot be unopened now. They'd been together 20 years, didn't have kids as they were enjoying the party lifestyle of cocaine, champagne, restaurants, and holidays; he was making the money and she was spending it, was the premise of the 20-year marriage. The more he drank, the louder he became and once we'd finished eating, I excused myself and went to the loo to check the timetable for the next train home.

When I returned, our dishes had been cleared and I watched Randy pour more wine into his glass. The waitress arrived with dessert menus and asked if we'd like anything else. Randy looks across to me and asks if I'd like to get another bottle of wine, to which I decline, so he orders a large glass for himself. "But you've already got a glass," I say, motioning to a full glass of red sitting in front of him.

He looks down at it and says, "Yes, that'll be done by the time she gets back with another." He excuses himself and bumbles to the gents. He still has his suit jacket and tie on and as he walks away, I shake my head, thinking that this was not what Kevin had described to me.

The waitress returns with his glass of red and asks if I would like anything else and I say, "No, nothing except the bill please."

"And anything else for your father?" she asks.

I'm about to say that I'm on a date but then involuntarily laugh out and say, "No, nothing for him, I think he's had quite enough already." We exchange smiles and she leaves me to chuckle to myself.

When Randy returns and takes his seat, he notices the two glasses of wine in front of him and he smiles and says, "Well, I've had a jolly nice time, Rachel."

He looks across at me and I'm rendered speechless. Is this what he calls a good time? All that I can force from my lips is, "Oh that's nice." He smiles as if I've paid him a compliment and then our waitress returns and places the bill on the table.

"What's this?" he says, looking up at her but she's already walked away.

"It's the bill. I have a train to catch in about 10 minutes," I say, reaching into my handbag to retrieve my purse.

"Oh, I was thinking we could go for another drink somewhere," he says, picking up the bill. "It comes to £101; that's without a tip, so if we round it up to £105, that'll be £52.50 each." I look at him, flabbergasted, and take £45 out of my purse.

The waitress arrives with the card machine, and I hand her a £5 note and say, "That's for you." I pop the £40 on the table and say, "My dad will take care of the rest."

I pick up my handbag, my jacket and walk out, hurrying down the steps toward the station, hoping that Randy hasn't followed me out, although he has got two glasses of wine to finish so I'm pretty sure he won't be leaving them. *The cheek of it*, I think, as I jostle through the oncoming crowd in the station. As I pass through the ticket barrier, I start singing, 'Another One Bites the Dust' and I imagine I'm dancing and singing all the way towards the waiting train until I hear the whistle blow and I run, jump on just before the sliding doors starts beeping and close. I sigh, I smile, I'm still humming my song as I search for a seat, sit down and close my eyes.

On my journey home, I decide to text Kevin saying, *'Well, I'm on my way home from yet another terrible date, this time with a bitter, older four-foot-five divorced man who didn't stop talking about his life, his ex-wife and he had a huge bulbous red nose. Thanks a bunch, Kev'.*

I didn't hear back from Kevin until the next time I saw him in the office the following week. He had placed a box of my favourite chocolates and a bottle of red on my desk with a note saying sorry. He told me later on that afternoon when I stopped ignoring him that Nina was mortified, she had only spoken to Randolph on the phone and he gave her the impression that life was grand, and that he was doing okay after the divorce and was ready to start dating. After I forgave him, I told him of our date and how I left the restaurant, with much laughter from him, especially when I told him that the waitress thought he was my father. He resigned himself to never get involved in my dating life again and to only be a willing listener. I agreed and accepted the chocolates and wine he had bought me by way of an apology.

Chapter Eleven

Mishaps, Bad Manners and Downright Disgusting

After my date with Randolph, I felt a little down with the quality of men I was meeting or maybe it was just the start of a new year that made me feel this way; I had high hopes a couple of weeks ago and now after my first date of the year was over, I thought things could only get better. I decided not to do a thing and just sit back and let the universe bring me what I was meant to experience.

Mishaps

I met Trevor through an ex-work colleague, Lorraine. She always got in touch in the new year for a catch-up. She wanted to know all the office gossip; she'd left the company a couple of years earlier and I think she regretted it. She felt micromanaged by her boss at her new place and was hoping that there would be an opening so she could come back. After learning that I was single, she spoke of her younger brother who had also started dating after coming out of a relationship eight months earlier. “He’s a stand-up comic, normal, nice-looking and funny, of course,” she said.

“Lorraine, I’m waiting for the ‘but’!”

“Well, he works evenings and weekends and is away a lot as he does a fair bit of travelling up and down the country going to his gigs.”

“And what makes you think that I’d want to go out with someone who works evenings, weekends and is away a lot?”

Anyway, in light of adhering to the quest, I agreed to a lunch date with him a week later on a Saturday, seeing as he’d be passing Windsor en route to Bristol for a gig that evening. We arranged to meet at mine at 2pm. It’s a complete blind date so when I open the door, I’m pleasantly surprised with what I’m confronted with. His smiling face puts me at ease and once we introduce ourselves, we nervously laugh at the situation that we’d been put in by his older sister. We strolled down Peascod Street chatting and I suggested Mo’s Kitchen to which he agreed to. Thankfully, Mo is not around to make a fuss and seeing as Trevor is working later that evening, he’s not drinking, so I decide to follow suit and we share a bottle of sparkling water and order lunch.

I find Trevor amazingly easy to talk to and feel comfortable in his company. He talks about his life on the road doing stand-up comedy and how he’s been doing it for years, just waiting for his big break. Our food arrives and as we tuck in, we exchange witty banter and I find myself chuckling all the way through lunch from his funny anecdotes and observations, and when one of the waiters comes over to check in on us, Trevor starts imitating his accent. I take my last mouthful of couscous as Trevor mimics the waiter again, which makes me laugh so much that I start coughing. I try to stifle my cough but find it hard to breathe. Trevor continues laughing and so I stand up and lean over the table, coughing, trying to signal to him to give me a slap on the back; only realising then that I'm in distress does he slap me hard in between my shoulder blades twice. I end up inhaling the couscous which gets sucked up into the back of my nasal cavity. Not only do I have tears streaming down my face, but I also have a runny nose; I must've looked a sight.

I made it to the toilets and coughed 'til I could cough no more, cleaned up my tears and blew my nose; it still felt like there were tiny bits of couscous stranded in that passage which I could not dislodge with any amount of coughing. Feeling completely embarrassed, I eventually made my way back to the table and apologised for causing such a commotion. Trevor, on the other hand, found the whole incident so amusing, saying that he would be incorporating it into his gig saying it was comic genius. I smiled at him and said that I was glad that I was contributing to his show.

We split the bill and he walked me back to the flat. He said he'd love to see me again and asked if I'd like to meet up, to which I agreed to, he then kissed me on the cheek and left. When I stared at my reflection in the bathroom mirror, I looked a mess. My mascara and eyeliner had run, my back hurt from his back blows and my pride was sorely bruised. I poured myself a glass of wine and sat in front of the TV for the rest of the day under the duvet, coughing.

Suffice to say, I never heard from Trevor again.

Bad Manners

A couple of weeks later, on a Saturday afternoon in February, I was mooching around the shops in Windsor. I stopped outside the posh cake shop, looking in through the window, salivating over the array of teeny-weeny cakes, tarts and sponges positioned beautifully on tiered stands looking all pretty on display, when I noticed someone inside, waving their hand in the air. I look up and recognise Luca; he beckons me in. I hadn't seen Luca in years; he was an old friend from college days. We always had a thing, but we never really got serious; we'd get drunk and high at house parties and snog but that's where it stopped.

"Hello, Luca, how are you?" I say, as we hug.

"I'm great, how are you, Rachel?"

"I'm doing okay, thanks." I look across to the lady who is seated at the table with him and say, "Hello."

"Rachel, this is my mum, Maria."

"Hello," she says, "why don't you join us, dear? I don't know any of Luca's friends."

"Oh, that would be lovely, thank you, but I'm just on my way to meet up with Naomi," I reply, looking over at Luca and lying through my teeth.

"Oh wow! You two still in touch?" Luca says, sounding surprised.

"Yes, I'm also in touch with Harriet."

"Say hello to them from me and let's get together for a catch-up some time," he says.

We exchange numbers, say goodbye and I head out of the café and make my way back to the flat. I think back and wonder why we never got together back then; he's tall, good-looking, with dark hair, hazel eyes, and he was a lovely, sweet guy. Maybe we were just too young to know what was right in front of us, but he was always my go-to guy in college if I needed a cuddle or a chat. That evening, I receive a text message from him saying how lovely it was to see me after all these years and to put down a date for a proper catch-up, so I got back to him, and we made a date for the following week.

We met up midweek at a local pub and after an initial five minutes of feeling a little unsure, we soon both settled into our comfortable banter. It turned out to be a lovely evening and I felt completely at ease with him. I discover that he's been single for a year, he says Lily left him because she needed a lot more attention and excitement. They'd been together seven years and she was 11 years younger than him, and she felt that he was getting boring and fuddy-duddy, not wanting to go out pubbing or clubbing. He tells me about his business as a landscape gardener and that he lives in a two-bedroom house, rent-free, in Slough, that belongs to his best mate.

"So, how come you don't pay rent, then, Luca?" I enquire.

"Well, I look after the house for Mick, you see, he has a number of properties and I sort of look after them all and he lets me live in one for free."

"Wow, that's generous of him," I remark.

Next time I meet up with Naomi and Harriet, I tell them about my catch-up with Luca and about how well he was doing. "His own business, lives rent-free and still the same old Luca."

"He always had a thing for you, Rache, I always thought you two might end up together," Harriet says.

"Yes, I suppose we always enjoyed each other's company," I reply.

"You mean you always enjoyed each other's tongue," Naomi says, laughing.

"Bravo, Naomi!" Harriet says, laughing.

"Yes, that too," I agree, blushing but joining them in their teasing.

I meet up with Luca a couple of more times and we fall back into our comfortable friendship and, come Valentine's Day, I invite him over to the flat for dinner. I'm not expecting anything but good company, dinner, drinks and lots of laughs, but when he arrives with flowers and chocolates, I call him a 'sucker' for being cliché. He laughs and we enjoy the evening and once dinner is eaten, we sit on the floor looking through old photos from college days, listening to the hits of the late '80s and early '90s and tuck into the chocolates that he'd bought over. I'm feeling so good for once; I'm not on a date, I feel relaxed and happy just being myself. I pop to the loo and on my return I find Luca rolling a joint on the coffee table.

"Oh! Okay, has the party started?" I say, laughing.

He looks up at me and says, "Oh, sorry, Rache, is this okay?"

"Yeah sure, I stopped smoking at the beginning of the year – cigarettes, that is – I haven't had a joint since I don't know... Last time was probably with you!" I say, as I go to the kitchen and get an ashtray from the cupboard under the sink.

I grab my hoodie and we make our way out to the balcony and sit down. Luca lights it up and passes it to me; I feel a bit nervous and take a drag and pass it back. "Rache, you can keep it a bit longer," he says, smiling, sensing my nerves.

"Yeah, I know, but, like I said, I haven't smoked in years and I'm pretty sure I got really paranoid last time I did."

"This is really good shit," he says, taking a long inhale of the joint, "you won't get paranoid, I promise." He winks at me as he passes it over.

The rest of the evening was spent relaxed on the sofa, laughing a lot, whilst watching a chick flick, after which, Luca gets ready to leave. I walk down the stairs after him to the front door and we kiss, just like we were back at college 20 years earlier. My head was spinning from the effects of the joint and the familiarity of kissing Luca was making my heart race, but everything felt like it was in slow motion. All I managed to do for the rest of the evening was brush my teeth, take my make-up off and crash out on the bed.

I awoke early after having had the deepest sleep ever and I bumbled out of bed, put some coffee on and started clearing up the lounge from the night before. I thought of Luca and then remembered the kiss and I smiled to myself as a flutter of excitement rushed through my body. That day at work I had a secret smile on my face that I couldn't shift. I was eagerly waiting to hear from Luca, but it wasn't until the evening that I received a text message from him saying how much he had enjoyed last night and the trip down memory lane and to see if I wanted to catch up again sometime. I invited him to Friday night drinks with the girls; he said that he would try to make it but was working on a job in London, so it would depend on traffic. I told him that we would be in The Drinking Ole from 5:30 onwards and left it with him.

The next day, after work, I made my way home to freshen up my make-up and walked to the bar to find Harriet and Naomi already there with a bottle of Prosecco sitting in an ice bucket. "What's all this, then?" I say, giving them a kiss.

"We thought you might have a bit of good news seeing as you had a dinner date on Valentine's," Naomi says, passing me a glass.

"Oh, I see. No, not yet, although we did kiss at the end of the night," I say, beaming.

"Well, that was a given," Harriet adds.

"Will he be making an appearance?" Naomi asks.

"Not sure, Nomes, he's working in town, so will try, he says."

We enjoy the rest of the Prosecco and just as we are about to leave, Luca arrives. We all stay for one more drink whilst Luca reacquaints himself with Naomi and Harriet, after which we all leave. I say goodbye to them both, and me and Luca stroll down Peascod Street. "Rache, do you fancy getting a takeout and heading back to yours?" he says.

"Yeah, sure."

We head to the chippy and place our order and whilst we're standing to the side, Luca decides to wait outside and as he's walking out past the queue of people waiting for their order to be taken, he lets out an enormous walking fart that sounded like a motorbike roaring by. I look up, startled by the noise, and then notice the look of disgust, shock and some silently laughing faces of those in line. He turns back and says, "Sorry, better out than in." He promptly walks out and waits for me outside. I feel so embarrassed and pretend that he's not with me, and when my name is called, I collect my order and walk out.

Two minutes later, we're back at the flat happily tucking into our fish and chips. Luca talks of his current job in London, and once we've finished eating, I change out of my work clothes and pop the kettle on. I find Luca out on the balcony having a joint and I make a 'T' sign with my fingers, to which he nods. I pop my hoodie on and join him on the balcony with the teas and he passes me the joint. "Do you smoke every day?" I ask, as I inhale.

"Yeah, I guess I do, don't suppose I really stopped," he says.

"What? Since college days, you've never had a break from it?" I say, astounded, as I take another draw on the joint.

"No, guess not, Rache. Why? Does that shock you?"

"I wouldn't say shock, I'm just surprised. I mean you clearly function okay on it, seeing as you've got a business, you're not psychotic—"

"Yet," he butts in, laughing and making scary eyes at me.

"You know what I mean, you've got your own business as well as looking after these houses for your best mate," I conclude, as I take my last inhale and pass it back.

"Wow, you're getting to enjoy it now, aren't you?" he says, smiling at me.

"Yeah, I always have but I don't think I would function well on it every day, I would become a complete dope, especially at work."

We finish the joint and tea outside on the balcony and then Luca makes a move to leave. "I've got work tomorrow, Rache; that's the downside to having your own business, when you've got a job on it isn't always Monday to Friday, nine-to-five."

We make our way downstairs and when we reach the front door, I say, "Okay, have a good weekend and I'll catch up with you soon." He opens the door and steps outside, turns back around, steps forward and we start kissing. A couple of minutes later, he leaves. I try not to think about it too much as I'm just enjoying things as they are and I'm feeling too relaxed from the joint to ponder too deeply.

The following few weeks are consumed with seeing Luca; nothing like dating at all, just hanging out as mates a couple of times a week. Sometimes on his way back home from work, early evening, he'll pop by for a cup of tea and a joint, we'll have a snog, and he leaves. I almost feel as though I'm back at college. The couple of times we have gone out have been brief; to pick up a takeaway and once to the supermarket, where he literally farted all the way around every aisle, pushing the trolley and trumping. "I've got a problem with my guts, Rache." I shook my head in embarrassment and left him to push the trolley while I picked up what I needed, only coming close to him to place the food items into the trolley. He said he couldn't control it, but the worst part was when we were at the till and as I was paying, he let rip. It sounded like an elephant was being tortured; the elderly couple next in line thought it was me and I couldn't get out of there fast enough.

"What is wrong with you, Luca? It's not right, you need to see a doctor!" I said in disgust, but he couldn't help but laugh and light up a joint.

"I can't hold it in, besides, it's not good to hold it in," he says, as he puts the shopping bags into the boot.

"Yes, but you can go to the loo and do it there," I snap back.

"Well, I'll be in there all day, I'd never get anything done," he says, still laughing.

I can't help but laugh, too, although still feeling cross with him. "Just as well you work outdoors by yourself, then," I say. "And you better put that out before you get in the car as well, I don't want my car smelling like a ganja-mobile."

When we get back to the flat, he helps me unload the shopping, I can't help not being cross with him; he has a kind nature and I love spending time with him. He's easy to be with but I feel like I don't know if we're just friends or if this thing will lead anywhere. I mean, we haven't actually been on a date, and it seems we only get to kissing at the end when he's leaving so, I decide to ask him if he'd like to go out for dinner sometime. "Yeah, sure, Rache," he says. Our evening is spent doing the usual; cooking, eating, getting stoned and a snog before he leaves.

The following week, Luca texts me. *'How does Friday sound for dinner?'*

I send him a message back. *'Sounds perfect'*.

He sends me his address, which is a couple of miles away in Slough. I've offered to drive as he only has a transit van for work, and I really don't want to travel to a restaurant in that all dressed up. Friday night arrives and I decide to wear a dress and heels; I want Luca to start seeing me in something more feminine than jogging pants and a hoodie. On my drive there,

I turn into a street that the satnav has bought me to. *Surely this can't be right*, I think. The houses look run down, the cars are parked all the way up on the pavement, most of the front gardens look untidy and overgrown with weeds, and one house has a ripped brown sofa sitting on the front lawn that's seen better days. The house where Luca lives, at least, looks better than the rest and as I walk up the path to the front door, I raise my hand to tap on the knocker, but Luca has opened it before I get a chance.

"Hi, will my car be safe out there, Luca?" I say, voicing my concern with a slightly worried expression.

"Yeah, it'll be fine, Rache, don't worry," he says as he steps to the side and lets me enter.

I walk inside to the hallway to what I can only describe as stepping back in time to run down student digs, where the floorboards are exposed but not in a good way; they haven't been varnished. It's the same on the stairs. Luca leads me into a room which spans the length of the house; it's much the same as the hallway, with no carpet. There's a mountain bike propped up against the wall, a double mattress on the floor at the far end of the room with a crumpled-up duvet. An ashtray sits on the floor beside the bed, filled with ash and joint ends, and a free-standing clothes rail stands in front of the back patio doors.

My face must look a picture, as Luca says, "I know it's bit of a shithole, Rache, but it's rent-free and the best part is..."

He walks out of the room and I follow him, saying, "There's a best part? I mean, your friend should be paying you to live here, Luca."

We walk up the stairs and he says, "He does, with this." He opens the door to one of the bedrooms. The room is filled with cannabis plants; all you can see is green, from floor to ceiling. My jaw drops down and I turn to look at him; he has a huge grin on his face like a kid in a sweet shop. I am left temporarily speechless as Luca shuts the bedroom door and opens the door to the second bedroom which is much the same as the first. I don't say a word, I couldn't, I wasn't sure what to say. I knew in that moment why Luca could never be a serious contender for my heart and that this life of his would remain as it is for however long he desired, and nothing or no one could change that. I walked down the stairs, opened the front door and stepped out of the house and in that moment, he looked at me and understood that we would never see each other again. I walked down the path onto the pavement, turned and saw him standing there at the doorway, watching me. I stopped, blew him a kiss and walked back to my car.

When I reached home, I burst out crying, I'm not sure why, but I felt lonely and sad for what could have been. I changed into my comfy clothes and had a tidy-up of the flat, popped the kettle on and made a cuppa. I noticed the ashtray on the table outside on the balcony and went to get it, only to find a half smoked joint sitting there, propped up against the side so I went back inside, picked up my tea and a lighter, and sat there and smoked it. I said goodbye to Luca and in that moment I just couldn't say 'another one bites the dust'.

Downright Disgusting

I wasn't really in the mood for meeting anyone after Luca; I think I must've given off those vibes too as no one approached me. I know I needed to just go out and try something different, like speed dating or some other organised singles event, but I just couldn't be bothered with the quest anymore and I even wished I hadn't started it.

I had to force myself out to a bar in Windsor, called Crowns, for Vince's 40th birthday celebrations a couple of weeks later; he had invited the usual crowd, bar Artisan. I wasn't sure if I was ready yet, if ever, to see her boobs and Gregory together. There were a few others there too that I hadn't met before, but it was a civilised affair with a free bar and canapés. Vince had organised a private section which overlooked the river. There wasn't really a dress code; Vince just said that he wanted us to look 'fabulous, darling'. So, I decided to wear my hair up in a loose bun with a few strands falling around my face, a black dress, heels, a string of pearls and my black faux fur jacket. When I arrived, the bar was buzzing; there were lots of small groups, a few couples and what looked like a hen night. I saw a signpost with a balloon attached to it, next to the spiral stairs, saying, 'Vince's private party', so I made my way up to a room filled with familiar faces. Harriet was the first one to see me and she walked over and gave me a hug and said, "Tell us all about it once you've got a drink and said hello to the birthday boy, Rache."

"Sure, where is he?" She points to the outside terrace area where I see Vince and Harry. I walk out over to them and give Vince a big hug and wish him a happy 40th.

"You've got this all to come, darling," he says, winking at me.

I greet Harry and turn to find a waiter holding a tray of pink Champagne standing close by. "Thank you," I say, as I take a glass. Harriet and Naomi join us on the terrace and we all clink glasses to Vince.

"You're the last man standing now, Rache," he says, blowing me a kiss.

"Yes, I hope I feel the same as you when it's my turn."

"I feel fabulous, darling," Vince replies, tossing his head up in the air and laughing.

"You look it, too, and thanks for not inviting Artisan, not sure I could've handled seeing those two tonight," I say.

"What, her boobs or her and Gregory?" Harriet says, laughing.

"Both," I say, laughing back.

"That bitch has truly gone!" Vince says with a flick of his head and a snap of his fingers as he struts away to greet more of his guests.

We all walk back indoors, and I run through what happened with Luca. "What, Rache, just because of his trumping?" Naomi says as Harriet starts to chuckle.

"No, Nomes, I could've coped with the constant farting, well, not in public places, but the fact is that he lived in this rundown house in Slough that looked like a student bedsit, which was also a cannabis factory."

"What!" she shrieked out so loudly that those that were standing close by stopped talking and looked over at us. Harriet smiled and put her hand up to her forehead to shield her face from the onlookers. "Sorry," Naomi whispered.

"The two bedrooms upstairs were full of marijuana plants; no wonder he wasn't paying any rent looking after all that for his best friend."

"Well, I'm not surprised he had a problem with farting, then," Naomi says.

Me and Harriet looked at each other and burst out laughing, Naomi stood there looking bewildered for a moment and then she joined in. She tried to explain to us that he was smoking so much dope that his anus had become so relaxed and that's why he had a problem with trumping so much. Me and Harriet were laughing so much that we had tears in our eyes, we both left her to her theories and popped to the loo to freshen up our make-up.

On our way down the stairs Harriet asks, "Are you okay, though, Rache?"

"Yes, absolutely fine now that Dr Nomes has diagnosed the problem," I reply, looking at her and laughing.

We both laugh our way down to the loo and on our way I catch the gaze of someone staring at me. He's with a small group of men standing at the end of the bar and as we pass, he smiles at me. When we return from the ladies, I notice that he and his friends have moved and are now standing next to the stairs, As me and Harriet pass them, he turns towards me and says, "Hi."

"Hello," I reply, with indifference.

"Can we join your party?" he asks, as we start making our way up.

"No, afraid not, it's a private party," I say, with a tilt of my head.

We continue walking up the stairs and Harriet says, "Why didn't you give him the time of day, Rache?"

"I don't know, he just looked so smarmy and full of himself."

"Well, he certainly liked the look of you, I noticed him staring at you when we were on our way down," she says, looking at me intently.

"I know, I know, the quest! I was thinking of giving it up," I reply.

"No, Rache, don't you dare! I haven't had this much fun in years listening to your stories," she says, grinning. I roll my eyes and pinch the side of her waist as we make our way to the table of canapés and plate up a selection, then head to the bar for some Champagne.

Vince's party came to a close at 11pm and on our way out, I noticed the guy from before standing outside with his friends. I walked past him and he smiled at me and, as he held out his hand, said, "Hi, I'm Ranj."

"I'm Rachel." He takes my hand and kisses the top of it. Vince, Harry, and a few others on their way out of Crowns notice and start whooping. I start to cringe. "I'm sorry, they're not with me," I say, laughing.

"I'd love to take you out sometime, Rachel," he says as he hands me his business card, "just get in touch if you want to."

I take the card, say 'night' and join the others who are all making their way back to Vince and Harry's to continue the party. After more Champagne, cutting the cake, dancing, followed by playing the love/hate game – which consists of admitting to one thing you love and one thing you hate about the birthday boy and hope he doesn't take offence – I eventually get home at 3am.

My weekend passed by with me nursing the hangover that I could've done without; I didn't even attempt to move too far or too fast as I forced myself out of bed, dragging the duvet behind me and collapsing on the sofa. After an hour, I made a coffee and then went to the bathroom to freshen up, which was followed by a mug of tea, toast with lashings of butter and marmalade, two paracetamol and then back to the sofa. I surfaced from the sofa feeling a lot more civilised and spent the afternoon getting ready for my working week, which entailed ironing, washing hair, and putting on a hydrating face mask. Later, I came across the business card in my clutch from the guy at Crowns last night. I wasn't really in the mood to make contact with him just yet; I felt as though he seemed a bit arrogant but then thought that I shouldn't be judgemental and tapped his number into my phone.

The next morning, I came to the realisation that I was halfway through my quest; it's the last week of March and the days are getting a little warmer and my mood has started to lift from the temporary blip of sadness that overcame me since Luca. I get ready for work and by the time I've reached the office, I've talked myself into continuing whole heartedly with the quest, so decide to send Ranj a message. *'Hi, this is Rachel, we met at Crowns on Saturday night, thought I'd get in touch'.*

Later that evening, I receive a message back from Ranj saying, *'Hi, Rachel, glad you did. How are you?'* We exchange messages and make a date to meet up for drinks on Friday evening.

That Friday after work, I get a bite to eat at home before meeting up with Ranj. I walk to Crowns and arrive with two minutes to spare; I take a quick scan around the bar area and then look outside on the terrace. The outdoor heaters are on and it's warm and inviting so I take a seat at a table. The waiter arrives and whilst taking my order, the roaring noise of a car driving up distracts our attention. It gets louder as it passes, and everyone seated outside, including the waiter, looks up. It's a black, flashy sports car and as it makes a left-hand turn towards the car park. I notice the driver; it's Ranj. I cringe. The waiter returns a few minutes later with my glass of red just as Ranj walks past towards the entrance. I take a sip of the wine, imagining how the evening will progress from here when I hear a chirpy voice behind me say, "Hello, stranger."

I turn and see Ranj just standing there, looking at me, as if we've known each other a lifetime. "Hi," I reply, looking a little bemused at his familiarity. He takes a seat and leans forward and pecks me on the cheek, which surprises me even more. "I've just—" I start to say, but I'm cut short.

"Firstly, I want to apologise for being 12 minutes late." He looks at his watch which also looks very flashy.

"That's fine," I say, but am cut short again.

"Well, I see you have a drink; good, okay," he says, trying to signal to the waiter by raising his hand in the air like he's trying to get the attention of the teacher in the classroom. Cringe again. The waiter approaches looking a little annoyed at being summoned in this way and Ranj orders a drink. "So, Rachel, I'm so pleased you got in touch," he says, smiling at me.

He's not bad looking; he has dark hair, he's clean shaven, dark brown eyes, lovely, tanned skin, with quite a big nose. He's not very tall – around five-foot-eight – but he's well-dressed, in jeans, a shirt, and a jumper. The waiter arrives back with his gin and tonic, we clink glasses, take a drink, and Ranj starts talking about his job at the airport as a manager in the terminal. He lives in London and also has a business – a shop.

"Oh, that sounds very interesting," I remark, enquiring as to what kind of shop it is.

"Well, it's actually my parents' shop; it's a newsagents that also sells food and alcohol," he says.

"Oh, so do you work there too?" I ask.

"No, we have staff, I just go in and collect the day's takings." His gaze shifts to look at something behind me and I instinctively turn around and notice a table with three Asian ladies seated behind us.

I talk a little about my job and we chat about holidays; he tells me that he's well-travelled, seeing as he works at the airport, loves sailing and enjoys the outdoors. "Oh, wow, well that sounds impressive." He doesn't seem like the outdoorsy kind of guy to me. "I've been out a few times on a dinghy with my family, who live on the south coast; where do you go sailing?" I ask. It seems we may have something in common, after all, I think.

"Well, I've not been out yet, but I'd love to sail the Aegean Sea," he says, looking a little flushed.

"Oh, I see. Pardon the pun!" I say, chuckling, but it goes over his head. I'm sure he said that he loves sailing, but I brush it aside and we continue chatting about holidays and places we have visited.

After a while, we make our way inside and order another drink; the bar area is busy and the change of scenery is a welcome sight. We find a space on a small, high table; the seats have been taken but I'm happy to stand. I pop to the loo and on my return, I see Ranj chatting to one of the Asian girls who were seated behind us outside. As she walks away, he keeps a lingering look on her. "Hi," I say as I take my drink and say cheers. "A friend of yours?" I enquire.

"No, I thought she worked at the airport but mistaken identity," he says.

"So, I take it you're of Asian descent," I say. "Yes. FBI." He pauses and then smiles. "Full-blooded Indian," he says, looking chuffed.

I start to laugh. "FBI, that's very funny," I say.

"And you?" he asks.

"Well, I'm also a FBI," I reply, smiling.

"Really?" he says, looking puzzled.

"Yes, full-blooded Irish. Touché!" I say, as we both chuckle, and he nudges my elbow affectionately with his. His manner is noticeably confident; he surveys the room like a meerkat then settles his gaze on me.

We finish our drinks and Ranj asks if I'd like another, to which I decline, so we decide to call it a night. On our way out, I again notice his tendency to glance around the room at other women, which I find quietly amusing; my instincts were right, he seems very full of himself. He offers to drive me home and I accept. "Is that the sports car you arrived in?" I say, pointing to the Porsche convertible.

"Yeah, that's my baby," he says.

I give him directions to the flat and he races there as if he's driving in Formula One. I tell him to slow down as we approach the flat and he comes to an abrupt stop just past it. I unbuckle my seatbelt and say, "Thank you, Lewis." He looks at me with a puzzled expression. "Hamilton," I say, with a wry smile, then open the door and climb out.

It goes over his head as he doesn't react, but says, "So, Rachel, do you fancy meeting up again?"

"Er, yeah, sure," I say, not sounding too enthusiastic but he seems too distracted with his phone to notice so I shut the door and he races off.

I meet up with the Indian prince a few days later after work when he calls to say that he's in the area. He picks me up and we go to a restaurant in Ascot that has an open fire and lovely big sofas. After ordering a few small plates and a bottle of wine, we settle on one of the sofas and I discover that he has a brother who's in prison for drug offences. I think back momentarily to a few weeks earlier, smoking pot with Luca, and smile to myself. "I swear on my son's life!" I hear him say as I snap back to reality.

"You have a son?" I say, surprised that he hadn't mentioned it on our first date.

"Yeah, I was married young, and I have a ten-year-old boy."

"Oh, so you're divorced?" I ask.

He then proceeds to tell me that his wife left him when she discovered text messages from another girl on his phone and when she confronted him he swore on his son's life that he didn't do anything, but she decided to give the girl a call. She'd told her that they'd been having an affair for years and that she also worked at the airport, and so his wife kicked him out. "So, do you have any kids or ever been married, Rachel?"

"No, on both accounts," I reply.

I notice his habit of staring at other women again, especially if they're sitting behind me and in his sightline. I'm starting to find it quite rude and think that maybe his wife was right in not trusting him, however, he has this confident way about him that you can't help being drawn to.

Since he has a bit of a drive home, we decide to call it a night and arrange to meet for dinner at the weekend. "You'll have to come to my neck of the woods, Rachel, I'd love to take you out for dinner, Indian-style," he says, putting on an Indian accent and doing a head wobble. I laugh and try to mimic the Indian neck move but fail miserably. We make our way to the car, and he opens the passenger door for me and then suddenly starts kissing me. I cautiously respond; at first it's gentle then it becomes a little more intense with his tongue in my mouth, his nose pressed up against my face moving up and down. I pull back gasping for air. "Well, I wasn't expecting that!" I say, not entirely sure that I liked it.

I get in the car, and he races down the country roads back to Windsor. I could feel something on my face; I wasn't sure if it was just his saliva, so I opened my handbag and took out my mirror and a tissue ready to wipe, when – eww – I find a bogey, a big white one, on my cheek. I quickly capture it with my tissue. It felt disgusting. Was it mine? No, it can't be, I check my face again to ensure that there's no more and quickly look up to check my nose; it's clean.

Ranj pulls up outside the flat 10 minutes later and jumps out. He opens the car door for me, which I find charming, and then continues the same assault on my face, but not as long this time. He stops, gets back into his car and roars off. I feel a little disgusted with his irreverent behaviour. Maybe I'm being too critical; *he is a few years younger than me*, I think as I walk up the stairs to the flat. I have that feeling of something on my face again, so my first point of call is the bathroom where I discover another huge bogey on my face, I'm so upset that after taking it off with a tissue, I exfoliate and put a face mask on and run the water for a bath.

Soaking in the tub, I start feeling embarrassed, thinking maybe it was mine and I had it sitting on my face the whole time I was with Ranj. I try not to think about it too much as I focus on our upcoming dinner date at the weekend, 'in his neck of the woods', as he puts it.

I text him the next day, saying, *'Hi and thank you for a lovely evening'* but there's no response until a couple of days later when I receive a text from him saying that he'd been busy with work and that he'd be free to meet up on Sunday at 6pm in Richmond. *Oh! So that's where he lives*, I think to myself, very nice too, but Sunday night is a bit of an odd first dinner date night, but what do I know, so I agree.

On Friday I meet up with the girls for a quick after-work drink at our usual. Of course, with being married, their stories revolve around husbands and children, so they're all ears when I've been on a date and are hungry for the latest instalment of the quest. Sometimes, I haven't even started talking when they just start laughing without rhyme or reason, I guess the expression on my face sets them off, but you can guarantee that Harriet will start laughing first, for the longest and the loudest, which sets Naomi off. This time, as soon as I mentioned what I found on my face after he had kissed me, twice, neither of them laughed. The expression on their faces were that of horror.

"What?" Naomi says.

"Urgh!" Harriet says.

"Yes, I know. The thing is, he just launched himself on to me, kissing me, his nose was pressed up against my face, I feel disgusted when I think back and now I can't stop looking in the mirror to check my nose is clean." Desperate for their input, I make a look of distaste which sets Harriet off laughing again. "Harriet! It's not funny," I say, holding back a chuckle but then succumbing once Naomi starts.

"Honey, it's not you, you've never had a bat in the cave, or one on your face, for that matter, ever, why would you suddenly have one now, especially after he's kissed you. It's him," she exclaims, with a nod of her head.

"I agree," says Naomi.

I tell them of our upcoming dinner date on Sunday before we leave and Harriet says, "Remember to take a tissue for him, Rache." I smile as we walk our separate ways.

Come Sunday afternoon I start getting ready for my dinner date and decide to wear my faithful date night outfit of jeans, with a halter neck top, heels, and leather jacket. I double-check my nose for any offending squatters and once satisfied, I grab my car keys and head out of the flat, picking up an extra tissue for Ranj. When I arrive in Richmond half an hour later, I find parking on the road just off the high street and give him a call. It's not far off 6pm, but there's no answer, so I walk down the main street, window shopping, when I receive a message saying to meet him at an Indian restaurant called Masala Home. I locate the restaurant on my phone and discover it's only a two-minute walk away.

It's a big restaurant with an open kitchen running along the back wall with clear glass, so you can see the chefs preparing the food. The aroma of spices and garlic saturate my senses and I become eager to sit down and eat. A waiter arrives to ask if I have a reservation; I say that I'm not sure as I didn't make the booking but ask him to check under Ranj's name but there doesn't seem to be one under his first name. Fortunately, they have a table available and as the waiter leads me to it, I scan the restaurant to make sure that Ranj is not already seated, waiting for me. The table is halfway down, on the end, next to the aisle and opposite the kitchen, so I have a bird's-eye view and am kept entertained watching the kitchen staff at work. I text Ranj to let him know that I'm at the restaurant but there's no response so once I've looked at the menu and decided on what I'd like to eat, I order a glass of Prosecco and wait for him.

I discreetly check my nose in the small mirror in my clutch and am satisfied that all is clean.

My Prosecco arrives and the waiter asks if I'm ready to order. "I am, but I'm afraid that my date hasn't arrived yet," I say, and just as he leaves, I see Ranj stroll in. My seat is facing the entrance, so he sees me straight away and as I take a sip of my drink he walks towards me with his hands in prayer.

"I'm so sorry, Rachel, I swear on my son's life, I got caught up in traffic," he says, lurching forward to give me a kiss.

I almost flinch and offer my cheek and say, "Traffic? I thought you said this was your neck of the woods!"

"Er, yeah, yeah, it is, I live down the road in Hounslow," he says.

"Oh right," I say, touching my cheek with my hand where he kissed me.

"So, I see you've got a drink in," he says, trying to deflect from his tardiness again.

"Well, yes, I've been waiting for over 20 minutes and a girl gets thirsty," I say, chuckling and trying to disguise my annoyance with him.

"Yeah, don't you love this place? I come here all the time. They do something called a 'thali', which is a big plate with a selection of different dishes," he says.

"Yes, I've already had a look at the menu," I butt in, smiling at him as I take my glass of Prosecco in hand.

"Yeah, that's what I need; a drink," he says, motioning to the waiter. His manner is abrupt, and he seems a little distracted, looking around and touching his nose and sniffing.

Our waiter arrives and takes Ranj's drinks order and asks if we're ready to place our meal order, to which I reply, "Yes, I am." I'm eager to feast on my thali of Indian delicacies. Ranj doesn't seem pleased with my response from the expression on his face. I proceed to order the vegetarian option with garlic naan; he places his order too and continues sniffing and looking around the restaurant. "Are you okay?" I ask, looking at him in slight amusement.

"Yeah, yeah, you see, the reason I was late was that I was at my mate's house chilling and before I left, I did a line, you know – coke," he says. I watch him talking and silently I just nod my head, half-smiling, not giving away any thoughts running through my mind of what an arrogant arse I think he is.

The waiter arrives with his gin and tonic and Ranj orders a beer to have with his meal; the waiter asks if I'd like another drink and I decline. Ranj takes his drink and I pick up mine to clink glasses, but he's already taken a mouthful. He then takes my hand and starts stroking it with his thumb and says, "You really do look gorgeous, Rachel."

"Why thank you, Ranj, you don't look so bad yourself," I say, as I pull my hand back to pick up my drink. And then I see it. He raises his head to take another drink and I see the offending perpetrator peeking out of his nose. Eww. I'm sure my face must've slightly grimaced when I noticed it, but he seems oblivious. He starts tapping his fingers on the table and I ask him if he smokes.

"Yes, I do, do you want one?" he replies.

"No, I gave up recently," I reply.

"Do you mind if I— "

"No, of course not," I butt in. I watch him swagger out of the restaurant and light up a cigarette. He runs his free hand through his thick black hair, his back leaning up against the glass front, and I notice his gaze shift from one passing female to the next.

A few minutes later, our waiter returns with two thalis of steaming hot food and a beer for Ranj. I decide to wait a couple of minutes for Ranj before the mouth-watering aromas overtake my patience and I reach for the garlic naan and make a start. I take a look outside and notice that Ranj is now talking on his phone and even if I wanted to get his attention, I couldn't. My garlic naan, aloo gobi and dhal are too enjoyable that I'm quite sure that having him sit opposite me with his nasal mucus on show would surely ruin my meal. I feel quietly satisfied eating alone and although there are a couple of glances in my direction from other diners, it doesn't bother me.

The table next to ours is empty and the waiter passes by and asks if my meal is okay. "It's delicious, thank you." He smiles and, with an Indian head wobble, leaves just as Ranj returns.

"Oh, wow, why didn't you come out and get me?" he asks.

"Well, you were on the phone, and I just couldn't tear myself away from the delicious food," I reply, breaking a piece of the naan and scooping up the yellow dhal.

I can smell the odour of the cigarette as he takes his seat and starts to tuck in, the bogey is still visible too as he sniffs and takes a mouthful of his beer. I'm close to finishing my meal and I take the final sip of my Prosecco and notice a couple of Asian girls following the waiter down the aisle. One of them is tall and simply stunning, with long dark hair and big brown eyes and as she passes our table, I suspect that Ranj will no doubt look, and he does. I pretend not to notice his distraction and finish my meal. However, watching him eat and constantly glance to the side of me to look at them makes me realise that my first impressions of him were accurate. I turn around and can see the pretty one sitting facing him. His complete disregard for women, and the disrespectful way he has behaved on the couple of dates we've been on, makes me realise that he can swear on his son's life all he wants but he will never change. I mentally calculate the cost of my meal and discreetly take £25 out of my clutch, which is easy as Ranj is so preoccupied. "Are you enjoying your meal, Ranj?"

"Mmm, yes, very much," he replies, as he licks his fingers and then cocks his head to look at the Indian beauty. I turn around again to see what he's looking at, making it obvious this time that I know who has captured his attention. When I turn back, he says, "I'm sure I know that girl from somewhere."

"Oh, really? I'm pretty sure you've used that line on me before, Ranj," I say, as I slip my jacket on, stand up and sidle out between the tables.

"Rachel, what? Wait, what's going on?"

As I stand to the side of him, I pop the money on the table and say, "I think that covers what I've had plus a tip." I bend forward and whisper, "By the way, you have a bat in the cave." I stand back up and my hand accidently catches the top of his thali which flips up and slides down onto his lap. I quickly walk away and catch our waiter's eye who approaches me and asks if everything is okay. "Yes, the meal was delicious, I've left £25 on the table for my meal plus your tip, however, I think my date has had a little accident."

I head to the door and as I turn back, I can't help but smile watching Ranj half-standing, trying to wipe away the dhal and chicken curry off his crotch with his napkin and back into the thali. I breathe a sigh of relief as I walk away, knowing that I will never have to see him or his bogeys again.

I stop at the traffic lights, waiting to cross the road, and recognise a face standing on the opposite end and once the lights have changed, we walk towards each other. She recognises me too and we stop and hug. "Sarah, hi, how are you?"

"Rachel Collins, wow! You haven't changed one bit," she remarks.

"Neither have you," I reply.

The lights change and we hurry across to her side of the road and chat. Sarah was a face from college, not a friend, but just someone in one of my classes that I always used to chat with.

"So, I live in Clapham with Martin, no children, and I ended up working in social care." Sarah is a petite black lady, very pretty and full of life, she talks very fast and tends to say whatever comes into her head. "So, are you married, single, lesbian, have children?" she spits out.

"No, not married, very much single, in fact, I'm just escaping from a disaster date and on my way home to Windsor."

"Ooh, very posh," she interjects.

"No children and I love men," I say, laughing.

"Okay, good, so my husband, Martin, is an artist and he's exhibiting his paintings in Clapham, and you must come; there'll be plenty of single men there and I'm sure you'll meet someone," she says, speaking so fast that I just about grasp what she's saying amid the noise from the passing vehicles.

"Um, okay, sure," I say, not sure whether I really want to travel to Clapham for an art exhibition but maybe it might be just what I need right now, to be in an environment where I meet cultured, interesting people and she did say there'll be lots of single guys there.

We exchange numbers and she says she'll be in touch. After another hug we say our goodbyes and I hastily make it to the car, hoping that I don't bump into Ranj on my travels. My drive home is quick and once I reach the flat I check my phone to see that I've had three missed calls from Ranj and a message saying, *'I'm not sure what I did wrong, Rachel, please call me'*. I didn't respond.

Chapter Twelve

The Art of Ashes

April showers bring the quest to a sodden halt, which suits me fine. I immerse myself in my forgotten pursuits and get back to swimming, hot yoga and reading. The next two weeks are fairly quiet apart from Easter with the Devon family and the weekly phone calls from Ranj, which I refuse to answer, his voice message pleading to know why I walked out on him. In my contemplation, I come to realise that it shows true character to be real and to be happy with who you are, and in not having to please anyone but yourself. So, on that note, I called Ranj back, not to judge him but to merely point out how his behaviour made me feel, in the hope that he could change. He asked for a second chance to prove himself but there was no way that I could possibly go back there.

The following Friday, after work, I met up with the girls for drinks, and after the post-date catch-up, they decide to treat me to a spa stay at a hotel just past Ascot. It's exactly what I need – a little pampering at a posh hotel, a massage, good food and drinks with my friends. It's booked for the following Friday, so I take a day off from work and, come Thursday, when I reach home, I pack an overnight bag and pop a bottle of Champagne in the fridge to chill for our pre-dinner room drinks.

I arrive at the hotel at noon the next day to find them both already there, waiting in the hotel lobby for me. "Hello," I say, beaming, greeting them with a kiss.

"The rooms will be ready at 2pm, Rache," Naomi says.

"So, in the meantime, we shall go for lunch," says Harriet.

We leave our bags with the bell boy and make our way to the dining room for the guests using the spa. A few people dressed in their white robes and slippers are already there milling around the buffet table. We're led to a table, and I already feel a shift in my being, a feeling of lightness overcomes me; it's only one night so I shall definitely make the most of it.

Harriet orders a bottle of Champagne straight away and says, "Let's get this party started, ladies."

The buffet has a big salad station of every item imaginable neatly displayed, a section with cut fruits, cold meats and cheeses, and an assortment of warm breads, inviting us to dive in. After lunch we make our way back to the reception to collect our room keys. Harriet and Naomi are walking in front of me and as we approach the door leading to the lobby, it's held open for us to walk through. As I pass, I look up to show my gratitude and am faced with Enrique Iglesias; okay, not him exactly, but his doppelganger. I whisper, "Thank you." Our eyes lock for a second. Harriet and Naomi start giggling. "Didn't he look like Enrique Iglesias?" I say, giggling too.

"Oh, Rache, he probably works here; he was holding the door open for us after all, how many men do that these days?" Naomi asks rhetorically.

We collect our keys and make our way to the rooms, which are all close to one another's. Our bags have already been taken up and so we make a plan to meet in half an hour. I take the bottle of Champagne out of my bag and pop it in the fridge and walk to the window to take in the view of the beautiful, manicured grounds and then flop on the king-size bed, lie there for a moment, close my eyes and enjoy a few minutes of peace and tranquillity before the excitement overflows from within and I jump up and get ready.

A knock on the door 20 minutes later from the girls signals our spa time and with bikini on under my jogging pants and sweat top, we head down. The spa is huge. It has an indoor pool that snakes around and leads through an opening to the outside of the hotel. After we all opt for the mud bath, I decide to wash it off early and go for a swim. I swim through to the outdoor pool where the water is warm; the sun is out but there's a slight chill. The heat rising from the pool looks enchanting. I swim across to the far end and, apart from a couple of people in the pool and a few on the sun loungers in their robes, the place is pretty quiet. I flip over on to my back and float like a starfish, meditating with the warmth of the sun on my face, I find pleasure in doing absolutely nothing but relaxing with random thoughts passing through my mind as I look at the clouds. Then I see Enrique lying down on one of the sun loungers in a white robe. He puts his book down and looks at me. I freeze, flip on to my front and start swimming away, then stop and realise that I'm being silly, so I roll onto my back looking up to the sky and just float. When I look up a few minutes later, he's gone.

The girls join me outside in the pool and we make plans to meet in my room for 6pm. I book an Indian head massage and stay in the spa for as long as possible, alternating between the sauna, cold shower, and steam room until it's time for my massage.

I float back to my room and start getting ready for dinner, after which I order up three Champagne flutes, open the snacks of olives and crisps that I brought along. At 6pm, the knock on the door signals the start of our evening. Harriet and Naomi enter, laden with chocolate truffles and cheese straws and as we enjoy our pre-dinner snacks and Champagne, I tell them of my brief encounter with Enrique. "He's a guest here; he had a white robe on, and he was by himself," I say.

"His partner might've been in the spa having a treatment, Rache," Naomi says.

"Yes, of course," I say, retreating back into my hopelessness. "She probably looks like Anna Kournikova, too," I say with a sigh, as they both start laughing.

We finish the Champagne and head down for dinner. After our main course, I couldn't possibly eat anything else, but Naomi always has to have a dessert and once she's finished, we make our way to the bar for a nightcap.

A huge open fire invites us into a room with Chesterfield sofas, ornate rugs and Regency-style armchairs. We take our seats by the fire and a waiter arrives to take our order. I make myself comfortable on the Chesterfield, with Naomi and Harriet taking the armchair. The waiter returns with our drinks and as we clink glasses, I thank them both for a wonderfully relaxing treat. Harriet asks if I've had any thoughts on my 40th, which is in five months' time. "You better start planning, Rache, things will get booked up," she says.

"Yes, I haven't really decided what to go for, maybe a dinner at a restaurant or a riverboat shuffle, and then there's Mum and Dad; I'm sure they'd want to throw a party, but you know me, I'm not really the big party kind of girl," I say, exasperated even talking about it.

"I like the idea of a boat trip on the Thames," Naomi pipes up.

"But what if it's wet, September can be beautiful and warm but the last thing you need is freak weather and you're stuck on the Thames dancing in the rain," Harriet says.

"Yes, point taken. Maybe, something like Vince's, but not at Crowns," I say smiling, thinking back to Ranj.

"Yes, you don't want to run into bogey face," Naomi quips.

We all have a little chuckle, then Harriet raises her eyebrows and motions with her head towards the bar. I turn to my right and see Enrique standing there, he turns and looks over at us. I half-smile and turn back and look at Harriet. "He's alone, Rache," she says, "he's walking over to us."

"What?" I blurt out.

Harriet bursts out laughing. "Only joking," she says.

After a short while, Naomi calls it a night and heads up to her room to give Neil a call. Harriet follows suit, taking her brandy with her. "Don't leave me, Hattie," I say, looking around.

"It's okay, he left a while ago, I'll see you down at breakfast," she says, blowing me a kiss.

"Okay, goodnight," I say, and I curl up on the sofa slowly becoming mesmerised, staring at the fire. My hand is cupping my glass of brandy and as I raise it to my mouth to take a sip. I can see a figure standing to the side of me which startles me so much that the brandy misses my mouth and ends up splashing onto my left cheek and down my chin. "Oh crap!" I say, putting the glass down on the table and reaching in my bag for a tissue.

"I'm so sorry, I didn't mean to make you jump," he says. It's Enrique, standing there all casual and handsome with a huge smile. I know he wants to laugh from the glint in his eye. "Hi, I'm Aiden," he says.

"Rachel," I reply, a little indignantly.

He nods, smiles, and then I start to laugh at the incident, as does he. "May I buy you another?" he offers.

"Sure," I reply. Aiden gets the attention of the waiter and orders me another brandy. "Do you often stand around waiting to scare the living daylights out of people?" I ask.

"Yes, especially when they've had a relaxing day in the spa," he says, laughing.

"Would you like to join me?" I offer when the waiter returns with my brandy.

"Yes, I'd love to." He sits at the other end of the Chesterfield, so I turn and sit sideways on the sofa facing him and notice how well-dressed he is. He wears dark denim jeans, a black leather belt with a dark blue shirt, unbuttoned to his chest, exposing his gold cross necklace. He has short, dark hair with olive skin and hazel-coloured eyes.

"Where are you from, Aiden?" I ask. Although his English is perfect, I feel as though he's not local.

"I was born here but I'm Maltese, and I travel between the two countries on business, and I always stay here rather than with family, who always have a habit of interfering in my life," he replies. "And you, Rachel? What's your story?"

"Well, I live in Windsor, my parents live not too far away in Ascot. I work as a PA, and this is simply a treat that my girlfriends surprised me with."

We chat for the next half hour sharing stories, laughing, a little flirting, and when it's time for me to leave, Aiden offers to walk me back to my room. On our way up, he asks for my number, saying, "Maybe we can meet up next time I'm in the country."

"Sure," I reply, and he taps my number into his phone.

When we reach my room, I say thank you and he asks if I'd like his company. I say no, but he leans towards me slowly and kisses me. I respond and we kiss passionately for a few moments, my body wanting more, and then he asks again, "Are you sure?" I nod my head and say goodnight. He steps back, says goodnight and walks away. I open the door to my room and kick off my heels, lay back on the bed and for a moment I think of jumping up and flinging open the door and calling after him to come back, but I don't. I quickly undress, get ready for bed, and snuggle under the soft, fresh duvet.

In the morning I meet the girls downstairs for breakfast. I'm a little late so am pleased to receive Naomi's text message saying that they're sitting at a table behind a pillar on the left-hand side of the dining room, as I'm sure I wouldn't have seen them otherwise. We catch up over breakfast and I tell them of my encounter with Aiden. "Do you think you'll see him again, Rache?" Naomi asks.

"Yes, I hope so, that's if he gets in touch next time he's over," I reply.

We finish our breakfast and head back to our rooms to pack our bags, I liberate the teeny-weeny amenities from the bathroom and put them into my bag before leaving. At the reception desk, I leave Harriet and Naomi to settle the bill, although I do offer but am shut down. "No, this was our treat to you, Rache," says Harriet.

It's another beautiful, warm day and I propose a final drink before we leave as a way of saying thanks to them both. We leave our bags with the bell boy and head out to the terrace. I order three glasses of pink Champagne and we simply enjoy the tranquillity of the gardens. When the Champagne arrives, we clink glasses and savour our last moments at the beautiful hotel. "I was thinking, when you both went up to bed last night, about my plans for my birthday."

Naomi butts in with, "Was that before or after you had Aiden's tongue in your mouth!"

"Naomi. Really!" I say laughing. "No, before that."

I pick up my flute and take a drink and then notice Aiden walk past. He's a few feet in front of our table but hasn't noticed us sitting there. I'm just about to shout out to him when I notice a woman who looks like Olive from the '70s sitcom, *On the Buses*, walking a few steps behind him. He turns to wait for her and catches our gaze; we all look at him and he quickly turns and hurriedly walks away with her following on. "Well, did you see that?" Naomi says. We all look at one another in surprise and Naomi continues. "It could've been his sister."

We can't help but laugh at her remark. "He had a wedding band on, though," Harriet says.

"Yes, something he didn't seem to be wearing last night," I say.

We all clink glasses and say, in unison, "Another one bites the dust."

We all head home, and once I've reached the flat, unpacked and had a light lunch, I decide to go for a bike ride. It's still warm out and, in keeping with what should've been a detoxing, healthy spa day, I think I need to balance the scales after all the drinking. I cycle through Windsor Great Park and feel exhilarated when I reach the top and look down at the majestic sight of the castle. On my way back home, just around the corner from the flat, I pass a man who smiles and puts his hand up to say hello, I smile back, not sure where I know him from. I cycle home and pop my bike back into the store room downstairs and take one step at a time, climbing the stairs up to the flat. My bike ride has certainly awakened some muscles that were dormant in my glutes, that's for sure.

After a lovely long soak, I start preparing my healthy meal for one. I receive a text message; for a moment, I think, *I hope it's not from Aiden as I'll be giving him an earful*, but it turns out to be Sarah with an invite to her husband's art exhibition in Clapham for the following Saturday night. I text back and accept the invitation; she comes back saying that she's got a couple of friends lined up that can't wait to meet me.

My Sunday is spent with Mum and Dad talking through my options for my 40th birthday; they may want to be part of the celebrations so it's only fair that I include them in my plans. "We could not possibly be anywhere else but with you, Rachel, celebrating 40 years on the day you were born," says Mum as we tucked into the Sunday roast.

"Rachel, we have a huge garden, why don't you consider having it here? We can get a marquee set up and have it catered if you want and us oldies can totter up to bed whenever the music gets too 'boom boom' for us," Dad says, with a chuckle.

"Yes, I'm happy to make my salmon mousse too, if that's what you'd like, dear," Mum says, smiling at me with so much love that I couldn't possibly say no to her.

"Okay, I'll pop it in the suggestion box then," I say, winking at her, thinking that, actually, it might be the best option after all. A marquee sounds a bit over the top, but I guess September can be a bit hit or miss with the weather. I leave feeling quietly pleased that they too have thought about it and have given me the option of having a party in their garden. I guess their garden is big, and it could be just perfect.

One Week Later

Saturday arrives and so does the spring sun; it must be the warmest day of the year so far and I decide to go for a more casual look for my night out. I opt for my three-quarter length skinny jeans, heels, with a sheer dark blue top and a long grey cardigan. I keep my hair loosely tied and hope I can pull off that look of intellectual, sassy girl vibe and hope no one asks me to give my interpretation of any of the paintings. My drive to Clapham is fairly easy-going, apart from pockets of traffic passing busy towns on a Saturday afternoon, but I arrive just after 6pm and manage to find parking on a side street round the corner from the address that Sarah had sent me.

I walk down a street lined with old Victorian houses and think that this can't be right, until I see an outdoor sign stand with the words 'ART EXHIBITION' and an arrow pointing up to a house. The door to the house is wide open, so I climb the steps up and enter to find an open-plan room with dark, wooden, exposed floorboards and huge oil paintings adorning the walls. On the right-hand side are stairs leading up and, bar a handful of people admiring the artwork, the place looks empty. I walk around looking at the oil paintings; they're pretty impressive, in striking bold colours of deep reds and midnight blues, and mainly skeletal images of animals. It's as if the picture is coming off the canvas. I slowly make my way around the room, admiring the paintings and hoping that I'll see Sarah, then decide to make my way up the stairs where I find more paintings. There's a table on one side of the room, piled up with photo albums, then I notice Sarah chatting to a man, and she turns and sees me.

"Hi, Rachel, you made it, then! Well, it was a much better day yesterday, the place was heaving and there were loads of single men here, shame you weren't here," she rattles off.

"Oh, that is a shame, but your invite did say Saturday, Sarah."

A man appears standing behind her. "Hi, I'm Martin, the artist," he says.

"Yes, this is my husband, Martin," Sarah adds, looping her arm through his. He offers his hand and as we shake.

I say, "Hello, I'm Rachel, your work is very impressive."

"Thank you," he says, and then gets distracted by someone and walks away.

"So, there's a couple of guys waiting to meet you," she says, "let me get you a drink, a glass of Prosecco, will that do?"

"Yes, thank you," I say.

"Did you drive here, Rachel?"

"Yes, I did," I reply.

"Oh, better not drink, then, I'll get you a water," she says, walking off and I'm left stunned and a little miffed at her presumptuousness.

I walk over to the table with the photo albums and start looking through them, there must be half a dozen albums filled with photos and lots more in piles stacked on the table. The first album I pick up is full of steam trains; I quickly go through the album and then move onto the next which has pictures of canal boats. I let out a sigh and then feel someone standing to the left of me and so I slide along the table, album in hand, to accommodate them. Suddenly I hear the voice from the person standing there say, "Hi, I'm Mathew, don't call me Mat." I raise my head from the canal boat album and look to my left. I'm confronted with a man wearing a dark blue jumper and jeans, he has a bald head but with curly fair hair to the sides. I'm surprised by his introduction, and he says it again, "Hi, I'm Mathew, don't call me Mat."

"Hi, I'm Rachel, you can call me Rache," I say, chuckling at his oddity.

Just then, Sarah arrives and hands me a plastic cup of water and says, "I see you've met Mathew." She whispers in my ear, "He's a lovely, sweet man, Rachel, and a very good friend of mine." She gives me a wink and a gentle squeeze of my arm and leaves us.

"So, Mat-thew." I've already nearly slipped up. "How do you know Sarah?" I ask.

"We live on the same street and just got chatting one day; this was about seven years ago now and ever since then she's always been there for me, always checking I'm okay. Her and Martin, always so good to me." I nod my head and carry on looking at the photos and think surely Sarah doesn't think that I'd be interested in 'Mathew, don't call me Mat'.

I move across the table and pick up another album that's full of old black and white photos of sea anchors and think to myself, *why*? Mathew sidles along the table closer to me, talking about the artwork, saying how wonderful an artist Martin is. "Yes, the oil paintings are magnificent," I say, as I walk along, looking up at the paintings, Mathew in tow. I stop at a table that's in the middle of the room and flip open one of the many albums sitting there; it's full of old black and white nudes. All of a sudden, a black man appears and says, "Hi, I'm Shak."

"Hi, I'm Rachel," I say, and then notice that Mathew has disappeared.

"You're Sarah's friend, right? I work at the Shard as security," he says, shifting around as if moving to music.

"Yes, I am," I reply.

"You should've come here yesterday, it was buzzing, man," he continues.

"Yes, I heard," I say, not sure if this is another one of Sarah's potential matches for me.

"If you come to the Shard, I'll try and get you in for free," he says.

"Okay, I'll bear that in mind if I ever visit," I reply as I put the album down and wander aimlessly to another wall and look intensely at the painting. Thankfully, Shak leaves me in peace, and I take a keen interest in the painting. The thick red paint depicting the blood of the slain physical form of a beast; even the skeletal bones look real. Lost in my thoughts I hear a voice say, "So what do you think?"

I turn to my right and find Martin standing there, looking up at the painting too. He's a lot older than Sarah and seems like an affable character. "I think your work is amazing, I want to touch the painting, it looks so real, as if it's about to jump off the canvas," I say.

He starts laughing and says, "Thank you."

"I don't really know much about oil paintings and was wondering how you manage to get that build-up of colour and texture? What do you use to illustrate the skeletal frame?" I enquire, interested to know how an artist creates such work, and trying to sound somewhat arty.

"I'll let you into a little secret, Rachel," he says, and then looks around as if to make sure that no one is close enough to listen. "Many years ago, one of my day jobs was working in a cemetery and at the end of the day, whatever was left over in the furnace is swept up and put in a big drum. Well, I started to take the remains from that drum home, so I've been using the ashes and bones in my paintings. They're real bones, I mix the ash with the paint, and this is the end result."

I cannot believe what I have just heard, and my wide-eyed expression of utter shock is evident on hearing this revelation. "Surely that's not legal or even ethical," I say.

"Well," he continues, trying to intellectually worm his way out of a hole, "you see, you could say that I'm bringing life to art or art to life. I mean, those ashes and bones would've been thrown away and I've used them artistically."

"Did you seek permission to use the remains from the relatives of the deceased?" I probe, not letting this go.

"Well, they will be alive forever in my works," he says abruptly, and walks away as if he's been summoned, raising his hand in the air as if waving to the invisible man behind me.

I feel sick and have seen and heard quite enough; I'm so glad I didn't touch the paintings now. I make my way down the stairs and quickly look around for Sarah; there's no sign of her so I walk to the front door and stand there looking around when a man who has just chained his bike to the black railings walks up the steps and stops before entering. He lights up a joint and the smell invites me to take a deep breath in. "I'm Leroy," he says, as he passes me the joint. He has a strong Jamaican accent. I step outside and take the joint.

"I'm Rachel, a friend of Sarah's," I reply, then I see Shak and Mathew walking down the stairs and I stand to the side, hoping that they haven't seen me.

"You stay here, sweet thing; I'm going to find Sarah." Leroy leaves me with the joint and walks inside, disappearing from view, so I walk down the steps and hurriedly make my way down the street around the corner to my car. I put out the joint and sit in my car for a moment, waiting to see if Leroy has followed me, and then I start the engine and slowly accelerate, and as I turn the corner and pass the house, I duck and drive.

I make it home an hour later and completely relax, the tension in my neck and shoulders has somewhat eased and with my stomach grumbling from lack of food, I prepare a cheese and tomato toastie and a mug of tea and start feeling a little less annoyed at the waste of a Saturday evening. I sit down and run through the evening, starting with my encounter with

Mathew 'don't call me Mat', to Shak from the Shard, then Martin and his macabre artwork, and then I remember sweet Leroy and the joint. Where is that joint? I check my cardigan pocket and apart from looking a little bent, it's okay. So, after finishing my toastie, I change into my comfy clothes and enjoy the joint out on the balcony with my cuppa. I feel a little guilty as I inhale, thinking of Leroy coming back to find his 'sweet thing' gone.

I never heard from Sarah again.

Chapter Thirteen

The Ending

My next Friday night with the girls was a dinner date at a restaurant overlooking the Thames. It was Naomi's birthday and since I hadn't seen them for a few weeks, Harriet decided to book a table so we could have a proper catch-up. It wasn't long before Harriet was howling with laughter when I spoke of Mathew 'don't call me Mat' and then went on to Shak from the Shard, but when I told them about the paintings, they were just as horrified as I was. "How do you get yourself into these situations, Rache?" Naomi asks.

"Who cares, they're funny as hell," Harriet howls out again.

"I must be giving off vibes that invite all loonies to apply, Nomes. The silver lining was Leroy, who looked at me and must've seen so much despair in my eyes that he passed me his joint when I was leaving, I really feel like I'm done with the quest now."

"No!" Harriet shrieks.

"Harriet, I can't keep doing it just for your amusement," I say, smiling at her whilst shaking my head.

"Well at least see it through 'til September, Rache," she says, giving me puppy dog eyes with her hands in prayer.

"Okay, but I'm not wasting my time with futile propositions from people I don't like the look of anymore. I'm changing the rules and not dating any old Tom, Dick or Mathew 'don't call me Mat'," I say, defiantly.

After dinner, Naomi and Harriet share a cab ride home. I walk the 10 minutes back to the flat and when I reach the bottom of Peascod Street, I recognise a man from a few weeks earlier who I had seen when I was on my way back home from my bike ride. He's on the other side of the street and as we pass, he puts his hand up to say hello. I wave back, then try to recollect where I may have met him, but it eludes me. I reach the flat and reconfirm my decision to continue the quest only if I can seriously see a future with the prospective suitor; loonies need not apply!

Part One – May Be 'The One'

May has arrived with the first Bank Holiday weekend of the month. I don't have any plans at all and see that it's raining out. "What's new on a Bank Holiday," I say, sighing. I stay in and have a proper spring clean; any surface that needs a wipe, dust, vacuum, brush, polish, and scrub gets attention. When I finish up, it's gone 4pm and after a soak in the tub, I pour myself a glass of red and snack on carrot sticks with houmous whilst lazing on the couch, reading. My mobile rings. "Hello," I answer.

"Hi, Rachel." There's a pause. "It's Demi," the voice says.

My heart flips. "Hi, how are you?" I say, the words slipping out of my mouth.

"Yes, I'm good." There's another pause. "I just wanted to let you know that I've just moved to Windsor," he says. There's another pause. My heart beats faster and my mind asks why. "I'm seeing someone who lives here, and I've just moved in with her; I just wanted to let you know in case we bumped into each other. I wouldn't want it to be awkward."

"That's really kind of you," I say, with a touch of sarcasm, not sure how to respond. "How's Alison and the baby?"

"Er, yes, okay. She had a girl. I still think of you, Rachel," he says.

My heart now in my throat, I take a deep breath to calm myself and wish things could've worked out with me and Demi, but there's no way back now. "Yes, so do I Demi."

"If you ever want to meet up, Rachel..."

I can hear the regret in his voice which softens me. "Listen, Demi, you take care and I hope things work out for you. Bye." I hang up before I say something I later end up regretting. I feel a little sad knowing that he's found someone, and not only has he moved in with her but he's in my home town and I'm stuck in Loveless Loonyville alone.

I pour myself another glass of red and give Luigi's, the Italian restaurant, a call and order a pizza. I'm in no mood for cooking and seeing as it's still raining, I'm definitely not in the mood for going out, especially now knowing that I may bump into Dimitri and his new love.

Half an hour later, the door buzzes and I take my purse and dash down the stairs. I open the door and make the exchange of money for pizza and say thank you. There's no time for hanging around as it's pelting down now and as I shut the door, I notice a postcard hanging down, suspended in mid-air from the letterbox. There is a picture of a cat on one side and writing on the other. I don't even like cats. *Who's this from?* I wonder. I flip it over and it's from David; who's David? *He must have the wrong place*, I think to myself as I make my way back upstairs, the aroma coming from the pizza box too tempting to delay eating and I leave the postcard on the kitchen worktop.

My Saturday night at home consists of me cosied up on the sofa, eating pizza and drinking red wine, the noise of the rain against the window pane, the TV on keeping me company, and everything is good. Even the phone call from Demi earlier has made me realise that all is not lost; he's managed to find someone who will accept him just the way he is, excess baggage and all, and although I'm happy for him, I just wish it wasn't on my doorstep. But it gives me hope that my someone is searching for me, as I am for him. I finish my pizza, pop the box in recycling, top up my wine and pick up the postcard from the kitchen counter, curl back up on the sofa and read.

'Hello, to the lady of the house. My name is David and I have seen you a few times now when I'm out walking. I hope you don't find this rude or strange to approach you in this way, but I want to ask if you'd like to go out for a drink sometime. If you're in a relationship, I apologise, and please forgive the intrusion, but, if you would like to meet up, please feel free to give me a call'.

His mobile number follows the message. I read it again and think that it must be the man who has been saying hello and waving at me recently. I leave the card on the coffee table, feeling intrigued, and decide to have an early night and read my book in bed. After the day of cleaning, my body is looking forward to a good night's sleep. The rain is still coming down and not after too long, I succumb to the warmth of the bed and drop off.

In the morning, I'm awoken by the rumbles of thunder and wonder if there's any point in getting out of bed. I look over to the bedside clock and it's just gone 7am. I groan, roll over and go back to sleep. The sun peeking through the sides of the blinds wakes me and after a lovely long stretch, I climb off the bed and pull the blind up to reveal sunshine on a rainy day. It's Sunday, and with no plans, I pull out my yoga mat and stretch and contort my body for the next hour. I finish off with some meditation, which is mostly only about 15 minutes of deep breathing. Trying to silence my mind from mundane thoughts wandering around causing a nuisance to the stillness I'm trying to achieve is proving futile; maybe one day I'll succeed. However, one thought that did bumble around my head was the postcard I received from David. After a shower, I prepare two poached eggs on toast, a mug of tea and watch the morning cooking programmes on TV. The postcard sitting on the coffee table invites me to read the message again and once I've read it three times, analysed, scrutinized, and deliberated over it, curiosity get the better of me and I compose a text message.

'Hello, David, my name is Rachel, I received a postcard from you last night. I'm sure you must have the wrong person. I can't recall seeing you on my travels, but I thought I'd say hello'.

I sent the text message, then instantly regretted it. I sat there for a moment then jumped up, nervously walked to the kitchen and put the kettle on. Then the phone starts to ring. I run back to the sofa and pause, not sure whether to pick up or let it go to voicemail. "Hello," I answer.

"Hi, Rachel, this is David."

"Hi, David," I nervously chuckle.

"I'm glad you got in touch, I've seen you a few times now; in fact, I saw you a couple of nights ago on Peascod Street. It was in the evening, and I waved at you," he says.

"Oh yes, I remember, that's you, okay," I say.

"You were on your bike a few weeks ago too when I saw you and I said hello," he goes on.

A mixture of excitement rushes through my body. "Yes, right," I say, "well, do you normally pop cards of pussies through people's doors?"

"What!" he says, roaring with laughter.

"I'm so sorry. I mean cats, kittens, pussy cats." I start laughing too and once we've diminished the nervousness of the situation; David asks me if I'd like to go out for a drink. I accept, and we arrange to meet the following Friday.

The rest of the Sunday is spent floating around the flat on air. I have a good feeling inside about David and I'm trying desperately to remember what he looks like; from what I can recall, he has short dark hair, he's medium build, not very tall. I didn't really pay any attention to him the couple of times we passed each other, so I have nothing else to go on apart from he looks okay. The rain hasn't eased and so I pack a bag and go over to the folks for the night. I have come to the decision that I will accept their offer of celebrating my 40th round theirs.

"Well, that's wonderful news, darling," Mum says, giving me a hug.

"We will organise a marquee for you, Rachel, you just tell me how many people and what you'd like," Dad says, looking pleased with my decision.

"I'm telling you now that you're not paying for anything else; I'll organise the food, drinks, music and the girls will help me with decorations," I say. "But you can make your salmon mousse, Mum," I conclude, smiling.

Most of the May Day bank holiday is spent talking about the party. Mum gets her notepad out and starts planning, making lists; a food list, a drinks list, a list of guests and before I've left to go home, she has pretty much put the cogs in motion. By the time I reach home later that Monday, I feel a lightness in me that I've not felt for a long time, and I feel a deep sense of gratitude to have these two people in my life that are my parents.

My short working week flies by and on Thursday, I receive a message from David saying that he'll pick me up at 7pm the following day.

It's Friday at 7pm and the door buzzes. I pick up my keys, clutch, jacket and head down the stairs. Before I open the front door, I take a big deep breath in and exhale slowly, not knowing what to expect, I open the door with a smile on my face and there he is, smiling back. "Hi, I'm Rachel." I hold my hand out.

"Hi, I'm David," he says as I step outside, and we stroll down Peascod Street.

"So, your card," I say.

"Yes, my card, I take it you didn't like it," he replies.

"I'm not a fan of cats," I say, smiling.

"I think cats were the least of my worries when I was writing it out to you," he laughs. "I'd seen you a few times and most recently when I saw you riding your bike, I just thought I'd say hello to see if you'd respond and you did. So, the other day when I saw you again, I followed you to see where you lived."

"Stalk much?" I say, laughing.

He laughs back. "Yes, I suppose that was a bit stalkerish, if that's a word. Well, I'm glad, because here we are!"

"Yes," I reply.

We reach the top of Peascod Street, cross the road, passing the statue of Queen Victoria, and pop into the first pub we come to. After finding a cosy corner to sit in, David asks me what I'd like to drink, then goes to the bar and returns with a bottle of red. We share stories and he tells me that he also lives in Windsor, he has a brother who is married with kids and his parents live close by and that he works in finance. The pub is getting busy and as I strain to listen to what he's saying, we move in closer to each other. I can smell his cologne and as he stretches his legs out, they softly slide against mine. "I'm sorry," he says.

"That's fine," I say, shaking my head slightly. With both our legs stretched out, touching one another's, it feels nice, and once we've finished the bottle of wine, David walks me back home.

"I've had a really lovely evening, Rachel," he says.

"Yes, me too," I reply, as we stand on the doorstep.

"Would you like to do this again, maybe, sometime?" he asks, as he nervously looks down at his feet.

"Hmm, yeah, sure," I say, chuckling.

He looks up and smiles at me. "Great, okay," he says, and we say goodbye.

I open the front door and run up the stairs to the flat, not feeling particularly giddy with excitement but also not disappointed with my first date with David. He's not unattractive, he has blue eyes, just a little taller than me, a little nerdy but nice just the same.

The next day I receive a text from him asking if I'm free for dinner the following Saturday, which I accept.

The following week is so consumed with the day job and any spare time devoted to planning my big birthday with Mum and Dad, that, when Friday arrives, I'm reminded of my dinner date when David texts me saying that he'll be over to pick me up at 6pm.

The next day I awake early and start my day with a coffee and then go for a run; it's bright, sunny and a little chilly but the sound of birds chirping, and the sight of the castle make for a beautiful start to the weekend. I finish my run and walk back from the park to Peascod Street; it's just gone 9am and the shops are opening up for the day. There are a few people around but, all in all, it's quiet, but give it a couple of hours and it will be heaving with shoppers, tourists, and visitors.

The rest of my day is spent doing house chores before getting ready for my dinner date with David. It's still warm and sunny out so I decide to wear a denim knee-length skirt with a black halter neck top and take a long cardigan with me, just in case. The door buzzes at 6pm and I'm greeted by David, who is smartly dressed in dark jeans and a black shirt. "Hi," he says, beaming.

"Hello, David," I reply as I shut the door.

After exchanging pleasantries, we walk a little and settle on Italian for dinner and make our way to Luigi's. Since we're early and haven't booked we are seated at the smallest round table in the corner, at the front of the restaurant; it's not too bad although it is very cramped, and once seated, there's not much room to manoeuvre, but it suits us just fine. "Rachel, I forgot to say how lovely you look," he says, our knees knocking under the table.

"Thank you, so do you," I reciprocate, blushing a little.

He orders a bottle of Prosecco and when the waiter returns, we place our meal order, both of us opting for pasta, and once we've had a drink, we loosen up. I discover that David is five years younger than me and his 35th birthday is in a few weeks' time. He seems easy-going, there's not any chemistry between us but I've decided not to expect anything and not to mentally criticize or judge him. He's not my type, but then, what is? I accept things just as they are and enjoy our evening together. He graciously pays for dinner and on our way back to the flat he slips his palm into mine and holds my hand. Whether it was the free limoncello that was offered to us at the end of our meal that had given him that extra aplomb, or he was just being chivalrous in giving me support walking in my heels on the cobbles, I'm not sure, but it felt nice all the same. When we reached the flat he asked me if I'd like to meet up to go for a bike ride sometime, which I agreed to, he then kissed me on the cheek, and we said goodbye.

The following morning, I receive a text message from David asking if I'm up for the bike ride; I really didn't think he meant so soon but since I've no plans, and like his spontaneity, I accept and after breakfast I start getting ready. It's a lovely warm day and I put on some leggings, a t-shirt, and a cap. He texts to say he's on his way over and so I make my way downstairs and retrieve my bike from the storage closet. By the time I'm out the front door with the bike, he's arrived. "Good morning, how are you?" he says, beaming, as we both stand there, holding onto our bikes.

"Morning, David, I'm good, thanks, I really didn't think you meant so soon for the bike ride when you mentioned it last night," I say, smiling.

"Yes, neither did I, but when I woke up and saw how beautiful it was I decided to go for a ride then thought I'd see, on the off-chance, if you were game," he replies.

"Well, here I am," I say, laughing, "always game." I pause and realise what I've said. "I don't mean I'm... Um, I mean, I'm game for having a laugh or..."

He laughs and says, "It's okay, Rachel, I know what you mean,"

"So, what's in the backpack?" I enquire.

"Oh, just some water and essentials," he says. I pass him my keys and ask if he wouldn't mind popping them in too seeing as I haven't brought a bag.

David says that he knows a place where he regularly cycles, which is off the beaten track, so we get on our bikes and I follow him until we reach the woodland that he was talking about and, for me, it seems a little hilly and not normally where I would venture. But I try the best I can, which ends up with me walking the bike to the top of the hill, but once we reach there, the views are amazing. David takes my bike and props it next to his and we both sit down on a log. He opens his backpack and pulls out a bottle of beer, twists the top off and hands it to me, and then gets one for himself. "Is this allowed?" I ask.

"What?" he says.

"Drink-riding," I reply, laughing, as we clink bottles.

David talks of his upcoming 35th birthday and asks if I'd like to be his plus-one. "What are you planning?" I ask, before committing to anything.

"Oh, it's nothing special, I'll just be meeting a few friends to watch a cricket match on the village green, have a picnic or lunch at the pub," he says.

"I'm sure you don't want me there if you're meeting your friends," I say, trying to wriggle out of it.

"Well, it's actually something we do every year, it just so happens that the cricket match falls around my birthday weekend. Plus, my friends bring their other halves so it's more of a relaxed, watching-the-cricket-match piss-up," he says, laughing nervously.

My face is not showing any sign of interest at the thought of meeting his friends and their partners so soon, seeing as we've only been out a couple of times. "Maybe, if I'm free, I'll let you know, also I have to survive getting me and the bike down this hill first," I say, smiling at him.

"Okay, sure," he says, and we continue chatting about places we've visited, and then we stumble upon the subject of exes; he tells me that he's never been married and that his last girlfriend broke up with him, and he has no idea why.

"What do you mean, you don't know why? Did you not ask her?" I enquire.

"Well, no, she broke up with me on the phone, saying that things weren't working out; we were only together for about eight months," he replies, as he shrugs his shoulders. I don't push it any further as I start to wonder what he may have done for her to not even give a reason. When he asks about my exes, I tell him that my last serious relationship was seven years ago but that I'm a serial dater and haven't found 'the one' yet.

We finish our beers and after making David stand guard whilst I crouch behind a bush and go for a pee, much to his amusement, I bumble back and start to laugh, watching him standing there, whistling, whilst keeping guard. "I'm not sure how I'm going to manage downhill after the beer, David," I say, as I take my bike and let out a big sigh.

"Don't worry, just follow my lead, we'll go the easy way down," he says, then he climbs on his bike and starts cycling through the woodland. There's a slight dip and I seem to be managing the downward traction, my hand gripping the handlebars and brake for dear life, releasing the brake a little then tightening the grip when it gets too fast. David has vanished from sight, which is a blessing as I'm not sure I want him to see me wimping out, but also a curse as I have no idea which route he's taken, so I slowly make my way down the bumpy path. As I near the end of the incline, I see David at the bottom. He shouts out to me, "Rachel, just let go and fly down."

What! Is he crazy? The last 20 feet of the path is the steepest part. I start loosening my grip on the brakes; I'm hurtling down, my heart is thumping, and my mind is focused on keeping my balance. Then I momentarily raise my head to look at David and I lose control when the front wheel hits a protruding tree root and I instantly squeeze hard on the brakes and fly forward, my hands still gripping the handlebars. I come crashing down onto the left side of my body with the bike still in between my legs, sliding down on the hard earth. I eventually come to a stop at the bottom of the path to an open-mouthed David. The look of panic in his eyes is undeniable. I take a look down and my leggings have a gaping tear in the crotch area down to my knee, the palms of my hands are badly grazed, and my pride is sorely bruised. "Oh my God! Rachel, are you okay?" David says, as he helps me disentangle myself from the bike.

“I’m not really sure,” I say, as I gently rub the dirt from my palms. “Thankfully, I’m not hurt too badly.” Then a searing pain on the side of my left foot registers and as I look down, I notice my ankle is bleeding.

“Oh, I’m so sorry, I shouldn’t have told you to let go, I should’ve just let you carry on at your own pace,” he says with a concerned look on his face.

“I’m fine, David, not sure about the bike, though.” We both look down at the twisted front wheel and smile. David takes hold of both bikes as we make our way back to his house, which is the closest point of refuge.

When we arrive, he opens the side gate and dumps the bikes on the grass, then walks back and opens the front door. I follow him in and down the hallway to the kitchen. “May I go and clean up,” I ask, looking around at how neat and tidy his kitchen is.

“Yes, of course,” he says, walking me to the cloakroom.

My palms sting as I wash off the mud and tiny stones embedded in the skin and then I tackle my ankle which is too painful to bear, I finish up and head back to the kitchen, passing the lounge on my way. Everything looks so old-fashioned that I feel like I’m in an old person’s home. David is waiting for me in the kitchen with a little white medical tin in his hand. “Oh, I see you’re prepared, but I’m really okay it’s just my ankle that needs a plaster,” I say, trying to play down how I’m really feeling.

"Okay, well let me clean that up and pop a bandage on anyway," he says, going through the tin and retrieving the necessary items.

"Okay," I reply, as he walks me through to the lounge. I take a seat on the sofa, and he places a cushion on the coffee table and raises my left leg, placing my foot on the cushion.

After cleaning it and bandaging my ankle he says, "I'd like you to remain still with your leg raised and I'll fix us some lunch."

"There's no need, David, I'm sure I can hobble home and—"

"No arguments, I'll drive you home after lunch. Is tomato soup okay?" he interjects.

"Yes." I nod my acceptance and smile as he leaves. I close my eyes for a moment and must've drifted off as, in no time, David has returned with a tray in hand which he places on my lap. "Blimey! I do feel like I'm in hospital now," I exclaim, chuckling. He chuckles too as he walks back into the kitchen; seconds later he returns with his tray of soup and buttered bun. He picks up the remote control, turns the TV on and after channel-surfing, settles on an antiques programme, which, given the choice, would've been my guilty pleasure too, but I'm not telling him that.

As I tuck into lunch, I take in the room; there are little figurines sitting on little white doylies on the window sill. Some of the doylies are crocheted, some made of lace but I'm in shock at seeing so many of them. There's a framed photo on the mantelpiece of David and an older couple who I assume are his parents. I get back to my soup to find David looking at me. "Is everything all right, Rachel?" he says. He must've seen me looking around the room.

"Yes, I was just admiring the figurines, are you a collector?"

"Oh God, no, my mum passes down things to me. I'm not sure if they're worth anything, but there you go," he chuckles.

"And the doylies?" I say, teasing him,. "Are they also a gift or did you buy them yourself?" I say, chuckling.

"Ha-ha, very funny," he laughs.

"I know what to get you for your birthday now," I say in jest, not realising the implication of my remark.

"So, you'll be coming to the cricket, then? That's fantastic! Great, I'll let the guys know," he says excitedly, and turns back to continue watching the TV.

Oh no! What have I said? Crap! No! I didn't say that. I continue eating and glance over at David and think about how this could be us; fast-forward 20 years from now, sitting in front of the telly watching antiques fair, a tray on our lap, eating our lunch on a

Sunday with the same figurines staring back at us. Oh dear! What a frightening thought. I finish my soup and tell David that I ought to get home to prepare for work the following morning, he obliges and drives me home.

"Do you need a hand up, Rachel?" he offers, as I make my way out of his car.

"No, you're all right, thanks, I can manage," I reply.

"Okay, I'll see if I can get your bike fixed," he says.

"Okay, but don't go to too much trouble; it's pretty old and that front wheel looked mangled," I say before we part ways and I hobble up the stairs to the flat.

I take off my leggings and look at the red, tender skin, which, in a day or two, will turn aubergine in colour and then I spend the rest of my Sunday feeling sorry for myself. I eventually muster up the energy to do the ironing, pour myself a large glass of red, put some music on and recollect my comment to David about his birthday. I'm not ready to meet any of his friends, especially seeing as we've only just started dating. How am I supposed to get out of it now? I start thinking of reasons of how to let him down when my mobile rings. I pick up. "Hello," I answer.

"Hi, Rachel, it's David, I just wanted to let you know that it's all booked up."

"Oh! What is?" I ask, unsure as to what he's referring to.

"The room," he says.

What room?" I press.

"For my birthday. You see, we all stay at this hotel every year; well, it's not a hotel, it's the pub, which has rooms and—"

"Oh!" I cut in, sounding surprised and not in a good way. "I didn't realise. Well, you never mentioned anything about staying over."

"Er, oh, didn't I? Well, you see, we all pile into the pub after the cricket, have a bite to eat and stay for the night and, um, or we can just get a cab back," he says.

"No, look I don't want to go changing your plans, let me check if I can make it," I say, thinking it will give me some time to think of a way out.

"Great, okay, I'll make sure there's a room for you," he says, before hanging up.

I want to call him back to tell him that I didn't agree to going to his cricket picnic birthday and I didn't agree to meeting his friends and now I feel cornered into spending the night too. Am I being uptight? I mean, we're not in a relationship; maybe he thinks we are, but we've only held hands? Why is dating such a minefield? I finish the ironing, pour myself another glass of wine to anaesthetize myself from overthinking about the conversation and decide not to be a grouch when my mind reminds me of the quest. Then conclude that I can always escape from David and his friends and return to my own room, should I need to.

The next morning, I wake up in a complete state of discomfort; my legs feel like I've run a marathon, the left side of my body is tender and as soon as the water hits the palm of my hands, the throbbing, stinging sensation becomes more evident. Not to mention that I'm walking like John Wayne. After a shower I put on the easiest outfit my body will allow, and when I arrive at work, half an hour late, I walk at a snail's pace to my desk, trying not to bring any attention to the pain that I'm experiencing. I notice Kevin peer over his computer at me. "What the hell's wrong with you, then?" he says as I sit down, cautiously adjusting my seating position to accommodate the saddle-sore.

"Oh, good morning to you, too," I say sarcastically, which sets him off laughing.

"Yeah, yeah, morning, what's happened?" he says, eager to know which malady has befallen me.

"Well, I went for a bike ride yesterday with this guy that I'm dating and— "

"Okay, stop right there, this sounds like it's going to be a good one, so let's save it for a lunchtime story so I can fully appreciate it, Rache," he says, beaming at me cheekily.

As expected, at 12:30, Kevin sets up his desk with his lunch items of what looks like a ham, cheese and tomato sandwich, an apple and a flapjack. He stands up and says, "Rache, would you like a tea or coffee with your lunch?"

"Oh my God! Look at you, you just can't wait to hear of my calamity, can you?" I reply, shaking my head and rolling my eyes.

After telling Kevin of the events of the previous day, he asks, "So will you be seeing him again, Rache?"

"Well, yes, I accidently might've accepted an invitation to a cricket match for his birthday picnic with his friends," I say, disgruntledly.

"How did you manage to do that?" he asks.

"I know, I was teasing him about the doylies in his lounge and—"

"Doylies?" he shouts out, laughing.

When I finished telling Kevin the whole story, figurines and doylies, and all, with him laughing all the way through, he only stopped teasing me when I reminded him of Randolph and only then did we get back to doing some work.

Later on, that afternoon I received a call from David asking how I was doing, and I told him that I wasn't great. He invited me over to his for dinner, but I declined and said maybe another time. I just wanted to get home and have a long soak in the bath, which I did when I reached the flat, throwing in a generous amount of Epsom salts and relaxing, so much so, that it was only when I heard the door buzzer sound that I awoke with a start, the bath water now lukewarm. I climbed out and popped my robe on. *Who is this disturbing me?* I think. Still, I'm glad they did as who knows how long I would've been asleep for. I pick up the entry phone. "Hello."

"Hi, Rachel, are you okay?"

"Um, yes," I reply, not recognising the voice.

"It's David. I tried texting and then called you but there was no response."

"Oh, I was in the bath."

"Look, I've just brought over a little something, I'll leave it on the doorstep," he says.

"I'll pop down," I reply. I gingerly walk down the stairs, crack open the door and invite David in. "Hi, I fell asleep in the bath," I say, adjusting my bath robe around me.

"I feel terrible about yesterday, and so I brought over a few bits I thought you'd like, I won't stay, I can see that you're—"

"Thank you, David," I interject as he passes me a gift bag, "that's really very kind of you but you shouldn't have gone to any trouble."

"I wanted to, Rachel. Look, take care and hopefully we can catch up in the week for dinner," he says.

"Yes, for sure, and thanks again," I say. He opens the door and leaves.

I head back upstairs and pop the bag on the kitchen counter. After emptying the bathwater, I change into my comfy clothes; my body feels a lot better after the soak. When I get a chance, I take out the contents from the bag to find a bottle of red wine, a scented candle, a box of chocolates and a small box of paracetamol. I chuckle to myself and send David a text message, thanking him for his thoughtfulness.

He got in touch a couple of days later, asking me over to his place for dinner on the Friday, which is normally my evening with the girls, but I accept his invitation and send a message to Harriet and Naomi. They're disappointed as we hadn't had a catch up for a few weeks now, but also intrigued to know more about David.

A couple of days later, at work, I receive a text message from David with his address; he only lives half a mile away from me, so I decide to wear a dress with flip flops, take a long cardigan, and walk to his house. When he opens the door, he seems a little nervous. He invites me in, and I breeze in straight through to the kitchen where I'm confronted with an older lady. "Oh, hello," I say, with a smile.

"This is my mother, Jill," David says, looking a little flushed.

"Hello," she offers, eyeing me up.

"Hi, I'm Rachel, lovely to meet you, Jill," I say, now realising why David was so jumpy when he answered the door.

"I popped by this afternoon with some plants that I picked up at the garden centre; I had no idea David would be entertaining," she adds, smiling.

"Oh, that's nice, why don't you join us for dinner?" I offer out of politeness, as I look over at David to concur.

"No, no, Mum was just leaving before you arrived," David jumps in, and then starts ushering her out of the kitchen.

"Thank you, Rachel, but I have to get back and prepare dinner for David's father," she says, as she walks through to the hallway towards the front door.

I watch David and his mum chat for a moment as they say their goodbyes, then she turns back and says goodbye to me, and I walk back into the kitchen. I hear David say goodbye and the front door being closed. "I'm so sorry, Mum just turned up when I was in the middle of dinner and wanted to know everything, and then I couldn't get her to leave," he says, exasperated as he reaches into the fridge and pulls out a bottle of white wine, twists open the cap and pours.

"It's fine, David," I say, chuckling.

He hands me a glass, wipes his brow with the back of his hand and takes a big gulp of wine and then looks over at me. “I’m so sorry,” he says. He tips his glass toward mine and says, “Cheers.” I reciprocate and take a drink of the chilled white wine.

“So, what are you making then?” I ask, as I look around at his spotless kitchen, no evidence of any cooking going on.

“I made a fish pie earlier, it’s in the fridge. Maybe a salad or steamed veg to go with it; you decide,” he replies, opening the fridge door and taking it out.

“I don’t mind, either is fine with me,” I say, smiling at him.

Our evening is pleasant enough; we sit at the table out in the back garden, talking and drinking, and since it’s still warm, we decide to eat out too. “You seem very close to your mum,” I say.

“Yes, I suppose I am. With me being the youngest, she has a habit of looking after me, getting me things like the plants that she bought from the garden centre earlier and other things for the house,” he replies with a chuckle.

“Oh yes, the doylies and the figurines, too,” I giggle.

David doesn’t take offence at my teasing him and once we’ve finished eating, I help him take the dishes back into the kitchen, which he efficiently rinses and places in the dishwasher. We finish off the wine with a slice of strawberry cheesecake; I don't normally have a sweet tooth but tonight, seeing as I'll be walking home, I decide to indulge myself. David offers to walk me home and 10 minutes later we arrive at the flat; it's still early so I invite him up for a drink which he happily accepts. We sit out on the balcony. I feel as though we don't have much in common when he talks of his pastimes, the places he's been to on holiday with his friends; they don't appeal to me, but I have to keep reminding myself to stop overanalysing everything, to just go with the flow and get to know him without the mental chatter going on in my head. After another glass of wine, I'm ready for bed and I walk David down to the front door, wondering if he'll make the first move and kiss me but he's either very shy or he's not interested, as he just says goodbye and leaves.

The next day, I pop over to Mum and Dad's to discuss birthday plans. I settled on inviting around 20 friends and I tell Mum and Dad to invite anyone they want to. I contacted Vince to organise the music; he has the best dancefloor tracks, and apart from food and drink, there was only the party decorations, which I roped Harriet and Naomi into helping me with. That only left me with sorting out an outfit and finding 'the one' to accompany me on the finale of the quest. *Easy, right!* I thought on my drive home later that evening. Just as I pulled up outside the flat, the phone rang and when I picked it up, I saw that it was David. "Hi."

"Hello, Rachel, how are you?"

"Yes, I'm good, thanks, how are you?" I reply.

"Just wondered if you're free for company?"

"Yeah, sure," I say, sounding a little miffed.

"Okay, I'll see you soon, bye," he says, and hangs up. He arrives 10 minutes later, and I buzz him up "Do you fancy going for a walk?" he asks.

"Okay, I've not done any exercise today; I just got back from my parents," I say, as we head back down the stairs and out onto the street.

"How are they?" he asks.

"Yes they're fine, we were going through plans for my 40th in September," I reply.

"Oh, crikey! That's a while yet," he says.

"Yes, but you see, my mum is the event planner, and she has to have everything just right," I say.

"Talking of birthdays, you haven't forgotten about mine? It's next weekend," he exclaims.

"Oh, that's the Bank Holiday weekend," I say, sounding a little surprised; I had forgotten and was really hoping to catch up with the girls. "What day is it, David?"

"Well, it all kicks off at mine on the Friday evening with drinks and nibbles with a few close friends and then my actual birthday is on the Saturday, where we can either take a picnic or have a pub lunch, watch the cricket, then it's back to the pub for the evening," he says triumphantly.

"Oh, okay, sounds like quite an event for your birthday," I add.

"Well, it's my 35th and seeing as we go to the cricket on the village green every year, we just combine it with my birthday," he says.

"Okay, shall I make a picnic?" I offer.

"You could throw a few things together, but I'd rather treat you to a pub lunch," he says.

"Okay, but I'm pretty sure I should be treating you on your birthday," I say.

We pop into a pub for a drink and on our walk back home, David takes my hand and this time he seems a lot more confident and surer of himself. When we reach the flat, he kisses me on the cheek and says, "Thank you, Rachel, I'm really looking forward to next weekend." He says goodnight and leaves. *Maybe he just likes to take things slow*, I ponder as I make my way up the stairs to the flat.

The next day I spend getting ready for my working week, getting an overnight bag ready for David's birthday stay at the pub and also contacting the girls to let them know that I'll be busy on Friday again.

Harriet is not amused but is happy that me and David are still seeing each other, however, insists that we meet the following Friday, no excuses. I agree as I'm missing them, and I go one step further and make plans for them to come to mine for dinner. "Will you be inviting David as well?" Naomi asks, when I call her.

"No, I wasn't planning to, Nomes... Er, maybe, let's see how his birthday goes first."

My week is kept busy with work, shopping for a present for David and putting together food and drinks for the picnic. I start feeling a little anxious about it all, especially with meeting his friends. I don't feel that we're a couple yet, I mean, we haven't even been intimate with one another and I guess we're just in the early stages of dating too. I shake off my nerves and pick out an outfit for his birthday bash, pull out my picnic basket, fill it with a few snacks and pop a bottle of Prosecco in the fridge to chill.

Come Friday, seeing as it's the start of the Bank Holiday weekend, the office is quiet and by 4:30, the few of us still working wind down for the day and make our way home. I take a shower, refresh my make-up and pop on my jeans, white t-shirt, flip flops, take my long cardigan and walk to David's. When I arrive, I notice the side gate is wide open so I walk through to the back garden; I can hear voices and music playing and I feel a slight knot in my stomach as I walk the few steps and turn onto the patio where I find David's friends. There are two couples, all standing with bottles of beer in hand, chatting away happily, oblivious to my presence until David walks out through the French doors into the garden and shouts out, "Rachel!" Everyone stops talking and they all turn and look at me; I notice one of the men has a stunned look on his face.

"Hi," I say, as David walks over to me and kisses me on the lips.

"Everyone, this is Rachel," David announces to the group and then proceeds to introduce me. "This is James." He's the one with the stunned expression.

"Hi, James," I say, as we shake hands.

"Well, hello, we thought David had made you up," he says, followed by a raucous laugh, much to everyone's amusement.

David continues to introduce me to Wendy, James' wife, and the other couple, Tim and Bina. "Rachel, let me get you a drink; wine or beer?" David asks.

"Wine, please," I say, and smile as he walks back through the French doors.

"So, Rachel, how did you and David meet?" James asks, questioningly raising an eyebrow.

"It wasn't one of those dating sites, was it?" Wendy adds, scoffing.

Thankfully, David appears with my wine, and I say 'cheers' and take a drink. I pass David the gift bag and wish him a happy birthday. "Oh, thank you, Rachel, but you shouldn't have, and in answer to your question, James, me and Rachel only met a few weeks ago whilst out shopping," he announces.

Well, that's a lie, I think to myself, glad I didn't mention the postcard he popped in my letterbox now. "It's only a bottle of wine," I say, as he takes the bottle out of the bag and looks at the label.

"Ooh, it's a nice one; Châteauneuf-du-Pape," James says.

"Oh, what's this?" David says as he pulls out the packet of white paper doylies that I bought him as a joke, not expecting him to be opening his present in front of his friends. I cringe. "Ha, ha, ha, very good," he laughs out, and then proceeds to open the pack and place them on the table for everyone to use. "Private joke," he adds, as he leans in and kisses me on the lips again. "Thank you," he says. I blush, feeling a little awkward with the PDA.

The evening is pleasant enough, although I'm unsure of how to behave towards David, not knowing whether I should be more attentive towards him, especially as I feel myself being studied by James. After a couple of glasses of wine, I loosen up and try to enjoy the evening as best I can. A few nibbles and another glass of wine later, I decide to call it a night. David walks me out and as we stand at the side gate, out of view of the others, he whispers, "Thank you for coming, thank you for my gifts, and I'll be over to pick you up tomorrow about 10am."

"Okay, sure, see you tomorrow," I reply. He then moves in closer and kisses me. We kiss softly for the briefest of moments until he suddenly stops, says goodnight and walks back to the garden. I walk home thinking about the kiss and wondering why he stopped so abruptly when I was just getting into it. I feel as though he goes so far and then just pulls back; I guess the weekend will reveal his true feelings.

I arrive home and head straight to bed in preparation for David's birthday weekend but after a dreadful, sleepless night, tossing and turning, I surrender to the futility of forcing myself to sleep and crawl out of bed, my mind busy with endless random thoughts. It's 5:30, so I get ready and go out for a run. When I return home, I feel a lot calmer. The shower helps to refresh me and after checking my overnight bag and preparing a few more items for the picnic, I have a breakfast of poached eggs on toast with chargrilled asparagus and a pot of tea.

By the time the clock reads 10am, I'm ready; overnight bag by the door, picnic hamper fully stocked with food, just the bottle of Prosecco to go in when David arrives. I pop to the bathroom to check on my make-up and my outfit; it's going to be a warm day, so I've opted for three-quarter length light grey skinny jeans with a dark blue sheer top, denim jacket and wedges. I take my bag downstairs and leave it in the hallway and pack the bottle of fizz in the hamper just as the door buzzes. "Hi, it's me," David says, excitedly.

"Hi, on my way down," I reply. I pick up the hamper, my handbag, and head downstairs and open the front door. "Happy Birthday!" I say, smiling at David, who's looking super cool in his blue jeans, white t-shirt and sunglasses. He leans in and gives me a kiss, takes the hamper and my overnight bag and pops them in the boot of his car.

"Wow, the hamper is pretty heavy, Rachel," he says.

"Yes, I've been up all night cooking," I reply, chuckling, as I lock the front door and then make myself comfortable in the passenger seat. He takes his sunglasses off and I turn to look at him. "Blimey, you're looking a bit worse for wear," I remark.

"Yes, hence the sunglasses," he says, sheepishly. "They didn't leave 'til after midnight. James just had to sing 'Happy Birthday' to me."

"Oh dear," I say, with a smile.

We arrive 40 minutes later, in a small village bustling with people, with colourful bunting suspended all the way through on both sides of the road. The village green has been set up for the cricket match and picnics and blankets edge one side of the pitch. It all looks very lovely, with a few gazebos set up with food stalls and what looks like a hog roast spit. David takes a left turn into the pub car park opposite the green and says, “We’re here!”

“Great, it all looks very civilised,” I exclaim. We get out of the car and retrieve our bags from the boot and make our way into the pub where David manages to attract the attention of the waiting staff. “Let me know how much for the room, David,” I say, just as the young man returns with a key.

“Here you are, it’s room 4, just up the stairs on the right,” he says, handing David the key.

“I thought there were two rooms booked?” I blurt out.

“Um, the booking is under a group name of James Sinclair, and all the rooms have now been taken; this is the last room key to be picked up,” he says and walks away back into the bar.

“There must be a mistake, I told James to book two rooms,” David says looking at me apologetically.

I’m not sure what to say as I wasn’t expecting to be put in this position. “Well, maybe James has the key to the second room,” I say, hoping he has.

We make our way up the stairs and David opens the door; we enter a dimly lit room with two single beds, a small TV sitting on a dark wooden table, with a small kettle on a tray with tea, coffee, milk pods and a couple of individually wrapped biscuits. The bathroom is small but adequate. “Well, this is—”

I'm interrupted with David saying, "I'm so sorry, Rachel, this isn't what I was expecting."

"It's okay, David, it's your birthday. Why don't we just freshen up and go out and enjoy the day," I say, unzipping my holdall and taking out my toiletry bag. I make my way to the bathroom, sit on the toilet and sigh, a tiredness overcomes me and then I remember that I didn't get much sleep last night.

I quickly freshen up and walk back into the room to find David on the phone, and from the gist of the conversation, he's talking to James. "No, James, I said two rooms, you wally. Okay, see you down there, bye." He hangs up and looks over at me with a downward smile. "So, apparently, he thought I meant two beds, not two rooms; why would I want two beds? The plonker." He places his arms around my waist and pulls me in close to him; it feels a little awkward at first and then he hugs me. I hug him back, not knowing where this is leading, when quite abruptly, he stops and says, "Okay, shall we make our way down to the green and meet up with the others, then?"

"Yeah, sure," I reply.

He pops to the bathroom, and I touch up my lipstick, a little blush and take the picnic blanket out of my holdall. The toilet flushes and a few moments later, David opens the door, and we make our way down. "You've come prepared, I see," he says, looking at the blanket under my arm.

"Yes," I reply, as we walk out to the car.

"I was going to treat us to a pub lunch, Rachel, but your hamper is so heavy; what's in there?" he asks.

"I've made some sandwiches, there's also a prawn salad, potato salad, sausage rolls, cheese and crackers, oh, and some crisps too. It's the bottle of Prosecco that's the culprit," I reply.

"Wow! You did all that for me?" he says, taking the hamper out of the boot.

"Well, yes, I hope to have some too and I thought maybe your friends might want some," I say.

"Thank you so much, Rachel," he says, sounding completely surprised. "I am truly in awe of you right now." He puts his arm around my waist as we cross the road and we walk over to the green; the cricket match is in full swing and as we make our way through a path in between blankets and picnickers, I notice James waving at us.

"Hello, mate, happy birthday," he says, putting a hand on David's shoulder affectionately. "Hello, Rachel," he says, looking over at me.

"Hello, James, how are you?" I say, but before he can answer, David butts in.

"Rachel has made us a proper picnic so no burger and chips from the van today."

They both roar with laughter. I feel as though I'm being watched and look across to a group of five women sitting close by on blankets; one of them is cradling a baby. Then I see Wendy and Bina in the group and go over to say hello. There's space for my blanket, and I lay it out and take a seat as Wendy introduces me to the other ladies; they all seem friendly and one of them says, "This is the first time Dave's ever brought anyone to the cricket match." A couple of them giggle.

"Oh! Really," I say, not sure how to respond.

"Rachel, would you like a drink?" Wendy says, holding up a can of beer.

"I have a bottle of Prosecco in the hamper that I wouldn't mind cracking open before it starts getting warm," I say, looking around for David, who's standing with a beer in his hand and when he catches my eye, he comes over with the hamper.

"Oops, sorry, Rachel," he says.

"It's okay, I just wanted to open the Prosecco whilst it's still nice and chilled," I reply.

He places the hamper down on the blanket, unbuckles the straps and flips open the lid to reveal the contents. "Wow!" I heard one of the ladies say, watching me take out the sandwiches, salads and other food items and laying them down on the blanket. I pass the bottle of Prosecco to David to open and take out the plastic flutes. David pops the cork and pours out a glass for me.

“Thank you, would anyone like a glass?” I say, looking around at the ladies.

“Ooh, yes please, I’ll have one,” says the lady with the baby. David then pours her a glass and passes it over.

“Would you like anything to eat, David?” I say, as I open up one of the containers with the sandwiches.

“Yes, I will, thanks.” He helps himself to one, before returning to James.

I offer the food to the rest of the ladies, and they politely decline so I tuck into my egg sandwich. They all seem to know each other well and are happily chatting away, occasionally stopping to ask me questions like ‘what do you do, Rachel?’ and ‘how did you and David meet?’

All the men are standing together, cans of beer in hand, talking whilst watching the cricket. David turns around from time to time, to smile and check in on me. “Aw, isn’t that sweet, he keeps turning and looking over at you, Rachel,” Bina remarks with a chuckle.

“Yes, he probably wants more food, I’m guessing,” I say, laughing back.

“The lads always drink all day and then, later on, end up getting a greasy burger from the van,” Bina says.

"We all do!" Wendy screams out laughing.

"Well, you're all welcome to help yourself if you get peckish," I say, as I open the big bag of cheese and onion crisps, take a few, and pass the bag round. I continue eating, making a start on the prawn salad, conscious of the fact that the food may start to turn in the heat, but it still feels nicely chilled, as does the bottle of Prosecco.

The men return 10 minutes later at the lunch interval and David sits down next to me and starts tucking into the sandwiches and sausage rolls. I unpack the remaining food from the hamper, and it doesn't take too long to get eaten by the group. The only remaining item is the cupcake that I bought for David, so I take it out and hand it to him, saying happy birthday. I hear a couple of the ladies say, "Aww".

James shouts out, "Where's the candle?"

"I do have one, but I need a lighter," I reply, as I look in the hamper and retrieve the tiny candle, push it down the centre of the cupcake that David is still holding in his hand, chuckling with embarrassment by all the attention solidly focused on him. James passes a lighter to Wendy who promptly shuffles towards David and lights the candle.

"There you go, David, now make a wish," she says.

We all quietly start singing happy birthday, which progressively gets louder as people sitting close by join in too, until we reach the end in joyous laughter; David is positively cringing with delight. I take one of the picnic knives off the lid of the hamper and pass it to David, who cuts the cupcake in quarters and offers it round to the ladies before taking a piece for himself. "I suppose you'll be getting the birthday drinks in then, mate," James says, looking at David with a huge grin on his face.

"I suppose I will," David says, standing up. "Beers all round?" I look up at David and hold out my hand for him to pull me up and we both walk, hand in hand, back to the pub.

The pub is heaving with the lunchtime rush, so we wait in the queue to make our way to the front. David is standing behind me; he gently places his arms around me and whispers in my ear, "I love you."

"What?" I say, but just then, a space opens up in front of me and I quickly step forward and lean on the counter, trying to get the attention of the bar staff. David slips in beside me and we eventually get served. We're given a tray for the beers, and I hold my glass of Prosecco in my hand as we cautiously make our way out through the crowd back to his friends. I look at David as we wait to cross the road and say, "What did you whisper in my ear?"

"Er, umm," he stutters, "I said that I love what you did, you know, with the cupcake and the picnic; it was so thoughtful." He looks a little flushed and when we reach the others, he hands out the beers, and I sit back down with the ladies just as the cricket match resumes.

David takes his position with the men at the sideline of the pitch, and I settle in and watch the match, occasionally joining in the conversation with the other ladies and when there's an afternoon tea interval, I pack away the hamper and buckle it up. The men meander back, and I stand up, hamper in hand. David asks me if everything is okay. "Yes, I just need to pee, so I thought I'd pop the hamper back in the boot."

"Okay, all the food gone then?" he asks.

"Yes, I'm afraid so, I've left the crisps and crackers on the blanket," I reply, as we look across and see James making a beeline for them. David takes the hamper from me and picks up the drinks tray from earlier and we make our way over to the pub car park where he puts the hamper back in the boot. "May I have the key, David? I'd rather go to the toilet in the room."

"Yeah, sure, here you go," he says, as he passes it to me, and I make my way to the room and freshen up, applying some lip gloss and a spray of perfume. As I open the door to leave, I find David standing outside. "Hi, I'm sorry, I didn't know you were coming up too," I say, as he heads into the room.

"Yes, the toilets were busy so I thought I may as well come up," he says, as he nips to the bathroom.

"Okay, I'll leave you to it," I say as I go to the door to leave.

"Wait, Rachel, I won't be a minute," he shouts out from inside the bathroom.

"Okay," I reply, taking a seat on the bed, which feels super soft and comfortable after sitting on the ground.

I hear a flush of the toilet and a minute later, the door opens and David walks out. I stand up and he walks towards me. He puts his hands around my waist and starts kissing me; I feel hot and a little wobbly from the drinks and steady myself by holding onto him, kissing him back, unaware that his hands have found their way under my top and unhooked my bra. He's cupping my breasts, one in each hand, with his thumb gently rubbing my nipples. We kiss harder, my tongue in his mouth, playing with his. My hand reaches down and touches his penis, sliding up and down. He groans, and I unbuckle his belt and pop the buttons on his jeans. I lift my top up and over my head and let my bra fall down through my arms onto the floor and then unzip my jeans and pull them down and sit back onto the bed and peel them off.

I look up at David standing in front of me in his white boxer shorts, his cock hard and defined, right in front of my face. I'm sure he'd like me to perform fellatio, but I stand up and he looks at me and says, "Wow." We start kissing slowly and he adopts the same position with his hands, cupping my breasts, pinching my nipples. I put my hand inside his shorts and pull his penis out, my thumb gently circling the wetness on top; he stops kissing me and watches me handle him and groans in excitement, licking his fingers and rubbing my nipples harder and faster. He takes his hand and puts it inside my knickers, his fingers sliding up and down my clitoris. I'm in ecstasy watching him arouse me and we start to kiss feverishly until he pulls me in and back on to the bed. We lie down on our sides, facing one another, our hands returning to their positions. He places his mouth over my nipple and starts kissing and sucking; I'm so turned on watching him. I gently pull down my knickers and his boxer shorts and with his foot, he pushes down and kicks them off. "Rachel."

"Yes," I whisper as he moves on top of me and gently guides his penis in. We kiss as he moves in and out, groaning with pleasure. I lick his nipples and raise my legs up so I can feel a deeper thrust, which he reacts to with a loud groan; a few more jerking movements and he slumps down in a wet, sweaty mess on top of me. As I lie there, I come to realise that our momentary act of passion has taken us to the next stage of the relationship, which I find a bit ironic since we were supposed to have separate rooms.

David moves over to his side and positions his leg over my body, his elbow propping his head up and the fingers of his free hand gently stroking my stomach. He looks at me, smiling. "Happy birthday," I say, chuckling. He laughs back.

"Well, I wasn't expecting another present, Rachel, the bottle of wine, the doylies and picnic was quite enough, but this..."

"Yes, well, this was not a birthday present I was planning on giving," I reply, with laughter. "I guess we better get back."

"Yes," David says as he kisses me and then rolls back off the bed where he proceeds to pop his clothes back on.

I pop to the bathroom and wrap a bath towel around me. "David, I'll meet you there, I'm going to take a shower."

"Okay, sure," he says, as I shut the bathroom door.

After my shower, I feel a lot better. My sleepless night and the lunchtime drinking in the sun had made me weary. I get ready, refresh my make-up and redo my hair before heading back down to the others. It's just coming up to 5pm and the bar seems a lot quieter, as does the village green. I walk over to the group and Emma, the lady with the baby, is getting ready to leave, and as she packs away her things, she passes me her baby to hold. The cricket match has ended and as the men make a slow walk back, David looks over at me holding the baby and smiles. I feel a little awkward, given the fact that we've just had sex, especially when James shouts out, "Wow! David, you're a quick worker." This is followed by his raucous laugh. Emma's partner comes over and thanks me as he relieves me of the bundle in my arms, and after saying their goodbyes, they leave.

David places his arm around me, and we watch the remaining couples chat, that is, apart from James, who has a beady eye on us. It unnerves me a little and so I look back at him and smile. We all head to the pub, and I pick up my picnic blanket, give it a shake, fold it up and, in our own time, we make our way across the road. Me and David head to his car and he pops the blanket in the boot. "Are you okay, Rachel?"

"Yes, why wouldn't I be?" I reply.

"No, I just thought..."

"I didn't get a good night's sleep last night and I guess it's catching up with me, but I'll be all right," I say, reassuringly. "How are you doing, birthday boy?"

"Really good, happy you're here with me," he says, as he comes forward and kisses me lightly on the lips.

"Oi! Oi, enough of that." We hear a loud voice and turn to see James standing by the entrance to the pub. "What you drinking, mate?" he shouts out.

David asks me what I'd like and shouts back to him, "A red wine and a beer, cheers."

We make our way back inside and join the others at a big table; already seated are Wendy, Tim and Bina, and another couple whose names I can't remember.

I take a seat and David helps James bring the drinks over. In one corner of the bar there's a couple of men setting up a stage for live music. I feel a little self-conscious as I'm the only one who isn't drinking beer, not to mention that most of them are very loud; that is, James, Wendy, Tim and Bina. I try to join in as much as I can, laughing at their stories, which are mostly about David seeing as it's his birthday.

As the evening progresses, the smell of the food wafting in from the kitchen is making me hungry so I walk over to the bar and pick up a couple of menus bringing them back to the table, but it seems it's only me and the other lady who is interested. She asks me what I'm having and before I can answer, she asks if I'd share a pizza with her. "Yes, as long as it's a margherita," I reply.

"Great, I'm a vegetarian so that's exactly what I was going to order; they're so big that I never finish it and the rest of them will go to the burger van later," she says, smiling at me.

"Okay, I'll go and order it, then," I say, smiling back at her, feeling relieved that I may have an ally. I let David know that I'll be getting a pizza and sharing it with... I look over at her.

"Oh yes, with Dee, she always orders the pizza but never manages to finish it," he says.

"Would you like anything?" I ask.

"No, you crack on, Rachel, we'll be popping out to the—"

"Burger van," I interject, finishing his sentence, which makes him smile and nod.

I place the order at the bar and make my way back to the table, and 20 minutes later, our pizza appears, hot and bubbling, sat on a round wooden board. Me and Dee make a start, leaving the others salivating. She wasn't wrong; it's huge. The rest of them soon make a quick exit out of the pub to the burger van. "Rachel, can I get you anything from the van?" David asks me before leaving.

"Eww, no thank you," I reply, grimacing at the thought of eating anything from a burger van. He chuckles, as does Dee, at my reaction and follows the others out. It's a welcome relief to have a break from David's friends, especially James, who likes to take centre stage and it seems the more he drinks, the louder he becomes.

Dee is very reserved but nice just the same. "I'm so pleased they've left," she says.

"Oh?" I say, questioningly.

"It's the same every year; they get so drunk, then get burger and chips from the van. At least it's earlier this year; normally they eat much later. James is like the ringleader. I'm so glad you're here, David never brings anyone along. If you weren't here, I'd be eating this pizza outside with them. It's so nice to have some peace and quiet for a bit." She offloads her sentiments and smiles at me.

"Well, I'm glad we're keeping each other company, Dee," I say, smiling back at her reassuringly. "So, how do you know David?"

"He's friends with my partner, Gavin. James, Gavin and David have been friends since secondary school. I've only been going out with Gavin for a couple of years now, but the other couples are all married and are awfully close," she says.

"Well, me and David have only been dating a few weeks."

"What!" she gasps. "Oh wow, I thought it was longer than that."

"I'm not even sure I'm supposed to be here. I mean, we'd only been on a couple of dates, and I wasn't quite sure that I was going to say yes when he asked me to come but I jokingly made a comment about a birthday present and next thing you know, he says he's booked the rooms," I say, taking my last slice of pizza and placing it on my plate.

"Oh, that's why you asked for two rooms," she says.

"You know about that?" I ask in disbelief, nearly choking on the pizza.

"Well, James was booking the rooms, as he does every year, and apparently, from what I overheard when

Gavin and James were chatting on the phone, James thought he'd play a prank on David and just book the one room, not believing that David was actually bringing someone, or that you were even real," she divulges.

"What!" I shriek out.

"Oh, please don't say anything, Rachel," Dee pleads.

"No, of course I won't, thanks for telling me, Dee. The reason I wanted my own room was because we'd only been on a couple of dates and—"

"Yeah, I get it, I would feel the same," she butts in. "They're coming back," she says, taking her last slice of pizza off the board.

"Dee, can I get you a drink, I'm getting a round in before I head up to bed."

"Yes, I'd love a red wine, if that's okay," she says.

"Yeah, sure." I smile and nod at her as the others make their way back to the table and David slides in next to me. "Hi, how was your meal?" I ask.

"Very nutritious," he says, chuckling.

"I'm going to get a round in, David."

"You don't have to do that, Rachel."

"I know, but I'd like to," I say, getting up and taking the plates and popping them on the pizza board and taking them up. I order the six beers and two red wines, pay for them, and ask the barman to take them to the table whilst I nip to the bathroom.

On my return, I find the barman popping the drinks on the table and James bellows out, "Where did these magically appear from?"

"Rachel," David says.

"Well, thank you and cheers, Rachel." James nods at me in appreciation; I smile and give him a little nod back. "She's a keeper, David," he continues, laughing out in a sarcastic manner. I look over at Dee and notice that we're the only two that have not joined in with the group laughter. She raises her wine glass, smiles and mouths 'thank you' to me.

The band setting up earlier have taken their positions, a few people start clapping followed by whistles, and they start playing. I'm so pleased that it drowns out James' voice, and he eventually has to stop talking when we all turn and focus on them. David holds my hand under the table and shuffles in closer to me. I can feel someone staring at me and I just know that it's James, but I refuse to acknowledge his presence and sit back in my seat and enjoy the music. After 20 minutes, a familiar intro to a song begins, and I instinctively start singing along to 'Hotel California'; it's one of the few songs I know all the words to, much to the shock of James, who turns and raises his eyebrows at me. David starts laughing at my boldness and once the song gets to the guitar solo, I turn to

David and we both chuckle. "Blimey, I wasn't expecting that, Rachel," he says.

"No, neither was I," I reply, laughing.

When the band stop for a break, James can't help but talk about the meaning of the song. I look at David and quietly say that I'm exhausted and off to bed, he nods his head, and we shuffle out of our seats. I say goodnight to the group and the only person to make a fuss is James, who shouts out, "It's only 9:45!" I ignore this. I turn to Dee and say, "It was lovely meeting you." Then I turn to the group and say, "Enjoy the rest of your night."

David walks me up to the room and asks if I'm okay. "Yes, absolutely fine, I'm just exhausted and can't drink anymore, I hope you don't mind," I say, as he unlocks the door and I step inside.

"No, I quite understand, I'll try not to make too much noise when I come in. I shouldn't be too late," he says.

"You take your time, it's your birthday, after all," I say, smiling. He then leans in, and we kiss before he makes his way back down to the bar. A sense of relief overcomes me, and I can't wait to wash away the day from my face and climb into bed. I pop the kettle on, followed by the TV and channel-surf until I eventually find a movie, *The Omen*. It's just started. Once I finish getting ready for bed, I make a cuppa, pick up a biscuit, settle in the single bed and watch the movie. I'm awoken with the sound of a chilling scream; it's the horror film. I bumble out of bed and catch the time on my phone, it's nearly 11pm, so I pop to the bathroom, turn the TV off and decide to call it a night.

I can't breathe, I feel as though I'm being suffocated, buried alive, I must be dreaming but I'm paralysed with fear, I can't move, I panic, gasping for air, there's a heavy weight on me; I manage to move my head up slightly, inhale and scream out. Something's on top of me, it moves. "Oh God, I'm so sorry," David says, as his hands push down on the bed to get balance and he clambers off, and slumps onto the other bed. I pick up my phone from the bedside table; it's 2am.

I roll over and fall back asleep but as soon as it gets light out, my sleep is disturbed again, and a foulness strikes my sense of smell; it's so overpowering that I no longer can afford the luxury of having a lie-in. I check the time; it's 6:30am. I look across at David, who's asleep, face down, snoring. I creep out of bed and make my way to the bathroom and as I step inside, my foot slides across the floor. I grab the side of the sink to steady myself and then switch the light on to discover the putrid offensive odour is vomit. My hands and feet contaminated, I take a bath towel and lay it on the floor and step into the bath and wash away the sick from my hands and feet, using the entire contents of the miniature shampoo bottle. After drying them with the other bath towel and placing it on the floor, I pick up my toiletry bag and exit the bathroom. I have to get out of the room as I'm starting to retch, so I pack away all my belongings into my holdall and leave the room.

Still in my shorts and t-shirt I make my way down the stairs to the toilets, where I manage to freshen up, changing into my jeans and a fresh t-shirt. I must've washed my hands four times as I kept smelling vomit, then realised that it must be the toilets that are in need of a clean too. I sprayed myself generously with perfume before leaving. The door to the bar is locked but the room opposite, which must be the dining area is open, so I take a seat at a table, closing my eyes, trying not to think of the last few hours. It's only just gone 7:15, and I wonder if breakfast is included in our stay, not that I could even think about eating right now, but a cup of tea would be lovely. There's not a sound, bar a few creaks from the wood now and again, I look around the room and notice a newspaper on one of the tables and I retrieve it. *The Sun;* not my choice of a good read, but *desperate times*, I think as I flick through the pages. My eyes feel heavy and I can't help but close them, until I hear a noise and then footsteps approaching. The sound of keys jangling, a door unlocks, and is opened by a man who enters the dining area and jumps out of his skin when he sees me. "Gave me a fright, you did," he says, holding onto his chest and taking a deep breath.

"I'm so sorry, I didn't mean to," I reply.

"What you doing down already? Breakfast won't be served for another hour, love," he says.

"Oh, I just couldn't sleep so I thought I'd get up," I say, trying not to alert any attention to how I'm really feeling or what has occurred in room 4.

"Okay, love, well I'm popping the kettle on if you fancy a brew," he says.

"Yes please, I'd love one. Milk, no sugar." I smile, he nods and goes back through the door from where he came. I hear the sound of the radio being switched on, then running water and the kettle being filled, and wonder whether I can wait a few more hours for David to surface or if I should just get a cab home.

The man returns with a huge mug and a couple of biscuits and pops them down on the table. "There you go, love, that'll brighten you up."

"Oh, that's lovely, thank you very much," I say, smiling at him.

"I'll have to get back to work, so when you finish up, just leave the mug on the table and mind how you go," he says, as he turns and walks back through the door.

"Will do, thanks again," I reply. I can hear him whistling away whilst he's working, and I get back to thinking about what to do. I know there's no way I'm going back up to the room and I'm not sure I really want to wait here and risk seeing the others when they come down either; that settles it then, I'll order a cab and make my way home. I enjoy my mug of tea and biscuits and wonder why David got himself in such a state, and then am reminded of the stench I woke up to.

I check the time on my phone and it's just gone 8:30, so I take a look around to see if there's a card for a local cab company pinned up anywhere and walk out of the dining room into the hallway where I find a noticeboard. I hear voices whispering and turn and watch Gavin and Dee making their way down the stairs. Dee looks up at me and says, "What are you doing down so early, Rachel?"

"Good morning," I say, as they both stand at the bottom of the stairs with their bags, "it's a long story, are you off home?" I ask, hoping they are.

"Yes, I've got a family thing later today and need to get back," Dee says.

"Any chance you're going anywhere near Windsor?" I quickly cut in before I lose my nerve to ask.

"Yes, we live in Datchet, it's on our way, we could drop you off," she says, smiling, although Gavin's face doesn't look happy but, at this point, I'm past caring.

"Great! I'll just get my bag." I turn and retrieve it from the dining room. I can hear them whispering as I make my way back.

Dee smiles at me again and says, "I'm driving."

"Okay, I live at the bottom of Peascod Street," I say, relieved that I'm leaving.

Gavin walks ahead of us and Dee whispers, "What happened?" I look at her and shake my head, rolling my eyes. She chuckles as we make our way outside to their car.

The journey back was mostly quiet. Gavin slumped in the front passenger seat whilst Dee and I made small talk. "I went up shortly after you, Rachel," she says.

"Oh, did you, well I settled in that single bed, popped the TV on and started watching *The Omen*, and fell asleep watching it." I look at her reflection in the rear-view mirror.

She looks across at Gavin and then quickly turns around to me and mouths 'what happened' then turns back, looks at me in the rear-view and so I try to mime that I was asleep, David threw up, I pinch my nose and then I shrug my shoulders. She grimaces then bursts out laughing, which sets me off. Gavin's head shoots up from his catnap and he says, "What happened?"

"Oh, you just missed this man, he was naked, just walking down the street with a newspaper under his arm," Dee says, looking at me in the mirror smiling.

"What a load of rubbish," he says, annoyed at being disturbed. Dee winks at me and we continue the rest of the journey in silence.

Thirty minutes later we arrive outside the flat; Dee steps out of the car, opens the boot and I take my bag out. "What really happened, Rachel?" I quickly run through what happened and she says, "That doesn't surprise me, James always gets him so drunk and then gets him to do something silly. Normally it's chatting up some random girl and asking her a pointless question or getting him to run around the car park naked. I can't tell you what happened last night as I went to bed shortly after you."

"It's okay, I'm just disappointed that it's ended like this but I'm glad to have met you and I really appreciate you dropping me home," I say, giving her a hug. She hugs me back and we say goodbye.

I feel so happy to be home. I put the key in the front door and think back to yesterday morning when I was leaving, and David was popping the picnic basket and my holdall into the boot of his car. Oh crap! My picnic basket is still in his car. Oh well, he may as well keep it as I'm really not sure that I want to see him again. When I enter the flat, I feel a welcoming hug from the warm familiar smell. I run a bath and turn my mobile off and take the landline off the hook; today is a day that I don't want to be disturbed in any way. I take off my clothes and slowly submerge myself into the steaming bath and wash away the putridity from David's excesses off my body.

After my soak, I put my hoodie and leggings on. It's warm out, but I feel a little cold, the last two nights of not having much sleep has left me feeling weary so I make a strong cup of coffee, get a cigarette from my emergency pack, sit out on the balcony and think back to the previous afternoon when me and David were intimate with one another. It wasn't planned, none of it was, I was meant to have my own room. Now I wonder if James had got him so drunk on purpose to see what would happen. Whatever the reason, he's going to be in shock when he wakes up and discovers that I'm not there but then who would seriously stay in that room after he pebble-dashed the bathroom with vomit, and how is he ever going to drive home? Well, it's not my concern, and I get back to my coffee and cigarette.

My Sunday turns out to be truly lazy. I unpack my holdall and then, come late afternoon, I talk myself into having a glass of red wine, my excuse being to cope with the trauma I had been put through. I made an early dinner of sausage and mash and by 8pm, I was relaxing in bed with a book.

Waking up early on Bank Holiday Monday has me feeling rejuvenated and instantly brightens my day, so I go for a run in Windsor Great Park. When I get home, I turn on my mobile phone, which pings through a couple of text messages; one from Naomi asking how the birthday picnic went and the other from David asking where I am, which, by the looks of it, was sent yesterday, late morning. I send Naomi a text back saying that all started off well but ended badly. She calls me straight away and I briefly go through the previous day's events. We arrange to have our usual Friday after work catch-up and she says she'll let Harriet know. Harriet texts me 10 minutes later saying how she's looking forward to catching up as she hasn't had a good laugh since our last get-together, which she pointed out was over a month ago. I send her a message back saying *'It's all about you, you, you!!! X'*. I remember that I had said weeks ago that the next Friday we meet would be dinner at mine, so I send them a message saying to meet at mine for Champagne cocktails followed by dinner at Mo's Kitchen. They're both delighted with the plan, and I too feel excited with my Friday night date with my besties, so I pop a bottle of pink Champagne in the fridge.

After taking a shower and having breakfast, I get ready to go out for a mooch around Windsor. I pop on my black joggers, white t-shirt, baseball cap, flip flops, and head out. It's a beautiful sunny day and the high street is already buzzing with people dining alfresco at the restaurants and cafés. I stroll up Peascod Street, passing a busker singing 'Yesterday' by The Beatles, and I smile to myself, remembering my yesterday, then open my purse and throw a 50 pence piece into his open guitar case. He winks at me as I walk on by. When I reach the top of the street, I take in the view of the castle then make a left turn and walk down the steep slope, making a stop at the fudge shop. I pop in and help myself to a couple of pieces of free fudge from the tray on the counter, shout out thank you and enjoy the sweet treat on my walk down by the river, passing Alexandra Gardens, where I recollect ice skating back in December with Gregory. I wonder whether he and Artisan are still together as I make my way back towards town and turn the corner back onto Peascod Street, I notice a small table at one of the cafes that's unoccupied and decide to stop for a coffee.

When my cappuccino and biscotti arrive, I prepare to dunk the biscotti into the frothy coffee when my mobile starts ringing, it startles me, and my heart jumps a beat when I see that it's David. I decline the call and get back to my coffee. I know I'll have to face this situation at some point but now is not that time. The phone pings to let me know that a voice message has been received; I sit back, relax, and soak up the warmth of the sun whilst watching people pass by. After a short while, the young waiter arrives, placing a small silver plate with the bill on the table and as I reach for my purse he says, "No, take your time, Signora."

I look up at him and smile but catch sight of Demi a few feet in front of me with a young girl, strolling by, holding hands and I instantly duck. "No, it's fine, take it now, I'll be leaving soon," I say, still ducking behind the waiter whilst taking some loose change out of my purse. I place it on the plate and hand it to him then look up and watch Demi and his companion walk on. The waiter turns to see what I'm looking at and then turns back to look at me. "Ex-boyfriend," I offer, as I take my last mouthful of the frothy coffee and stand up. He smiles at me, and I step out onto the street.

A couple of minutes later I'm opening the front door to the flat and pick up an envelope that's sitting on the mat and head upstairs. *Whew!* I think, *that was a close shave, not sure seeing Demi with his girlfriend face to face today would've brightened up my day.* I open up the envelope and have a feeling that it's from David from the handwriting. The picture on the front of the card is of a cute puppy and inside are the words 'I'm sorry'. I leave the card on the coffee table and remember his phone call, so I listen to his voice message. "Rachel, I don't know what to say but sorry, please call me." I delete the message.

The next day at work turns out to be exactly what I need. I get back to the structure of my working week and, come Friday, I'm looking forward to getting together with Naomi and Harriet. On my way home I pick up a few items from the deli and prepare a tray of canapes to accompany the Champagne. I take a quick shower and slip into a rose gold strappy dress and heels. Harriet is the first to arrive, we hug like we haven't seen each other in years, laugh and then I task her with opening the Champagne whilst I take the canapes out of the fridge. Naomi arrives just as we head out to the balcony, and I buzz her up. "Don't start without me," she hollers as she hurries up the stairs.

"We would never do that," I say, giving her a hug and then looking over at Harriet, who's just about to take a sip of her Champagne but then stops, greets Naomi, and pours her a glass. We all sit down, clink glasses and take that first sip of chilled pink Champagne, closely followed by another sip.

"Oh, Rachel, this looks so lovely," Naomi says, eyeing up the canapes.

"Dig in, Nomes," I say, as they both lean forward and help themselves.

"So, come on, what's been happening, Rache? It's been weeks since we last caught up when Naomi got paralytic at our last dinner," Harriet says, chuckling.

"Gosh, so much has happened, I'm not sure where to begin," I say, picking up a salmon blini. "Well, it all started after our last night out, when I was walking home..." I told them about the cat postcard, the bike ride, meeting David's mum and then meeting his best mate, James and friends last Friday evening. Then the next day at the birthday cricket picnic, us sleeping together and what ensued. By the time I got to the end of the story, we had finished the bottle of Champagne and, thankfully, we had eaten the canapes way before I got to the part of what I stepped on when I entered the bathroom. Through their laughter, gasps and final 'ewws', I ended the latest saga of the quest with the puppy card and the voice message. No one uttered another word.

We all stood up and in turn visited the bathroom to freshen up, and then made our way downstairs and strolled over to Mo's Kitchen. Still not a word spoken, until we arrived at Mo's where he greeted us and showed us to our table. Once settled in our seats, Harriet bursts out laughing, me and Naomi look at her and can't help but join in. "Well, I have to tell you something else," I say.

But Harriet jumps in and says, "We need more drinks, Rache, if there's more to come." She decidedly looks up and nods to Mo, who rushes over. Harriet orders a bottle of red wine, some houmous and flat bread to start and we scan the menu but inevitably end up ordering the same dishes we always do.

I start telling them about the night I received the phone call from Demi. “He says he’s met someone who lives in Windsor and has now moved in with her and basically just wanted to give me the heads-up in case we should bump into each other, he says he doesn’t want there to be any awkwardness.”

“Well, that’s generous of him,” Harriet says sarcastically, which sets Naomi off laughing. Mo arrives back at our table. He uncorks the bottle of red and asks if we’ll be singing tonight; his two trusted musicians haven’t yet arrived, but he expects us to be up there kicking off proceedings. Me and Naomi instantly shake our heads ‘no’.

“Depends how much free red wine you ply us with, Mo,” Harriet says, smiling seductively and then winking at him. He nods his head, smiling as he pours a little wine in her glass for her to try, chuckling with us at her cheeky request. We all have a little banter with Mo as he pours the wine, we place our food order and he leaves us to it as it gets busy, with more diners arriving, and I get back to the Demi story.

“So, Rache, what else did he say?” Naomi asks as she takes a piece of the pitta bread and scoops up the houmous.

“Just that he still thinks of me. Anyway, I cut the conversation short, but...” I take a sip of the wine. “On

Monday I went for a walk and stopped at a café, and just as I was enjoying my cappuccino, I saw him walking past. I'm sure he didn't see me because I ducked, and the waiter was standing in front of me, so it was easy for me to hide behind him. I told him it was an ex." Harriet bursts out laughing, and a piece of the pitta bread comes flying out of her mouth, which makes her laugh even more. "Anyway, he was with his new girlfriend, although I didn't get a proper look, but she looked a lot younger than him," I say, with a shrug of my shoulders. "So, I got up and made a dash for it once they'd passed by; last thing I needed after my weekend with David and his friends was bumping into Demi and his new love."

"You know you're going to have to speak with him?" Harriet says.

"Who? Demi?" I say.

"No – David. It sounds like he overindulged and I'm wondering whether his friend, James, had anything to do with it. I mean, you've been out with him a few times now, at least find out what happened, he may have got food poisoning from the burger van," she says, sniggering. Naomi smiles and nods in agreement. I roll my eyes and agree.

Our meals arrive with another bottle of red, compliments of Mo. Harriet blows him a kiss and he points to the small stage where the musicians are getting ready to play. "I hope you've got a song lined up, Harriet," Naomi says.

"Always, darling, always," Harriet replies. Harriet does actually have a good singing voice, it's me and Naomi who have worried looks on our faces, but I figure after another glass of red, we won't really care how we sound. We finish our meals, pass on dessert and enjoy our free bottle of red whilst listening to the MoMo's; that's the stage name of the two musicians. They're both named Mohammed and they play traditional Moroccan folk songs, with one of the Mo's playing the guitar and the other Mo singing. A lot of clapping accompanies the songs but once their hour is over, they have a break, and the floor opens up for anyone brave enough. They've just finished their set and I look nervously across at Naomi and burst out laughing when she displays a face full of horror at the thought of standing up and singing. I top up our glasses and nip to the loo. When I return, Mo is stood beside our table, pen and paper in hand. Harriet gives him two songs, and he leaves, satisfied, and promptly goes around to other tables trying to get more takers. "Hattie, what are you going to sing?" I ask, taking a sip of wine.

"She's going to start with Sade's 'Your Love is King'," Naomi blurts out.

"And you two will join me after for 'Dancing Queen', because we all know the words to that one, don't we?" she says, smiling eagerly.

"I think I need a shot," Naomi says, looking around the restaurant; every table is occupied.

"Hopefully, no one will care when we go up, Nomes, they're all still eating and chatting away, don't worry," I say, trying to convince myself too.

Harriet pops to the loo, and I reapply my lipstick and notice Mo at the stage with his laptop. He looks over at our table, smiles and gives us the thumbs up. I smile back at him. We're sat in a booth halfway down the side of the restaurant, with the stage about 10 feet away on the far end; we only have to manoeuvre past two tables to reach it. Harriet returns just in the nick of time; the MoMo's are making their way to the seats on the stage, we sit and wait with bated breath until one of the Mo's picks up the mic and says, "We have a special guest singer, please welcome Harry." Harriet looks across at us and we all burst out laughing. The whole restaurant starts clapping, and Harriet stands up and shimmies to the stage. She exchanges pleasantries with the MoMo's, adjusts the mic on the stand and when the music starts, her sultry voice starts singing.

"Your love is king, Crown you in my heart, Your love is king, Never need to part..."

She looks sensational and as I take a look around, everyone seems mesmerised with her. When the song comes to an end, the rapturous applause is overwhelming and she takes a bow. Naomi pinches me, nervously laughing, Harriet looks over at us both and nods, neither of us able to move until she says, "I'd like to welcome Raquel and Nolene to the stage for the next song." We both slowly make our way over, standing either side of her. The music starts and in unison we sway from side to side.

"You can dance, you can jive. Having the time of your life, ooh. See that girl, watch that scene, Diggin' the dancing queen."

Me and Naomi starting off a little shaky but as soon as it gets to the next verse, we get into the swing of it. We're singing and gyrating to the music and mostly every lady is singing along with us. We synchronize our dance moves, pointing straight ahead, singing, "You can dance, You can jive, having the time of your life." We're singing to whoever is in our sightline. I see Mo's smiling face; he's swaying from side to side, clapping and standing next to him is Demi. He catches my eye and I pretend I haven't seen him, but I feel conscious that he's there; he's smiling and clapping along. When the song comes to an end, the applause and delight from the room is palpable; me and Naomi shuffle back to our booth whilst Harriet is loving the attention and takes her time.

When we sit down, I tell Naomi that I saw Demi. "What? Where?" she says.

"He was standing right next to Mo when we were singing."

"Noooo!" she says, looking from around the booth to see.

Harriet arrives back, giddy with laughter. "What's going on?" she asks.

"I saw Demi," I say. Harriet then does a meerkat impression and looks around the restaurant. The MoMo's start singing again as none of the other diners have dared to step up, then Mo arrives at our table with the bill and three small glasses.

"Ladies, thank you, this is for you, it is a Moroccan digestif, please enjoy," he says, as he places the glasses down on the table.

We each pick one up, clink glasses, "Here's to Harry, Raquel and Nolene," I say, giggling.

"Not sure I like Nolene," Naomi says, with a disgruntled look.

Me and Harriet look at each other and start to chuckle and start singing, to the music of Dolly Parton's 'Jolene', "Nolene, Nolene, Nolene, Noleeene." Naomi doesn't find this amusing but can't help but laugh too.

Harriet then promptly stands up, takes the glass, downs it in one and walks back to the stage. After a quick chat with the MoMo's and a tap of the keys on the laptop, the music starts, and she starts singing 'Jolene', much to Mo's delight. Harriet savours the applause once again and when the song comes to an end, we all make a move to leave.

I approach the bar to settle the bill and leave Naomi and Harriet with Mo, who is desperately trying to persuade her to stay, enticing her with more alcohol. I follow them out of the restaurant giving Mo a hug on my way out and just as we're about to leave, I hear a voice shout out my name. I turn and see Demi standing just outside the door of the restaurant. "Hi, Demi." My heart skips a beat. Naomi and Harriet stop in their tracks and turn to look at him. We just stare at each other for a moment. I'm waiting for him to speak and then I notice a girl sitting alone at a table by the window, watching us. "Demi, I think your friend is waiting for you."

He turns and looks at her, then turns back to me. "You were wonderful tonight, Rachel." I smile at him endearingly, say thank you, turn and walk away.

Harriet and Naomi look at me and both say, "You were wonderful tonight, Rachel." We all have a giggle as we walk up Peascod Street.

"So, that was Demi," Naomi remarks, "he's very handsome."

"He still has it bad for you, Rache," Harriet says, as we walk to the taxi rank. We hug.

"I can't go back there with Demi, besides, I have enough to deal with at the moment with David." They climb into the cab and leave, and I walk home singing 'Jolene' and then think of the stranger as I pass the alley where we collided. It's dark, and so I carry on with my walk back to the flat.

The next morning, I wake up feeling a little jaded from the previous night's excesses. I stretch out in bed and smile as I think back to the singing, the dancing and seeing Demi. 'Jolene' is still on play in my head and as I make my way out of bed to the kitchen to pop the kettle on, I fish out my phone from my purse and discover a missed call from David and a text message from Demi. The message from Demi reads *'Rachel, it was so good to see you tonight, you looked amazing and if you ever want to meet up, please call. Demi x'*. I don't respond to either Demi or David but send a message to the girls saying thank you and that the previous night was exactly what I needed, then I realise that it is now June and I have three months left before the quest comes to an end.

My Saturday is consumed with cleaning the flat, and after breakfast I pop out to do a food shop, stocking up on Champagne and wine for my birthday. On my return, I notice a car outside the flat and as I approach the front door, James climbs out. "Rachel!" he shouts out as I place the shopping bags down in the hallway, I turn around and he pops open the boot of his car and pulls out my picnic basket. "Hi," he says.

"Hello, James."

"I, um, have your picnic basket. David wanted me to return it in case you needed it."

"Okay, thank you," I say, taking the basket from him.

"You see, he, er, well I think it was all my fault," he says.

"What was, James?" I enquire.

"You see, I got David so drunk that he, well, you know," he continues. "We're always ribbing one another, and I think I took it too far," he says, smiling at me, as if his explanation is satisfactory.

"Well, how nice for you both," I reply, not giving him an inch.

"I'm sorry, Rachel, he's sorry, he says that he's tried calling but you won't pick up."

"You see, James, I had only met David a few weeks before his birthday and I wasn't actually planning on going, seeing as we were only dating but he asked me, and I only decided to come on the condition I had my own room but, somehow, even that got messed up."

"Yes, yes, I take complete responsibility for that," he says sheepishly. I can see the guilt on his face.

"Thanks for returning my basket, James, goodbye." I turn and walk into the hallway, shut the door behind me, pick up the shopping bags and head upstairs. The basket is heavy, and when I reach the kitchen, I pop it on the counter and unbuckle it. Inside I find a bottle of Champagne and an envelope. I pop the shopping away and make some lunch. 'Jolene' is still buzzing away in my head. I make a cuppa, sit out on the balcony and open the envelope, there's a letter with a gift card for a spa day at a hotel.

The letter reads, *'Dear Rachel, I can't imagine what you must have gone through having to be woken up in the middle of the night with me slumped on top of you, and then subsequently encountered what state the bathroom was in. I am mortified beyond belief at my behaviour, and quite understand if you never want to see me again'.*

His letter went on in that vein, saying how very sorry he was and hoped that I would accept the bottle of Champagne and gift of the spa day as way of an apology. After reading it, I felt indifferent, I hadn't really established a deep emotional connection with David to feel any sense of loss, my sentiments about the situation was that he was too immature to value the effort I had made for him on his birthday and allowed himself to get into such a state, all because his friend encouraged him to. I packed away the picnic basket and popped the bottle of Champagne with the rest of the bottles I had bought earlier for my party.

The next day, after my morning run, a shower and breakfast, I packed up the car with the drinks for my party and headed off to Mum and Dad's. Turning into their road, I glanced over at a man on the opposite side washing his car; he looks across at me as I pass. I park up on the drive and walk to the boot, taking out the box of Champagne bottles and place them on the ground. The man washing his car raises his hand and waves at me, I wave back, and he starts walking towards me. He crosses the road and I slowly begin to recognise him. "Simon?" I say, as we approach one another.

"Rachel, how are you?" he says, beaming at me. Simon was my first ever crush, and kiss, for that matter. He's a few years older than me but as a teenager, I wished that someday he would be my boyfriend.

What's he doing back here? I wonder. "I'm really good, thanks, and you? I haven't seen you in years," I reply, checking him out. He's still good-looking, a few greys running through his blonde hair, with blue eyes and a boyish charm that warms you.

"I'm just visiting Mum and Dad; it's been a long while since I've been back this way. I'm okay although me and Tina got divorced, she's moved on, you know, life just happens and before you know it, you're back home in your old bedroom, wondering where all the time went," he says, looking down at the box of Champagne bottles. "Are you having a party?" he asks, looking up at me with a chuckle.

"Oh, yes, in September, for my 40th," I reply.

"Wow, 40! Rachel, you look amazing, you married?"

"No, hasn't happened yet, still waiting to be swept off my feet," I say, blushing, now wishing I hadn't said that last bit.

We look at each other and I get taken back to my first kiss. I was 17 and he was 25; he and Tina had just got engaged. She looked like Shirlie from the '80s pop group Pepsi & Shirlie and Simon looked like John

Taylor from Duran Duran. It was his last day living across the road at his parents; him and Tina were moving in together, and I remember watching him from my bedroom window packing his car up, feeling sad that I'd never see him again. I went outside to go for a walk, hoping that by the time I came back, his car would be gone and that way I wouldn't have to see him drive away. I got to the top of the road and heard a voice shout out, "Rachel." I turned and saw Simon in his car, the passenger window wound down and my heart skipped a beat; I walked over to the window. "Get in, Rache," he said. A feeling of excitement rushed through my body as I sat down in the passenger seat of his Ford Capri. Madonna's 'Crazy For You' playing on the radio.

He drove up the road for a mile and then took a turn into a dirt track that led to some stables. All the while, I kept thinking that he was going to tell me that he and Tina had broken up and that he was going to ask me to run away with him. He stopped the car in a clearing at the side of the road, turned the engine off and turned to me. "I wanted to give you a present before I left, Rachel," he said, and then he moved toward me and kissed me. His mouth pressed against mine, I didn't know what to do, I hadn't kissed anyone before, apart from practise kissing on the mirror in my bedroom, or on my arm. It was my first kiss, and my mind was whirring with thoughts. He stopped and asked me if I was okay, and I remember just nodding. I was more than okay; in that moment it felt like all my dreams had come true. He smiled and continued kissing me, this time his tongue opening my mouth and furiously circling mine, his hand reaching under my t-shirt, grabbing my breasts. It was the most exciting thing to have ever happened to me and then he suddenly stopped, started the car and drove back home.

When we reached home a few minutes later, he walked me down the path at the side of the house where we couldn't be seen and said, "I don't know when I'm going to see you again, Rachel." He turned to walk away, so I took hold of his hand and stepped forward to kiss him. He kissed me back, harder this time, my body pinned to the wall by his, his hands reaching under my t-shirt, one on each breast, massaging them, my mouth open, letting his tongue swirl around. I was in heaven. He stopped abruptly when we heard a noise, stroked my cheek, and walked away and I watched him drive off. I was heartbroken.

"Rachel!" I hear Dad's voice and look across at Simon and Dad looking at me.

"Hi, Dad," I say, giving him a kiss on the cheek.

"I was saying how long it's been since we last saw Simon."

"Yes, I was saying the same thing, too," I reply.

"If you're free one night, feel free to pop over for dinner, Simon," Dad says, looking across at me.

"Oh, yes, sure, let me know which day and I'll make it over too, as long as it's not a school night," I reply, not sure why Dad has invited him.

"Okay why not, how does Friday sound?" Simon says, looking at Dad.

"Absolutely fine, I'll let Katherine know," Dad says, picking up the box of Champagne and walking back indoors.

"Guess you better get back to washing the car," I say, smiling at him.

"Yep, well, looks like I'll be seeing you on Friday, then, Rachel," he says, with that winning smile as he turns and walks back across the road. I watch him and can't believe after all these years he's back; he turns and catches me looking at him and waves, I wave back and then chuckle to myself as I make my way indoors.

I find Mum and Dad in the kitchen talking about Simon. I give Mum a kiss hello. "Rachel, darling, you used to have a little crush on him, didn't you?" she says, winking at me.

"Hmm, did I? Maybe, I can't remember, it was such a long time ago," I say, chuckling nervously, wondering how she knew.

After lunch, we all go out for a walk, and me and Mum finalise the food for the party and after an early evening G and T in the garden, I say my goodbyes and leave. When I reach home, I play songs by Duran Duran and think of Simon whilst prepping a salad for dinner, dancing around the flat pretending to be 17 again.

My working week flies by, with a couple of staff on their summer holidays, my workload has tripled but it's all good as I can't wait to see Simon again. When I finish work on Friday, I dash home to shower and get dolled up, wearing my denim knee-length skirt with a black blouse, kitten heels and I'm off out. I reach Mum and Dad's at 6:30 to find Simon already seated in the garden with a drink. "Hi," I say, as I walk through the patio doors. They all look up and Simon gets up.

"Hi, you look lovely, Rachel," he says.

"Thanks," I reply, giving him a kiss on the cheek, then turn and greet Mum and Dad in the same way.

"How was work, dear?" Mum asks, as Dad pours me a glass of wine.

"Yes, it was okay, bit of a busy week with people away on their hols," I reply, clinking glasses with Simon and saying cheers. I take a sip of the crisp chilled wine. "Mm, this is very nice."

"Yes, Simon bought it over, it's a Sancerre," Dad says, giving Simon a nod of appreciation.

We all chat for a while until Mum gets up to go inside, taking her wine in hand. "Do you need a hand, Mum?" I offer.

"No, everything is prepared, dear, besides, I've got your dad here to help," she says, winking at Dad, who takes his wine and follows her inside.

"Oh, Rachel, how sweet are they, they still seem ever so much in love."

"Yes, don't they," I reply, with a giggle.

We talk about our lives, our jobs and then he says, "Do you remember that day when I was leaving and we—"

"Yes," I butt in, "when you took advantage of a 17-year-old."

"What!" he spits out. "I thought you were older than that, Rache, well, you looked older," he says.

"No, I was 17 and had such a terrible crush on you and then you got engaged and left," I say, resentfully. He looks at me and we both burst out laughing.

"Well, I'm glad we can laugh about it, but since we're being honest, I had a thing for you too, always did," he says, sliding his leg against mine. We look at each other, our eyes locked until we hear Mum's voice.

"Would you like to eat outdoors?" We look over to her standing at the patio doors.

"Yes, Mum, outside is fine with me."

"Yes, me too, Katherine," Simon adds. I get up and help Dad bring out the plates and Simon helps Mum with the fish pie and vegetables.

After dinner, me and Simon take the dishes into the kitchen, and I make a start on putting them in the dishwasher. "Here, Rachel, let me do that," he says.

"No, it's okay, tell you what, you can open another bottle of wine; should be one in the fridge," I reply. I leave Simon to sort out the wine while I make an Eton mess with meringue, cream, and whatever berries I can find in the fridge.

We make our way back outside with the wine and dessert, much to Mum's delight. Simon pours the wine and I stop at my second glass. Simon looks at me questioningly. "I've got to drive home."

"You can stay the night, love," Dad says.

"Yes, I know, but I wasn't planning on staying and haven't got anything with me," I reply.

"I'm sure you can use anything of mine, darling," Mum says, and before I can answer, Simon has already topped up my glass. We tuck into dessert, and I look across at Simon chatting with Mum and Dad. I almost feel as though we could already be married, everything seems so natural and easy. Mum pops into the kitchen and I help with the dessert dishes while she makes some coffee. "Rachel, you and Simon seem to be getting along, what do you think of him?" she says.

"Well, I'm not sure, Mum, he's only just got divorced from what he's told me, and I really don't know him well enough yet." She gives me a squeeze, makes two coffees, and kisses me goodnight then heads outside to say goodnight to Simon, and then her and dad head inside for the night.

I put some music on, and Simon chats about the past, his marriage to Tina and him opening a hair salon in London. "I can't believe you're still a hairdresser, Simon."

"I'm a hair director. I think that's the technical word they use these days," he quips, laughing. "Yes, I've still got the salon although I employ four stylists now."

"Wow, good for you, you always had great hair. You know I always thought you looked like John Taylor from Duran Duran." He bursts out laughing and leans towards me and I run my fingers through his hair. "I've always wanted to do that," I say, blushing.

"Have I made your dreams come true," he says.

"Not quite," I reply, and we continue to laugh and flirt with each other.

When we finish the wine, I suggest calling it a night. It's gone 11, and as we walk down the side of the house, Simon turns to me. "Do you remember what happened here?"

I look up at him and say, "Yes."

I sense his hesitation, so I take his hand, as I did back then at 17. He moves towards me. This time I know exactly how to kiss, with my back against the wall he presses his body onto mine and we kiss; it's a sexy, longing, wet kiss. His hands re-enact our first encounter, sliding up underneath my blouse and he touches my breasts, but this time he strokes them softly. My hand reaches down to his hard penis. He groans. "Rachel, come back to mine, Mum and Dad will be asleep."

He takes my hand, and we walk across the road and enter the house, creeping up the stairs and when we reach his bedroom, he says, "Their bedroom is downstairs at the back, they won't hear a thing." He closes the door behind me, then we resume our act, my back against the door with us kissing. I pull my blouse up over my head whilst he unbuttons his jeans, and we move over to the edge of the bed, the streetlight shining through the window casting enough light to show off our physical forms. He takes off his jeans and t-shirt and sits down on the bed, his manhood evident through his boxer shorts. I stand in front of him in my black bra, my bosoms waiting to be stroked again. I unzip my skirt and let it fall down to the floor and he places his hands on my hips and pulls me in; I part my legs and sit on top of him as we start kissing. He then unhooks my bra, takes my breasts in his hands and kisses my nipples. I'm in ecstasy as we press hard against each other. He lays back on the bed and I straddle him, rocking against his cock with my breasts in his face. I fall to the side and take hold of him in my hand and stroke his hardness; he places his hand in my knickers and plays with my wet clitoris and we gently kiss each other, moaning with the pleasure of each other's touch. My mind is racing with thoughts of Duran Duran's John Taylor and the dreams of that 17-year-old coming true at last. He slips off his shorts and peels my knickers off. I part my legs and he enters me hard and forcefully and in that moment, I feel blissfully happy. He raises his upper body and rests on his forearms, his face directly on top of mine panting; I can see beads of sweat on his forehead as he rides me, the beads start dripping onto my face, and the faster he jerks, the quicker they drop. My face is covered with his sweat, dropping into my eyes and mouth until he climaxes and shouts out, "I love you. I love you so much, Tina!" Then he slumps on top of me. I can hardly breathe, and I try to wriggle myself from underneath the sweaty mess but it's useless, until he slides off me.

I roll off the bed and hunt around for my clothes; I find my bra and knickers on the floor with the rest of my clothes close by and quickly put them on, when suddenly Simon rears his head and says, "Tina, what you doing?"

I pick up my heels and say, "It's Rachel." I walk out of his room, down the stairs and out of the house. Thankfully, Mum and Dad are asleep, so I clear the garden table of the glasses, head upstairs, take a shower and go to bed.

The next morning, I awake to the sound of Mum and Dad in the kitchen chatting, the radio is on and although I feel a little disappointed in Simon, I realise that he's not over Tina and it's good that I know before

I invested anymore time and energy in him. I stretch out in bed and feel warm and fuzzy, the safe, familiar feeling of being in my old bedroom embraces me and then I recall my sexual encounter from last night, how much I enjoyed it up until the profuse sweating and being called Tina. I drag myself out of bed when the smell of freshly brewed coffee hits my nostrils and put on the jogging pants and t-shirt that Mum has left in the bedroom for me. After a quick freshen up, I go downstairs to find them both in the garden. "Good morning, darling," Mum says, followed by Dad.

"Good morning," I reply, as I take a seat and pour myself a coffee from the cafetière.

"How was your night?" Mum asks, as I pour milk into my cup and give it a stir.

"Yes, it was really nice, Mum, it was lovely catching up with Simon; he hasn't changed a bit." I take a drink of the coffee. "Shame he's not over Tina," I say, casually.

"Yes, he was talking about her yesterday before you arrived, apparently she left him after discovering inappropriate messages and pictures on his phone; he said that they were his clients who wanted more than just a haircut," Mum divulges, shaking her head.

"Oh dear! Well, he didn't quite go into that much detail with me, Mum."

"He probably didn't want you to think bad of him, Rachel," Dad says.

"Hmm, I guess. Poor Tina," I add, feeling sorry for her.

After showering and washing Simon's sweat out of my hair, I get dressed and go back down to find breakfast laid out on the kitchen island, which is a welcome sight as I'm famished, and the mushroom omelette followed by toast and marmalade goes down a treat. I leave Mum and Dad to the rest of their Saturday. Dad walks me out to the car, and I give him a kiss goodbye and as I turn, I notice Simon staring at me from his bedroom window. He quickly moves back. I get into the car and wind down the window, reverse out of the drive, and take one more look up at his bedroom. He appears, so I put my hand up to wave at him; he raises his hand and waves back. I smile and drive off.

My weekend floats by on a cloud of sweet delights. I'm not sure if it's to do with getting intimate with Simon after years of holding him in my heart as my teenage crush, and making my fantasy become a reality, but I'm savouring every moment, reliving the act, apart from the bit at the end. Even the irony of me driving away with him standing at his bedroom window was the icing on the cake.

My working week is much the same and, come Friday, when I meet up with the girls after work, we have a good laugh when we hark back to the last time we met and had dinner at Mo's Kitchen. I tell them of my encounter with James when he dropped off my picnic basket and the letter from David. "Aw, Rache, why not give him another chance?" Naomi says. "After all, he has been trying to contact you to apologise. He could've been a right coward and just left it; he must really like you," she concludes, with a sad downward smile.

"Okay, Nolene, less of the dramatics," I say, as we all have a chuckle. "Please remember, I did step into his vomit and go sliding across the bathroom floor. I could've slipped and cracked my head open on the sink, then where would I have been?"

"Okay, Raquel, less of the dramatics," Harriet quips, laughing.

"Touché," Naomi adds.

"Okay, okay," I reply, in defeat. "So, I've got something else to tell you," I say, smiling smugly.

"Ooh, go on," Harriet says.

"Well, do you remember Simon? Lived across the road from me when we were kids. John Taylor lookalike," I say.

Harriet nods her head and Naomi says, "Yes, we all had a massive crush on him."

"Yes, well, he came back home a couple of weeks ago and..." I continued telling them the story of my dalliance with Simon, and when I got to the bit at the end with the sweat dripping on my face, I could see the corners of Harriet's mouth turning up, ready to start laughing. "Nooo, what a shame, he was so gorgeous," Naomi says.

"Yes, but, Nomes, Mum told me the following morning that Tina had found inappropriate messages and pictures from other women on his phone, so bit of a sleaze really."

We finish our drinks and call it a night, and walk out onto Peascod Street, the sun is still shining, and we make our way down towards the flat when suddenly I hear someone shout out my name. We all turn around and watch David half-running towards us. He looks a little overwhelmed by the time he reaches us, and also a little out of breath. "Hi," I say.

"Hi," he replies, "I saw you coming out of The Drinking Ole and..." He pauses, catching his breath.

"Harriet, Naomi, this is David," I say. He says hello and shakes their hands. He looks very smart in a dark blue suit and lilac-coloured shirt. "You look very smart," I say.

"Yes, I just had an appointment with a client," he says.

"So, this is the infamous David. We've heard a lot about you," Harriet says with her trademark smile. She turns to me and says, "We'll catch up next week, Rache. Lovely to put a face to a name, David." Naomi kisses me and says goodbye as Harriet pulls her away.

"Your friends seem nice," David says, blushing a little.

"Yes, they are."

"You got your picnic basket back okay?" he asks.

"Yes, I did thanks, and thank you for the Champagne and gift card but you shouldn't have," I reply, looking at him blankly.

"Yes, I should. I should have done a lot of things, Rachel, that I didn't, like making sure that James had booked two rooms, not getting carried away with drinking too much and then throwing up – which I'm most ashamed of – and not being able to clean it up. I, er—"

"You forgot about the part where you were slumped on top of me when I was asleep," I interject.

"Yes, yes, I'm sorry, I had no idea where I was, all I know is that I needed to lie down and... Look, Rachel, I have no excuse for what I did that night, all I can say is that it will never happen again and offer you my sincerest apologies for my disgraceful behaviour." He pauses, and then asks, "May I take you for a drink, er, or a coffee?"

"I've had hell of a week, David, with work, so maybe another time." All I can think of is picking up some cod and chips on the way home and devouring them in the peace and quiet of the flat.

"Do you mean that?" he says.

"What?" I reply.

"Another time. You're not just saying that to get rid of me and then I'll never hear from you again?" he says, eager to close the deal.

"Look, how about sometime this weekend, send me a message and I'll see if I'm free," I say, abruptly, desperate for a wee.

"Okay, great, will do," he says, his eyes lighting up.

"Okay, see you," I say as I turn and walk down the street, heading to the chippy.

"Okay, bye, Rachel," I hear him say as I'm walking away.

I place my order of cod and chips and stand to the side, smiling to myself, remembering the time I was here with Luca and his terrible flatulence. My name gets called out and I pick up my warm paper parcel and rush home. After eating, I pour myself a glass of wine and check my phone. There's a message from Naomi asking what happened with David. I give her a quick call and tell her that I'll be meeting up with him over the weekend. "He looked very nice, a bit shorter than I imagined but seemed like a genuine sort," she says.

"Yes, I must admit he did seem sincere in his apology, I'll see what happens when we meet up, Nomes."

"Anyway, I wanted to remind you that it's Harry's birthday in a couple of weeks and Vince is organising a riverboat shuffle from Windsor promenade," she says.

"Yes, I hadn't forgotten, Nomes, is it a big one? I can't remember."

"Um, I don't think so. Anyway, he's sent us an email with all the details and told me to remind you that you're not to be planning any dates for that night."

"Okay, sure," I say, laughing. We hang up and I get back to my wine and check my email for the invite and mark it in my diary.

The following day, I receive a text message from David asking if I'm free on Sunday for an afternoon walk. I text back saying yes and we arrange for him to come by at 3pm. I decide to give him the benefit of the doubt, to listen to what he has to say and to respond truthfully. If I choose not to see him again after our walk, well, at least I can say I tried.

I wake up early on Sunday and go for a run, after which I get work clothes organised for the week and then get myself ready for my walk with David. He arrives on time and when I open the front door, he's standing there with a cool box and my picnic blanket. "Hi," I say, looking at the cool box, the blanket and then back at him.

"Hi, Rachel, I found your blanket in the boot of my car and then thought I'd put a little something together for us," he says, looking a tad uncertain as to what my response will be.

"I guess the walk is off, then," I reply, smiling.

"No, we can still go for a walk, I'll just carry this—" he says.

"No, it's fine, I went for a run this morning anyway," I interject.

We chit-chat on our way to The Long Walk; it's a little overcast but it's a warm day, and we find a quiet spot under a tree not far from the castle. I help him lay the blanket down. He opens the cool box and pulls out the bottle of red wine that I bought him for his birthday. "I thought it was only fair that I share this with you seeing as it's a nice one," he says as he takes a couple of plastic wine glasses out of the cool box and passes them to me.

"Thanks, that's kind of you," I reply.

"Well, I sort of thought that if you decide to never see me again after today, then at least I've had the pleasure of sharing this expensive wine with you, and I won't feel so bad. I mean, I will feel bad if you never want to see me again," he says.

I start to laugh. "Yes, I think I know what you're trying to say, David."

He laughs back. "I opened it a couple of hours ago to let it breathe," he says, as he pulls the cork out. I hold up the glasses as David pours the wine, and we both enjoy the delicious aroma enticing us before taking a sip. "It's very nice indeed," he says, taking another sip.

"Yes, shame we have to drink it from a plastic glass," I say, chuckling, as I take another sip.

"Sorry, my bad," he says.

"It's okay, I'm only messing," I jump in.

David unpacks the cool box and says, "I haven't made anything, Rachel, it's all shop-bought, so I hope that's okay with you."

"Yes, that's fine, I wasn't expecting this, so it's a nice treat. Also, I've just noticed the selection of cheeses and Comte and Manchego are favourites of mine, so I'm happy," I reply.

His smile widens, and he says, "Well, I've done something right so far, then."

The rest of the afternoon slips by with us both enjoying the mini picnic, the wine, and the lazy Sunday afternoon together. After making a huge dent in the cheese and the baguette, David addresses the elephant in the room and talks about why he got into such a state on his birthday. I listened to him tell me that James had bought along a bottle of malt whisky and after the pub had called last orders, they all went back to his and Wendy's room for a nightcap and just carried on drinking. Once he'd finished talking, he looked over at me. I didn't know how to react, so I thought it only fair to tell him how his behaviour made me feel, and once I'd finished talking he said, "So where do we go from here, Rachel?"

"I'm not sure, but I'm glad we've spoken," I reply.

"Okay, I just want you to know that I like you and hope you give me the chance to redeem myself. If you decide to never see me again then I'll understand and wish you all the best," he says, reaching for the bottle of wine and topping up our glasses.

We sit in silence, taking in the late afternoon sunshine and after a while I look at him and say, "I'm reading this book which is all about living in the present moment, not looking back to the past or even looking forward to the future, so I'm willing to give you a chance, David, to give us a chance, to see where this goes."

"Thank you, Rachel," he says, nodding and smiling at me. He pours out the remaining wine and we clink glasses and enjoy the rest of the Châteauneuf-du-Pape. Once we've finished, we pack away the picnic and make our way back towards the castle. After a short while David takes hold of my hand; he seems lighter in his demeaner and when we reach the flat he asks if I'm free to meet in the week for dinner, to which I accept. He then kisses me on the cheek, and we say goodbye. I watch him walk away and as I pop the key in the front door, he turns around, smiling and gives me a wave. I wave back and enter the flat feeling pleased that I gave him the opportunity to take responsibility for his actions; ordinarily I wouldn't have bothered to give him any more of my time, not even to apologise. So, it seems the quest has found me examining and improving aspects of myself that I never thought I would ever compromise on.

My week starts off on a high note and on Tuesday, I receive a message from David with an invitation for dinner on Saturday at 6pm. I accept, and on Friday when I meet up with the girls, they're eager to know what transpired. I tell them about the mini picnic, his apology, and our upcoming dinner date. "Well, I'm glad you're giving him another chance, Rache, he seemed like a nice guy," Naomi says.

"Yes, a bit too nice, I hope he has a bit more to him, otherwise you'll get bored with him," Harriet says.

"Yes, I agree on both counts, I've got three months left of the quest, so let's see how long this one lasts, shall we?" I say, with a wry smile.

"Have you asked him to accompany you to Harry's birthday?" Naomi asks.

"No, I've decided not to, Nomes, it's only a week away and I just want to have fun without having to babysit him," I say, with a chuckle. "Besides, I'd like to get to know him a bit better before I unleash you lot on him." I pause for a moment and think maybe that's not such a bad idea, seeing as I met his friends on his birthday, let's see how he copes when it's his turn. "I've changed my mind! I'll see how our dinner date goes and if all goes well, I'll invite him. I had to endure a whole day and evening with his friends, he can enjoy an evening with mine," I conclude, emphatically.

"We promise we'll be gentle with him, Rache," Harriet says, laughing.

I send Vince a message the next day saying that I may be bringing a plus-one to Harry's birthday party. He's intrigued to know more, so I call him and give him a brief rundown which he actually doesn't need as Naomi has already filled him in with all the news. "What sort of man can't clean up his own vom? Poor you, Rache, sliding across that bathroom floor." He then starts singing a line from Shania Twain's song 'That Don't Impress Me Much' and starts laughing, I can't help but laugh too and after we hang up, I slowly start getting ready for my date with David. My mind is now transfixed on singing 'That Don't Impress Me Much' on a continuous loop, until, at 6pm, when the door buzzes, I snap out of it. I pick up the phone and tell David I'm on my way down, and take one more look at myself in the bathroom mirror. I'm wearing my black halter neck dress, black strappy heels and I take my blue denim jacket and slip it on as I make my way down the stairs.

When I open the door I'm presented with a huge bouquet of flowers. "Wow!" I say, smiling. "They're beautiful. I wasn't expecting this, I would've buzzed you up. Thank you, David." I make a U-turn and head back upstairs, David follows. I open the door and we both enter the flat. "Hello," I say, taking the bouquet from him.

"Hi," he replies, with a big smile.

"Thank you again," I say, blushing a little as I retrieve a vase and half fill it with water.

"My pleasure," he says, looking around the flat.

"So, this is my one-bedroom flat; you've been in before, though," I say.

"Yes, we had a drink out on the balcony," he replies.

"Well, feel free to have a look around, but I warn you now, the bedroom is a right mess."

He laughs and wanders around, popping his head in the bathroom, bedroom and then walking over and looking out at the balcony. "It's really cute, Rachel, it suits you," he says.

"Cute!" I say, laughing. "What, like a puppy?" He bursts out laughing.

Once I finish arranging the flowers in the vase, we make our way out and walk up Peascod Street and make a right at the top. We walk along until he stops at The Regal, which is a lovely posh hotel that I've never been to before so I'm excited when we walk up the steps and enter through the revolving doors. The hotel is very grand and opulent with crystal chandeliers, I feel a little underdressed in my denim jacket, so I take it off as we make our way to the restaurant where the maître d' shows us to our table. "Rachel, you look lovely," David says, as we take our seats.

"Thank you," I reply. "I've always wanted to come here but never had an occasion to." The waiter arrives and leaves us with the menus and wine list. David asks me if I'd like some Champagne and I respond, in a plummy accent, "Yes, of course, darling, would be rude not to." I look up from the menu at David and start giggling, he joins in and when the waiter returns, he takes our drinks order. "So, have you been here before?" I ask.

"No, like you, I've walked past it a hundred times and have always wanted to but never had a reason or a special occasion to warrant a visit," he says, just as the waiter returns with a bottle of Champagne.

"So, is this a special occasion?" the waiter asks, as he takes the foil off and pops the cork.

"Yes," I reply, much to the surprise of David, "it's our anniversary." I stretch my arm across the table towards David, who plays along, holding my hand tenderly trying not to give the game away.

The waiter finishes pouring the Champagne into the flutes and places the bottle in the standing ice bucket and says, "Happy anniversary." Then leaves us to our deceitfulness. Once he's out of sight, I start to chuckle, and we take our flutes and say happy anniversary to each other and take a sip.

"You're so bad, Rachel!"

"I know, I'm sorry, I just couldn't help it, maybe we might get a free drink or something," I say, giggling away, feeling a little naughty for telling a white lie. David laughs and we exchange a moment of unbridled happiness.

We place our food order; I decide to go for the pear, blue cheese, and walnut salad to start and the trio of salmon for my main, and David opts for the duck pate followed by the fillet of beef. The evening is wonderful, from the Champagne to the delicious food and the ambience. When the waiter arrives with the dessert menu, I'm happy not to indulge, however, David orders the tarte Tatin and when the waiter returns with his dessert, he also places two glasses of complimentary Champagne and a small plate of chocolate truffles on the table and wishes us a happy anniversary again. "Oh, how lovely, thank you so much," I say, as he stands beside the table, smiling, asking us if we'd like anything else before leaving us to our freebie.

"Well, Rachel," David says raising his flute, "here's to you." We clink glasses. When the bill arrives, David refuses to entertain the idea of me contributing. "I invited you to dinner, Rachel," he says.

"Well, thank you, it's been such a treat to come here, David."

"You're welcome. Besides, it's not going to look good if we go Dutch on our anniversary, is it?" he says, softly chuckling.

Once David has settled the bill, we leave arm in arm, strolling back down Peascod Street, our arms still looped until we reach the flat. I open the door and we make our way up the stairs. I'm not sure what to do. I don't want to sleep with David out of obligation, just because he's paid a huge amount of money on dinner, but I do want to just to get over the slight awkwardness that still remains between us from his birthday. "Would you like a drink, David?" I ask.

"I'd love to, but I'm going to have to decline. I've got an early start; I'm doing an off-road bike ride with James," he says, shaking his head slightly and rolling his eyes. "Something I could do without now I'm standing here with you, but it was organised weeks ago."

Whew! I think, *that's sorted that out, then.* I feel relieved, and I smile at him. He steps in closer to me and waits, not sure of himself, so I take the lead and pull him in towards me; after that, he needs no prompting. He kisses me, it's soft, gentle and feels different from the first time we kissed. I place my arms around him and kiss him back, I can feel our excitement build but it comes to an abrupt halt as he pulls back and says, "As much as I'd like to, Rachel, I don't want to rush anything."

"Yes, of course, I agree," I say. "I'd love to, too, seeing as it's our anniversary and all, but..." We both start laughing which breaks the nervous tension still lingering and we head downstairs. I open the door and we kiss goodbye.

He turns and says, "Happy anniversary, Mrs. Andrews." I blow him a kiss and watch him walk down the street before closing the door and running up the stairs, feeling content with my date with David Andrews, and for the first time in a long while, think that he may be 'the one'.

It's still early, but I start getting ready for bed, excited for the next time we meet. By the time I crawl into bed, David has already messaged me, thanking me for a wonderful night. I message back saying the same and wish him luck on his bike ride before drifting off to sleep. When I awake the next morning, I think of David on his bike up a mountain with James. I make a cuppa and grimace thinking back to my bike ride with David and then take delight in enjoying my lazy Sunday, before forcing myself out for a run and picking up a birthday card for Harry on the way back.

Later that evening, whilst preparing dinner, I receive a call from David. "Hello, Mr Andrews," I answer.

"Hi, Rachel, how are you?"

"Yes, I'm good, how was your bike ride?" I enquire.

"Yes, very good, James has just left; I'm a little battered and bruised but all okay otherwise. Anyway, I just called to see how you are," he says. I tell David of my lazy Sunday and ask him if he's free on Saturday to be my plus-one to Harry's party. He happily accepts, and we make plans to catch up in the week. When I hang up the phone I get that warm fuzzy feeling and continue with making dinner, all the while thinking of him.

Midweek at work, I receive a message from David, asking if I'm free to meet later that day. I text back saying that I am, and for him to pop over to mine for dinner, which he agrees to. Then I go into panic mode about what to cook, whether the flat is clean and then I stop myself from having a meltdown when I recall that, a few weeks earlier, I stepped into this man's vomit, and nothing can be as bad as that. On my way home from work, I pick up a few bits and make a tomato sauce to go with linguine and prawns. I have a quick tidy up, open a bottle of red and 10 minutes later, David arrives, punctual as ever. I buzz him up and open the door to the flat; he enters with a bottle of rosé in hand. "Hi," he says, as he walks in and nervously stands watching me in the kitchen.

"Hi, David, come in," I reply, walking over to him. He gives me a peck on the lips, smiles, and hands me the bottle of wine.

"Ooh, thank you, this is lovely and chilled," I remark, as I retrieve two wine glasses and leave David to open the bottle whilst I busy myself slicing the baguette and taking the antipasti out of the fridge. David hands me a glass of wine and we head out on the balcony.

"Rachel, you shouldn't have gone to so much trouble, we could've just got a takeaway," he says, popping an olive into his mouth.

"It's no trouble, I'm only making a prawn linguine, if that's okay with you?"

"Yes, that sounds lovely," he says, beaming.

"Yes, all the carbs tonight; bread and pasta," I laugh. "And I hope you're okay with lots of garlic and a little chilli," I say.

"Mm, yes, I guess I better kiss you now then," he says, leaning over. I move toward him and reciprocate the sentiment; we kiss longer than I anticipated and only break away when his phone rings. He looks down and says, "It's James."

"Take it," I say, as I get up and pop to the bathroom. On my return, I find David leaning against the kitchen counter. "That was quick," I say, looking at him quizzically.

"I didn't take it... He interrupted our..." But before he could finish, I had already made my way over to him and planted my lips back onto his; we kiss each other soft and lovingly. I want to take him to the bedroom but want him to initiate. He stops, and he looks at me as if he's reading my mind and says, "Shall we get more comfortable?"

I nod and lead him into the bedroom, where we slowly take each other's clothes off, down to our underwear, whilst still kissing. There's a gentleness between us; the warm and sensual feel of our bodies softly reacting to each kiss, touch, and stroke. I climax during foreplay with David gently sliding his fingers around my clitoris and his tongue sweetly licking my nipples. When he enters me, the rush of exhilaration sweeps through me. The gentle rocking motion of our bodies in sync, the hardness inside of me, awakens the lustful animal in me. I breathlessly whisper his name as he pushes in quicker and more forcefully, until he lays on top of me, the weight of his body stuck to mine like glue, the pulsing inside me as his manhood retreats. He props himself up on his forearms and looks at me and we both smile and then inadvertently burst out laughing, any remaining tension between us escaping. "Are you okay?" he asks, as he slides off me and over to one side. I nod as we face each other and start kissing again; I'm easily aroused when he lightly strokes my breasts, and sigh with pleasure. "Rachel, you are very sexy, you have an amazing body."

"Thank you, but I'm sure my cellulite and wobbly bits would disagree with you," I say, my face snuggling up into the crook of his neck as I nibble on his earlobe.

"Your cellulite and wobbly bits can disagree as much as they like, I love them too," he says, chuckling.

After a little more kissing, we get dressed and I make my way to the bathroom to freshen up. David retrieves the wine glasses and tops them up whilst I continue with preparing dinner. "May I do anything to help?"

he asks, as he brings in the bread and antipasti from outside and pops it on the kitchen counter.

"Yes, you can put some music on and then sit down and relax." He walks over to the hi-fi and presses play on the CD. Teddy Pendergrass kicks in and I smile over at him as he makes his way back to the counter, takes a seat on a stool and watches me. Once the tomato sauce, linguine and prawns have been tossed together, I serve up in bowls, and we head back out to the balcony. Maybe it's the music or our earlier act of love that has softened the edges, but the easiness between us now is clearly evident; even eating the pasta with sauce slopping around our faces is not the most graceful exhibition but we're both relaxed enough with each other not to feel self-conscious about it.

Once we've finished, David is quick to help with the dishes and we take our wine and settle on the sofa. He asks about Harry's birthday party on Saturday. "It's a riverboat shuffle, leaving from Windsor promenade at 7pm," I reply.

"Okay, is there a dress code?" he asks, sounding a little nervous.

"Not that I'm aware of," I reply.

"Shall we go for a bite to eat beforehand?" he asks.

"Hmm, yes, why not," I say.

Once we've finished the wine, David makes a move to leave. I walk him down the stairs to the front door and we embrace each other tightly. He whispers in my ear, "Thank you, Rachel."

I whisper back, "You're welcome." Our lips connect for the final time.

I go to bed feeling sexy about my wobbly bits and must've fallen asleep tout de suite with a smile on my face, but am awoken with the sound of buzzing. I frantically jump out of bed and notice that it's only 7am and pick up the entry phone. "Hello."

"Hi, Rachel, it's David." He sounds panicked. I buzz him up and then unlock the door to the flat and he rushes up and says, "Is my phone here?"

"Um, I don't know, when did you last use it?" I ask as he looks around the kitchen. I walk over to the balcony and see it sitting on the table. "It's here, David," I say, opening the door, picking it up, and handing it to him.

"Thank God!" he says. "I thought I must've dropped it on my way home last night." He looks up at me relieved. "Did I wake you?"

"Well, yes," I reply, as I realise I'm in my negligee. "Oh, I must look a right mess," I say, patting down my hair.

"You look beautiful," he says, laughing.

"The laughing is not convincing me, David," I say, giving him the look and then laughing too. He's already dressed in his suit for work, looking and smelling lovely and fresh. "You're up early," I say, walking to the bedroom to retrieve my dressing gown.

"Yes, I've got a meeting in Oxford at 9:30," he says, following me into the bedroom, "but I guess I could spare a few minutes." He takes hold of me from behind and kisses my neck. I turn around and he takes his suit jacket off and lays it down on the chair.

"David, I haven't even brushed my teeth," I say, as he starts to kiss me.

"Your morning breath is fine," he says, slipping the straps of the negligee off my shoulders. It falls to the floor, and he looks at my body and continues to kiss me. Caressing my breasts, he unbuckles his belt as I stroke his penis; he's so hard and groans in a desperate yearning. I sit back on the bed and watch him hurriedly take his clothes off, delicately laying them on the chair and he climbs on top of me, kissing me as we dry hump for a few moments before we peel off our underwear and fuck. There's no gentleness like the day before; this is a raw longing desire to feel that instant pleasure, it's a hard, thrusting, pounding joy that excites us both. I don't want it to end but I know it will soon, so my body enjoys every moment, and once David has made his deposit, he looks down at me and says, "Sorry."

"Why?" I reply. "I loved every minute of it." I start laughing.

"Yes, it probably was only about a minute," he says, laughing too and then continues to kiss me. "Rachel, I have to get on the road."

"Yes, I know, just come round here, use me and leave," I say, as I watch him dress.

I slip my dressing gown on, and David finishes getting ready and pops to the loo. I pick up his mobile phone and when he returns from the bathroom, he kisses me. "I'll make it up to you," he says. I hand him his phone and he's gone, shouting out bye on his way down the stairs.

Well, that was an unexpected start to the day, I think as I take a shower and get ready for work. I'm ravenous, so I make some toast and a cuppa whilst preparing my packed lunch. Work floats by in a daze, a transfixed smile on my face. Kevin comes into the office after lunch and takes one look at me and blurts out, "Good God! What's up with you?"

"What?" I reply.

"You have a look of an air stewardess with a deranged smile plastered on her face," he says, scoffing.

"Nothing," I reply. "Well, I think I might have a proper boyfriend, Kev," I say, excitedly.

"Oh, thank heavens for that," he says. "Come on, tell Uncle Kev all about it," he continues, rubbing his hands together.

"No, I'm not telling you anything yet, you'll only jinx it," I say, as I turn away and get back to work.

"Okay, suit yourself, but I need a good laugh, so whenever you're ready, let me know," he says.

On my way home from work, I receive a message from David saying hello and what a beautiful start to his day it was, and we arrange a time to meet early on Saturday. My Friday night catch-up with the girls is cancelled, seeing as we'll be seeing each other for Harry's party, so I have a quiet night in and organise an outfit for the following night. I pull out my black faux leather skinny jeans with a black silk halter neck top, dark blue faux fur jacket and heels. I have a relaxing soak in the bath, put on a face mask, and once I've scrubbed and exfoliated every inch of my body, I have an early night.

Saturday morning after my usual routine of run, breakfast and tidy-up, I start getting ready for Harry's party. I decide to wear my hair up in a loose ponytail with a few strands teased out around my face. David arrives at 5pm, so I make my way down and when I open the door, I find him dressed in black jeans and a white t-shirt, holding a black blazer. "Wow!" he remarks.

"Wow, yourself," I reply, as he kisses me lightly on the lips. We walk up Peascod Street and he takes my hand to steady me; heels and cobbles do not go well together. "Do you fancy Greek?" I ask.

"I fancy you," he says, grinning. I shake my head, smiling back and rolling my eyes playfully, and he starts laughing. "Yes, that sounds great."

"Okay, there's a restaurant that's close to the promenade that we could go to," I add. He nods and squeezes my hand tighter; he seems different, more confident with a spring in his step, eager to get to the restaurant. Or maybe it's nerves, seeing as he'll be meeting my friends properly tonight.

We arrive at the restaurant and quickly peruse the menu, ordering a selection of small plates to share, some bread and wine. Our bottle of red arrives shortly after with the flat bread and houmous, and not long after, the remaining plates descend upon the table. I finish eating, feeling satiated and leave the last pieces of flat bread for David. With half an hour to go before meeting up, I pop to the toilets to freshen up and on my way back, pay the bill before returning to the table. We both sit back and finish the wine, and when David visits the bathroom, I reapply my lipstick and get ready to leave. "Shall we make a move?" I say, standing up, picking up my clutch, jacket, and Harry's birthday card.

"Yes," David replies, taking his glass and finishing his wine. We make our way out and walk across the road towards the promenade; I can see a throng of people waiting by a boat, slowly shuffling on. Suddenly, David shouts out, "We didn't pay!"

"Oh no!" I react, looking shocked and placing a hand over my mouth. He turns and starts walking back to the restaurant. "David, it's okay, I paid already," I shout out, smiling at him.

"You did?" I nod. "Thank you, Rachel, I wasn't expecting you to pay, I was..."

"It's okay, and you're welcome. Besides, after that beautiful dinner at the hotel last week, I'm pretty sure it was my turn to treat you." He kisses me gently on the lips and looks at me tenderly, his blue eyes wide, staring straight into mine. I become a little nervous and blink. "Come on, we better get on that boat," I say, averting my attention from his gaze. It's too soon for me to hear those three little words, especially since I'm not ready to reciprocate just yet, if that's what his gaze was leading to.

We walk onto the promenade to find Harry and Vince standing by the boat, welcoming all their guests onboard and as me and David approach, Vince shouts out, "Rachel plus one, make your way to the front of the queue please." Then he shrieks out with laughter, blows me a kiss and resumes his meet and greet. Me and David walk to the end of the small queue, chuckling. I look across and see Harriet and Naomi all aboard with a glass of Champagne in hand.

As we shuffle up to the gangplank, I introduce David to Harry and Vince. "This is David," I say to them both, "and this is the birthday boy, Harry, and this is Vince." They all shake hands.

"Happy Birthday," David says. He seems a little nervous.

"Plus-one, we will be grilling you later," Vince says, shrieking with laughter again.

I hug him and then give Harry a kiss. "Happy birthday, darling."

"Thank you, Rache." David holds his hand out to me as we walk onboard and are greeted with a waiter offering us a glass of Champagne. We mingle through the crowd, saying hello to familiar faces and manage to wind our way through to the back of the boat where the girls are stood.

"Hello, Rache," John says, the first one to see me.

"Hello, John, she let you out again?" I say, motioning over to Harriet, and then introduce David to everyone. "You've met Harriet and Naomi, and this is John and Neil, their better halves," I say, smiling. We make small talk until the boat starts slowly moving off; there's a whoop from the crowd and Vince takes the mic.

"Hello party people, we are gathered here today to celebrate the wedding of, oops, sorry, wrong speech." Everyone starts laughing and he continues. "Harry's birthday, don't ask him his age but he's forty something, not quite hit the fifth floor but getting very close." There's another cheer. "So please enjoy the music, the drinks, the food, and if you can't swim and need a lifejacket, please leave now." We all cheer and laugh, and the music starts with Harry's favourite song, 'Born to be Wild'.

David holds my hand and whispers in my ear, "I really like your friends, Rachel."

"Yes, so do I," I reply, looking at him and smiling.

Vince arrives with Harry following on behind and they join the group. We all clink glasses and wish Harry a happy birthday. Vince looks over at David and says, "So, this is David, we need to know a few things about you." He then changes his voice into a Gestapo and says, "Who are you? Where are you from? And, most importantly, what are your intentions with our fräulein?" Vince screams with laughter, and snorts; none of us can keep a straight face. And then in his normal voice, Vince says, "It's nice to see Rachel with someone for a change." He gives me a wink. Harry saunters off, singing, mingling with the rest of his friends. David, John, and Neil start chatting, giving us girls and Vince a chance to catch up in our own little circle.

"So, how are things going?" Naomi asks, looking at me.

"Yes, really good," I reply.

"Rachel, I must admit that you would not have entertained the idea of seeing him, so he must be doing something right," Harriet adds.

"I was just about to say, in my little intro, that if anyone needed to throw up, to do it overboard and not in the loo but I thought better of it," Vince says.

"Oh, thank God you didn't, Vince, I would've cringed," I say.

"He seems nice, Rache, not what I would've picked for you, but..." Vince says, shrugging his shoulders. "Okay, I'm off to mingle, ladies." With that, Vince minces off.

We all catch up with each other's news and I tell them about dinner at the hotel. "Oh, Rachel, it's so good to see you happy," Naomi says.

We both look over at Harriet. "Yes, yes, I'm happy that you're happy, but I was so enjoying our Friday night *Jackanory* sessions; those were the only times I got to have a proper good laugh," she says, sulking.

"It's okay, Hattie, I'm sure I'll have some funny stories for you again," I say, rolling my eyes and chuckling.

"Yes, I'm going to miss them too, but look, this is good news, the quest is finished. You've found him, Rache!" Naomi shrieks. No one hears over the music, thankfully.

"Yes, maybe I have," I say, looking across at David, who's engrossed in conversation with John and Neil. He notices me looking over at him and I smile, and he winks back. "Although, there is still two months before my 40th, so anything could happen."

We finish our drinks and head to the bar, stopping along the way to say hello to mutual friends. After picking up our drinks, we head back to the men, who are happy to see that we've brought beer for them.

David gives me a kiss. "Well, I didn't get a kiss!" Naomi says, looking over at Neil.

"Oh God! Look what you've started, mate," Neil says to David, laughing, and then gives Naomi a peck.

David turns to me, and I ask him if he's okay. "Yes, yes, absolutely fine, Rachel," he says, giving me that dreamy look again. Then suddenly the music changes and 'Dancing Queen' starts to play. I look across at the girls; we all burst out laughing and start singing as Vince struts over to us and takes centre stage, dancing in the middle of the circle. We're all dancing and singing; poor John, Neil and David shuffling nervously back, hoping that Vince doesn't pull them in the middle to dance.

An hour later, Vince announces that food is being served inside. Me and David hang back and look out at the houses lining the Thames. He stands behind me with his arms around my waist. The sun is setting but it's still warm, the music has mellowed, and the evening has a romantic feel to it. "Rachel," David whispers in my ear.

"Yes," I reply, thinking *oh God, he's not going to say what I think he's going to say.* "I really do like... Your friends." I burst out laughing in relief and turn to him. His face looks puzzled from my reaction.

"That's great! I'm really glad you do; I think they like you too," I say, just as Harriet and John return holding a plate of food, shortly followed by Naomi and Neil.

"You better grab a plate before it all goes, Rache," Naomi says, as she arrives back.

"We had a bite to eat beforehand, Nomes," I reply.

"Yes, so did we," she says with a chortle.

We make our way inside and pick up a plate. I go for the salad whilst David fills his plate with everything on offer. We manage to find an empty bench to sit down and eat. "I feel a bit naughty eating a second dinner," I say, as I look to the side at him and watch him take a huge bite of the chicken drumstick and nod in agreement. I burst out laughing.

"What?" he mumbles, trying not to laugh and spit out any chicken.

"You know, this is a good idea – a boat party – I did think of it for my 40th," I say, sighing.

"What are you planning to do for it, Rache?"

"Aww, that's the first time you've called me 'Rache'," I say, smiling. "I'm planning to have it at Mum and Dad's, in the garden. Music, dancing, food and Champagne; what more could a girl ask for!"

"Are they happy with that?" he asks.

"Yes, they suggested it; they want to be with me celebrating and I want them to be part of it too. Besides, they know most of my friends and nothing shocks them anymore."

He looks at me and smiles. "They sound really cool."

"Yes, you know what, they are," I add, feeling proud that my parents are relaxed, easy-going, and mostly that they let me be who I want to be, and there's no judgement. And even if I didn't find my perfect imperfect soulmate, then I know that they'd just want me to be happy. I sit in silence for a moment, not thinking about a thing, feeling peaceful, and then I look around at the smiling faces, people dancing, eating, drinking, and talking. I look over at my friends and then at David, and I feel content.

"Rachel!" I hear David's voice.

"Sorry, what?" I mumble.

"I was just checking to see if you were okay; I was chatting away to you, I thought I must've bored you into silence," he says with a chuckle.

"No, I just drifted off in my own thoughts for a moment, sorry, what were you saying?" I reply, giving him my full attention.

"It was nothing serious, Rache."

We join the others after we've finished eating and as the sun sets, the boat is all lit up and the music changes to a slower more romantic pace; a few couples are intertwined, their bodies gently swaying side to side. I look across to Vince and Harry dancing to their favourite slow song, Otis Reading's 'I've Been Loving

You Too Long' and smile at the tender way they're gazing at each other. I watch Harriet and John embrace and move rhythmically to the music, then me and Naomi both look behind us at Neil and David jabbering away, probably too engrossed to even notice that the ambience has shifted. We smile at each other, and Naomi says, "He's all right, Rache, he's not your usual strapping, drop-dead gorgeous manly man, and despite that initial hiccup, he seems to fit in well with us."

"Yes, Nomes, I do feel like maybe he's the one, but I don't want to rush into anything." I feel arms embrace me from behind and then Neil appears and takes Naomi by the hand to dance. I turn my head to the side and say, "I think you like it from behind, don't you?"

David bursts out laughing. "What?" I realise what I've said and turn to face him, and we both laugh, embracing one another.

"What I meant was..." I whisper in his ear.

"I know what you meant." He laughs again. He looks at me and says, "You really are something else, Rachel." He kisses me gently on the lips as we move to Otis, like we're the only ones on that boat.

When the boat arrives back to Windsor we all shuffle off, hugging, kissing, and saying our goodbyes. Me and David walk through the town centre, chatting and laughing along the way. It's only just gone 11pm and when we reach the flat, I unlock the front door and step inside, but David remains standing on the doorstep. "Are you not coming in?"

"Um, well it's late and—" he starts to say.

"Oh, I thought you'd be staying over," I butt in.

"Yes, that would be nice, but I don't have a toothbrush and..."

I look at him and smile. "I'm sure I have a spare toothbrush for you," I say, "but, if you'd rather not—"

Before I could finish, he steps inside, shuts the door, and kisses me. We make our way up and once inside, I ask if he'd like a cuppa. "Yeah, sure, if you're having one, I will," he says, looking over at me and smiling as he walks to the bathroom. I walk to the bedroom and kick off my heels, lower the blinds, pop the bedside lamp on and change into my joggers and a t-shirt and then make my way back to the kitchen to make the tea. David returns from the bathroom, kicks off his shoes and we settle on the sofa and pop the TV on. After finishing my tea and after endless yawning, I pop to the bathroom to get ready for bed. I manage to find a toothbrush in one of those airplane comfort kits and hand it to David. "Thank you, Rache," he says, as he takes the little bag and heads to the bathroom.

I turn off the TV and head to the bedroom. Taking off my joggers, I climb into bed and then remember the last time we spent the night in the same room. *I hope nothing like that occurs tonight*, I think to myself as

I apply my face cream. David returns and I watch him undress down to his boxer shorts; he climbs into bed, lies back and I snuggle my head in the crook of his neck.

"I had such a great time tonight, meeting your friends and—" Before he could finish I place my lips on his and we kiss. Exploring each other's mouths with our tongues, our hands stroking and touching in all the right places, we remove our underwear, and he lifts my t-shirt up and over my head and climbs on top of me. I part my legs as he moves down, kissing my nipples, his hands firmly holding my breasts as his tongue flicks up and down. I feel so aroused that I just want him inside me, then he moves lower down, and his tongue finds my wet clitoris.

I can't hold back and purr with pleasure, murmuring, "Oh David." His hands reach up and pinch my nipples as he goes down on me. With the light from the lampshade, I watch him excite me until I climax and as soon as I come, he enters me. Throbbing, hard, fast fucking. He kisses me and I can taste and smell me on his lips. He comes too soon but we are both satisfied, and he stays on top of me for a moment then props himself up on his elbows; we kiss, wanting more.

"Rachel, was that okay?"

"Yes, that was more than okay; that was... Mmm." He laughs and slides off me and I snuggle back into him and fall asleep.

I wake up needing to go for a wee, so I crawl out of bed trying not to make a sound, hoping that I haven't disturbed David. My sleep was restless as I'm not used to having another body in bed with me and will need to get used to it, I think to myself as I creep back into the bedroom and slide back under the covers. David stirs and opens his eyes. "Morning," I whisper, as our bodies lock in an embrace and we fall back to sleep.

I'm woken by David's hard penis pressed against my lower back. I reach my arm back to stroke his leg which instantly engages him, and he reaches his hand around to my breasts, softly stroking them. I can feel his mouth kissing my back, and I push my bottom out and grind against him, turning my head around to kiss him. His hand lowers to my vagina and he stimulates me. We resume our intimacy from a few hours earlier, and, post-coital, remain in bed, snoozing until the sound of rain against the window pane stirs us, and we get out of bed.

"This calls for a duvet day," I say, dragging the duvet off the bed. David smiles at me, watching my naked body stroll to the lounge, duvet following on behind. "Would you like tea, coffee or a shower, David?" I ask, as I walk back into the bedroom and put my dressing gown on.

"I guess I'll have a shower first, Rache," he says, as he retrieves his boxer shorts from the floor and pops his t-shirt on.

"Okay, I'll get you a towel."

We take turns to shower and then settle on the sofa with our tea and toast. Most of the day is spent lazing under the duvet in front of the TV; the rain is falling lightly now but neither of us are energised to do anything. The lack of sleep has rendered us immobile, and we only move off the sofa to make another cuppa or to prepare a late lunch, which I leave David to do. I assist as his sous chef as he prepares a veggie omelette and potato rösti. I'm pleasantly surprised with his effort and after lunch, the sofa beckons, and the remainder of the rainy summer day is spent under the duvet until late afternoon when David makes a move to leave. When the rain eases, we stand on the doorstep embracing. He whispers in my ear, "Are we official?"

"Official?" I whisper back, knowing full well what he's getting at.

"Yes, may I call you my girlfriend, Rachel?"

"Hmm, well, I'm not sure," I say, looking at him with a thoughtful expression. He squeezes my waist and starts to tickle me, and I start to laugh. "I guess you might have to," I whisper in his ear, and we kiss a final time before he leaves for home.

Part Two – My 40th

It's less than two months to go 'til my big four-zero, the end of the quest and the start of my new life of not being beholden to date every man that shows any interest. Me and David are officially a couple, and everything is all right with the world in Windsor. My birthday party plans are going well; Vince has taken charge of the music, Mum is happily organising the food, Dad is sorting out the garden and I'm stocking up on the alcohol. David is eager to help but I've told him that everything is covered, and I've asked him if he'd like to invite James and Wendy, too, as I want him to feel comfortable, especially seeing as he'll be meeting Mum and Dad for the first time.

Me and David settle into a comfortable routine of seeing each other once in the week after work and on the weekends if neither one of us has other plans with family or friends, tending to go to the pub, or a restaurant, walks in Windsor Great Park, cooking at home and once to a garden centre where he spent an hour looking at plants. The most exciting excursion was staying the night at a spa hotel, which was due to the gift card he had bought me weeks earlier.

So, during our spa break, we get to talking about holidays. I always go away on holiday after my birthday and this year I've planned to go back to Ibiza for a week to chill out on the beach, drink sangria, maybe take a trip on the boat to the hippy market, but basically to do absolutely nothing but eat seafood and swim. I haven't mentioned it to David, as it's too early in the relationship and holidays are always one of those times where it can make or break a relationship. We've only been seeing each other for a couple of months and going on holiday together can be a daunting experience; spending 24/7 with someone you hardly know – the full-on living and being together experience – can be a recipe for disaster. "Are you planning a summer holiday this year, Rache? I mean, I know you're busy with planning your 40th and that," he asks.

"Well, I was looking at going away after my birthday to Ibiza," I reply, as I make a move to relax in the hot tub.

"Oh, okay, who you going with?" he asks, as he sits down across from me.

"No one; everyone tends to have already been on their holidays by the time I go, although, a few years ago, the girls did come along to Ibiza with me, and then John and Neil ended up coming too, last minute. How about you?"

"I'm going away for a long weekend on a boys' holiday to Zante," he says, cringing.

"Aren't you a bit old for Zante? Isn't that where all the uni kids go for a bit of fun?" I say, teasing him.

"Um, I don't know, I didn't book it. James has organised it and I think there's about eight of us going," he says. "Well, if you'd like company in Ibiza, then I'd love to come too."

"Er, yeah sure, I guess so, I didn't ask you because I wasn't sure if we'd— "

"It's okay, Rache, I understand, we've only just started seeing each other and it's early on in the relationship," he jumps in.

"And we're still getting to know one another," I say, sinking down to my neck in the hot tub.

"Okay, then we better start looking at booking flights and a hotel and I promise to be on my best behaviour," he says, excitedly. *What does he mean by his best behaviour?* I think, as I sit up in the hot tub. Maybe he's referring to the way he behaved on his birthday. I don't ponder too deeply on it and get back to enjoying the spa.

David gets straight into booking our trip to Ibiza; he books car hire too, even though I tell him that I love taking the bus around the island, but he says he's happy to drive. We go holiday shopping together and I slowly start feeling a little more comfortable in our relationship, getting to know him, with his little quirks and his silly Mr Bean voice; it seems we don't really have a lot in common apart from our love of red wine and sex.

With the end of summer approaching, and a few weeks until my birthday, I'm making final preparations for the party. My anxiety levels are rising. Me and David are still together, although we may have hit a 'relation blip', I tell Naomi and Harriet when we get together for our Friday night drinks a couple of weeks before the party. "Why? What's happened, Rache?" Naomi asks.

"Well, nothing's happened, that's just it; we've only been seeing each other for a few months, and we should be in the honeymoon phase of the relationship, but I feel like we're at the slippers and cocoa stage."

Harriet bursts out laughing. "He doesn't seem to want to do anything exciting; we go out to the pub or to dinner and that's only because I've suggested it. He'd be happier if we stayed in and cooked or went out to a garden centre every Sunday. The most exciting thing we've done is going on the spa break for a night," I say, disheartened.

"You're still getting to know one another, Rache!" Naomi exclaims.

"Yes, I guess so, I just thought I'd have butterflies and have that longing to be with him, but I don't. I mean, the sex is great, but it feels like there's something missing."

I look over at Harriet, who smiles at me and says, "Rache, when you meet 'the one', you'll know, and so will he, and no matter what you do, whether it's going out or staying in, it won't matter a jot because everything will just click into place, and you'll not find yourself questioning whether he's the one or not." I nod and smile, acknowledging that what she's said is absolutely right.

"So, are you going to break up with him, Rache?" Naomi asks.

"Well, I'm not sure, Nomes, he's coming to my birthday party with his best friends, James and Wendy, and we're going on holiday the day after, so maybe I'll see how things go and decide when we get back from Ibiza."

"You'll know when you're together on holiday, Rache, spending all that time together will reveal all," Harriet says, winking at me. We finish our drinks and catch up on birthday talk, arranging to meet at Mum and Dad's the day before to get the garden party-ready.

The next two weeks are spent packing for Ibiza and organising an outfit for my 40th, which I've narrowed down to a dark blue halter neck lace bodycon dress, or black skinny jeans with a black off-the-shoulder top, dependant on weather and dance appropriateness. I'll take both outfits and decide on the day. Work keeps me busy during the day and the rest of the time is spent last-minute party shopping, dropping things off at Mum and Dad's and preparing as much as I can. I've not seen David for over a week since he went on his boys' holiday to Zante and when he returned home, he was unwell and was staying over with James and Wendy for a few days, which I found a bit strange but didn't question it. I'd been so consumed with my party prep anyhow that, when we spoke on the phone, and he said that he had booked The Regal for my birthday dinner the following Thursday I assumed all was well.

I spoke with Mum and Dad about David, telling them not to get too excited as we'd only been seeing one another for a few months and it's very early doors. They're eager to meet him but I'm having a few reservations now. Since coming back from his boys' holiday, he's been distant and when he calls me and makes arrangements to pick me up on Thursday for my birthday dinner, he sounds different.

Thursday – two days before my Party

The door buzzes at 6pm and I let David up; he walks into the flat carrying a big box adorned in gold gift wrap. "Hello, what could that be?" I ask excitedly, as he hands me the box and gives me a peck on the lips.

"You'll have to wait and see," he says, looking at me and smiling, all glowing and tanned after his trip to Zante.

"How are you? You're looking good," I say, picking up my clutch, keys, and jacket.

"Yes, I feel a lot better, thanks, I guess it was overdoing it on holiday which got the better of me," he says, looking at me sheepishly.

"Okay, you can tell me all about it on our way to the hotel," I say, making my way to the door.

David tells me of the drunken antics that went on in Zante; it all sounds very childish to me, but I don't react or express any emotion, even when he tells of how, one night, one of the guys threw up in the pool at the complex where they were staying. All the while, I'm thinking, *I hope it wasn't him.*

When we arrive at the hotel, we're shown to a table which has been decorated with a huge 40th birthday balloon. "Oh wow! Well, I'm certainly not going to forget this," I laugh, as we take our seats. "I cannot believe that you would do this to me, David!" I say, cringing.

"Well, you only turn 40 once, Rache," he says, laughing. I lean over and kiss him, saying thank you. Our waiter returns with a bottle of Champagne and proceeds to pop the cork and pour, wishing me a happy 40th birthday before leaving too.

"Oh, David, this is so lovely, thank you." We clink glasses.

"Happy Birthday, Rache." The first glass goes down far too quickly and when the waiter returns, he tops up our flutes and lays the napkin down on our laps. After a short while he returns with an amuse-bouche.

"Ooh, what's going on here, then?" I say, smiling at David as we tuck into the tiny morsels of food.

"You told me once what your favourite meal would be if you were stuck on a desert island," he says.

"Did I? How drunk was I?" I laugh.

"So, I have organised it for you," he says.

"Ooh, lobster? Caviar? It's got to be pizza, hmm." He shakes his head to all my guesses. "I know what it is, David."

"You do?" he says.

"Yes, but I'm not going to ruin the surprise," I say, then I pause. "But it's fish and chips!" I blurt out, laughing. He joins me in my laughter and when the waiter arrives to clear our plates, he promptly sets down the fish and chips.

"I remember you saying one night that you would be happy with a bag of fish and chips and a glass of Champagne," he says.

"And you're right, this is perfect. Thank you, I love it," I say, picking up a chip and biting it in half. After we've eaten and our plates are cleared, I'm further surprised with the waiter bringing over a plate with a chocolate torte sitting atop, singing 'Happy Birthday'. It was all a little embarrassing, especially when a few of the other diners sang along too, but I went along with it. Me and David shared the dessert and on leaving, I untied my balloon and we walked back to the flat. I opened the front door and stepped inside, but David remained standing on the doorstep.

"Are you not coming in?"

"Um, no, not tonight. I've got a few things to do, which includes packing for Ibiza," he says.

I step back out and embrace him, we kiss, and I whisper, "I wanted to thank you properly, it feels like ages since we've—"

"Yes, you can thank me properly when we're on holiday," he cuts in, then he kisses me on the tip of my nose. "I'll see you on Saturday. Oh yes, I forgot to mention, is it okay for James' sister to come, too? She's been staying over at theirs; she's just broken up with her fiancé and ..."

"Yes, of course it is," I reply.

"Great! Okay, goodnight, Rache."

"Bye and thanks again," I shout out as he walks away. I walk me and my birthday balloon up to the flat, feeling a little miffed; in my head this was not how it was meant to play out. Me and David should be having sex right now but we're not; he seemed to be here in body, but his mind was elsewhere. I'm left feeling horny and confused. *I guess I'll have to park it for now and unravel the mystery when we're away in Ibiza*, I think to myself as I sit out on the balcony with a glass of red wine, and a pre-birthday emergency cigarette. With my birthday tomorrow, I haven't got time to deal with any drama that David may have going on, so I enjoy my last night as a 39-year-old.

I have an early night, and as I lie in bed, contemplating this time last year when I was in the middle of celebrating my last year of being 30-something, of dreaming up the 'quest' and having palpitations about approaching 40, I think back at all the men I've dated that I would not have ordinarily considered. And how, in one year, I'm in a relationship, and still unsure if David is my perfect imperfect soulmate, but I guess time will tell and, as Harriet said, our holiday will surely tell if we're meant to be. I drift off feeling happy, relaxed, and not one bit anxious about tomorrow; I'm looking forward to it, in a weird kind of way, and as I fall into a deep slumber, my encounter with the 'stranger' sweeps through my thoughts momentarily.

Friday 21st September 2007

I wake up to a beautiful sunny morning and jump out of bed, take a look in the mirror to see if whether, overnight, I have any more frown lines and grey hairs than the day before, then after my morning coffee, I go for a run. By the time I reach home, I've already received a few text messages wishing me happy birthday, from the girls and Vince and Harry. It's only just gone 9am and the phone rings; it can only be Mum and Dad calling this early, and they proceed to sing to me down the phone. I then open the only present I've received so far, which is from David. It is a black, knee-length coat; I'm not sure whether I may have mentioned that I needed one or maybe he saw me looking at it when we went holiday shopping, but it's very nice. I send him a text message thanking him for the gift but don't get a response. I crack on with packing my overnight bag and getting my party outfits ready. Once everything is meticulously lined up in the lounge, ready to be put in the car, I make breakfast. Naomi calls and has arranged to pick up Harriet at 2pm, and then they'll head over to Mum and Dad's, so I get ready and make my way over. As soon as I park up on the drive, Dad rushes out and gives me a hug. He helps me unpack the car and when I enter the kitchen, I can smell the smoked salmon that Mum is in the middle of preparing.

"Happy birthday, darling," Mum says, flinging her arms around me.

"Thank you, Mum," I say, kissing her on the cheek. "You've started on the salmon mousse, then."

"Yes, darling, now don't worry about a thing, everything is under control with the catering," she says, and then goes on to tell me that the Devon family will be coming, and that Uncle Terry will be doing the BBQ.

"Oh, that's wonderful news, Mum," I say, before taking my belongings and popping them in the bedroom.

I help Dad set up the gazebo before Naomi and Harriet arrive and me and Mum go over the checklist and, as per usual, Mum and Dad have organised everything; all I need to do is decorate the garden.

When the girls arrive with a huge bag of decorations, old photos of us through our teenage years with our bold make-up and drawn on beauty spots, big, permed hair that makes us look like we were in a terrible music video, we all have a good laugh. Dad cracks open a bottle of Champagne and Mum brings out her salmon mousse for us to sample with some crackers. The day is spent decorating the garden and getting it party-ready, and, by 6pm, it has been transformed. A huge disco ball is suspended from the centre of the gazebo, lights edge the frame, coloured streamers twisted and taped anywhere where they can stick, and Naomi has made a chain of photos and has strung them anywhere she's able to. At the back of the garden where it's a little secluded and private, we have created a seating area with benches and scattered some huge cushions on the grass with blankets. Me and Harriet create a bar area housing all the alcohol, with two huge stainless-steel buckets for the Champagne and beer, which we'll fill with ice tomorrow. We've popped a table next to the bar for the food, and once we've organised the plates, cutlery, glasses, and serviettes, we all sit back down and sigh. Dad opens another bottle of Champagne as we admire our creative talents. "Not bad, girls," he says, looking at the garden. The hanging decorations softly swaying, the butterfly craftwork clipped in and around the garden, with tall candy-stripe candles staked into the ground ready to be lit tomorrow evening makes it look enchanting.

Mum brings out a big tray of antipasti, cheese and freshly made focaccia and gasps, "How lovely!" She sets the food down and looks at the change in the garden from a couple of hours earlier.

Later on, after I've cut the cake and heard another rendition of 'happy birthday', Naomi and Harriet leave. Me and Mum finish up doing as much as we can in preparation for the party, and she makes the coffee and settles down in the lounge with Dad. I pour myself a glass of red and sit in the garden and realise that I haven't checked my phone all day; I'm sure David must've been in touch but there's no missed call or even a text message from him. It seems a bit strange, but I guess I only saw him yesterday so think nothing of it and take a walk around the garden and feel excited about having my favourite people here celebrating my 40th with me tomorrow. After a while, I head up to bed and again find myself thinking about the quest and whether I've achieved anything from putting myself through a year of hopeless dates, although I'm pretty sure Harriet would say it was worth every effort, for all the laughs she's had listening to my stories. But even though I'm in a relationship with David, why do I still feel very much single? I sigh and wonder what he's up to and then drift off.

The day of my party I wake up to another beautiful sunny day. I pop my dressing gown on and rush downstairs like a child on Christmas morning and open the patio doors to the garden; it still looks magical. I can hear Mum and Dad in the kitchen chatting away. "Good morning," I say as I wander in, smiling, taking a mug from out of the cupboard.

"Good morning, darling," Mum says, pouring some tea out of the teapot for me.

"Rachel, the only thing I've yet to do is get the BBQ out of the shed for your Uncle Terry and make some more ice," Dad says. Mum and Dad have one of those huge fridge freezers that has an ice-making function, so Dad has been making bags of ice for the last two weeks now.

"Dad, I'm sure you've made enough," I say, smiling over at him.

"He has, darling, half of the freezer is taken up with bags of ice," Mum says, rolling her eyes. We smile at each other and tease Dad.

After my cuppa, I freshen up and help Mum in the kitchen making sandwiches, cutting them in cute triangles and arranging them on trays, covering the tray with clingfilm and popping them in the fridge, eating a couple along the way. After making up four trays, I make cheese and pineapple on cocktail sticks, Mum makes a pavlova followed by a cheesecake and I prepare the cheese and crackers and grapes on a tray. Dad organises the drinks on the bar outside, all the while listening to songs from the year I was born; all of which they know and sing along to.

By 1:30, the stage is set, and I run up and take a shower and put my make-up on. The Devon family arrive so I change into my comfy clothes and dash down to greet them. They fuss over me and once they've settled in, we all have a late lunch followed by a glass of Champagne, Dad and Uncle Terry opting for an ale whilst they get to organising the BBQ. Me and Mum leave them to it as we make final preparations, including slicing lemons for the G and T drinkers, popping olives and nuts in bowls and slicing burger buns.

By 3pm, with an hour to go before the party is due to start, I rush upstairs and freshen up my make-up, slip into the blue halter neck dress and strappy heels. When Mum comes up to get ready, she backcombs my hair in a Brigitte Bardot half-updo-style; I'm pleased with my look and splash on my favourite perfume and head downstairs. I'm met with photos of me as a baby through to my teenage years pinned around the house and garden, which I've no doubt my cousins are guilty of displaying. I make my way to the side of the house to make sure the side gate is open to find a huge

40th birthday banner and balloons lining the way. The gate is wide open, and I notice a taxi pull up. Vince and Harry climb out and I smile as I watch them, excited for the party to begin. I hear a wolf whistle as they walk up the drive. "Well, chick, it's arrived, the big four-zero; Happy birthday, Rache," Vince says. "You look sexy as," he continues, as we hug.

"Happy birthday, my love," Harry says. "I don't want to mess up your make-up, so it's air kisses." I laugh, leading them through to the garden and leave them to say hello to the family, whilst I rope in my young cousins to man the bar and to start pouring the Champagne. Vince sorts out the music, playing a chilled-out selection which makes me feel as though I'm already in Ibiza. Harriet, John, Naomi, and Neil are the next to arrive, and I start feeling a little less nervous at the thought of David and his friends arriving.

Harriet notices my slight unease. "Rache, did you speak with David yesterday?" she asks, raising an eyebrow.

"No, he didn't call," I reply.

"Not even to wish you a happy birthday?" she continues.

"No, but I guess I did see him on Thursday night," I say, trying to shrug it off.

"Still!" she exclaims.

"When will he be arriving?" Naomi asks.

"Well, I told everyone else to get here for 5pm, so I guess at 5," I say, with a cheeky smile. Vince and Harriet howl with laughter. "I just wanted to have a drink with my besties first," I say, laughing too. Mum and Auntie Jean descend upon us, each holding a tray of sandwiches and offering them around.

"What's so funny, darling?" Mum says, smiling at me.

"Oh, no, nothing, Mum, I was just saying that I told everyone else to get here for 5pm, so I could spend time with my favourite people first, that's all," I reply, helping myself to a prawn mayonnaise triangle.

"Oh, Rachel, you are naughty," she says, smiling and shaking her head. She and Auntie Jean leave the trays on the table and head back inside, but a few of the neighbours who Mum had invited soon start trickling in, and once I've spent time chatting with them, it's close to 5pm anyway. I help Mum bring out some of the trays of food until I'm shooed away and told to enjoy the evening, at which point I pick up a bottle of Champagne from the ice bucket and join Naomi and Harriet under the gazebo. Vince and Harry are engrossed in looking at the old photos, with an occasional shriek of laughter from Vince when he gets to our teenage bad hair years. John and Neil are happily chatting away with the neighbours. Dad and Uncle Terry command the BBQ, ale in hand, and my cousins are pleased to be manning the bar. It could not have been more perfect, with the sun shining down on the garden.

Me and the girls walk to the back of the garden to the chill-out area and take a seat on the benches. I top up our glasses and we sit facing the top of the garden so I can see when people arrive. "I must say that you're looking very sexy, Rache, the dress, the hair, those killer heels; if I was a bloke, I would," Harriet says, with a giggle.

Naomi nods. "Yes, I think David's eyes will pop out of his head."

"Thank you, Mum did my hair, but I think I may have to change into my jeans later, so I can dance." I say, taking a sip of my Champagne.

"Talking of David, isn't that him?" Harriet says, motioning with her head towards the patio. We all look over and he's standing with James, Wendy and another lady. We all stand up.

"Oh my God! Has he brought a date?" Naomi says. Harriet shrieks out with laughter, and Vince, hearing Harriet's scream, saunters over with Harry.

"Ladies, what's occurring?" Vince says, picking up the bottle of Champagne.

"David has arrived with a date," Naomi says.

"No, Nomes, I think that's James' sister. David asked me if he could invite her seeing as she's staying over with them; she's just broken up with her fiancé," I say, before making my way over to greet them.

"Rachel!" James says, noticing me walk over. "Happy birthday!" he says, giving me a kiss on the cheek.

"Thank you, James," I reply.

"This is my sister, Jenny."

"Hello, lovely to meet you," I say, shaking her hand.

Wendy greets me with an awkward half-hug, mumbling happy birthday as she does, and then I turn to David. "Hello."

"Hi, you look amazing," he says, giving me a kiss on the cheek which strikes me as odd.

"Thanks, let me get you some drinks; as you can see there's a bar which is manned by my cousins," I say, leading them a few steps down from the patio towards the table. "They can fix you a cocktail, or just help yourself to the wine, beer or Champagne in the ice buckets and please help yourself to the food." I take David by the hand and lead him into the kitchen. "Hi," I say, giving him a kiss on the lips.

He places his hands around my waist. "I wasn't sure whether to kiss you in front of everyone," he says. I sense a nervousness from him.

"Why?" I ask, just as Mum and Auntie Jean walk in.

"Hello, love," Mum says, and then notices David's arms around me. "Oh, hello, you must be David." She walks over to us, and I introduce David to Mum and Auntie Jean. "It's lovely to meet you, David," she says, looking at him. "Rachel hasn't brought a boyfriend round in years," she says, which makes David chuckle.

"Mum! Okay, I'd better introduce you to Dad," I say, chuckling too and taking David by the hand and leading him out. We walk over to Dad and Uncle Terry, who are firing up the BBQ. It's all very civil, with handshakes, and we leave them to it. "Let's get you a drink," I say, as we make our way over to the bar.

David picks up a beer and says, "Where's yours?"

"I think I left my glass at the back of the garden with the girls." We stroll over to the benches where they're all sat, and they all welcome David. "I'm just going to grab another one," I say to David as I pick up the empty Champagne bottle and head back to the bar. As I pass James, Wendy, and Jenny, I say, "Hi, why don't you come and join us at the back of the garden?"

"Is that the VIP area?" James scoffs, as they slowly make their way over to the others.

I notice a few more of my friends arriving, including Kevin and Nina, so I go over to greet them and introduce them to the family whilst also organising drinks for them. Mostly everyone invited has arrived now and I feel a lot more relaxed, so I pop inside to freshen up. As I reapply my lipstick in the cloakroom,

I hear voices outside. "I'm not sure what David sees in her, really, she seems high maintenance to me, only drinks wine and Champagne," one of the voices says scornfully.

"Well, she's very pretty," says the other voice. I open the door to find Wendy and Jenny standing outside, both startled when they see me walk out, wondering whether I'd heard what they'd said.

"Hello," I say, gliding past them, "are you both okay?"

"Yes," Wendy mutters, as she makes a hasty retreat into the toilet, leaving Jenny to face me, who lowers her head and looks down at her feet.

"I'm so sorry to hear about your break-up, I hope you don't mind me saying, David told me the other day," I say, looking at her and smiling warmly.

"Oh, thank you," she says, looking up and smiling back. The sound of the toilet flushing is my cue to leave.

"I hope you enjoy the evening, Jenny." I walk back out to the garden and look around at happy smiling faces, which warms me, and I make my way to the bar, pick up a bottle of Champagne and go around topping up glasses, stopping to chat. By the time I reach the gazebo, the bottle is empty, so I retrieve another and find Harriet and Naomi.

"Hello, Rache," Naomi says, with a look of concern, "are you okay?"

"Yes, I was until I went to the loo and overheard James' wife, Wendy, talking to Jenny about me, calling me high maintenance and wondering what David was doing with me."

"What?" Harriet says loudly. "That bitch! Who does she think she is?"

"It's okay, Hattie, she's allowed to have an opinion, it doesn't bother me but the look on her face when I walked out of the loo was priceless."

"Well, that husband of hers is a right bore who loves the sound of his own foghorn," Harriet says, looking over at him. Me and Naomi start to laugh in agreement with her.

"Ladies, are you ready to switch it up?" Vince shouts out to us as he taps on his phone, which is positioned in the docking station of his mobile speaker. We all turn to look at him as he walks over to us, just as 'Dancing Queen' starts playing. He takes the bottle of Champagne out of my hand and swings me around under the disco ball. Harriet and Naomi join me in dancing and singing along and there's a 'whoop' from Vince when Mum and Auntie Jean join us. Vince takes Mum by the hand and twirls her around. I notice Wendy and Jenny looking over at us as they walk past the gazebo, heading towards the back of the garden and I beckon them over to join us, but Jenny waves and smiles whilst Wendy, who has her hands full carrying three bottles of beer, just nods and carries on walking by. Harriet looks at me and we both burst out laughing as we move our bodies to the music. When the song ends, Mum and Auntie Jean walk away giggling.

Vince's disco playlist manages to get mostly everyone up to dance, apart from David and his friends. Even Dad and Uncle Terry, who were firmly fixed to the BBQ, prised themselves away for Mum and Auntie Jean. Kevin from work also gave me a twirl around the dancefloor to The Bee Gees' 'More Than a Woman'. "I thought you said you had a boyfriend, Rache?" he asks.

"Yeah, he's standing over there with his friends," I reply, pointing towards the back of the garden.

"Oh, right," Kevin says, looking miffed.

"Yes, I know, Kev," I say, shrugging my shoulders, giving him a look to say, 'I know what you're thinking from the expression on your face'. I give him a kiss on the cheek when the song ends, and he makes his way back to Nina.

I walk over to the bar to get a drink and as I'm pouring the Champagne into a flute, I feel someone standing behind me, and arms wrap around my waist. "Oh, you've finally come to talk to me," I say, imagining it's David.

“I’ll always have time for you, Rache,” Vince says.

“Oh, sorry, Vince, I thought you were David,” I say, turning around.

“Hmm, what’s he up to? I don’t think I’ve seen you two together at all tonight,” he exclaims.

“Yes, I know, he’s not moved from that spot for the last two hours,” I say, motioning to the back of the garden.

“Anyway, Katherine has just asked me...” He places his hands under his face like a cherub and bats his eyelashes. “To make an announcement.”

“What does Mum want you to announce?”

“She wants me to tell everyone that the food is ready,” he says, kissing me lightly on the nose.

“Okay,” I say, smiling at him as he disappears on his mission. I head back to the girls who have been joined by John and Neil.

“We were just saying how strange it is that David hasn’t spent much time with you, Rache?” Harriet says.

“Yes, Vince just said the same thing.” We all look over at him and his friends standing at the back of the garden in their own little cocoon.

"I mean, it almost looks as though they're a couple, David and..." Naomi pauses.

"Jenny," I add.

"Yes, David and Jenny," Naomi continues, looking at Harriet to concur.

"Yes, well, I'm quickly going off him, Rache," Harriet says, taking a sip of her Champagne.

We are distracted by a clinking sound and look across to see Vince standing on the patio tapping a spoon against his flute. "Ladies and gentlemen, I'd like to welcome the bride and... Oops, sorry, wrong speech." Everyone laughs, and he continues, "The food is served, please form an orderly queue, thank you." He shrieks with laughter, turns, flicking his head, as if he's on a fashion catwalk and walks inside. Me, Harriet, and Harry walk over to the bar, laughing at his theatrics.

"He's hilarious," Harriet says, still giggling as she loops her arm through mine. Harry tops up our drinks as we watch Naomi head for the table. Filling her plate, she turns, waves and smiles at us. Me and Harriet chuckle and smile at one another.

"He's very funny," we hear a voice say. We both turn around to see David and Jenny standing behind us.

"Yes, he is," Harriet quips, looking at them suspiciously.

"Hi, how you all doing?" I say, trying to cut the tension.

"Yeah, we're okay, thanks," David replies, looking a little nervous from Harriet's glare.

"Are you on your way to get something to eat?" I ask.

"Yes," they both say simultaneously.

"And to get a plate for James and Wendy, too," Jenny adds.

"Okay," I say, as they smile awkwardly and walk away.

"Why? Is something wrong with their legs?" Harriet says, under her breath. "Can you believe it?" she continues, once they're out of earshot. "Honey, I'm not surprised you were having doubts about him, things don't seem right to me." Harriet says, shaking her head.

"Maybe he's just keeping her company seeing as she's just broken up with her fiancé, Hattie," I say, trying to convince myself that him ignoring me is justifiable.

"Well, whatever it is, Rache, it seems awry to me." We watch Naomi walk over to the BBQ, Dad places a sausage on her plate, and she takes a seat at the table on the patio.

"Shall we go and join her?" I say.

"No, the boys can sit with her, let's go inside," Harriet replies. We wait until everyone has taken a plate and then we help ourselves, going inside to the kitchen and sitting on the stools, and Dad and Uncle Terry come in and join us. Occasionally, we hear Vince shriek out with laughter, followed by Mum and Auntie Jean giggling.

"Are you having fun, Rachel?" Dad says, looking at me with beer goggles.

"Dad, how much have you two had to drink?" I remark, chuckling. "Yes, everything is perfect," I reply.

"Not nearly enough yet," says Uncle Terry, snorting with laughter.

When we finish eating, I give Dad a kiss on the forehead and me and Harriet head upstairs to freshen up. I change into my second outfit while she's in the bathroom and when she returns, she says, "Knock 'em dead, honey."

"That dress was skin tight, Hattie, at least now I'll be able to dance."

"You look like Sandy from *Grease* in that outfit," she says.

"Well, I think my Danny has gone AWOL."

"Rache, you never know, he might want some 'Summer Lovin' when he sees you in that," she says, laughing. I can't help but laugh too. We make our way down the stairs, singing 'Summer Lovin' until we reach the bottom and see David standing outside the cloakroom.

"Wow, Rachel, you've changed."

"Yes Danny, I mean David," I say, as me and Harriet chuckle.

"You look..." he begins to say and pauses.

"I'll see you outside, darling," Harriet says, leaving us alone.

The toilet flushes, the door opens, and Dad walks out and says, "Darling, you look sensational, I think is what he's trying to say." Then he walks back into the kitchen.

"Yes, that's exactly what I was—"

I cut him dead in his tracks, I've become bored of his obvious lack of attention towards me these last couple of weeks and tonight has confirmed that. "Are you going to the..." I say, motioning towards the cloakroom.

"Um, yes," he says.

"Okay, I'll see you outside," I say, walking off.

It's only just gone 8pm and it's still warm out; the outdoor lights have been turned on and someone has lit the tall candles dotted around the garden. I walk out onto the patio and Vince wolf whistles, I smile at him and join them seated at the table. "You're looking very daring, Rachel, where's that boyfriend of yours?" Mum asks.

"In the loo, Mum," I reply.

"I hope he's not throwing up," Vince quips with a snort and Harriet howls out laughing.

"Oh, is he unwell, Rachel?" Mum asks, looking mildly worried.

"No, Mum, I don't think so," I say, laughing too. "I'm going to get a drink; would you like one?" I say, looking over at Mum and Auntie Jean.

"No, love," Mum says, and Auntie Jean shakes her head.

I walk over to the bar and David walks out of the house at the same time and I stop as he walks towards me. "Do you come here often?" I say, trying to inject some humour. He laughs, we both get a drink and walk to the gazebo.

"The garden looks amazing," he says.

"Yes, me and the girls decorated it yesterday, with help from Dad."

"I would've helped, you should've called me," he says.

"Well, yes, it would've been lovely if you were here to help but I thought you must've been busy seeing as I didn't get a response from the text I sent you in the morning," I reply.

"Oh, I'm sorry, Rachel, I've been a bit out of sorts lately," he says, looking over to the back of the garden at his friends.

"Anything I can help with?" I say, taking hold of his hand. But before he could answer the music switches and the intro of Earth, Wind & Fire's 'September' blares out of the speaker. I look across to hear Harriet whoop and jump up, closely followed by Naomi, and they dance their way over to the gazebo. Vince and Harry join them too, and we all start dancing and singing along.

"Do you remember, the 21st night of September."

Mum and Auntie Jean and few more friends have joined us and as I look across at everyone singing and getting down, Vince grabs my hand and pulls me in the middle to dance and everyone circles us. I scream with laughter and perform my best disco moves, finishing with a spin and pointing at whoever's in my sightline when I stop, which is Kevin, who is quick to jump in and dance. When he has his turn, he pulls Mum and Auntie Jean into the middle, and we all let out a whoop as they both get down. We all carry on dancing to the disco tunes, dropping in and out to get a drink, and I manage to dance with mostly everyone apart from David. "So, where did David go?" I ask, looking over at the girls.

"Oh, Rache, he scarpered as soon as Vince pulled you up to dance in the middle," Naomi says.

"Yes, he was like a little piggy running away!" Harriet screams out laughing and making a running gesture with her fingers.

"Gosh! I thought he would've at least danced with me." I shake my head. "He said that he's been out of sorts lately, whatever that means, all I can say is that this holiday to Ibiza is going to be fun." I say, sarcastically. I look over at him and his friends still sat on the benches at the back of the garden and regret having invited them. I'm too merry to waste my energy on them and get back to dancing. Vince plays all my favourites and then changes the music to the 'golden oldies' for Mum, starting with 'California Dreamin''. Her and Auntie Jean are delighted when Dad and Uncle Terry make it back on the dancefloor and join them. I leave them to it and head inside to freshen up, taking any empty dishes with me into the kitchen.

Whilst sitting on the loo, I wonder why David is 'out of sorts', as he puts it, I'm sure to find out when we're in Ibiza in a couple of days' time but since his break to Zante, I've noticed a change in him towards me. I finish up and head back out, picking up a cheese and pickle sandwich on the way, then refill my flute. I watch the couples slow dancing to 'Unchained Melody' as I ponder why David isn't here dancing with me, I see that even James and Wendy have managed to pry themselves away and walk 20 feet to the gazebo to dance. I take a sip of my Champagne and walk to the back of the garden and when I near the chill-out area, I see the back of David and Jenny sitting on the bench, his arm draped around her shoulder, her head nestled in the crook of his neck, and his hand stroking her arm. I take a deep breath in, contemplating whether I should disturb their cosy nesting and then pause for a moment, turn and walk away.

When I reach the gazebo, Dad catches my eye, and he senses my upset. He beckons me over and takes me in his arms and we dance. "Rachel, what's happened?" he whispers, as we gently sway to the music.

"No, nothing, Dad," I say, faking a smile.

"I know something's up, girl," he says, stroking my hair.

"I guess I'm just a bit emotional about turning 40, not being married or having children and I guess I'm a little tipsy too," I say, chuckling and then resting my head on his shoulder.

"You've just not met anyone worthy enough to have you, Rachel, and as for kids, you've still got time, my love. Listen," he says, as he pauses, "don't be upset for what you don't have, just be grateful for what you do, and everything else will just happen when it's meant to, and if it doesn't, then it wasn't meant to."

I look up at him. "I love you, Dad."

He smiles and says, "I know."

When the song comes to an end, we stop dancing and in that moment, I feel an energy between us that is so strong, so calming, an unrestrained feeling of pure love. Mum joins us and the three of us dance, holding hands, until Vince arrives and whisks Mum away. The next thing I know, I'm being ushered towards the patio by Harriet and Naomi and as we get closer I can see the table with the pavlova and baked cheesecake with a '40' candle, lit, sitting on top. Vince shushes everyone and the music to Stevie Wonder's 'Happy Birthday' plays in the background. I blow out the candles amid the shouts of 'make a wish' and 'do another quest', which I'm sure sounded like Harriet, and 'speech! speech!'. I cut the cake and Mum carries on with slicing and plating it and I look across at everyone and notice that David is nowhere in sight.

"It's been such a lovely evening," I start to say.

"It's not over yet, Rache!" someone shouts out, followed by laughter.

"This time last year, I embarked on a quest to date as many men as I could in a bid to find my perfect imperfect soulmate and I'm pleased to say that the quest is over."

"And you still haven't found him." Vince howls out with laughter. I chuckle, as does Harriet and Naomi.

"So, I would just like to say thank you all for coming and sharing my special day with me. Some of you know that I had trouble processing the thought of turning forty, but I think I'm going to be all right, so please, have some cake, have another glass of Champagne and enjoy the night." I turn and give Mum and Dad a hug.

"Rachel, what on earth is the quest?" Mum says.

"I'll tell you all about it one day, Mum." Dad and Uncle Terry light up the fire pit, whilst Mum and Auntie Jean dish out the cake for everyone.

"Where the hell was David?" Harriet says, a bit too loud.

"I hear you, girl," Vince says, agreeing with her as he walks off to the gazebo. A few seconds later and the intro to 'Another One Bites The Dust' starts playing and we all turn to look at him. He starts to grin as he passes the bar, picks up a bottle of Champagne and starts singing into it. We all fall about laughing, no one outside of our group knowing why, but laughing along, too, at his frivolity. He pops open the bottle and tops us all up and we all start singing along with him. Naomi taps me on the arm and points to the garden. I turn and see David and his friends slowly walking towards the patio, our singing slowly peters out as we watch James and Wendy stop and pick up a beer from the ice bucket.

David approaches us tentatively. "Rachel, did I miss you cut the cake?" he says, looking over at the table with the remaining cake.

"Yes, you did, David! We thought that maybe the sound of us singing happy birthday to Rachel might've given it away," Harriet says sarcastically.

"Well said!" Naomi whispers, looking over at Harriet.

David stands there, motionless, looking at me. "Oh, I'm really sorry, James was talking and..." he tries to offer as an apology.

"It's okay, don't worry," I say, just as James, Wendy and Jenny join him.

"Ooh is that cheesecake I see," James says, making his way over to the table.

"Why don't you get some cake, David," I say, getting up and walking them over to the table where James is helping himself to a piece of everything on offer, even popping the cheese and crackers on the same plate.

I briefly turn to look at the girls and can tell that Harriet is fuming; she looks as though she's ready to punch both David and James on the nose, and probably Wendy too but I can't help but get a fit of the giggles when I walk back over to the table, which in turn makes her laugh out loud. Wendy and Jenny both twitch and turn to see what we're laughing at, which inevitably makes her howl even louder, which starts Vince off, snorting with laughter too. Mum walks over to us, half-laughing herself, and says, "What's going on?"

"Mum, I think Harriet wants to punch David," I say, as Harriet nods her head.

"Well, if she doesn't, I will," Mum says. Well, after that, none of us could hold back from laughing. David and his friends stand around the firepit, eating their cake and once the laughing had died down, David made his way over to us, standing on the outskirts. Mum turns to him and says, "David, are you looking forward to going on holiday on Monday?"

"Yes, very much, Katherine," he replies.

"Rachel, I'm sure you must be," Mum says, looking at me and smiling.

"Yes, I can't wait to be in my bikini, on the beach, with a jug of Sangria, Mum."

"Ooh, I wish I was coming too," Harriet purrs, smiling at me with a knowing look.

We smile at each other, and I turn to David. "So, what's the plan for Monday, then?"

"Er, I'll come and pick you up, shall I?" he offers.

"Okay sure, our flight's at 1:35, so I'll be ready to leave by 11."

"Great, okay," he says, looking a little less intimidated now that everyone has left us alone to talk. We make small talk, and he attempts to apologise again for not being there when I was cutting the cake, but mid-sentence, Harriet shouts out to me. Amy Winehouse's 'You know I'm No Good' starts to play. I look over at her in the gazebo, waving her hand, beckoning me over to join them.

I look at David and say, "Come on, let's go and join them."

Kevin, Nina, and a few others make a move to leave not long after, so I accompany them to the front of the house where we say our goodbyes. When I return, I notice David has disappeared again. "Where's David?" I ask, looking around.

"Well, as soon as you left, he skulked back to his friends," Naomi says, rolling her eyes. We all continue with our frivolous behaviour until the only ones left on the dancefloor are me, Vince, and the girls, shortly joining the others who are sat by the firepit enjoying the warmth radiating from it. Vince changes the music to a mellow pace and Chris Isaak's 'Wicked Game' starts to play. I look over at him and he smiles and winks at me; I smile back thinking how apt the song is. I'm not left long to linger on my thoughts as a tray of hot sausage rolls passes in front of me. We all relax, listening to the soft, haunting music.

Mum and Auntie Jean appear with a pot of coffee, a bottle of brandy and a plate of chocolate truffles and tell us to help ourselves. "Katherine, when can I move in?" Vince says, chuckling and blowing Mum a kiss. She giggles and walks back inside, returning with coffee cups and brandy glasses and as she sets them down on the table, her gaze is transfixed on the back of the garden, and we all turn to see what she's looking at.

David and his friends are walking slowly towards the patio; it looks like a scene from a zombie movie, the four of them appearing from the dark, and as they get closer, I can see the nervous look on David's face as he tries to feign a smile. "Good grief! Rachel, I thought they'd left," Mum says, looking at them as they approach the table. Harriet is the first to unleash her laughter, Vince following in second place.

"No, Mum," I reply, cringing with embarrassment.

"Hi," I say, as they hover around the table, "we thought you'd all left."

Then a voice bellows out, "Ooh, is that sausage rolls I see."

We all look across at James; no one responds to his observation. The awkwardness is palpable, the music still playing in the background helps to soften the atmosphere, and after what seemed like a long silence, David says, "Our taxi must've arrived." They all shuffle out, murmuring bye and I walk David out through the side gate to the front where a taxi is parked; I watch them disappear into the waiting car and say goodbye to David. He leans in to kiss me, and I flinch, turning my face and offering him my cheek.

"Okay, Rachel, I'll see you Monday then," he says, walking away.

"Night," I say, turning around, and as I make my way back down the side of the house, I can hear Vince and Harriet laughing.

I jump out of my skin when I hear a voice shout out, "Rachel!" I turn around and David is running towards me; maybe he's come back to say sorry for being a total arse all night. "Would you mind if I, um... Well James and Wendy would like a drink for the road," he says, panting and looking embarrassed.

"Oh, right, help yourself," I say, incredulously. He didn't wait long enough to notice the expression on my face as he ran past me down the side of the house, and then stopped just before reaching the patio and waited for me. I watch him walk towards the bar, and I look across at everyone; they've stopped talking and are watching him retrieve two beers from the ice bucket. He tries to conceal them as he makes a quick getaway, shouting out thanks. The jaw-dropping looks on Harriet and Naomi's face is hilarious as I walk back and take a seat.

"Rachel, what on earth was he doing?" Mum asks, with a bemused look on her face. There's a roar of laughter from the usual suspects.

"Mum, he went to get a couple of beers; James and Wendy needed one for the road," I reply.

"What dreadful people!" Mum exclaims, and everyone chuckles. I could hear Mum and Auntie Jean talking about how ill-mannered they all were, not mixing with anyone and how they stayed at the back of the garden the entire evening, and I felt so disappointed in David. After saying their goodbyes, the family headed in for the night.

"Rachel, how do you feel?" Naomi asks, sighing.

"I know how I'd feel!" Harriet says, shaking her head in disbelief.

"Well, I know it's over, I guess it's just a matter of trying to enjoy next week in Ibiza with him."

"You know, you don't have to go, Rache," Harry says.

"Yes, I know, Harry, but I'd like to, I've been looking forward to this holiday, so I'll be making the most of it."

We stayed up listening to music and chatting, Harriet trying to persuade me to do another quest after she recalled and laughed through the one's she found most hilarious, after which they all left. I bumbled up the stairs, and it wasn't long before my tired body succumbed to the warmth softness of the bed.

My eyes felt like they were glued shut; it took time, but I forced them open, only to find myself standing on the roof of my flat. I feel frightened, a panic stirs in my stomach like as tornado making its way up to my throat but somehow I know I have to take a leap. I look around and the morning sun is spreading a warm bright glow against the wispy sky. I can't look down; I daren't. I open my arms and step off the roof, drop for a millisecond then the thermal breeze lifts me up and I find myself gliding. I can't help but smile as I look down at the rooftop of the flat, but after a few wobbles, I gain confidence, my arms outstretched wide like a 747 soaring high above the buildings. But most of all I feel an overwhelming sense of calm, an inner peace, and elation engulfs my whole being. I look across and smile at a fellow flying companion, who is watching me swoop down, turn, and then fly back up. For a split second, I close my eyes, a sense of falling backwards overtakes me, the blue sky slowly disappearing from view. My landing is abrupt but soft, and I open my eyes with a start to find myself in bed. I snuggle the duvet around my neck and bask in its warmth and ponder on my dream until I fall back asleep.

My Sunday morning is spent getting the garden back to normal; my cousins help Dad with the gazebo whilst I collect the glasses, bottles, and any rubbish. When I reach the back of the garden, I recalled the image of David and Jenny sitting on the bench, his arm around her, it may have been innocent, but it just didn't seem right. There must've been 30 or so empty beer bottles strewn around the benches, and I imagined James and Wendy ploughing through most of them. After our clean-up, Mum and Auntie Jean called us in for brunch, and shortly after, I said my goodbyes and made my way home.

Part Three - Stepping Stones

I wake up at the start of my holiday feeling refreshed and well rested after having an early night. I had the most wonderful deep sleep and a mug of tea later, I got to answering text messages and then I have a strong coffee before taking a shower. With my suitcase packed, my handbag checked and then double checked for the essentials, my plane outfit sorted, I make breakfast, using up any vegetables from the fridge and rustle up an omelette. David arrived 15 minutes late, and I decided to lock up and go straight down with my case, rather than buzz him up. He's stood by the open boot of a car that I don't recognise and when I look across, I see James sitting at the wheel. "Good morning," I say, wheeling my small case to the back of the car.

"Hi." He helps me place it in the boot. "James offered to drive us to the airport," he says, kissing me on the cheek.

"Yes, I see that," I reply, as he shuts the boot. "Hello James, how nice of you to drive," I say, as I take a seat in the back.

"Well, hello to you, Rachel," he shouts out, as if I'm standing 20 feet away. "Shall we go then?" he says, looking across at David, who's sitting in the front passenger seat. David nods and we set off to Heathrow. I'm pleased it's a short journey as listening to James' voice any longer than 15 minutes would surely drive me insane. They talk amongst themselves, which gives me the opportunity to text Harriet and tell her of my misfortune of having to see James again. She texts back saying that she's laughing but also feels my pain.

When we arrive at Heathrow, I jump out of the car, open the boot and retrieve my case, and stand at the side, waiting for David as he finishes saying goodbye to his friend. He eventually shuts the car door, takes out his case and we make our way in to the terminal. I feel completely disconnected from him, it's as though we're strangers. The lack of emotion in our interaction is evident and when the lady at the check-in desk asks us where we'd like to sit, I say window and David says aisle. She looks up at us, smiles and then prints off our boarding cards. We have over an hour before boarding so I suggest going for a pre-holiday drink once we've cleared security. "Yes, okay, but I have to pick up some sun cream and a few other bits," he says. We meander through the duty-free shop, and I come across a sign for a restaurant aptly named Runways.

"I'll leave you to your shopping, then. I'll be in there when you're done," I say, pointing to the restaurant. He nods and walks away. I make my way over, taking a seat on a stool at the bar and order a glass of fizz.

"Going anywhere nice?" the barman asks, as he places the flute down.

"Ibiza," I reply, smiling at him.

"By yourself?" he questions, giving me a cheeky smile.

"No, I'm going with someone, he's around somewhere," I say, glancing towards the entrance.

"Someone?" he says, raising an eyebrow.

"Yes," I say chuckling, "he's not a significant someone, but he's..." I pause, not knowing if I should divulge any more but the barman is distracted by someone waiting to order and leaves.

I busy myself with answering the 'bon voyage' message on my phone from Naomi, and then he returns, standing across the counter from me, smiling. "You were saying that he's insignificant," he says, with a wry smile.

"I said no such thing!" I reply, indignantly, and we both start laughing.

"All I'm saying is that if you start the holiday off drinking alone, then...." He pauses, shrugs his shoulders and curls his lips.

"Who are you? The holiday relationship guru," I say, with slight sarcasm. We both chuckle, and we continue to enjoy the innocent banter.

"Okay, what time's your flight?" he asks, propping his elbow on the counter and resting his chin in the palm of his hand.

I take out my boarding card from my handbag. "Boarding is at 5 past 1."

"Okay, so you've got about 40 minutes," he says, looking at his watch. "I bet that the insignificant someone doesn't make it here before you finish your drink and have to leave." He then nods at me and walks away to serve someone.

"Really!" I reply, looking across at him, all cocky and sure of himself, his Irish accent melting through his rogue exterior. He has thick dark hair and piercing green eyes, and he glances over at me, catching me checking him out; he winks and smiles. I take a look around to see if David is anywhere to be seen; there's half an hour before boarding, so I stand up and look over to the barman. He looks over and I mouth that I'm popping to the toilets; he smiles and nods his head. I take my time to freshen up, reapplying my lipstick, a little blush and then make my way back to my seat, hoping to see David, but there's no sign of him or the barman. I notice the bill on a small silver plate on the counter next to my flute and open it up. It reads *'told yer he wouldn't show, the drink is on me. Liam'*, followed by his phone number and a kiss. I smile as I read it again and look around to say thank you but he's nowhere to be seen, so I finish the drink and pop the note in my handbag and leave.

On my walk to the boarding gate, I give David a call, but his phone is engaged so I send him a message saying that I'm on my way to the gate. It's a good 10-minute walk and when I reach there, boarding has already commenced. I join the queue, looking out for him, maybe he's already onboard, I think, as I inch closer to the plane. I make my way to my seat, which is in the last row at the back and take my seat by the window, check my phone for any messages, then turn it off and pop it away in my handbag, retrieving my book but keeping an eye out, but there's no sign of David in the throng of people waiting to get to their seats. Maybe he's decided not to come, I mean, he has been acting very strange of late, and we haven't exactly been close these last couple of weeks. I close my eyes for a moment and then hear a voice. "Hi."

I look up to see a young Asian man with a big smile looking at me. "Hi," I reply, smiling back.

"I think I'm next to you," he says, in a strong Brummie accent.

"Okay," I say, as I adjust myself on the seat moving closer to the window whilst he manoeuvres into the middle seat.

"I'm Sunny," he says.

"Hi Sunny, I'm Rachel, nice to meet you."

Sunny continues talking about what time he got up in the morning to make the flight, that he's travelled all the way from Birmingham and how he's going to his friends stag do. "All my mates are already there giving it large," he says, bopping his head to a beat whilst talking.

I switch off listening to Sunny jabbering on, and my mind wanders off in thoughts of Liam the barman and what he said to me about starting off the holiday drinking alone, and then I wonder if I should send him a message to say thanks for the drink. I reach down to get my phone out of my handbag and hear a voice call out my name. I look up to see a flushed-faced David standing in the aisle. "Oh, you made it then," I say, placing my phone back in my handbag.

He places his bag in the overhead locker and sits down, sighs and then says, "I've just run all the way here; I went to the bar but didn't see you."

"Well, I did try calling you, David, but...."

"Do you two know each other? I'm Sunny, by the way," Sunny butts in, looking at David and they start chatting, which gives me the opportunity to buckle my seat belt and absorb myself in my book, which is a futile option while sitting next to Sunny, who is now relaying his story to David. I switch off and lean against the window and close my eyes, only opening them when the plane is ready for take-off.

The two-hour flight seemed to drag, listening to our Brummie neighbour talk nonstop, calling the stewardess 'babs' when she came round with the drinks trolley. I pull out a Tupperware box that mum had given me which was filled with sausage rolls and cheese and crackers, which was met with delight from Sunny and David when I offered them out. When we landed, the stewardess opened the door at the back of the plane, and we made our way down the steps onto the bus waiting to take us to the terminal building.

Sunny chatted the entire time, saying that we must meet up, and I left it to David to make conversation whilst I enjoyed the heat caress my body, smiling and nodding to show some interest. Our luggage was quick to arrive and after loading them onto the trolley, we said goodbye to Sunny and made our way out. "I'll go and sort the car out," David says, half-smiling at me.

"Yeah, sure, I'm going to get a coffee, would you like one?" I ask, pointing to the café.

"Yes, okay," he replies, so I take the trolley off his hands. He leans in and gives me a kiss on the cheek, and we walk away in opposite directions. I manage to order two coffees in Spanish quite easily and wait for David at the side. By the time he returns, I've finished my coffee and I'm sure his must be cold, but he drinks it, nonetheless. We make our way out to where the hire car is parked; it's a little hatchback and we just about manage to get our luggage in the boot. David drives whilst I navigate our journey to the hotel, which is not more than 20 minutes away.

We find parking on a side street and a short stroll later, we walk through sliding doors into a huge, bright lobby, where the view of the beach and the sea are visible through a glass partition. After checking in, we take the lift up to the second floor where we find our room; it's huge with two small double beds on one side and a sitting room on the other, there are two bathrooms too, either side of the door, one with a shower cubicle and the other with a bath. "Wow! This is perfect, we have our own bed and even our own bathroom," I say, laughing, as I walk out of one of the bathrooms toward the lounge. I slide open the door to the balcony; the view isn't great but that doesn't matter to me, seeing as we'll be on the beach most of the time. I turn back and walk through to the lounge and notice that David has disappeared into one of the bathrooms, so I open my case and take out my toiletry bag and claim the other bathroom. I continue to unpack my case, placing my belongings around the room and hanging up a few things and then I hear the toilet flush and a few moments later David emerges.

"Well, this is rather big!" he exclaims, beaming.

"Yes, it's wonderful, although the view from the balcony isn't, but I don't mind," I respond, excitedly. He smiles over at me as he unzips his case and takes out his belongings and places them on one of the beds.

"Are you okay, David? You look a little clammy."

"Yes, I'm fine, just hot, I guess," he replies.

"Okay, I'm going to take a shower and start getting ready for dinner," I say, as I make my way to the bathroom, and as I close the door, I hear him shout out 'okay'. Twenty minutes later I'm ready to start exploring, eager to get out on the beach, dip my toes in the sea and have a chilled glass of cava with some tapas.

David is still standing over his suitcase when I finish up in the bathroom. He eventually heads to his bathroom and as he shuts the door, I let out a sigh. A second later the door opens, and he says, "My bathroom only has a hand-held shower in the bathtub, do you mind if I use yours?"

"No, not at all," I reply, picking up my bag, "I'm going down, I'll see you at the pool bar," I shout out as I open the door to leave. I hear the shower running and him shout out 'okay'.

The hotel is situated in a quiet, residential part of the island, past the bustling area of Playa d'en Bossa, so the clientele are much older and don't look like the clubbing type, but as I make my way down, I can hear music. The lift door opens onto the lobby and the restaurant is busy. There's a band on the stage belting out 'Macarena', and I walk past, out onto the terrace to the pool, but my gaze is firmly fixed on the sea. I take my flip-flops off once I reach the beach and walk towards the water, my feet sink into the sand and I breathe in the evening sun and drink in the view. After a little stroll, I come across a few restaurants opposite the promenade and I make my way over to look at their menus, which leaves me salivating, so I make my way back to our hotel in search of David but there's no sign of him. So, I resign myself to a seat at the pool bar and order a glass of cava. My mind reflects back to the image of me earlier in the day, sitting at a bar alone, waiting for David. It's becoming a little annoying, waiting for him again, I start to think. Then I pull out the receipt from my bag with Liam's number and smile to myself, remembering what he'd said in his Irish accent. “If you start the holiday off drinking alone then...”

“Hi.” I hear a voice and I look up to see David.

“Hi, you made it,” I blurt out.

“What’s that?” he says, looking down at the piece of paper clearly showing Liam’s name and number.

“Oh, nothing,” I reply, folding it back up and placing it back in my bag. He sits down and orders a beer, and I tell him of the restaurants I saw on my walk, which he agrees is good with him, seeing as he hasn’t had much sleep these last few nights. “Oh! Why’s that?” I press, eager to know.

“Um, well I’ve been staying over at James and Wendy’s, and you know what they’re like, late nights and nonstop drinking,” he replies, with a nervous laugh, realising he may have said too much.

“All sounds very cosy,” I remark, remembering that James’ sister, Jenny, is also staying with them. “Was Jenny there too?” I ask as he’s taking a gulp of his beer. I can see his brain going into overdrive, his eyes widen and then he suddenly loses control and coughs and splutters his way out of answering. His coughing fit lasting a few minutes and attracts glances from those who are seated close by.

He eventually composes himself and says, “Sorry, went down the wrong way.”

"Shall we go?" I say, finishing my cava and standing up, not waiting for a response. He scrambles up out of his seat and follows me out towards the beach and we walk in silence. He slips his arm around my waist, and I momentarily get swept away in that warm feeling of belonging until his phone starts to ring, which makes us both jump. His arm is swiftly withdrawn from around my waist as he retrieves it from the pocket of his jeans; he looks down and silences it. "Who is it?" I enquire, looking at him. He can't cough and splutter his way out of this one.

"It's James," he replies in a carefree manner, "he probably just wants to know how we're doing, I guess."

I refuse to entertain a conversation about James and smile at him as we walk to and settle on the first restaurant we arrive at.

After another drink, we both loosen up and it almost feels like we're getting back to that closeness that I'd been missing. I ordered tapas, whilst David opted for chicken and chips and on our stroll back to the hotel, he takes hold of my hand, gently stroking it with his thumb. The wine has left me tipsy, and I feel a sensuality in me rise. By the time we reach the hotel and are alone in the lift, we start to kiss with a longing, as though this is the first time we've seen each other in a long while. That familiar taste and smell invading our senses, and when we arrive at our room, we're both hungry for more, unashamedly pulling each other's clothes off, kissing, groping, and moaning until we are both physically erupting with pleasure. I lie back on the bed, and David slides down, kissing my body as he goes, stopping at my open legs and licking my clitoris until she throbs. No words are needed as my body shudders with pure delight, and I let out a moan, yearning to be entered. We fuck. His penis sliding in and out easily, my vagina bursting with tiny bubbles as he soon climaxes. As he lays on top of me, I feel a satisfaction that I had not felt for a long while. He slides over to the side, and we kiss and caress each other as we had many times before.

I slept in a contented slumber, and when I awoke the following morning, the warm smile of inner happiness from the night before slowly starts to dissipate when I find David's side of the bed is empty and cold. I can hear his voice; it's quiet but audible enough for me to make out him chuckling softly. I climb out of bed, naked, curious to know who he's talking to so early in the morning. As I get closer to his bathroom door, I hear water splashing and sounds like he's having a bath. *Maybe he's just talking to himself*, I think, *in which case I'll join him for a soak.* I open the door, and as I thought, he's lying back in the tub. "Buenos días," I say, in a sexy soft Spanish voice as I walk in. He looks up at me with a shocked expression, his face turns red, and I can hear a female voice on the other end of the phone. His upper body shoots up, and he loses grip of his phone; it slips out of his hand and into the water with a splosh.

"Oh my God!" he screams as he quickly picks the phone up and looks at it. "Rachel, pass me a towel, quick!" I ignore his request, turn and walk out.

I lock myself in my bathroom, walk into the shower cubicle, turn it on and burst out crying. I'm not sure how long I was in there for, but I didn't stop until I had washed away the taint of the previous night. When I finished, I felt as though a weight had been lifted off me, and as I slathered the factor 30 over my body, I decided that this was my holiday, and I wasn't going to let anyone spoil it. I wrapped the bath sheet around my body, unlocked the door and walked out. The door to David's bathroom was shut. I put on my dark blue bikini and slipped into the dress from last night, slid my feet into my flip-flops and then noticed the door to the balcony was open, so I stepped out and saw that David had placed his phone on the table. The morning sun was a tonic to my soul. I reached my arms out and overhead placing them together in prayer, then slid them down to rest at my heart space and I silently prayed that I'm given the strength to face any challenges with love and grace. I bow my head down to meet my hands and relish the peaceful warmth, although my peace is quickly disturbed with the sound of footsteps. "Well, I'm really hoping it's going to dry out here," David says, as he comes up behind me and places his arms around my waist. "What are you doing? Praying?" he chuckles. "Well, say one for my phone, too," he continues, his arms tightening around me. "Listen, I'm sorry about before," he whispers. I turn to face him. "You see, I was on the phone, and you startled me, coming in all sexy and naked." He smiles apologetically.

"Who were you talking to, David? And please don't say James, as that would be really weird," I say, keeping his gaze. His grip around me loosens and he looks down at his feet briefly.

"It was my mum," he mumbles. The lie was evident. I didn't even have to say another word, his face was dripping with deceit.

"I'm going down for breakfast." I picked up my handbag and left.

Harriet's voice ringing through my ears as I made my way down to the restaurant. I can just imagine her saying, "He was talking to his mum whilst naked in the bath, yeah sure." Followed by her howling with laughter. I can't help but laugh too at the notion that he would be chatting to his mother whilst having a bath and that he actually thought that was a plausible lie. The first day of our holiday and the minor fractures in the relationship have now made an appearance as major cracks that can't be skimmed over. I sit in the restaurant with my café con leche, contemplating how, a couple of months ago, I was so sure he was 'the one', to now knowing he definitely is not.

"Hi," David says, as he takes a seat opposite me.

"Hi," I reply, trying to sound light and carefree.

"The phone looks completely buggered, think I'll take it out and see if it dries out in the heat," he says, avoiding eye contact with me.

"Yes, good idea, your mum must be worried wondering what happened, you're welcome to use my phone if you want to call her back," I say, reaching in and taking my phone out of my bag and holding it out to him.

"No, Rachel, it's fine, it wasn't important," he concludes.

"Okay, I'm popping over to get some breakfast, would you like me to get you anything?" I ask, getting up from my seat.

"No, I'll come up in a moment," he says, half-smiling. Breakfast was eaten pretty much in silence, David making a few observations about the hotel and other guests in the restaurant to make conversation. "So, what's the plan of action today then?" he asks, desperate for some input from me.

"How about the beach?" I say, laughing, a touch of sarcasm in my voice, but not enough for him to pick up on.

"How about the place you were telling me about where they have a saxophonist playing on the beach?" he adds.

"Yes, it's at a restaurant in Salinas, I suppose we can get the bus," I reply.

"No, we've got the car, I'll drive, we can go there for lunch," he offers.

"Yeah sure," I say, faking a smiling and nodding at him, not in the mood to contest his decision to drive.

After breakfast, I head up to the room to freshen up. I slip on my blue denim shorts and white halter neck top, pack my beach bag with all the essentials, pop some lip gloss on and dust my face with a little bronzer before heading back down. I find David sitting outside on the terrace, his phone taking centre stage as he stares at it, hoping for signs of life. "Hi, shall we go?" I say, startling him from his stupor. He jumps up out of his seat and I watch him as he takes his phone off the table and slides it into the side pocket of his khaki shorts.

Our drive to Salinas is a little tense with David driving; his lack of concentration at the roundabout nearly causing an accident. The road is also very busy and when we arrive half an hour later, I navigate David down a dirt track to the beach car park. Boulders line the path, and as he drives slowly around the winding path, the car suddenly launches forward, crossing the oncoming cars. I scream out, but before David has time to react, he has already crashed into one of the boulders. The look of shock on the people walking by, making their way to the beach, and the rubbernecking from passing cars, makes me cringe. I look across at David; his face beetroot as he reverses the car and proceeds in forward motion. As soon as he parks up, he jumps out. I can hear him swearing under his breath as he makes his way to the front of the car to survey the damage. I join him, both of us staring down at the indentation in the bumper. "What happened, David?"

"I don't know, my foot slipped, and I hit the wrong pedal, doesn't help wearing these flip-flops," he says, looking desperately embarrassed.

There's a long pause. "Oh well, no harm done," I offer, as I head back to the car to retrieve my bag. I hunt around for my lip gloss, and reapply whilst watching David mutter to himself, standing motionless, looking at the damage. "David," I shout out. He looks up. "I'm desperate for a wee, so I'm going to head to the restaurant, okay." I give him a sympathetic look.

"Okay, sure, see you there," he snaps back, a little irritated that I'm leaving him to it.

"Look, no one was hurt, that's the main thing," I say, but he doesn't respond. As I walk away, I turn back and shout out to him, "It's the restaurant at the far end on the left, I'll see you soon." He raises his hand up in acknowledgment, and I continue my walk, feeling a touch relieved to be out of the car and have the sun shining down on me. I slip out of my flip-flops when I reach the beach and hold them as I make my way to the restaurant, passing beautiful, tanned bodies stretched out in the sand. The familiar aroma of Marijuana is wafting through the air, and the sound of chill-out music eases my demeanour. I look across at the water, glistening in the sun, inviting me in, the vivid colours embracing me and massaging away any tension from my eventful morning thus far.

As I approach the restaurant, the music becomes louder, and I wind my way through people relaxing on the beach. After popping to the loo, I join the small queue of people waiting to be served at the bar. Everyone is friendly, smiling, happy, and I must've said 'hola' to nearly a dozen passers-by from just my walk from the car park. Then I hear someone say, "Hi." They pass by me, and I turn and am faced with a tall Adonis wearing a short-sleeved white linen shirt, that's unbuttoned, revealing a tanned physique, and denim shorts. My eyes take me up to a handsome face that has a rugged look, and wavy blonde hair.

"Hi," I reply, smiling at him, trying to fix my eyes on his face and not his bronzed, bare chest. He's holding a bottle of Champagne, and a straw hat.

"I'm Nick," he says, beaming at me playfully.

"Rachel," I respond, smiling back and chuckling softly.

"I'm sitting out there with my friends, if you fancy joining us for a drink," he says, motioning with his head towards the beach.

"I'd love to but I'm waiting for someone," I reply, tilting my head to one side and giving him a look to suggest that it's a fait accompli.

"Okay, well, if you change your mind," he says, winking at me before he walks away.

I can't help smiling, and the feeling of complete freedom I now find myself in ignites my passion to do as I please. I order a jug of sangria and take a seat at a table on the terrace and look across the beach to see if David is on his way, but there's no sign of a man in khaki shorts and white t-shirt, so I pour out my first glass of sangria. I can see Nick standing up with his hat on, looking over at me. He raises his glass of Champagne at me to say cheers, and I raise my glass of sangria back at him. I enjoy the brief solitude as I contemplate the morning's events. The first glass of sangria has gone down far too quickly and there's still no sign of David, so I decide to make a bold move and with the jug of Sangria in hand, I make my way over to Nick. "Hi," I say, as I tentatively approach the group. There are three men, including Nick, and four girls. Two of the girls are on the sun loungers; they both look up and smile at me, the rest are sitting on colourful bohemian blankets.

"Rachel!" Nick says, and then introduces me to his friends. He pours out a glass of Champagne for me, and I pass him the jug of sangria, which he sets down on the table.

"Are you celebrating?" I ask, as we clink glasses.

"Yes! It's my birthday; 40th," he says, as his friends let out a 'whoop', excitedly raising their glasses.

"What, today?" I ask. He nods. I wish him a happy birthday and we both sit down on the blanket, a joint is passed to me, and I take a couple of tokes, and pass it to Nick, whose face has a permanent smile. He takes the joint, swaying his body to the music. I look at him as he inhales and smile, thinking how his open, childlike friendliness has made me feel so welcome. He passes the joint back to me and after taking another drag, I pass it on.

"Rachel, where's your friend?" Nick asks, looking at me suspiciously.

"Oh yeah! I almost forgot about him. I have no idea, he crashed into one of those boulders on the drive into the car park and..." Nick bursts out laughing, as does a couple of his friends who are close enough to hear what I've said, which sets me off too. Mid-laughter I notice a figure walking on the beach towards the restaurant. It's David. He's taken his t-shirt off, revealing a farmers tan; his forearms and face are tanned but the rest of his upper body is pale. I feel a knot in my stomach and feel myself cringing as he gets closer. I shout out to him but he hasn't heard me and so I stand up as he passes.

He stops in his tracks, almost unsure that it's me, and says, "Hi." Then he glances over at Nick.

"Hi, where did you get to?" I ask, but don't wait for him to answer as I turn to Nick and say thank you. He stands up and picks up the jug of sangria. "No, it's all right, Nick, you guys have it," I say, smiling at him. He winks at me as I turn and walk away.

Me and David make our way to the restaurant; the table I was sitting at on the terrace has been taken and while I wait inside, David pops to the loo and thankfully puts his t-shirt back on. A table inside becomes available, which I take. I order another jug of sangria and peruse the menu; I already know that I'm going to order the garlic aioli, bread and either sardines or prawns. David returns looking a little less flushed and sits down opposite me. "So, I see you've made some friends," he remarks, his smile disingenuous.

"Oh, yes, well, I was invited over for a glass of Champagne, so I thought, why not! What took you so long?"

"I was just trying to see if I could somehow bang the dent out of the bumper," he says, pursing his lips. The waitress arrives with the sangria and takes our lunch order. David orders a cheese and ham baguette and a beer.

"Would you like a glass of sangria?" I ask, as I pour myself one.

"Yeah, sure, why not!" he replies, in a tone mimicking my answer in accepting Nick's offer of a drink. I pay no attention as I pour him a glass; he places his mobile phone on the table, and I ask if it's working. "No, sadly not," he replies with a downward smile. The conversation between us is strained, and after talking about the weather, the beautiful beach, and the relaxing vibe that Salinas offers, there's not much else for us to talk about. So, when the waitress delivers our lunch, I'm relieved for the excuse of not having to make pointless conversation with David. The prawns arrive still sizzling in the small skillet, the bread and aioli fresh and inviting, and the baguette and a beer for David. I top up my glass with sangria and scoop up the garlic mayonnaise with a piece of bread, my stomach grumbling away and my mouth anticipating it's arrival. And once the prawns have cooled a touch, they, too, I start to devour.

"How's your baguette?" I ask, looking up at David. He doesn't reply as he's mid-bite, so I continue eating, until I hear him mumbling. I look up at him and he's still holding onto the baguette mid-bite, his eyes watering. I want to laugh but have to control myself, the side effects of smoking a joint awakening my sense of humour. He eventually manages to tear the baguette away from his mouth and places it down on the plate. He takes the serviette and places it over his mouth. "What's happened?" I whisper, a little alarmed by the pain evident on his face.

"My bridge, it's my bridge, I think it's..." David stops talking, and I watch him as his tongue moves around his front teeth. He pushes his plate away and excuses himself. I continue eating my lunch, mopping up any sauce from my prawns with the remaining bread. The waitress returns to clear our plates, and not sure whether David wants his baguette, I ask her to leave it and pay the bill.

When David returns, he picks up his phone from the table and motions to the waitress for the bill. "I've settled the bill, David," I reply, as I pick up my bag and put my purse away.

"Oh, okay thanks," he mumbles as he picks up his beer and leaves the baguette. I top up my glass with the remaining sangria and follow him out onto the beach, which has got busier. The sun loungers are all occupied apart from one that's right at the end, which has a parasol, so I start making a beeline for it. As I pass Nick and his friends, he shouts out my name and beckons me over.

I walk over to him, smiling. "Hi," I say, chuckling softly.

"Hi, did you have a nice lunch?" he asks, his eyes squinting, his laughter lines clearly visible.

"Yes, I did, thanks."

"Look, if you feel like ditching your friend, you're welcome here," he says. Then he leans in, and I slightly turn my head to see where David is, and as I turn back, our lips accidently meet, he places something in my hand and, as we part, winks at me before I walk away. I can feel Nick's eyes watching me as I make my way towards David, who has put his sunglasses on and is trying not to make it look obvious that he's watching me too.

"What was that all about?" David asks, as he places his towel on the lounger, I pop my drink on the table and open my other hand to find a joint. I look over at Nick and give him a wave to say thank you.

"Oh, nothing," I reply, much to David's annoyance. I take my beach blanket and lie it down on the sand next to the table, under the shade of the parasol and slip off my shorts and sit down cross-legged, facing the sea. "So, what's going on, David?"

"I could ask you the same thing!" he says. I can feel his glare through the sunglasses. I can't help but chuckle. "What?" he says.

"I mean at lunch, with the baguette, what happened?"

"Oh, well, it was so hard, that when I took a bite, it damaged my bridge," he says.

"Oh," I say, not knowing what a bridge is, but thinking it's got something to do with his teeth. "How come you have a bridge?"

He takes a big gulp of his beer and proceeds to tell me the story. "Well, when I was around 18, maybe 19, me, James and Gavin were in a pub having a few drinks. James had been eyeing up this girl all night and when her boyfriend noticed, he came over to us. James started to talk his way out of it, saying that she'd been looking at him but the guy just wanted a fight and so I stepped in, trying to explain that it was much ado about nothing, and he punched me square in the face.

Anyway, he knocked my front teeth out and that's why I have a bridge."

I gasped, open-mouthed in shock. "You didn't actually say 'much ado about nothing' I hope!" I cry out, chuckling.

He chuckles too. "No, hmm, well I'm not sure, quite possibly."

"God! I'm not surprised he punched you, if you came out with that," I say, bursting out with laughter. "I'm sorry, I didn't mean that, it just seems like you always tend to be James' fall guy."

He looks at me with a puzzled expression. "What does that mean?" he asks, a little indignantly.

"No, nothing," I reply, pausing to think whether I should continue the conversation.

David gets up from the lounger and says, "I'm going to get another beer, do you want anything?"

"I'd love a bottle of water, please." I watch him walk towards the restaurant and come to think what a loyal friend he is to James and then my eye catches Nick, who's standing up, looking cool in his blue shorts and unbuttoned white shirt, dancing away on his birthday. I get a waft of sweet marijuana and remember the joint he gave me. After rooting around in my bag, I find a lighter and spark it up. David returns with the drinks and passes me the water.

"Where did you get that from?" he asks, just as I inhale.

I exhale slowly enjoying the taste, the smell, the euphoric feeling and, smiling at him sweetly, I reply, "Nick gave it to me." I motion with my head to where Nick is dancing. I offer it to him, he hesitates, and then takes it and inhales, and coughs a little before inhaling again.

"I haven't smoked this since college days and even then I didn't take to it," he says, taking another drag before passing it back to me.

I lay back in the shade of the parasol, my body soaking up the heat, enjoying the chilled-out vibe of Salinas even more so after the smoke, occasionally cooling down in the sea. David remained firmly glued on the sun lounger, only moving to visit the toilet or checking to see if his phone was working, and when he bought a beer from a beach hawker, I had to question his decision. "Are you going to be okay to drive, David?"

"Yes, why?" he snaps back, sounding annoyed that I should even ask.

"Well, you didn't have lunch, and you've already had a prang in the car," I reply.

"I am on holiday; besides I can't bite down since damaging my bridge on that hard baguette," he replies, sounding like a petulant teenager.

"What's going on with you, David?" I ask, looking at him incredulously.

"Well, let's see, my phone is buggered, I've crashed the car and now I can't eat because my bridge is broken," he spits out, as if that gives him carte blanche to do whatever he pleases.

"No, you've been acting off with me for weeks. I noticed it at my party too; it's as though we weren't even a couple," I blurt out, unable to contain my thoughts any longer.

He looks at me and I can feel his glare through his sunglasses again. "Well, you and your friends never really made us feel welcome," he replies, in retaliation. I could feel the anger in me rise, any feelings of relaxation disappearing fast. I had to stop Jack from springing out of the box and remain calm.

"What do you mean by 'us'? You and your friends chose not to mix with anyone, staying at the back of the garden the whole time. The only time we saw you was when you came to get food and drinks." I could've gone on but decided to stop before I said something I'd later regret.

"I was trying to please everyone, as well as look after Jenny." The realisation of what he'd just said stopped him from saying any more; we both looked at each other expressionless.

"And there it is, David."

"What?" he says, looking at me, hot and bothered.

"Jenny," I say, pausing for a moment. "I saw you with her, I took a walk to the back of the garden and the two of you were... Well, you had your arm around her and..."

"That's ridiculous!" he interrupts, not willing to hear any more. He picks up his beer and uses it to shield his face from my stare. I turn away from him and sit, looking out at the sea, satisfied that I've aired my feelings and now no more needs to be said. "Look, Rachel," he starts, but I no longer have any desire to hear his voice so I get up and walk away to cleanse myself of any doubts and fears that I may be holding onto.

The water refreshes my soul and now I know that there's no turning back, no going forward, either, with him. My body dances with the gentle waves of the Balearic sea, and I lie back, floating like a starfish, looking up at the clear blue sky. The ambient sound of a saxophone and cheering disturbs my floating meditation, and a smile covers my face. I stand up and look over towards the restaurant where the harmonic instrument is being played, and swim back to shore returning to my position on the blanket to enjoy the live music. "Hi," I say, half-smiling at David when he turns back to look at me.

"Hi, he's very good," he says. I nod in agreement, before lying down on my stomach, and resting my head on my hands.

Our first day on the beach passes by and, come late afternoon, the beach gets a lot busier. The sound of balls ping-ponging from one bat to another as people play beach tennis can be heard. I gently shake the sand from my blanket, folding it and placing it back in my bag. "David, are you ready to leave?" I slip on my shorts, as he looks up from his book.

"Yes," he replies, and puts his book down on the table. He stands up and stumbles, catching hold of the parasol to steady himself.

"Are you okay?"

"Yes, I just remembered that I haven't eaten," he replies, as he sits back down on the lounger for a moment.

"Maybe it's best I drive," I say, as I pop my top back on and pick up my flip-flops. He doesn't respond, and on our walk back to the car, I remember Nick and turn back to see if I can see him, but the beach is too crowded. When we reach the car, David passes me the keys and our drive back to the hotel is in silence. His eyes are closed, which makes it easier not to force conversation and as we near the hotel, I notice a sign for a tapas bar called El Drinking Ole and I scream out. "Look, that's where me and the girls go to in Windsor – El Drinking Ole," I say in a Spanish accent. "We have to go; I've got to take a picture," I say excitedly, as I take the turning down the road and park the car. I look across at David, who gives me a wry grin as I unbuckle my seatbelt and climb out of the car. He takes his time getting out, so I toss over the car keys for him to lock up. I happily make my way down the steep descent onto the beach, turning to face the restaurants on the promenade, but I can't see it. I look up and down the line of bars and restaurants, but there's no sign, and then David arrives.

"Where is it then?" he asks.

"I don't know, can you see it?" I ask, as he takes a look around.

"No, can't see it, are you sure you saw a sign for it?" he says, smiling smugly.

"Yes, it said El Drinking Ole. I'm sure it said tapas bar. Oh! Never mind," I sigh disappointedly.

"Well, I'm hungry, so we may as well get a bite to eat here," he says.

"Yeah sure," I reply absently, still looking for the bar as we walk towards the promenade.

"Look! There's a place there that says, El... Something," he says, pointing to a restaurant on the beach, but as we get closer, we see it says El Pirates. We decide to eat there; the tables are set out on the beach so you can sit with your feet in the sand. It's a small place with a boho look about it, the smell of incense getting stronger as we approach it and take a seat at a table at the far end where it's a little quieter.

"Would you like to share a bottle of red, David?"

"Um, no thanks, I think I'll stick to the beer," he replies, playing with his front teeth with his tongue.

"How're your teeth?"

"Not great, not sure what I'm going to order seeing as I can't bite down without it hurting," he replies, looking at the menu.

"How about sharing the paella with me," I offer, looking up at him, hopeful that he'll be happy with my suggestion.

"No, I've already said that I can't bite down," he says sternly, with a definite hint of hostility in his tone.

"Maybe you can ask if they'll liquidise it for you," I snap back, chuckling.

We sit in silence until the waitress arrives to take our order, I opt for a glass of Rioja and some tapas; David orders a beer and asks if they have any soup. The waitress offers their homemade bean stew which he agrees to. We resume our silence once she's left, and I take a look around at the other diners; chatting, laughing, loving, and I recollect when I used to notice couples who sat in silence looking like they'd had an argument, only to find myself in the same predicament on holiday with a man that I'm not in love with. I look over at David, who has become a phone zombie. "Is it working?" I ask, just as the waitress arrives with our drinks and sets them down.

"No, doesn't look like it," he sighs heavily, as he places it down on the table. Our food follows shortly after, and I tuck into my tapas. David struggles with his stew.

"How is it?" I ask tentatively, not wanting another terse response.

"Well, it's very spicy for one thing, and I can't really chew the meat or the beans," he replies, a little sarcastically, reverting back to his moody teenager act, and takes a huge swig of his beer.

"How about if you squish the beans down with the spoon?" But as soon as I said it, I realised it was the wrong thing to say and would be met with scorn, so I quickly picked up my glass and said, "Cheers." He followed suit, taking another drink of his beer. I savoured my potato tortilla, salad, and ate the bread that accompanied his stew, seeing as he wasn't going to. He did manage to eat the liquid part of the stew and once he'd finished he ordered another beer.

"Do you want another drink, Rachel?"

"No, I've got to drive."

"The hotel's not far from here, we can leave the car and pick it up tomorrow," he says. When our drinks arrive, David reaches across the table, takes my hand and says, "I know things haven't started off well with the holiday, with me nearly missing the flight, the mishap with my phone, and then earlier on at lunch, but I just hope we're okay." He seems pissed as he's talking, his eyes glazed and then the foulest smell, like a sewer, infiltrates my nostrils and I can't help but cover my nose with the napkin.

"Eww, what's that smell?" I say. David looks around and then inhales, his nostrils flaring. He excuses himself from the table and hurriedly walks inside the restaurant, the smell following him. The look of disgust on my face must be evident to anyone who is privy to our conversation. I pick up my Rioja and take a sip to neutralise the foulness that I may have ingested and then I hear a phone ringing. I check my bag but it's not mine, and then I see the corner of David's phone poking out from under his napkin. Should I pick it up? I question myself, maybe it's his mum? I lift up the napkin, pick up the phone and press the green button. A voice, a female voice; she sounds anxious, but relieved.

"Oh, David! I've been so worried, what happened? The phone just went dead, I've tried calling you so many times. Hello, David?"

"Hello, Jenny," I answer calmly. "David has just had a little accident and has popped to the loo. Oh, hold on, he's just on his way back, I'll pass you over to him." I could almost hear her gulp in fear of the realisation of her frantic outburst. I stand up, phone in hand and watch him walk towards our table. As he gets closer, the quizzical look on his face, asking why I'm standing up with his phone in my hand, slowly changes to horror and his steps quicken. He reaches the table, his face ashen, not knowing what to expect.

"Rachel, what?" His voice is almost pleading.

"You're a piece of work, aren't you? It's Jenny, she's worried, she wants to know what happened when you were in the bath and suddenly the phone went dead." I place the phone down on the table and he momentarily hesitates before picking it up and lifting it to his ear.

I watch him as he says, "Hello, Jenny?" I turn and leave, the tears stinging my eyes, I'm not sure why – I don't love him – it's the humiliation, the betrayal, being made a fool of, that hurts. I hear him call out my name and I start to run, my bare feet hitting the sand and then I remember my bag and flip-flops, but it doesn't matter. I hear him call out my name again and again. I run past people out for an early evening walk, running through the people playing beach tennis and those just sitting down, catching the last rays of sun. I don't want to go back, and I don't want to hear any more lies. I slowly come to a stop and walk towards the water and soak my feet. I'm all cried out.

I walk along the shore, back to the hotel. The young man at the reception desk looks at me with concern in his eyes; I ask for my room key and make my way up. David's not there. I take a shower and wash away the day, then separate the beds, pushing mine up against the wall and lay down, trying to fall asleep before he returns. I'm not sure how much time had passed when I heard the door being opened and his footsteps enter but I was just dropping off. My body instantly tensed up and as he turned the lights on and saw me in bed, I sensed him creep closer to me. My eyes shut, I hear him sigh and whisper my name. I daren't move, I don't want a long-winded conversation leading to nowhere; for me, it's over, it has been since I'm not sure when. Was it my party? Or when he came back from Zante and things had changed; he had changed and had become distant. All I know is, not tonight, I want to sleep and leave this day behind me, wake up to a new beginning, a new day, a new Rachel, who's 40, single and free. I hear his footsteps retreat into the bathroom. I take a deep breath and fall asleep.

I'm not sure what woke me, whether it was David's snoring or the foul stench coming from his side of the room, but I quietly climbed out of bed and was glad to see that he'd brought back my bag and flip-flops. I picked them up, along with whatever clothes came to hand and went to the bathroom to freshen up. It had only gone 6am, so I slipped on my shorts and a white t-shirt and left the room. The sun was rising as I walked along the beach; it was quiet, calm, and peaceful. I looked across at the hotels I passed and saw a man cleaning out the pool with a long fishnet pole, and couples sitting out on their balconies enjoying the view with their first coffee. I keep walking, not knowing where it'll take me, until I find myself at the restaurant from last night. I can't help but smile and wish I'd been a fly on the wall listening to David and Jenny's conversation but, then again, no. The look on his face when he saw me holding his phone, the dread in his eyes, I have to feel sorry for him, he had the worst day ever yesterday. I start to laugh remembering all that befell him, from dropping his phone in the bath, driving into the boulder, biting into the baguette and causing damage to his bridge, resulting in him not being able to eat, to the finale at this restaurant last night.

As I pass, I look at the road where I parked the car and am pulled in that direction. I wander up to see if the car is still there, I hope it is, as David was not in a fit state to be driving last night. I walk 200 yards up the incline and see the car parked just where I'd left it. I turn and walk back towards the beach when I see the sign for 'El Drinking Ole' and I smile as I walk towards it. Taking my throwaway camera out of my beach bag, I take a picture of it and then cross the road and peer through the shop front. It's empty, no tables or chairs and as I'm looking in, I notice two men at the back of the shop looking at me. It startles me, and I turn and hurry down the hill back to the beach. The sound of Bob Marley's 'Is this Love' coming from one of the apartments invites me to slow down and be still and enjoy the music. I sit down on the sand cross-legged, looking at the water, waking up to the golden sun, and I soak in the pure energy of this beautiful day.

There's a tower of white pebbles stacked a few feet in front of me. I start to count them, each one sitting on top of the other, all performing a balancing act and supporting each other. I start reflecting on this last year of the quest, on all the dates, of all the men I've encountered that have led me here, to sit in this very spot on this beach looking at a tower of white pebbles. I smile as I come to the realisation that maybe the people you meet in life are like these pebbles, like stepping stones, joining you along your life's journey. Some come along to help you in a fun, positive way and other's arrive to perhaps prepare you, to challenge you, to test your strength of character by revealing who you really are, and thus leading you to discovering your true nature. Inevitably the outcome remains the same, in that we are constantly facing our truths, our beliefs, our integrity being pushed to its limits, all to ultimately help us to evolve and learn from each experience, to love and understand our true selves.

This last year has found me running from people, from situations, even from myself, and now as I sit here on this beach, I have nowhere to run. My eyes well up, and as I look out at the sea, a figure stops in front of me, and I hear a voice, a Spanish voice. "Rachel?"

I instinctively say, "Si." The sun blurs my vision, and his outstretched hand helps me to my feet. I look at the man standing in front of me, my hand still in his, and he smiles.

"You are always running," he says.

I somehow recognise him, his smell, his touch, his aura, his warmth floods my senses, his deep brown eyes look into mine and my mind flashes back to that alleyway in Windsor where we first kissed.

The End...

Lightning Source UK Ltd.
Milton Keynes UK
UKHW010840101122
411908UK00002B/71